VIKING

SAGA OF SOULS
BOOK ONE

Derek Nelsen

Summit Pen

Edited by Amanda Ashby
Copy Edited by Will Clifton
Cover Design by Dan Van Oss

Published by Summit Pen
eBook ISBN: 978-1-7351240-0-1
Paperback ISBN: 978-1-7351240-1-8

My father taught me that any good sailor dedicates his first boat to the woman he loves.

Lisa, this book is for you.

Thank you for giving me your heart to love, a home to return to, and three wonderful children to give us something to talk about on date night.

CONTENTS

STRANGERS ARRIVE

I cy fog hung so thick in the air it blocked both sun and fjord the day the strangers arrived. Too late in the season to be out in open sea, the dragon-headed ship, filled with water and regret, looked like it had lost a great battle with wind and wave. No oars touched the water; only remnants of a tattered and sun-bleached sail urged the craft along amid churning currents.

The dragon slipped silently past chunks of floating ice. The few boys still fishing ran home to be the first to tell their fathers.

Three large ravens soared above a broken mast. Their black wings cut the gray as if the sky were being torn open from the other side. The largest raven lit onto the dragonhead before croaking a deep *kraaa, kraaa, kraaa* from its shaggy throat, announcing the ship's arrival. The cold sucked the sound from the air before it had a chance to echo off the surrounding cliffs.

As if steered by a ghost, the dragon found safe harbor. Quietly it bumped against a jetty that reached out into the fjord like the stone arm of some great giant. Its failing hull scrubbed against the rocks with each passing wave like a dog scratching at the door to come in from the cold.

TOR AND VIGI: THE LAST HUNT

Something was out there.

Tor held his breath as he scanned the dark forest to spot whatever had snapped the branch.

He was a great thick man, over six and half feet tall. His reddish blonde hair and red beard were highlighted with gray, the color of a stag half into its winter coat.

Snow blanketed the ground, dampening the sound of movement. Nocking an arrow on a string of cured bear gut, Tor leaned against the oak to break up his outline. Senses heightened. He peered around the white birch, careful not to scratch his bow against its bark.

Come on. Be a moose or a fat doe. Odin, you owe me that much. Tor exhaled into his heavy coat to conceal the fog of his breath.

Vigi raised his head. Tor took his hand away from the string and scratched his old friend behind the ear.

"Easy, boy. Let's see what we've got here," Tor dared to whisper. He ran his fingers up the old dog's ears. They were alert as ever but colder than he remembered. "Better to die doing what you love than to live doing anything else. Eh, boy?" He breathed heat across numbing fingers before returning them to the taut string.

The dog pedalled his front paws in a silent rhythm, his head bobbing ever so slightly.

"Here it comes." He slowly raised his bow to expose a sharpened iron tip toward whatever may come.

Although not five leagues from home, Tor was alone. He

and Vigi were farther up the mountain than any man dared or cared to go. Any man from *his* village, anyway. Goats had led him to this spot.

The one part of farming Tor could do right, it seemed, was to breed goats. But his tended to escape—and disappear. Although he was gifted at carving wood, he wasn't so talented at maintaining fences. And fences, it turned out, were important if you wanted to keep goats.

Tor's goats did not suffer from superstition. Other than occasionally raiding a neighbor's turnips, they rarely stuck to the main roads, often wandering where farmers did not want to go. Luckily for Tor, he had lost his tolerance for superstition long ago.

As long as they stayed away from the ledges and the cliff's, Tor would eventually find them. But right now, goats weren't what he was after.

Vigi furrowed his brow as he crouched, barely an inch, but it was enough to set Tor on edge. Another branch snapped. Probably just another bird or a squirrel. Hard to tell. It was dry powder this time of year, when the snow first began to fall, and the world rolled into its white blanket like an old man with cold feet.

"There she is," Tor whispered, wiping sweat off onto his bear hide cloak.

Even when it was cold enough to freeze rivers, when playing games of hide and seek, any sign of movement would make even an experienced predator's heart race. For a hunter, it was a feeling that couldn't be matched by drink or horn in house or hall.

He raised his bow but did not draw the string. He knew from where it would come, but how long would it make them wait?

A large red deer eased her head into the clearing. Something wasn't right. The deer took another step and stopped again.

Tor's stomach growled.

3

Vigi turned his head up as if his master had broken some solemn code. Tor cast his eyes in apology to his old friend. The deer stopped. An ear cocked left, then right. Then two yearlings passed their mother and loped into the clearing.

Tor did not move. The light tension he had on the string numbed his fingers. He began to draw back the bow, then eased it to. Vigi stamped his front feet, then lowered his entire body into a full-on crouch. Tor looked down angrily, and Vigi's sharp ears drooped like a scolded puppy. The old dog wasn't used to being corrected.

The big doe eyed the woods. Tor held his breath, every muscle tensed. She stared at him, turned to look back, then eased into the clearing. Tor looked behind her but saw nothing but dark wood.

Vigi held steady except for licking his pink nose. Tor did not draw the bow. Vigi looked up to his master, as if not sure what to make of his hesitation. The large red deer snapped her head backward and coughed, then darted through the opening, her two yearlings bolting off close behind.

Tor stared after them, not sure what he had become. The man he used to be would've taken the doe, then killed the confused yearlings while they hopelessly urged their mother to get back to her feet.

All was quiet. Then something moved. Vigi panted. That always made the old Elkhound look like he was smiling. Tor's fingers tensed around the string. His breathing slowed as he raised his bow again. The dog stared intently at the hole in the dark forest not twenty paces from where they hid.

Without a sound, the opening filled with dark brown. The bear was big—fifty, maybe even sixty stone. The old bear had been stocking up for winter, the same as every farm in the village. He was, by any stretch, one of the largest bears Tor had ever seen.

Could this be the one? The same bear that Erik saw years

ago, running off into the forest after raiding their house? For years his little boy swore it had been a troll wearing a bearskin suit. Could this be the brute that stole his little Gefn? She would've been about fourteen herself now. Tor allowed himself to think about his beautiful baby girl, all big now. Had it been seven years since the bear had turned their happy life upside down?

Tor didn't need to be reminded that he, or his dog, could easily be mauled before even a perfect shot could drop such an animal.

Something between revenge and regret spread from the ache in his heart, and despite the cold his body began to burn. Old Vigi's lip curled and he bared his teeth, but he made no noise.

The old bear put his nose up into the small dry branches at shoulder height. Then he stretched up on his back legs as if he wanted a better look around. He sniffed the trunk of a heavy tree before giving his left eye a good scratch. Claws as long as kitchen knives hung off the massive paw. Truly, this was the king of the forest.

Tor froze. Did the bear know they were there? There must've been something off about their setup. Vigi had done his part, rolling in two types of scat on the way out. Even frozen, that would be enough to cover his scent. Maybe it was from when Tor stoked the fire or fed the horse. Or maybe it was the smell of goat. They had found twelve meandering around the mountain this trip.

The bear raised his nose and sniffed again, and just like the deer, seemed to stare right into Tor's eyes. Finally, he dropped his nose to the ground and sniffed his way out into the clearing, his large lumbering gate dredging the fresh powder, leaving pigeon toed tracks in his wake.

Tor's ice blue eyes caught fire as he drew back the string.

The bear crouched when the string snapped. All game does. Even the king of the forest walks warily. Tor expected it to duck, so he aimed low, something he'd learned from

5

his father—something he'd taught his sons. But there was something off about the shot. The bear broke too hard. No arrow was perfect. Maybe one of the fletchings came loose, or the shaft bowed as it cured. That happened sometimes. Or maybe he just blew the shot. Vigi stared up whimpering, waiting to be released.

"Too early boy. Give it a chance to bleed out a little." Vigi's ears were tweaking left and right, audibly following the bear. Tor rubbed the dog's thick coat, grabbing handfuls of skin and fur along the back of his neck.

Tor thought about the shot. The arrow veered right and met its target low. Instead of hitting the heart and lungs, it looked like a gut shot. As soon as it passed through, the bear tore a new path into the woods, away from where it came, and away from Tor. That's what injured prey did. They went away from everything, and they did it fast. But still, Tor knew he got lucky.

He'd never been hit with an arrow, but he knew men who had. The ones that survived said it felt like getting punched, then it burned like a bee sting. The shock of it stifled the pain, like the brain hadn't had time to figure out just how bad things were. With a heart-shot the bear would've just ran and ran, not realizing it was already dead. It probably never had a chance to feel what came next.

After the bee sting comes the burn. Like a thousand wasps stinging both places where the arrow broke skin. With a good shot death would probably come too fast for that. With a good shot, every beat of the bear's dying heart would paint the snow red with blood. Until the crash, where its legs would give out mid-stride, its heart pumping nothing to power its legs but red froth as it drowned in its own blood. Every time he took a life Tor thought of it. Not because of what happened on the hunt, but because he'd held the heads of his own men up out of the mud and watched the life leave their eyes—and add weight to their departing souls.

A good shot meant a quick death. That was the best scenario for the one who got the arrow and the one still holding the bow.

But Tor didn't make a good shot.

"Vigi." The dog was as excited as a pup. He'd pawed the ground down to wet leaves while waiting for what came next. "Go get 'im."

Vigi knew where the bear had gone. He'd watched it run off, but he stopped in the clearing anyway, putting his nose to the ground and circling the spot until he took in the full scent of it.

Tor checked the area. There was very little blood. The arrow's shaft was coated in a smelly grease and tufts of brown coarse hair. Just as Tor thought. *Gut shot.*

There are many things that could go wrong when hunting, but one of the most dangerous was stalking an injured animal. Even reindeer had been known to impale a careless hunter who went in too close, too soon. Moose that can barely stand still find a way to run down grown men. And bears are different animals altogether. They can outrun horses in a short sprint and can climb up or drop down out of a fifty-foot tree as easily as a man can mount a horse. Once, Tor heard a story of a sow attacking a group of armed warriors just for happening upon her cubs. She killed one and injured two more before escaping into the woods without losing so much as a clump of fur. The same sow will teach her cubs to hunt by turning them against moose three times their size.

The bear Tor shot was a full-grown male in its prime. It was out there hiding. It would be confused and aggressive. It would kill for a chance to lick its wounds and die alone, in peace.

Vigi had always been a good tracker. He'd been bred for this. He moved silently, the black curtain over his high arched tail wagged in excitement, like a flag leading Tor farther up the mountain. Every now and again Tor would

7

find blood or tufts of fur making the tracking easy, only to suddenly stop, the wound likely clogged from the gut or something the bear ate. That's how it worked with this kind of wound.

Tor had to hustle to keep up. He loosed his coat to keep from overheating. He could already feel the sweat and his shirt clinging to his chest. He still had to get back, and the cold could kill him just as easily as the bear. Vigi barked. Tor dried his palms, then regripped. He was holding a seax in one hand and a two-handed axe in the other. He would've preferred a spear. Something he'd wished he had with him at least once per trip, but still never carried in. Too long for the woods. Heavy too. There also wasn't a trip he hadn't wished, at least once, he'd had more clothes, or more food, or just one piece of dry wood.

The thick brush finally opened up. They were back on the trail. He'd been walking head down to follow the tracks, arms up to keep the raking limbs out of his face. He didn't realize they'd circled so close to camp. *Wouldn't it be lucky if it'd crawled up onto the sledge to take its final nap?*

Tor was glad to be able to stand up straight again. Vigi was staring into a thicket of briars and stunted trees.

Vigi broke his crouch, the standing hair settling back down the length of his back. *Maybe it's dead.*

"Where is he boy?" It was snowing again. "I wish we had more light." A little chunk of snow plopped onto Tor's shoulder. He couldn't believe they might not find that bear. There was nothing worse than waking up in the middle of the night to the sound of wolves running down an animal you stuck with an arrow. If they didn't claim that bear tonight, by morning there wouldn't be enough left for the ravens.

Tor looked at old Vigi, nose down to the ground again. *Could he have lost the scent?* Maybe it was time to start bringing Jakl or Sterkr on these trips. He'd known it was coming, but it would kill Vigi to be left at home. He was old, but he lived for these hunting trips.

The sun was already tucking itself behind the mountain. "The days are already getting so short." More heavy chunks of snow fell. Tor looked up to see how much daylight they had left, but then Vigi started to growl. The hair on the back of his neck bristled to life as he crouched again. Tor sheathed his knife and raised the axe high over his shoulder with both hands.

A squirrel ran out of the thicket, saw Vigi, and cut hard up the trail. "Vigi, hold!" Tor stopped his old friend before he broke down the trail, too. "Come on, let's get back to camp." Another hunk fell on his shoulder. He knocked it off. There was a green mash on his fingers. Vigi sniffed his hand and then put his nose down hard, turning around in tight circles as if he was chasing his tail.

A piece of bark fell to the ground. Then another. Tor pushed Vigi's nose away and picked it up. As he turned his head to the sky, hunks of bark and branch rained down as if the pine were shedding its skin.

The quiet wood exploded with the sound of four-inch claws raking down the length of the tall pine. The bear fell from overhead as if dropping out of the waning sun. It stood, a giant between them.

Vigi barked wildly, confusing the old bear.

Tor saw an opening and went for the throat. He threw his hands up bringing the axe's sharp edge shaving along the giant's jaw. It caught no bone, bore no blood. Tor roared as loud as the bear, knowing that was his one chance. He was too close and too unlucky to get another. He raised the handle to block the coming teeth or claws, but they didn't come.

The bear wailed in pain and spun away.

Like a cork being pulled from a wineskin, Vigi opened the bear's side. The bite might have loosed the cork, but the arrow had done the work. Blood and fat and half-digested food that had been collecting in the animal's gut splashed out onto the snow, filling the air with a putrid stench.

The bear roared and reared, turning its attention to the biter.

Vigi was fearless, growling through the black fur he'd taken for his prize. Then he was gone.

With a swipe of his paw the beast sent Vigi hard into the brush. From the shadows Tor heard the whimper of a hurt puppy. The only proof that Vigi had been there at all was the swatch of black fur.

Vigi had given Tor his second chance, and this time he hit his mark. Down came the axe, catching the bear at the base of its massive skull. The sharp edge locked in with a crunch, and the bear fell for the last time.

"Vigi!" Tor ran to the brush where he last saw his old friend. But Vigi met him halfway. He was limping, and his tail hung low. The old dog walked past Tor, gingerly lifted his injured leg, and relieved himself on his prize.

WELCOME HOME

"Well, this is the way for a man to be greeted when he returns home from a successful hunt." Tor smiled to see his sons running out to meet him at the gate. Vigi popped his head up from the sledge where he'd been sleeping with the bear. "You boys are going to want to hear about this one."

"Father!" Erik, Tor's youngest, arrived first and out of breath. His eager eyes turned bitter when he saw the dead beast on the sledge. Then, as quick as the snap of a twig, he perked up again. "There are Vikings."

Tor dropped his smile and picked up his axe. His eyes narrowed and turned toward the house, then scanned the surrounding wood line.

"Nice bear, Father." Toren, Tor's eldest, rubbed Vigi's thick coat. "A ship washed in, and there are survivors."

"They're in the hall," Erik added. "And there's a girl."

"How many?"

"One ship, four survivors, maybe five," replied Toren.

"Three Vikings." Erik scowled at his older brother for telling his story. "One's a giant. Biggest man anyone's ever seen."

"They have a lot of tattoos," added Toren.

"And the girl," Erik stepped between Toren and his father. "She's got red hair."

"Erik, I need you to —" Tor raised a crooked finger, then couldn't help but smile. "Red hair, eh?"

Erik and Toren smiled back.

Tor looked over his shoulder to see his beautiful wife, Runa, waiting in the doorway. "I think your stepmother wants to see me." He petted Vigi's ears—still too cold for his liking. "Toren, help Vigi down from the sledge. Be careful, he got injured saving me from the bear."

The boys' eyes grew wide. Vigi panted like a proud puppy.

Tor handed the reins to his youngest. "Erik, you take care of the horse. Only after he's watered and brushed can you start on the bear."

ANOTHER BEAR

"**A**nother bear," Runa frowned.

Tor pretended not to notice his wife watching Erik as the boy gutted the beast and emptied the contents of its stomach into a wooden pail. It was a ritual he'd performed on every bear his father had brought home since the day he allowed one to run off with his little sister.

"Stupid boy," she muttered loud enough for him to hear. "What does he think he'll find, anyway?"

Erik looked toward the still open door, then got back to his task.

"Let him be, Runa." That was about as much of a rebuke as Tor dared mutter to her about *that*. He had learned over the years that there was no relationship to salvage between the two and the less he got involved the better it was for his son.

Tor understood her grief. A pain was seeded in both their hearts when they lost their baby girl. But Runa's seemed to grow a little every time he brought home another bear. He'd have gladly left them to rot in the woods, but an empty larder would not heal her scars. It would only make things worse for Erik.

Tor knew this of his wife. Although she had not inherited her father's green thumb, she knew how to care for a grudge. The scorn she felt for Erik over that little girl was well maintained, even after these many years.

Tor put his arm around his wife. Maybe she would

accept his comfort. Runa shrugged him off. He shook his head, "Trade it with the butcher!" He didn't mean to raise his voice. "Whatever that bear brings will help round out the stores for winter."

"I'll make it work," she whispered. "I always do."

They had loved each other once, and maybe they would again. But right now, it seemed hopeless. They were two ships drifting farther and farther apart—the wind and tides just seemed to be against them. They had been for a long time.

The fire in the house was warmer than his wife's greeting. Tor guessed she still remembered the argument they'd had before he left. There was always an argument. It might be up to him to fix that. Maybe after something to eat and drink. Tor watched the white leave his knuckles as she eased the long-handled axe from his strong grip and set it down by the door. He had forgotten he was carrying it.

"Before I go back up the mountain, I'll stop by the Hall to see about the Vikings. Try to talk some sense into our neighbors. Fools should have put a hole in the ship and sent it straight to the bottom of the fjord."

Runa frowned. "You haven't even taken off your coat and you're already talking about leaving?"

"Do you know how many goats are still missing?" Tor did not like this game. She knew he had responsibilities.

"We will be missing more if you leave your sons in charge of fixing the fences!" Runa took a deep breath and exhaled slowly, noticeably, then poured her husband a cup of hot mead. "How do you know your neighbors won't talk some sense into you?" she said, before plopping in a sprig of pine.

"What do they know about Vikings?" Tor said sarcastically. If he was trying to fix their quarrel, then he was doing a poor job of it.

"Maybe they know more about them than you think," Runa replied, raising an eyebrow.

"Can we talk about something else? I'd like to wait until I see what we're talking about before anyone tries to change my mind, all right?"

The house smelled of fresh bread. It was obvious she had planned a much warmer reception. She cut off the crusty end and put it on the table next to a bowl of lapskaus. "Pedar offered his home to nurse some of the survivors back to health."

Was she trying to upset him? She had a knack of making him feel like he wasn't living up to her expectations.

"Ja. Well I'm sure he'll try to work this for his benefit." Tor took a bite of bread softened by the broth. "I don't care what others do. No Viking will step foot into this house.

Apparently, Runa hadn't finished her point. "My father would have-"

"Ja. He would take them in. He took my family in, didn't he? And look at what that got him." He smiled to lighten the mood. She did not return it. "Well, I am not so-"

"Watch what you say, husband. My father was a great man."

This woman. Tor thought about grabbing the axe and making himself a new doorway. Instead he hunched over his food like a dog protecting a bone, took a deep breath, and replied with what he thought could only be taken as a compliment. "Your father was the greatest man. Better than a father to me."

Runa's smile looked forced. "One of the Vikings, the fat one, talks in his sleep, something about treasure. There could be profit in helping them."

"Is that what everyone's thinking?" Tor asked. "Hoping for the generosity of Vikings?" The wooden spoon clacked the bowl as he shovelled down the white stew. It was time to go, before he made things worse. He brushed wet soup and dry crumbs from his beard with a cloth as he pushed away from the table. He took a deep breath; this was his last chance to make things right.

15

Runa pulled her soul out from underneath her shirt. The gold-covered ring was being used like a little picture frame, and inside it held a relief of the goddess Freyja. Tor did not believe in much of anything, but Runa did. So, he carved it for her as a bridal gift at her request.

That felt like so long ago.

"Pedar thinks their arrival could be a gift from the gods." She kissed the little graven image of the goddess. Tor approached his wife, closed her hand around her soul, and held it tight to pull himself close. Runa smiled, as if expecting an apology, or a kiss. With his other hand he pulled at the top of her blouse. Her smile grew. Then he shook her hand until she dropped the little idol back from where it came. "The only gift gods or Vikings will bring is death." He let go of her and emptied his cup of lukewarm mead.

He did not have the time or energy to fix this today.

Tor swung the door open and breathed deep. He liked the cold outside better than the chill he felt within. "Thank God for goats!" He shouted. His sons turned toward their father. "At least we won't starve, not this winter." He guessed he would have to acknowledge his own accomplishments. No one else seemed to want to.

Tor stuffed his bread into his mouth, mumbled something through the crumbs, and left Runa standing in the door.

BEARS AND VIKINGS

T he boys were still trying to drag the unwilling goats back into the old fenced-in garden, now only good for growing weeds and the occasional stubborn volunteer vegetable. That fence, originally built to keep the goats out, now was the only one that stood a chance of keeping them in.

"Father?" Erik asked. "What about the Vikings?"

"I'm going to the hall now. Dry my things, I'll be back this afternoon. Then I've got to make another trip up the mountain." He grabbed the horn of a black spotted billy. "Got to gather more of the escapees."

"Can I come with?" asked Toren.

"In the spring. I promise," said Tor. "Right now, you need to learn how to manage the farm. This will all be yours someday, and a well-run farm can produce more food than any man can drag out of the woods."

"Can I go, then?" asked Erik.

"I need you both here to protect the farm." Tor put a strong handed grip around the back of each son's neck.

"From Vikings?" Erik scowled as he put his hand on the hilt of his seax.

"From the cold." Tor frowned. "Keep the fire burning for your stepmother, and mend the fences so I don't see any of these goats again while I'm up on the mountain."

"Ragi says Old Erik thinks we should forge an alliance with the Vikings," Toren blurted. "I think he's right."

Tor put his arm around his eldest. "Are you a politician,

now?"

"Everyone's saying there's no better traders than Vikings," added Erik.

Tor mounted a fresh horse. "Vikings are also supposed to be good seamen, but every boy with a rowboat knows not to be caught near open water this time of year."

REHABILITATING VIKINGS

"**A**h, Tor. Perfect. Give us a hand, will you?" It was as if Tor's closest neighbors were having a meeting in the woodshed next to the hall.

Outside, it was a bright, snowy autumn afternoon—a good day for work. There was no event, no occasion, and no reason he should smell meat roasting or bread baking—no reason he should hear so many voices inside.

"Here to see some old friends?" Pedar Thordsen stood in front of the door as if he was waiting to greet guests into his own house.

"I'm here to meet your Vikings," replied Tor. *Old friends?*

Arn Halvarsen and Bor Jonsen stood at either end of a rack full of limbs and logs that were about as long as Tor was tall. Bor joined Arn at the far side of the pile, leaving the near end open for Tor.

"Will they live?" Tor asked.

"Ja. Elsa's bringing them around with one of her special brews." Pedar edged past Tor and made his way to the center of the log. He always liked being in the middle of things.

Tor's lip curled. He'd survived Elsa's treatments before.

"Where's the ship?" he asked.

"You haven't seen it?" Bor responded. "It's a longship. Half sunk in the fjord. Not far from Pedar's."

Pedar glared at Bor as if he was interrupting. Bor owned

a farm near the village, the third largest behind Pedar's and Tor's.

"Should be able to get it out in the Spring," Arn added. Both Pedar and Bor glared at him as if he'd spoken out of turn. Arn followed Bor, and Bor followed Pedar, and Pedar followed Tor. And Tor only followed goats.

"Alright, I did not come here to hear about Vikings ten feet from the door. Are you ready?"

The others nodded.

"One." Tor started the count.

Arn and Bor both warmed their hands, and Pedar picked at the bark with a manicured nail.

"Two," Tor continued.

Arn and Bor both took hold of their end of the white birch, Tor grabbed hold of his end, and Pedar pulled away an area of its loose papery skin like he might a piece of lint on a coat.

"Three!" Three of the men heaved.

Pedar rested his hands atop the log. "I think the big one is Jarl Olaf."

Arn and Bor dropped their end, and when it bounced Tor lost his grip and nearly smashed his fingers.

He wondered who to hit first, "Either help, or get out of the way!"

"Olaf the Soul-less," Bor nodded. "I think you're right."

"He's big, but he's not a giant, is he?" Arn looked anxious.

"He's emaciated," argued Pedar.

"Wait'll we see him on his feet. Bet he's a head taller than Tor," added Bor.

Tor's face was starting to burn. *Why does everyone want to keep me from getting in the hall?* He started walking toward the door.

"Wait, wait. Just help us with this one," Arn begged. "I lost a bet."

Tor shook his head, grabbed the log, and started to count.

"One."

"Olaf's supposed to wear a necklace made of other men's souls," Bor slipped in.

"Two." Tor's voice lowered. "Pedar, get the door."

"No man is strong enough to carry another man's soul!" Arn got the words out just in time, then inhaled heavily through clenched, yellowing teeth.

Tor longed for the mountain—it had been a lot quieter.

"Three!" Tor's face turned to stone as he lifted the log up and over the rack. Bor and Arn both grunted as if to argue that their end was heavier.

"Even I can carry a soul if it's given to me." Pedar's soft, gold-ringed fingers tugged at the tall door's handle. He sucked in his pot belly, trying to stay out of the way as the log staggered into the hall.

Faces of men Tor knew came into focus as his eyes adjusted. Many loitered around the waist-high troughs of stacked stone that were in the center and around the edge of the hall.

Elsa hefted a beer at Arn as he passed. "That doesn't count," she said. "You got help." *Was Arn trying to smile at the ugly maid?* It looked more like a growl, as if he couldn't quite raise a smile and the log at the same time. His cheeks were splotchy red, and he had a string of spittle that curled in and out with each labored breath.

She smiled back at him. As if things weren't painful enough.

Again, gravity viciously snatched the log from Tor's grasp, because, without warning, Arn and Bor dumped their end into the first raised trough they passed.

"Uff-da!" Tor coughed as fiery embers flew up into his face. Then the white papery skin of the birch caught fire, nearly blinding him with a sudden burst of heat and light. Arn and Bor surrounded him with apologies, one knocking orange embers off his bearskin coat while the other forced a horn of beer to his mouth to help with the coughing. *Lazy buggers.* The fire closest to the door was always the one with the most wood.

Tor regained his bearings in time to see the dry wood ignite, illuminating a pillar of smoke that climbed high into the heavy oak rafters until being drawn out of one of the covered chimneys by a passing breeze.

He drank his beer, warmed his hands, and gathered his thoughts. For some time, he could not even look at his friends. Instead, he calmed himself by watching ancient oak timbers dance in a play of light and shadows from orange and yellow fires.

Wood blazed in stone and black iron braziers atop many of the long oak tables. This was not uncommon in the evenings, or during the long winter months — but it was still light outside, and there was plenty to be done at home before the snows set in. What was most odd was how many of the long fires were burning. The hall was so stoked with fires that it was actually warm.

Tor pushed through the spectators.

Three men slept on straw mats made up on the riser next to the empty throne.

Elsa, Pedar's maid, moved from one mat to the next, pouring spoonfuls of warm broth into each unconscious man's mouth before tucking them into thick wool blankets. Two of the three thanked her by spitting out the broth and kicking off their covers. But the giant one lay still as a corpse, other than the occasional gasp, as if he was struggling to tread water in a sea of bad dreams.

Tor's heart stopped. After all this time, he couldn't believe his past had found him now.

Here.

He gripped the handle of his seax and gave the fat one a nudge with his boot. *Come on Orri, give me a reason.* The heavily tattooed man's eyes opened, then grew wide. Tor pulled back.

He recognizes me. I should end this all right now.

22

He looked over his shoulder. The entire hall was watching. *Or I could come back tonight. If I killed them all, who would take up the law against me?* Tor hadn't killed a man in so long. The fat Viking grumbled something, then his eyes fell closed again. Nothing felt right to Tor now. He took his hand off the hilt of his seax. He would not add assassination to his list of sins.

Tor raised himself up and looked to Elsa, the unfortunate nurse. "What's wrong with them?"

"They're deprived, is all." Elsa was the ugliest thing in Pedar's house and worth every grimace. "Deprived of sleep, of food, of water. They'll be alright once I get enough of my tonic in 'em." As bad as it usually tasted, she did have the recipe for healing.

Tor thought of the men spitting unconsciously. *They would rather die than drink the troll's brew.* He could relate. One time he pretended to get better just so his wife would stop making him take it. He doubted he was the only one.

"Take care this one survives, Elsa." Pedar timidly pulled at the giant's collar. His voice came back when he backed away. "He is Jarl Olaf, the Soul-less. Do you see the string of rings around his neck?"

The hall leaned in.

"What do you hope to gain out of this, Pedar?" Tor asked. "You already trade with half the Sogn."

"Vikings have gold and silver, and livestock on faraway lands," said Bor.

"What have you been telling these men, Pedar?" Tor felt like he was being forced to eat bad lutefisk, the kind you only ate when the pantry was empty and spring refused to come. "Keep your trade in the northern villages. Whatever you do there, keep it there. Leave this place sacred."

"Sacred? You speak of sacred when you —" Pedar broke off, as if trying to choose his words carefully. "When was the last time you sacrificed to the gods?"

"It's been quite a while, hasn't it, Tor?" another voice

said.

Of course, Old Erik would be there. The decrepit old priest needed a staff to steady himself, but somehow he was always there when big decisions were being made. His brother, Afi, was probably around the hall somewhere, too. Old Afi he liked. He was more of a listener. Tor always joked that those two should have been dead ten years before he even arrived, and that was thirteen years ago.

It wasn't long after he found this place that Old Erik encouraged him to take the empty throne. He said he had a natural way about him that people would follow. Tor never told anyone that. He didn't want to find out who agreed with the old man.

Since then, he kept his distance from the priest. He never liked people who encouraged him to do or take what he wanted. Who needs council for that? From then on, he noticed, if anyone was looking for someone wise to tell them why it was alright to do something selfish, they'd make a sacrifice just so they'd have a reason to talk to Old Erik. He'd make them feel much better about it. Tor seemed to be the only person who noticed that.

The last time he saw Old Erik, he was heading off on a long hunting trip. When the old man smiled and wished him luck, he immediately felt guilty for leaving—like he was abandoning his family or something.

"What do you think, Tor? Look like Olaf to you?" Old Erik winked with his green eye.

Why is he smiling like a forest cat? Tor exhaled deeply. The hall smelled like farmers in the fall. Like sweat stained clothes, earth, and smoke.

"It's not Olaf. It's one of his sons." He wiped the damp from his forehead and shook off his outer coat. *When did it get so hot?* "Olaf only asks for the soul rings of his thingmen. In exchange they get a larger share from the raids, and one of his arm rings. Look." He pointed to the Vikings' arms. Each was wearing one silver band. The one with long, black hair had two. "Olaf wears at least five so he has some to give away. To get one is an honor." Everyone had gotten quiet. They were all listening now. "Before I left Olaf's army, I had three. Solid gold."

The hall murmured.

"I was second only to Olaf himself. I had wealth and power." Tor withdrew his seax, dug its tip into the table, and leaned on its hilt. "Men have sold their souls for less." With it he cut the leather thong from around his neck and held up his gold-plated ring. "Here's what it cost me. This is what I made with some of that precious gold." He frowned when he looked at it. "What a beautiful forgery." He felt like he was confessing his sins to his late wife's priest. His eyes glanced up as if to heaven. *Could he still be listening now?*

Tor sheathed his seax and snatched Pedar by the wrist. Pedar tried to withdraw but his strength was no match. Tor twisted and squeezed until Pedar's palm forced open. Then he dropped the little gold soul ring into his hand and let go.

The room erupted in whispers. Tor could make out the general sentiment. *He's lifting it!*

No one looked more surprised than poor Pedar. He half expected to have broken an arm or at least had his hand smashed into the table.

"It's just a ring!" They were hardly whispers anymore.

Pedar stared at the little golden ring reflecting firelight in his hand. Tor felt flush as he could only imagine what Pedar was thinking. It was a poor forgery. So plain. Maybe even a touch small. Tor always kept it hidden in his shirt. Now they all knew why. Soon everyone would know.

Tor took the ring back, then patted Pedar on the shoulder. "Did I hurt your wrist?"

Pedar shook his head blankly.

Tor held the ring up to his eye and looked at it, then dropped it into the fire. That was a lie he'd been carrying for far too long. *The priest was right, confession is good for the...*

Well, it may have been too late for his soul, but not for his conscience.

He looked for the stunned faces, but they weren't there. "Men like these," Tor motioned to the platform, "cost me my soul."

Tor stared at blank faces. Maybe they were missing the point. So he said it more plainly, "I was Viking." The whispers stopped — but there was still no surprise. Men he knew well refused to look him in the eye. Some bit their lips and stared at the fire. If anything, they looked worried about the gold melting away in its coals, enough to cover their own dirty souls if they could just get their hands on it. *They knew!* Tor shook his head. He never was good at secrets; he had only been fooling himself. *They already knew.*

THE GIRL

A rn climbed up on one of the benches. "To Tor!" He raised a horn of ale. "May his past, and past friendships, bring security and opportunity to us all!"

Horns of beer and cups of mead were raised in raucous agreement. Tor pulled Arn down from the bench and the noise fizzled like foam on flat ale.

"I have no friends among Vikings." Tor cleared the last of the excitement from the room. "I left because I no longer wanted to be a part of that life."

"That life you left offers trade and opportunity. This land offers onions," Arn persisted. "I have sons to worry about."

"We all do," Bor reminded. "What future do you have to offer your youngest son, Erik? What's he got to look forward to with no inheritance? Plowing fields for his older brother?"

"Catching goats is more like it." Arn laughed into his cup.

"They'll never be your allies," Tor scolded. "Not without a cost."

"Well, I'll not make enemies of them; that's for sure," said Bor, "or their fathers."

"I've got to go." Tor glared at Arn with narrow eyes. "I've got goats to catch." Then he looked to Pedar. "There was a girl?"

"Ja," said Pedar. "Hiding over there. Old Afi's with her."

A waif of a girl was huddled up on a bench close to the trough of embers near the back. The Vikings were the draw here, and she looked to be sitting as far away from the commotion as possible.

"Where is she from?"

"She's one of them," replied Bor.

"The gods must have favored her," added Arn. "How could that girl have come off that ship in better shape than these men?"

"My wife figure's they must have given up their rations for her," Bor added.

"My wife thinks she's a witch," said Pedar.

Tor shook his head. "If anybody's a witch, it's your wife," Tor whispered under his breath as he skulked over to grab a few pieces of wood, then returned to the girl.

Her head was bowed. He nodded to Old Afi. The old man nodded back. It was good she wasn't alone.

Tor eased the wood into the coals closest to her, knocked the bark off his hands, and lifted her chin. A burst of flames brought warmth to the chilly corner.

She was dirty, but pretty. Her strawberry blond hair matched the color still visible through the filth on her dress.

"Can you speak?"

She didn't reply. He lifted her hand. Broken blisters had formed thick callouses.

"She's no witch," said Tor. "She's been pulling the oar. If anything, she was meant to be a slave."

"How else could she have survived?" asked Pedar.

Tor ignored him and lowered himself to her level. She could have been his daughter.

"Are you alright?" he asked in broken English, dredging his memory for the right words to use.

"What did you say?" Arn leaned in, his eyes curious.

Tor ignored him and kept his focus on the girl. "I won't let anyone hurt you." He ran his hand down her shoulder and held her hand gently. He cast a look over to the three unconscious Vikings, then back to her. Her eyes were green and sad. "I'm sorry for whatever they did to you, but you are safe now. This is not their village."

As he began to stand, she tightened her grip around his fingers. Tears made two clean lines down dirty cheeks. "I'm cold," she replied in English no better than his, only seasoned with a Gaelic rasp.

Tor raised an eyebrow, put her hand gently down, stood, and walked toward the door.

"Where are you going?" asked Pedar.

Tor returned with his bear skin cloak and put it around the girl's shoulders. It covered her head to toe. Then he refilled her empty bowl from the large iron pot hanging under the hearth, broke off a fresh piece of bread and put it on the table beside her.

"Are you from Ireland or Scotland?" He hadn't spoken Irish since his first wife died in Runa's father's own bed. Toren was probably only three then, and Erik just a baby.

"Ireland." She hovered her hands over the steaming bowl.

Tor hung his head. He had raided there many times. Olaf had a thing about it. He smiled as his mind shifted back to his first wife. Her hair was red too. She taught him how to love—and forgive. He looked at Old Afi. "My wife will care for the girl through winter. I'll send the boys over to get her."

"What about the others?" asked Bor.

"Stop treating them. Put an axe in each of their hands and let them go to Valhalla where they will only kill more of Odin's favorites."

Blank faces.

Tor lowered his eyes and shook his head. "If you want Elsa to keep torturing them, have her do it somewhere else."

More blank faces.

"This is a common hall not a boarding house. If they wake up here, they'll empty the casks, then come for the women." Tor remembered how his first wife was the reason he left the Viking life in the first place. He looked back at the girl. Red heads fetched twice as much as other women in much of the world.

The door slammed as he exited the hall. It was snowing again.

RUNA

The boys knocked over a chair on their way out, excited to be going to the village — and to collect the girl.

"How are we going to take care of her?" Runa stared at Tor — her mouth tight with annoyance. "We barely have enough to feed ourselves. Those sons of yours will have eaten half of our stores before the lake freezes."

Does leaving always have to be a fight? Tor thought.

"It's not their fault the ground here is fallow," he murmured under his breath.

"It was never fallow when I was growing up."

"Well it is now. Everything your father sold me was fallow," he said — then wished he hadn't.

Runa's eyes flared, and she threw a stale loaf at him. He caught it, broke off a piece of crust, and crushed it in his hand, more mad at himself than at his wife. He dropped the crumbs to the floor. A little dog scurried from under the table, retrieved the scrap, and retreated to his spot in front of the fire.

Tor put his hand on his wife's shoulder. Her muscles were bunched, but her breathing softened. Then he crossed to the other side of the room. After pushing a thin linen curtain to one side, he dragged the stuffed mat they used for a bed to one side and lifted a loose plank from the floor. From inside a small hole he pulled out a little wooden box, ornately carved and trimmed with brass. He weighed it in his hands as he walked it back and put it on the table.

Runa started sweeping up crumbs the dog hadn't bothered to clean.

Other than the fine red velvet lining, there were three gold coins, two silvers, five coppers, and a few small, colorful jewels. Everything else was gone. Tor's brow furrowed as he fingered the contents of the box.

"What have you done?"

"If you spent less time on the mountain and more time tending to the farm I wouldn't have had to." Her eyes narrowed and she raised a hand. "Did you think I could run this farm by myself while you and your sons went hunting? When I was a girl my father had twenty hands running this place."

Tor's eyes burned as he fought to keep it together. He stalked across the room and started stuffing heavy clothes into a bag.

She ran around in front of him.

"What about the animals? If you can't grow feed, then we have to buy it, don't we? Or did you think the horses eat what you carry out of the woods on your shoulder?

His mind raced through the argument he did not dare to have. This woman had no idea what that small fortune cost him. How dare she use it. And for what? To prop up what was left of her father's failing farm? To pretend to still be somebody. They should have sold it all to Pedar and built a cabin in the woods, something easy to keep up. Let the weeds have this barrow, a shrine to what used to be. His knuckles cracked as he tried to keep from breaking something of hers.

Tor closed his eyes and breathed deeply. He almost prayed for peace, something his first wife had taught him how to do, long ago. But he gave up on that after she died. The gods ask too much. Odin only wants you if you take. Jesus only wants you if you give.

The only good he had from his past was knowing he had something to leave to his sons. And now that was gone. Tor pulled on his heavy fur lined boots, the ones with the toes nearly worn through. He belted his axe and his seax.

"Your oldest son will inherit my father's farm one day. Think about that before you complain. Some of that money went to make sure he has a house worthy of that girl's hand. Did you think the roof would fix itself?" Runa taunted him.

"I fixed the roof." Tor ducked through the door, out of the dark house into the bright, snow-covered world.

"Where did you think we got our stores all these years?" She followed him out to the barn, still pulling on her new winter coat. "What do we have for sacrifices? Pedar makes regular offerings to the gods and look at how they've blessed him."

"You've given Old Erik our choicest yearlings." Tor was near growling now. He checked his bow string and counted the arrows in his quiver before fixing it to the top of a sledge that was already packed, always ready.

"Well, apparently the gods are sick of goat. As am I!" his wife derided.

"Tell me you haven't been stealing from my sons' inheritance to sacrifice to those greedy gods. It's never going to be enough, you know. Ask Old Erik. They'll take everything from you, until finally you give them your soul. Yours looks beautiful, by the way. At least all of the coin wasn't squandered on keeping up the farm."

She stared back at him. "Inheritance? You have to eat if you want to live long enough to worry about that."

"Well thanks to you and Pedar, the priest will outlive us all," he said, as he stuffed some small things in his pockets.

"You cannot go. What are we going to do with the girl?"

Tor pressed a gold piece into the palm of his wife's hand. "Take this to Pedar. Buy provisions for winter, enough for our growing boys and that waif of a girl. I doubt she'll eat much."

Tor strapped on a pair of skis and grabbed his spear.

"None of it goes to Old Erik. None of it goes to the

upkeep of those Vikings. They can sleep with Pedar's chickens for all I care. But not the girl. Take care of her as if she was-"

Runa's eyes cut him off. He knew he was walking on thin ice. "Where are you going?" she asked.

"Anywhere but here." Tor skied off, towing the sledge behind as he *shooshed* across the top of the deep, powdery snow shouting "Wip, wip, wip!" Two dogs ran out from the woods to greet him, and Vigi, a little slower, trotted out of the barn. "Not you, boy. You've got to stay back and help protect the farm, alright?" Tor hated leaving Vigi behind, and Vigi didn't look like he understood. The last thing he heard was Vigi whimpering lowly to himself.

Before disappearing into the forest, his tone lifted as he praised the only things in his life that never argued, never complained, and were always happy to see him. "How are you feeling today pups? Ready to do some hunting? Me too."

PEDAR'S OFFER

"Tor, can we talk?"

"I've really got to get going, Pedar." All Tor wanted was to get out of this village.

"It's important." To him, everything was important.

"Alright," Tor thought of a solution, "only if you take this goat to your farm and hold her for me until I get back. I was trying to go hunting when I saw her, and I really don't want to go home right now."

Pedar looked confused when Tor handed him the rope. "Will you be able to find her again if I have the men just put her in with mine?"

Sometimes Tor couldn't believe this man held the biggest farm in the village. "They wear my mark. I can always find my own."

Pedar didn't look like he believed him. "Tor, that was quite a moment you had back in the hall. How are you doing?"

"Is that what you stopped me for?"

Pedar shook his head. "You could've been the leader of this village."

What is this man talking about? "I never wanted that, Pedar." Tor looked up at the sun, he guessed he still had some time. "I support the council of our elders. I never wanted the empty throne."

Pedar looked scared of the little goat. "I understand. You are loyal to this village and to Old Erik and Afi. That is not in question. But you saw that Viking. You are the only one in this village even capable of standing against men like that."

"Give her to me." Tor tied the little nanny to the back of Pedar's horse. "Would you have me take the throne and end our tradition of self-rule under a common law? Of abiding under something greater than a man?"

"No, no, no." Pedar cleaned his hands in the snow, then shook them off, as if afraid to defile his fur coat. "I would have you convince the elders we need to forge an alliance with Jarl Adar, to unite the Sogn."

"Adar? The merchant?" Tor could not believe this man stopped him to talk about politics, now of all times. "Pedar, it's cold out here, and I've got to get going. Can't we talk about this over a beer sometime in the hall? We've got all winter for this."

"You never want to talk about these things," said Pedar. "If you'd let me talk about it in the hall without constantly changing the subject then I wouldn't have to stand out here freezing just to get your attention. This is urgent. Things are about to change around here."

"Why?" Tor asked. "Because three Vikings shipwrecked on our shores? Why would that make me want to pledge to a man like Adar? No matter how much men like you want to believe it, wealth does not make a leader. And since when did Adar become a jarl?"

"He negotiated an alliance with Sveinn and Jǫfurr. That covers the villages to the North. And Kál Ólisen, which brings in the South. He's got the Fjord already—you just didn't know it. Joining voluntarily ensures opportunity for men like us and our families."

This man is delusional. "Men like us?"

The goat butted Pedar on the knee. He kicked at it and shooed it away. "And will protect our neighbors from the threat of Vikings like Vidar's father."

"Right now, I just want to protect them from Vidar." Tor

knocked the snow off his skis, trying to drop the hint that he was going somewhere. Then he leaned back on his poles. "Adar has no experience in war. If anything, a Sogn united behind a man like that makes it more of a target for men like Olaf."

"Before becoming jarl, Adar presided over a vast area with many villages along the southern shore of the fjord." Pedar struggled back atop his horse. Fjord horses weren't tall, but neither was Pedar. "I have traded with Adar for many years. His people live well, and he also leaves an empty throne as a reminder that he governs under the law, not under some priest speaking on behalf of the gods or in service to a would-be king like Harald Fairhair."

"Kings or gods or jarls or elder councils, I have seen little difference in my life. All are manipulated. Whether by women or ambitious men, they are all under the influence of trolls of some kind, from this world or another." Tor began to ski into the forest.

Pedar dodged limbs as he followed on horseback, goat in tow. "You speak in rants of sentimentality, as if nothing will change as long as you believe it shouldn't." He spat after having his teeth brushed by pine needles. "You said it yourself; wealth does not make a leader. This village needs a warrior to give us position in a changing world. If you won't align with the Vikings, then help me convince these people to ally with the rest of the fjord."

Tor kept skiing, pulling his sledge of supplies through forest too dense to be traversed on horseback. "If you're coming with me, maybe you'd have an easier time of it riding on the back of that goat."

"Tor!" Pedar sounded upset. "Stop for one second, please! This spring, Adar is hosting a Gulating, the first for all the villages of the Sogn. After the laws have been spoken and the ceremonies are finished, Adar will choose his thingmen. Our families need to be there to represent this village."

Tor stopped skiing and looked intently at his friend. *Am I just a pawn to this man?* "How long have you been planning this alliance with your trading partners, Pedar? What has Adar promised you?"

Pedar looked flustered. "Can I tell you a secret? I wish you'd have taken control of the village when you first arrived. No one would've tried to stop you. Afi would have stepped down, and maybe you'd have been the one to unite the Sogn. Things could have been different—for all of us."

"You say this to me now? After fifteen years? I never wanted anything here to change." *Wait, is this man blaming this on me?* "Pedar, how many years have you been silently watching Adar grab his power? And this is the first you've mentioned it. Does Afi know?"

"None of that matters, does it? The time for you to act passed years ago. Now, we must ally with someone who showed ambition while there was still opportunity. The only question now is whose kingdom will we join? After the Gulathing of Sogn, even Jarl Adar will be strong enough to take us if he wants. We might as well profit from it. Gain a position."

Tor dropped his gaze and just shook his head.

"Why are you so stubborn?" asked Pedar. "Are you so principled that you're willing to let this village change hands without even trying to direct where it falls? Are you willing to throw away this chance at prosperity? Your sons' only chance—if I am being honest?"

"My sons?" replied Tor. "I am trying to protect *our* sons, and daughters." Tor looked into Pedar's nervous eyes. "But maybe it's too late for that. I believe you are trying to think of the village as much as yourself, here. But I understand these types of men. In some ways, jarls and kings are worse than Vikings. Unless you have an army, there's no allying with them. It's why Vikings raid and move on, because politics are too dangerous.

What happens when the next village refuses to join Jarl

Adar? Do you think he and his council will act any different than Olaf? No. The more power he gains the more authority he'll demand."

Tor loosened his grip when he heard his ski poles begin to crack. He'd only been home one day, and he felt like all the arrows of his past were being shot toward his home — and his neighbors were lining up to help pull back the bowstring.

Tor had one more point. "Peaceful Adar will lead us into war, maybe not with Olaf at first, maybe with that small defiant village, like us. Maybe it won't be for conquest, but in the name of peace, or food, or water. Maybe it will be to help some king up north we didn't know we'd agreed to protect. And for war or peace, it doesn't matter which, Adar and his council will form an army. And our children will be the ones who are sacrificed.

"I would choose we have that fight on our own terms, right here. We are under no threat right now. Our village is still hidden, is it not?"

Pedar's cheeks flushed red. "Of course, it is. Tor, don't you see. You've made my point for me. We can choose our own destiny, choose whether we will fight a fight we cannot win, or join someone who can and will reward us for our allegiance. For our children's sake, shouldn't we make sure we're on the winning side?"

"Stop it with the children already." Tor skied deeper into the trees.

"Can we stop them now? They are here!" Pedar melted some snow against his red cheeks. "You can thank the gods for any arrangements I've made with Adar. Because alliances must be forged before the powerful arrive at your door. Not after."

Tor always told his sons, even a small axe will eventually fell a mighty oak. Pedar had made his point. As Tor started his ascent up the mountain, he felt an uneasy peace, the kind you get when you finally understand. He knew the true enemy and understood what needed to be done.

A GIRL IN THE HOUSE

K iara was not expected or wanted, but Tor's pet arrived just the same.

"Set the table, girl." Runa's shoulders were as tight as if Freyja herself were dropping by for a cup of spruce tea. She was not friendly to 'the Christian' or 'the girl', for those were things she called her, but it didn't take long before she warmed to the idea of having a servant.

Kiara turned out to be a good one. In preparing for the guests she juggled stirring the pot, stoking the fire, and putting out bread and cheese and lingonberry jam.

In the spring, Toren was to marry Anja, Pedar and Skadi's daughter. Runa and Skadi had been negotiating the details of the arrangement since Toren got his soul.

During better days, Runa's father had built servants' quarters that Runa had been busy preparing for the marriage. The house would make up the bulk of the bride price. In return, Anja's dowry was generous enough to provide solvency for Runa's father's farm. It was a good match.

Dogs barked. Runa peeked out the door. "Hurry girl. And do something with yourself. You look terrible." Runa jerked the copper pan out of Kiara's hand, the one she used for a mirror, and checked herself one more time.

Anja came in first. She looked Kiara up and down, pulled off her fur hat, pushed it into the girl's hands, and walked directly to the fire. "I miss the sun already." Her pink lips pouted. Even after trudging in from the snow Anja was beautiful. The cold gave her cheeks a faint blush. Just opening the door made Kiara's cheeks as red as her hair. Anja's long brown mane held together in a long, tight, perfect braid, woven in a way that it lay neatly over her right shoulder. Kiara's untameable hair lifted off her head and crackled with electricity the second she took Anja's hat.

"Don't be dramatic, Anja. There are still some leaves on the trees," said her mother. Skadi walked past Kiara, took off her furs, and handed them to Runa. She looked Kiara up and down like she was examining a fish at the market.

Skadi was striking. With long, black, perfectly combed hair and pale, soft skin, she hardly looked like she'd been outside at all. Skadi pushed a piece of Kiara's hair out of her face and tucked it behind her left ear. Then she took her daughter's hat from the girl's hand and added it to the pile, tucking it under Runa's chin.

"She's prettier than you let on, Runa."

"Do you think so? I don't know —"

The door opened, and Toren walked in. "I gave the horses something to eat." He stopped in the doorway to look at Kiara, then Anja, as if surprised to see them together. Toren's future was established. He was seventeen — a good age for marriage, and as Tor's eldest son, someday he would inherit everything — including the care of his stepmother.

And this match would make sure he could afford to do it well.

Erik slipped sideways past his big brother.

He pushed Anja to the side so he could warm his hands. "Make way woman, it's cold out there."

"Erik, go back where you came from. No one is here to see you." As the youngest son, Erik had no right to anything. Runa felt like he forgot this sometimes. So, she reminded him of it daily.

Anja pushed Erik back. "Are *you* still here?"

"Not much longer, that I can promise you." Runa reminded him of *that* daily, too.

42

"Toren, beat up your little brother for me." Anja played with men the way a broke musician might browse through a room full of overpriced instruments.

"Little? You and I are the same age."

Runa shoved a small sack in Erik's hand and pushed him toward the door. "Out, out. You are supposed to be cutting firewood."

Erik twisted out of her grip and stole cheese off the table, stuffed it in his mouth, and slipped out the door.

Erik had a natural charm that made mothers of eligible daughters despise him almost as much as Runa.

Skadi scowled at Anja until she stopped smiling. "I thought he'd be gone by now, Runa. I don't know how you manage to feed everyone." Skadi tended to sound tired when she was being a witch. Poor thing. "Now you've got her to worry about." She turned her scowl toward Kiara.

The future in-laws had never been friends, but they were pragmatic for the sake of their shared interests. Wealth, power, and position—and the children. Of course, the children.

"Erik will be gone after the thaw." Runa wanted to be clear. "He gets his soul ring this year, then he's off."

Kiara looked at Toren, as if he would explain. Runa was sure Anja noticed the look, too. "Don't you have something you should be doing?" Everyone stared at Kiara as she scurried back to the kitchen, which was only four feet away from where she had been standing.

Runa tolerated Kiara, but unless she needed something, she mostly treated her as if she wasn't there. "I think Erik's got the girl confused. I think he likes her a little and doesn't realize how hard that makes it for her to know her place."

Kiara seasoned the pot.

"Maybe they're both confused." Skadi wouldn't take her eyes off the girl. "Do you know who she reminds me of?"

Runa corralled the couple toward the door. "Toren, why don't you take Anja for a walk?"

"She looks like Toren and Erik's mother, doesn't she?" Skadi couldn't help but stir up trouble.

Toren's head snapped toward the girl. Kiara kept stirring an over-stirred pot.

Witch. "It's been so long since she passed." Runa tried to pretend she hadn't noticed. "Maybe that awful red hair."

"It's more than that. Surely Tor's mentioned it?"

"No." Runa hurried into her bedroom, then emerged again with Anja's coat and hat. Kiara was still stirring, and Toren was still staring. "Toren, show your betrothed the progress on the house. You don't want to hear our gossip and scheming." Runa shuttled them outside. "But stay close, I doubt her mother plans to stay long."

"You're lucky Tor grabbed her. I know you can use the help."

Runa was tired of Skadi telling her how lucky she was.

Skadi smiled. "I don't know what I'd do without Elsa."

Everything Skadi said was as painful as a cut finger, but at least she'd stopped talking about the boy's mother.

"I'm glad to have some help in the house, but it's a job just keeping the girl straight. It was almost easier doing everything myself."

"Girl, I think you've stirred that pot enough," Skadi laughed.

You should talk. Runa started thinking of ways she could get this woman out of her house. Until she could figure out how, she pretended she was happy. She'd become adept at that over the years. "The girl is actually a pretty good cook. Apparently, stew is as common in Ireland as it is in Norway."

Skadi spooned through the lapskaus until she found a piece of meat. "Mmm. Apparently." She pushed the bowl away and pretended to be confiding in Runa. "I think I'm just used to the way Elsa makes it."

Runa eyed the knife next to the loaf of bread and considered the consequences of murder. "The boys have really been helpful, lately. Fences are getting mended, and animals are getting fed without complaint. How's Ragi been? Has he decided to learn a little something about farming, or is he going to be more of a hunter or fisherman?" Runa knew she shouldn't bring up Skadi's stepson's incompetence, but it felt good to remind her neighbor that not everything about her life was a blessing from the gods.

"You don't want to talk about farming, do you?" Skadi looked bored. "We have tenant's and servants for all of that. Ragnall's got a mind for trading, like his father."

So far, the only thing the fifteen-year-old had managed to succeed in was to build himself a second chin and a soft belly. Runa really did hope that he would become half the man he envisioned himself to be, though. Maybe he would hire Erik and send him off to trade somewhere far away.

Skadi crushed the end off the bread with the knife. "When did your boys start helping out more? Was it after the girl moved in?" She put the crumpled loaf next to Runa's bowl.

Runa pushed her bowl and bread away, both untouched. "What are you getting at?"

"I'm not sure if it's wise to have my future son-in-law under the same roof with this foreigner. Maybe red hair has some power over the men in your family. Pedar said Tor wanted to drown the Vikings, yet he offered his house to help this...Christian slave." She rubbed the crumbs from her fingers onto the table. "Some of our men even said they thought she might be a witch."

"She understands what we're saying, you know," said Runa. "The Vikings spent all summer at her village before they were forced to take to sea. Even an idiot would learn something after all that."

Skadi stood and stared at the girl.

Kiara was back to stirring.

"Is that true?" asked Skadi. "Have you been listening in

on us?"

Kiara looked down at her mistress.

Runa smiled and nodded.

Kiara hesitated, then looked into Skadi's piercing green eyes, and nodded to the lady. "No."

"Get me my things," hissed Skadi.

"I mean, ja, I understand, but no, I haven't been listening!" Kiara was flustered and ran into the back room.

Skadi had to get the last word. "I don't approve of this girl living in the same house as the boy who may become my son-in-law."

"*May* become your son in-law?" Runa was just glad she was leaving. There was only one witch in her house, and she had black hair, not red.

"Who knows what she's learning from your family. She won't likely have any loyalty to our little village once she's gone, will she?"

"Gone? What do you mean?" That caught Runa off guard.

"Well, she isn't yours." Skadi looked at Runa as if she felt sorry to be the one to remind her. "Once our Viking gets well, he'll be wanting his slave girl back. Or had you forgotten?" Skadi smiled, put on her furs, and let the door slam shut as she left.

Runa watched as a tear formed in Kiara's eye. Well, she had to find out sometime. Anyway, the girl had done something right for once. The witch was gone.

FAT ORRI

"I've only seen one man cut wood like that," a voice said.

Erik's heart leapt in his chest. When he caught a glimpse of the fat Viking from the hall, he tripped over a piece of wood and landed painfully in the pile. The snow-white kid he displaced climbed back up to its perch and butted him on the shoulder, apparently willing to fight to take back its spot at the top.

"And that's the ugliest dog I've ever seen."

You should talk. Erik looked out into the forest, thick with a low hanging fog. He was alone.

"I didn't see you." He flailed like a turtle trying to get back on his feet. It was no use.

The Viking shooed the little goat away before offering Erik a hand.

Erik wasn't sure.

"Come on boy. When a man offers you a hand, don't keep him waiting, because if he wanted to keep you down, you'd get the boot. I'm Orri."

Erik slowed down, pushed a particularly sharp piece of ash away from his side, planted one of his hatchets in it, and accepted the strangers help. As soon as he took Orri's hand he came straight to his feet.

"There you go." Orri made a grunting noise when he leaned back. But it was fake. "I din' mean to startle you. Just trying to be friendly." There was an unpleasant tang in his voice. Also, fake. Maybe he was trying to *sound* friendly, too. "And what's your name, boy?"

"Erik, Tor's son." He and his friends had played kill the Vikings a hundred times. He had imagined cutting them down as easily as he would a spindly pine. Cutting this one down wouldn't be that easy.

"Your father's name is Tor?" asked Orri.

"Ja." This was not going the way Erik had envisioned it. At least the Viking wasn't armed. He was sure he could kill this man if he tried anything. If he had to.

"Gangly one, aren't you?"

"I can hold my own." Erik felt the blood rise in his face, not sure if for the embarrassment of being caught off guard or the anger at being called gangly by a fat man. Orri was covered in tattoos, but the one that most drew Erik's attention was a pair of snakes running up his neck and onto his bald head. Getting that one had to have hurt.

"I didn't mean to scare you, boy. I was out for a walk and I heard the chopping. Thought I'd find two men with axes, instead I find one boy with two hatchets."

"I'm older than I look." Erik was beginning to wonder why he'd wanted to meet these Vikings so badly.

"'Ave you seen your soul, yet?" Orri asked.

Erik shook his head. "This year." He did not like the way this Viking was staring at him.

"I meant no disrespect, boy."

Boy? Erik was liking this man less and less. He wrenched the second axe back out from the ash.

"Well, Erik," said Orri. "What'er you gonna do with that goat?"

"What?" Erik couldn't tell if he'd hit his head, or if the Viking had lost his mind at sea.

"Well, there's wood, and a goat, and I'm sick of eating Elsa's broth." Orri made a funny face. "And Bor's wife's cooking idn't much better."

Erik smiled. He couldn't help it. Elsa was famous for brewing up terrible remedies. One time he feigned he was cured just to stop being force fed the briny, lumpy stuff.

Orri smiled back. "'at's it. You can smile. That troll must have poisoned you a time or two." Then Orri dug in his pocket and pulled out two pieces of silver. "If I had more, I'd buy that girl from you right here — but I think I'll need to hold on to this. It's all I've got. Everything else is on the ship."

Erik lowered his axes and swallowed hard. *Silver.* "This little goat is one of ours. We've got 'em scattered all over the mountain."

Orri smiled. "I'm not surprised. Your father's no farmer."

"How do you know my father?" This Viking didn't seem so bad.

"Oh, Tor and I go way back. But I can't talk about that now. Too hungry. After nearly starving on that ship I just can't stand the feeling of it no more." Orri looked around. "If we can't eat her, have you got anything else?"

Erik couldn't imagine this man had ever starved. He bet it took four men just to carry him off the ship.

"Just this." Erik lifted a sack up from beside the tree. One piece of dried fish, no bigger than two of his fingers put together, and a cold potato, boiled yesterday.

"'At's all you got left?" Orri asked.

"That's all I ever get. Runa's squirreling food away for winter."

"Runa? Who's that?"

"My father's wife."

"I must not have seen who I thought I saw. The man I knew would never let his sons go hungry. Not Tor. He was a Viking among Vikings. The proud son of Ove Strongbow." Orri started walking away. "I must be out of my mind. Should've known it couldn't be him. That Elsa's filling me full of poison, she is. She's made my eyes as worthless as Ubbi's tongue."

"Wait," Erik said. "I always thought I'd make a good

Viking."

Orri turned and eyed him up and down. "Maybe if you were bigger."

"Like you?" Erik knew he shouldn't have said it. But he didn't like being called small any more than he liked being called boy. He was only fifteen, after all.

The fat Viking shot him a hard look, then as if his face muscles couldn't keep it up, he let his jowls fall.

"I doubt your mother would like that idea. Besides, you're as worthless as your father."

Erik's blood boiled. He scraped the blades of his axes together.

"Whoa," Orri held up his hands. "They won't give me a weapon, here." Then he lifted his coat and spun around as if to show he was unarmed. His fat rolled over his belt the entire way. "All I meant was, a Viking wouldn't starve while protecting a tasty goat as if it was his favorite pet."

"My family needs it." Erik didn't know if he was trying to convince Orri or himself. His older brother got plenty to eat. So did Runa. He was the second son, so none of it would be his, not one acre of land. Not one goat. Why did he care anyway?

"I tell you what." Orri walked back. "Do you want to eat regular? You want to see a real treasure?" Orri threw the silver coins in the air and held them out toward Erik. "Not this silver-coated tin they spend across the sea." He shoved the coins back in his pocket. "Then give me an axe."

Erik stalled. "What?"

"I'm not going to ask you again. Are you hungry or not?"

Erik held out one of the axes.

Orri reached out and took it, slowly. Then smiled.

Erik's heart raced, half excited at the idea of treasure, and half worried he had just armed a Viking. Although he looked slow, he also looked more menacing with an axe in his hand. And that twisted smile.

Orri took the axe by the steel and tested it on the back of

his hand as he walked over to the log pile. It shaved. Then he reached out slowly to the kid.

"There now little one." He whispered, and rubbed its fur, as if it was a puppy. "I think I'm going to call you, let's see," he winked at Erik, "Runa. There, there, you wouldn't buck me would you, Runa." And as he lulled the little goat with his soft voice and his gentle hand, he ran the blade across one side of its throat as unthinking as Erik might run it along a piece of leather to keep it sharp. It was sharp. The little goat just stood there, its snow-white coat turning crimson in pulses, until, without a bleat, it eased to its knees, then lay down on top of the wood pile, the same place where Erik lay helpless only minutes before.

"All right." Orri kept talking in that soft soothing voice. "Get a fire going, then clean her up so we can eat." He didn't stop petting it until it took its final breath. "I'm starving."

Erik stood somewhere between impressed and in shock.

"Now, I'm going to tell you about a Viking treasure, and how you can earn a little bit of it for yourself. And maybe you can tell me a little more about your father. You're tough, kid. Maybe he is the Tor I knew after all."

It wasn't long before Erik and Orri were filling their empty stomachs and laughing over the fat man's stories. They were full of adventure and survival, wealth and women, and memories of friends he'd lost along the way. Erik could tell he was leaving out a lot of the details, details that could be the difference between humor and horror. But as Orri said more than once, a lot depends on which side of the door you're on, and who's doing the knocking.

Erik learned a few survival tricks, too. Orri told him how to clean the goat's bladder, and how by adding a few sprigs of pine for flavor it could be used to melt snow for drinking.

Orri seemed to find Erik's near retching amusing. "The problem with that trick, which will keep you alive of course, is no matter how much pine you add, it still tastes like minty goat piss." He handed Erik a skin he'd been hiding in his coat. "This ought to freshen your breath." It was half-full of wine he'd borrowed from Bor.

Orri was very curious about things in the village. Erik told him how to get to Ubbi, who was staying at Arn's. When he found out the boys in the village weren't being trained to fight, he volunteered Ubbi for the job.

Since they were being generous, Erik volunteered that Kiara was staying at his house.

"Who?" Orri couldn't place her.

"The girl?" Erik reminded him. "Very pretty. Red hair. Only speaks a little Norse."

"Oh, the slave. She made it, eh? Is she the only one?"

"There were just the four of you." Erik reminded him.

"Ja, ja." Orri's eyes got distant. He threw another log on the fire and rubbed his fat hands together as if he'd just caught a chill. "I knew that." It took a swing of the axe to free the back leg of the goat from its socket. As he bit into it, grease coated his lips out to his plump sagging cheeks. "Any news about my captain, Vidar? He's staying with that Ruiner of Appetites, Elsa. I think she works for a merchant."

"The giant? He's not doing that well." Erik didn't want to upset him. "My friend Ragi, the merchant's son, said they're worried he may not wake up."

"That's what Bor said, too." Orri stared at Erik as if watching to see how he felt about the news. After only one bite, Orri threw the leg in the fire. "Listen. You want to make your father proud, and maybe get out of this hole with more than a few pieces of silver in your pocket? I need you to get something for me."

RACE TO THE HIDDEN FJORD

T he boys waited for the warmest part of the day, but the cold breath of winter was already breathing down autumn's neck. The sky was gray with the falling snow, and the cold was chasing the sun away from the afternoon sky faster than the last leaves could fall off the trees.

Erik and Magnus bounced on the heels of their sleds, trying to eek out a little extra speed. This was the best hill in the Hidden Fjord, where the sleds could almost outrun the dogs — the stretch that took them all the way to the water's edge.

It was going to be close.

"Hyahhh!" Erik bent low. The wind was cold, but it felt good. "Dig Kratr, dig. Come on boy, you can catch 'em!" *Why did I let him have Sterkr?* Erik always second guessed himself when he was losing.

It was always the same, no matter which dog he had. Erik won the uphills, and Magnus won the down. *Can't lose again to that short, fat goblin.* Erik knew Magnus wasn't fat; he was solid as a pine knot, but he would never let Magnus know that.

"Jakl! Here boy!" Erik reached out, grabbed Jakl by the collar, and leaned back, letting him feel his weight. Dogs pulled harder when they felt the weight. "Get 'im, boy! Come on!"

"Skinny, cheating, dog!" Magnus yelled as he leaned into the hill, as if that would help. It didn't. Erik broke out of the woods first.

Both sleds stopped, and all three dogs went frantic, yelping and yipping and rolling in the snow. Smoke effervesced from their pink noses all the way down to their heavy coats, already thick to fend off Winter's bite.

"Hey, we were saving Jakl for the trip back," Magnus wheezed.

Toren was on skis, following in the sleds' deep tracks. Near the bottom, he leaned back to pick up speed, turned hard, and *poof*, his brother disappeared in a sparkling white cloud. "Erik cheated, two dogs to one." He looked past the boys at the fog swirling above the water. "Magnus wins."

"Yeah, cheater." Magnus was out of breath, but Erik didn't know why—Sterkr had done all the work.

"You're fat and slow, Magnus. Blame your mother, not me." Erik and Magnus repeated different versions of the same japes as they disappeared back into the trees with axes in hand. Toren stayed with the dogs so they could all catch their breath.

Kratr, Jakl, and Sterk were Vigi's sons. Toren and Erik had the dogs since they were pups. Tor trained them all to be like their father, and their mother, Etja. To hunt, pull, and protect the boys and the farm. Protecting the farm meant they wouldn't dig up onions or eat chickens or goats— unless the boys slipped it to them from the table.

Magnus's wolf, Garmr, was somewhere around too. He was half brother to the Elkhounds. A year younger and twice as large, he didn't share their masked faces, their medium build, or the thick tail that curled high over their backs. They were all strong, thick dogs, but Garmr was as tall and lanky as Magnus was short and stout. Garmr looked wild and dangerous. Apparently, their mother Etja had a romp with a black wolf—and Garmr took mostly after his father.

The same could be said for Magnus, because he definitely didn't take after his mother, Elsa. Where she was tall, he was short, where she was mushy, he was solid. Neither were thin.

Despite his conversation with Orri, the boys had no idea what was waiting in the Viking's ship, so they brought two sleds, just in case they were lucky enough to need them. Erik dreamed of having to help the dogs pull the sleds home, weighed down with gold and silver and precious gems.

Erik heard a horse approaching, and his heart sank. He and Magnus came out of the woods carrying armfuls of kindling and firewood. But it was just Ragi, sitting high on his old mare, talking to Toren.

"What are you doing here?" Erik asked.

"I saw you all mushing along the wood line, out past the old barn."

"Well, you found us," Erik said. "Go on, then. We've got things to do, and the days are short."

"I want to see," said Ragi.

Erik felt his left eye begin to twitch. All he could think to do was to keep staring, trying to look uninviting. He didn't hate Ragi. They were all friends, really, but the big Viking was at his house, and Ragi had a big mouth. The last thing they wanted was for the giant to hear they had been snooping around his ship.

In a span of silence no longer than the time it took Sterkr to scratch his belly, Ragi confessed. "Anja told me."

Toren just shook his head.

"I knew it." Erik tried to burn a hole through Toren with his stare. "Is there anything you don't tell her?"

"It's Viking treasure." Toren sounded oddly defensive. "Like the games we all played when we were little."

"Ja," Erik remembered. "Until you got a girlfriend."

"Now Ragi's your best friend, eh?" asked Magnus.

"He's going to be my brother-in-law." Toren sighed.

"Don't worry, I won't tell anyone," Ragi promised.

"You'd better not." Erik held up a finger as if to scold him, then he stopped. "You don't get credit for this." He looked at Toren. "Neither of you." He put the wood on the sled and took hold of Kratr's lead. "Come on, Magnus." Then he mushed off along the shoreline toward the dragon-headed ship.

"I'm not going to tell anyone," said Ragi, as his mare cantered up beside Magnus. "I can't believe you didn't tell me. You're acting like greedy trolls."

ROBBING THE DRAGON

The idea of going into the slush was almost unthinkable. With no inheritance and no prospects, and with the fjord quickly turning to ice, neither Erik nor Magnus felt like they had a choice.

"What if we get caught?" Ragi asked from high atop his old mare.

"We?" Erik asked. He guessed it was universal. Boys just like watching each other do stupid things.

"Ja, have you got a nisse in your pocket?" Even though Orri the Fat, which is what the boys called him behind his back, was wintering over at Bor's, Erik was the only one he told about the treasure. It was Erik that convinced him that Magnus could be trusted to help.

"My hands are freezing," Ragi complained. "Whose idea was this, anyway?"

"Your hands are freezing? I wish I had gloves as fine as yours," replied Magnus. "Besides, it's not even winter yet. It's barely past harvest." A snowball flew past Ragi's head. "That Fjord horse is the only one of you two who should be complaining here."

"Harvest?" asked Ragi. "What harvest? You mean from that potato field and goat pasture you call a farm?"

"Why are you here, Ragi?" Erik was sick of hearing about how hard winter was going to be this year. Runa had already pounded it into his head.

"Your two families together only put up half the stores

DEREK NELSEN

we did."

"Again, with the 'we'." Erik shook his head. "Ragi, have you ever pulled a weed?"

Another snowball sailed.

"Hey, cut it out," Toren ordered. "There it is."

The dragon lay sleeping, half drowned. Its hull leaned to one side from the push of a mass of ice trying to follow the tides out of the Hidden Fjord.

As Ragi dismounted, Toren, Erik, and Magnus took the harnesses off Kratr, Jakl, and Sterk. The three dogs lapped up icy water. Then as if on cue, they all raised their heads, keened their ears, and raced back into the woods.

Ragi fed his horse a treat and watched Erik use his hatchet to split and then quarter calf sized pieces of white birch he'd carried to the site on his sled.

"Next time you need wood let me know. I can help."

Erik put down the wood, walked up to Ragi and held out his hatchet. "We could use some more wood."

Magnus began to take off his layers of thick outer clothes and lay them on his sledge.

Ragi ignored the hatchet and changed the subject. "Would you strip down before going out there?" A small glacier steamed as it floated by.

"Ragi, too bad your father's coin has made you an idiot. If I get my clothes wet, I'll be a block of ice before we get past your father's farm." It warmed Magnus to have a chance to pick on Ragi—it was one of his favorite things to do.

Within six tries, Toren used a pair of stones and a pocket of dry tinder to turn some kindling and split birch into a nice little fire.

"One of these days I'm going to get you to teach me how you do that so quickly," said Ragi.

"Nobody's stopping you from trying it right now." Toren didn't even raise his head. "You won't learn anything by standing there petting that old nag."

58

"Hmmm." Ragi stroked his horse's nose. "Next time let me know before you start so I can see your trick."

Magnus pulled off all his shirts at once. "I'll show you a trick." Dropping his pants around his ankles, he bent over to display his freezing, reddening backside to the jockey and asked, "Ever seen a faerie burp?"

Ragi covered his eyes, looked over at the half-frozen fjord, and shivered. "You're insane."

"It would be insane to stand around petting a horse and wishing it was warmer," said Magnus. "While more silver and gold than I'll see in a lifetime sink to the bottom of the fjord in the belly of that ship."

"If that fat Viking didn't think this was as crazy as feeding the nisse in the barn, he'd be out here doing this himself," replied Ragi.

The smile left Magnus's face when his naked toes first touched the water. "Aaaayyyy!" His jaw fell and stayed open as he concentrated on balancing along an exposed edge of the ship's prow. Ice flowed around the ship in bands like a false floor. Balance began to fail as Magnus's eyes shifted between floating ice biting his ankles and stone shore falling fathoms farther away with every outgoing step.

"My father wants us to be the ones to save the jarl's son. That's why he insisted Elsa care for him at our house. That'll be worth more than anything you find in there."

"That's funny." By now Erik was naked, except for his long shirt, turning like a pig on a spit in front of the fire. "The giant's the one our father wanted to tie to the anchor of that ship before sinking it to the bottom of the fjord."

"Shut up you two," Toren growled. "Careful Magnus, do you see it?"

"I think so. Of course, it had to be all the way back near the tiller." Magnus chattered. "I think that's—" the ship lurched, legs stiffened, toes clung, but it was no use. Magnus sprawled face first across a remnant of cloth sail into stacked oars and chests of clothes half floating in a saltwater slush. Long seconds after the splash, he bobbed to the top again, gasping to catch his breath as if in shock from the icy plunge.

Erik ran past the dragon's prow and down the rocky jetty before losing his footing and tripping into a dive. The breath knocked out of him when he hit the slurry. Forgetting to swim in his panic, he gagged on icy slush as he gulped for air. Frozen, time stood still, an eternity between breaths, his mind preoccupied with sinking. How far he would fall before reaching the bottom of the deep fjord?

"Erik!"

Toren! With a feeble kick, Erik followed his brother's cries back to the surface. After what felt like an eternity, Erik emerged as far out as the belly of the ship.

"Whoah!" Magnus's face was the color of death, but his voice was lively, as if he was trying to convince himself everything would be alright. "This water is freezing!" His pain echoed off the face of the stone as if the mountain itself was agreeing, having spent its eons also trying to climb up out of the cold North Sea.

Everything inside Erik called him back to shore, but he fought both the urge and the current, put his head down and swam toward his over-zealous friend.

"Ragi," Toren commanded as he started tying the dog harnesses together. "Bring me your horse."

Suddenly, a piece of white birch splashed Erik in the face as it landed in the belly of the ship. Erik was confused, but he pressed on. By the time he reached Magnus he had found his footing on the submerged ledge near the aft of the ship.

"Er-r-rik," Magnus's teeth chattered as he pulled him close.

"I'm alright," Erik sputtered. "F-f-f-freezing, but alright."

They were both splashed this time. A white piece of birch floated nearby.

"Swim to the float," Ragi yelped.

Confused, Erik saw a rope from the float to the shore. Instinctively, he leaned for it, but Magnus caught him by the shoulder before he lunged.

"Wait!" Magnus yelled right in his ear. "The chest. It's right there. I couldn't manage. But togeth-th-ther—" his breaths were shallow, "we can get it."

"Don't be stupid," yelled Ragi.

Erik started drifting, but Magnus pulled him back to upright.

"When will we ever have this ch-ch-chance again?" Magnus's eyes looked wild.

"Forget it!" yelled Toren. He was knee deep, probably near the ledge where the land fell off into the depths. "A Viking's favor is not worth dying over."

"Not for you!" Erik yelled back. "You have an inheritance." Then he looked wild-eyed into the water.

"Just wait." Magnus's skin was pale, his blue lips shivered. "Be still for a second, and look." His finger shook violently as it pointed toward a submerged chest slid against the aft rail near the tiller. "That's got to be it. It's the only one not fl-fl-floating." His eyebrows were white ice. "I tried but I can't manage it. That's got to be it."

"Get out of there, Erik. Magnus, don't be stupid." Ragi's words could be heard as echoes from the shore.

"What else have we got, Erik?" Magnus pleaded. "We may never have a chance like this again."

Erik stopped his struggle. He craned his neck to the side with a shiver that ran the length of his body, his wool shirt weighed heavy on twitchy muscles and cold bones. "We are idiot's, aren't we?" Then he started to count. "On three." He gasped as he mouthed *One, two*. Then both took a deep breath and dropped down under the icy slush. Erik's eyes burned from the salt and cold, but he forced them open to find the chest. The cold crippled his lungs and it felt like he was out of air the second his face hit the water.

Erik couldn't believe how tough Magnus was, and refused to be the one to quit first. The chest was heavy, and the weight of it planted his feet firmly to the sunken deck. The ship lurched as they moved forward, and Magnus finally dropped the load, breaking Erik's grip, allowing him to swim up to refill his aching lungs.

Immediately, Magnus started counting again. On three, they filled the air with a smoky exhale, gasped in another shallow breath, and back down they went.

With everything Erik had he stayed with Magnus. They had to climb the tilted wreck, sometimes falling to a knee, and pulling their way up, one foot at a time. This time Erik grabbed Magnus's shoulder, and both swam the one foot to fresh air.

"Whoo, huhhh, whoo, huhhh." They had made it to the belly of the dragon.

"Last time." And Magnus skipped the counting, inhaled heavily, and pushed up with his hands to force himself back down. Erik followed. The two had a rhythm of sorts, moving the chest a foot then dropping it, a foot further then dropping it again. The chest was moving, but when Magnus's grip failed on the third, Erik fell forward hard, then Magnus pulled on his shirt to drag him back up.

This time they could stand. After filling their lungs with ever shallower breaths, Erik led this time. He leaned his chest into the water, and craning his neck, he found his grip. "I've got it!" he cried out as if they'd already won.

Magnus was shorter, so he buried his face, then whipped Erik with his hair when he splashed back out again.

"Aaaghh!" He looked like he was going to cry. "I can't lift it," his voice was beaten. "My hands are dead." He coughed white smoke and his body shivered uncontrollably. "I c-c-can't hold on." He held up his hands. They were bluer than before. His fingers were curled and lifeless.

"Magnus, Erik." Toren was less than seven paces away,

"you've got to get out of there. Grab the rope and I'll pull you in."

Erik coughed, "M-M-Magnus." He shivered. "I'll get the chest. You go back to the fire." Not waiting for a response, Erik grabbed the rope and dropped back down into the water.

"If you drown, I'm not going to try to save you." Ragi paced back and forth in front of the warm fire. "It's only money. Stupid fools."

Erik emerged from the slush. Magnus's eyebrows had re-frozen back to white. "*Pull.*" he wheezed, not able to manage a shout.

Toren grabbed Ragi's coat and pushed him up his mount. "Pull!"

Ragi complained as he mounted the horse and nudged her on.

"Father was right." Toren stripped off layers of shirts and his waterlogged boots. "I wish Ran's daughters had dragged this dragon down to the depths and presented it to Hella herself." Toren grimaced as he watched the horse steadily edge away from the shore.

Erik grabbed Magnus by the waist with one numb arm and tried to hold the rope with the other, but his grip failed, and the lifeline sank below the surface.

Toren cursed every god he could think of as he splashed into the icy water. The ship teetered, then lurched, sinking them all down to their chins. He swam around behind and grabbed the birch floating at the end of the rope. "Grab onto me," he choked. "Pull Ragi!" he chided. "Pull faster!" Toren was robbed of his commanding voice, but it was enough.

The boys fell face first into the snow next to the fire as the horse dragged all three ashore.

"Ragi, over here." Toren's hands shook violently as he held up fistfuls of clothes he'd left laying by the fire. Dry Magnus off and help him put on wh-wh-whatever's dry."

"T-T-Toren." Erik could barely hear himself speak. "The

chest. Get the chest."

"Stupid fools. If you die over that box, I promise in the next life I'll hunt you down and kill you again myself."

Erik heard the crunch of his frozen shirt as Toren stripped it off his back, dried him as best he could, and put him back in dry clothes. Toren stoked the fire until it was so hot Erik began to itch all over.

"Ragi," Toren said, sounding worried. "Rig up Magnus's sledge to the back of the horse."

"Why don't you do it?" Ragi held his hands to the fire.

"I'm going to make sure these fools don't die for nothing. Best you do as I say, or I'll take you with me."

The shock on Ragi's face from the threat mirrored the look on Toren's when he entered the water for a second time. Minutes later, Tor's eldest son heaved a wooden chest, brass trimmed and leaking water, up over the bow and onto the safety of the shore.

Ragi left Erik and Magnus by the dwindling fire to look at the prize, but Toren's scowl sent him back. Taking a minute to warm his hands, Toren said nothing as he pulled on his damp undershirt, wet pants, and soggy boots, grabbed two hatchets, and hustled into the forest.

As the fire started dwindling for a second time, Toren had decided they had to risk making the trip home or they'd lose the benefit of the waning sun.

If only for the use of his horse, it was good that Ragi had come. The old Fjord horse towed both sleds home, the first with Erik and the loot, the second with an unconscious Magnus strapped aboard and covered with anything left that could be considered warm and dry.

From his back, Erik watched his brother ski home with the help of the three dogs. Toren was as blue as the dwindling Hidden Fjord, clad only in his undershirt, icicle lined trousers, and frozen boots.

THE GIANT AWAKES

"So, you're finally waking up. They didn't think you were going to make it for awhile, there. Master Pedar was right to leave you with me." A tall, hunched, well-fed woman with bulging gray eyes lurched over and put a cold hand on Vidar's forehead.

"Where am I?" Vidar grunted as he sat. He pushed away covers of reindeer skins and odd pelts and caught his breath as if drowning from heat and deep sleep. His legs were hanging over the end of the straw-filled mattress, his heels lay heavily on the floor.

"Take it slow now, don't hurt yourself." The woman smiled an awkward, flirtatious grin. "I am Elsa." Her teeth were stained as yellow as a buttercup. "You've been asleep for a long time." Her loose neck swung a little when she talked, hanging under her jowls like a sheep's udder.

He winced at the sight of the old maid. She didn't seem to notice.

"Magnus," she sung in a sour note. A short stocky boy around sixteen lumbered into the room. "'Ats a boy. Bring me some of that broth, will you dear?"

Magnus grabbed a bowl, then stopped at the sight of Vidar. Elsa filled it with a chunky, foul smelling broth.

"Sorry, I don't know your name," she said.

The boy moved slowly, soup sloshing from a shaking hand. He stopped short. His face pale, he stared as if someone had been raised from the dead.

"Vidar." He took the bowl before the boy made him wear it. "Relax. I'm not a draugr." His voice was deep and gruff, even for him.

Elsa put her arm around the boy, beaming. "This is my son, Magnus."

Lucky for the boy, he didn't get his looks from his mother.

"Short as you are tall, Magnus is," she feigned a whisper.

The boy stood up straighter, his pale cheeks flushed with color.

"Oh, don't be so sensitive. Tell master Pedar the Viking, er, Vidar's awake."

"He's not my master." The rest of Magnus's face turned red as a harvest beet.

"As long as he's putting a roof over our heads, he is. Go on now. I'd better not hear you talking like that again, you hear me?"

Magnus slammed the door behind him before she could finish her sentence.

Someone needs to beat some humility into this boy, Vidar thought to himself.

Elsa looked apologetic. "Boys with their tempers. Best if you don't mention that to the master, eh? Magnus'll be getting his soul ring this year, and my lands he's full of himself. He's lucky to be alive, really." It was just the two of them, but the woman sidled up to Vidar as if she was telling some dark secret. "Just this week, he and some of his friends fell through the ice playing at the fjord. Nearly froze to death."

For the first time since he woke, Vidar wanted this woman to keep talking. "What were they doing at the fjord?" he asked.

She shrugged her broad shoulders, blushed, then leaned in closer. "He needs a good role model. Poor boy never knew his father." Her mouth curved into a sultry smile, then she winked awkwardly, like a horse blinking a fly out of its eye.

Pretending he didn't follow where the troll was going with all her weak and unwelcome flirting, Vidar held up the bowl and nodded as if happy for something to eat. He was hungry. Despite the odor of onions, and whatever the color brown smelled like, he poured its contents into his empty stomach. His face went blank as he looked at the old maid in despair.

On unsure legs, he lurched to make his way to the door and slammed his head into a beam along the ceiling. He swallowed some of it, which was something he was trying to avoid.

His stomach wasn't interested. Immediately he began to retch and hobbled to the door, flung it open, and stepped outside into the snow.

At first, he spit out anything still swirling, simultaneously sickening and burning every harshly awoken taste bud. Then he began to gag.

The contents of his stomach painted the white snow. After he was done, Vidar reached his thick fingers back into his mouth, and freed some type of organ from between his back teeth. What had she given him? He threw the thing down and it skidded, still smoking, across the top of the snow. It was something from a small animal, hopefully just a chicken. He gagged again just considering the alternatives.

Three ravens flew down from the roof and attacked the offering, fighting over the heart or stomach, or whatever it was, before it had a chance to freeze solid.

Eyes squinting in the bright morning light, his back cracked as he stood up straight. He was sweating from the retching, and the cold air felt good. At least I am alive, he thought.

As he watched the black birds fight, he turned to one side to relieve himself, adding dark yellow rings around the still smoking brown-colored snow.

The satisfied birds flitted close to his head before landing deftly atop the snow-covered roof.

Maybe it was the bite of cold, maybe it was the ravens, but Vidar's mind took him back to the sea.

The last thing he remembered before losing consciousness was looking up at three ravens. Could've been these same birds, looking down at him just like this. Mocking him. As if to remind him he should have never been on the water that late in the season. As if Odin himself had sent his spies to report how the son of Olaf was to die.

These couldn't be the same birds, could they?

He remembered how he cursed them. From their perch atop the broken mast they reminded him that dying at sea would not get him into Valhalla. That his father and his brother would meet there someday, after a glorious death with a sword in their hand, and only then find out that Vidar had died with an oar in his. Drowning or dying of starvation at sea would not earn him a seat at Odin's table.

Would my father even care? Is he searching for me now? No, probably not.

Vidar hated being alone with his thoughts.

No, these were different birds. He was still alive. In a panic, the rough tips of his gnarled fingers scratched his neck until he found the rings. They were still there, held tight to his throat on braids of tanned leather. Each a soul lost while under his care. He tallied each one. *Twenty-four.*

He thought of the strong men his father put in his care. How they sustained him. How they looked at him with their dead eyes as he stripped them of their souls. How his stomach turned after their corpses began to rot on that ship that somehow seemed to shrink with every new empty seat. How the tiny fish sheltering under the dragon's cracked hull swarmed to feed after he pushed what was left of them into the waves. The small fish always ate first. Then the sharks would come.

The smaller of the birds rescued him from that dark place

with a mocking *toc-toc-toc.*

Vidar sneered, grabbed a handful of snow off the roof, and threw it in their direction. "Tell the trickster Odin that I'm not dead yet." They flitted quietly out of the way, only to land back where they started, and continued to stare at him with tilted heads. Then the larger threw in a deep rattle as if in protest of the assault.

Vidar belched, cringed at the taste, and scratched his stomach. He looked down at his own emaciated frame, running his fingers along his ribs. Then he glanced down at the meager contents of the cup he was holding and rolled his eyes.

"Uff-da."

Throwing the cup down into the snow, he stood naked, the heat effervescing from his body as it met the cold morning air. He looked around and saw he was on a farm.

Up on the hill there was a large house, away from the barn and the servant's quarters nearby. Magnus emerged from the red front door, leading a boy about his age onto the porch, then ran off into the woods.

The boy waited, then a man emerged. He looked down at Vidar, turned back toward the door, waited, looked down at Vidar again, then went back inside. The boy went back in and a moment later the two of them emerged again. *What are they doing?*

Elsa met him at the door with the reindeer skin he'd shed and put it back over his shoulders. "Aren't you cold, dear? Ah, there's the master now."

Vidar stepped off the porch and started walking up the hill. The man saw him and went back inside.

Elsa followed him. "Wait, let me get your clothes."

Vidar kept walking. He was finished talking to the servants.

Elsa ran ahead of him, went inside, then opened the door.

"Master Pedar invites you in."

Vidar grabbed pants, his naked hips knocking the rest of his clothes onto the porch as he ducked inside.

THE TRADER

The splotchy-cheeked man seemed to be posing by the fire. Uncomfortable. Maybe even nervous. Which, from the size of him, was understandable.

He teetered at no more than five and a half feet tall and had a backward tilt. Likely something he'd picked up to offset the weight of his paunch belly.

"I am Pedar, son of Thord, son of Ralph. And this is my son, Ragnall."

Who could miss the unremarkable boy? Pudgy and red cheeked, he cowered behind his father—like a fat chicken trying to hide behind a crooked fencepost.

"This is your farm?" Vidar doubted either had ever touched a plow.

"Ja." Pedar stood up straighter when he said it, making his pot belly stick out with pride. "My grandfather was the first to settle this land. It feeds my family and my workers, and there's usually enough left over to sell."

I'll bet there is. Vidar didn't like false modesty. Just from what he saw walking up the hill, there were enough harvested fields on this farm to feed a small village.

"My maid Elsa has been taking very good care of you while you were recovering. I made sure she kept a close eye on you."

Vidar pretended he didn't see Elsa staring. That woman had a smile that could cure fish. "Er, boy, were you with Magnus when he fell into the fjord last week?"

Ragi stretched his neck to peek out from behind his

father. "Ja."

Was this boy an imbecile? "And?" Vidar grabbed his shirt from Elsa and pulled it over his head. It smelled like her. He wished it didn't.

"We saved your treasure." He looked to his father as if this would make him proud.

Instead, Pedar looked nervously at Vidar, as if waiting to see which way the wind would blow.

"Don't worry," Ragi added. "Orri's got it. He's the one who told Erik about it. Offered two gold pieces to Erik and Magnus to get it. Toren and I were there, but we didn't get anything."

Did Ragnall just wink to his father? Vidar couldn't help but think to himself, if he had landed here on a raid he would have already killed these two.

"Erik is Tor's youngest son." Pedar's voice faded as soon as he started talking.

"And Toren's his oldest," added Ragi.

"Orri?" Vidar slowly shook his head. "He did this without me?"

"Nobody thought you ever would wake up."

Then Vidar thought he ought to smile before Pedar ran away from his own house.

Ragi smiled back like a dog waiting for a pat on the head. Pedar like he'd pissed himself.

"That was an impressive ship you came in on." Pedar the Fencepost changed the subject.

The man's coat was of stitched weasel. That seemed appropriate. Vidar decided to not say anything. One of the few things he'd learned from his father was to see if a man hated silence enough to fill it himself. His father was drunk when he said it, and he said it to his thingmen, not to Vidar. But it was useful advice just the same.

"Built for open water, eh?" Pedar cleared his throat. "I have a ship as well. I'm a trader."

Vidar didn't want to take the bait. Whether raiding or

trading, everywhere he'd been there'd been some local merchant telling him how valuable they'd be as a trading partner — usually after being discovered hiding in the barn loft.

"Just a little trading business, mostly around the fjord."

Here it comes.

"I would love to meet your father."

This man was an idiot. No one wanted to meet his father.

"Do you know who my father is?"

"You are Vidar, Jarl Olaf's son. One of my friends recognized the resemblance. He's been here a long time, so you probably wouldn't know him." Pedar held his hand up high over his head. "Big man, somewhere between you and Ubbi. His name is Tor Ovesen.

"Tor Ovesen is here?" Vidar felt a chill, then wiped sweat from his brow.

Pedar looked pleased with himself to have made a connection.

"He's in the farm just past those trees. Found us twelve or thirteen years ago."

Vidar took a deep breath to calm his thoughts. Every man in his father's service had heard of Tor Ovesen. He was the ghost that Vidar could never measure up to. Didn't matter what he or his brother Egil did, his father and Tor had done it better when they were that age.

"After you're better, of course. I'm sure there are opportunities for you, too."

What was this crooked little man stammering on about?

"There are things my neighbors need, and I'm sure I can get him crops and meat much cheaper than anyone he's working with now. I haven't any competition here. Can set my own prices, if you understand." Pedar raised an eyebrow. It was the one muscle he had that looked well exercised.

The little man had gotten much more comfortable since he started talking about his willingness to cheat his neighbors.

"I'm not here to make trade deals or introductions to my father. I'm feeling tired."

Pedar smiled. "I understand. Elsa, please take our guest back to your house where you can take good care of him. And get him some real food. We wouldn't want him to be hungry."

Vidar really was tired. Before walking back down the hill, he took another look at Pedar's house. Servants, high ceilings, wood stacked neatly by a roaring fire. And the kitchen was in another room altogether. And it smelled as if beef was simmering. The maid and her son lived in a single room small house that smelled only of potatoes and onions. Something to remember. The smell made his stomach burn for meat and bread and mead. How long had he been living on Elsa's terrible broth?

VIKING SLAVE

"Ahh." Kiara looked up into the beautiful blue sky. Days were short, but she loved to feel the sun, no matter how impotent it's warmth. "Whew!" She shivered and began to trot. As soon as she felt the chill, she had learned not to wait. It was time to get moving. This time the shiver felt like it crept slowly down, from the top of her head and down her back, leaving a trail of goosebumps in its wake.

The borrowed dress she wore was a size too big, and it let the cold air in like a door not quite shut. The way the wind can find a crack to spoil a koselig room, no matter how hot the fire was burning.

Koselig. The word finally started to make sense. After spending most of the last year with the Vikings, that was one expression she never really grasped. The raiders would come into her house and tell her mother how koselig everything was — as if they were guests thanking a willing hosts hospitality.

Even though she'd learned a bit of Norse during the siege, that word never resonated with her. Was the home she grew up in supposed to feel nice and welcoming when assumed by invaders who sat at her father's table and ate their food? Ending each meal with a clap on the back and a smile, as if they were old friends over for a nice visit. Was she supposed to have a warm feeling in her heart, even though she lived with the fear that she would be the next girl one of the Viking fish eaters would start to take a liking to?

She must have lost her senses after all this time. Or maybe, she was finding hope. Compared to what her life was like just a about a year earlier-*had it been that long?* — things now were at least...Well, not like then. In a place so cold it was like nothing she'd ever felt before, she started to get its meaning, just a little. She prayed to God every night that her hope, and that feeling, would last.

She was running now, and her tears felt like they were freezing to the sides of her face. The more she ran the warmer she felt and the farther she got from that dark, stifling house. Farther from Runa, a woman who seemed like she'd lost something and wouldn't let anyone help her find it. The only warmth she showed in that house was to her little dog Jeger, as if she didn't have a family to care for.

What Kiara wouldn't do to see her family again. She found herself so lonely for her mother that she thought if she could just get Runa to smile or to lay her hand on her back, just a whisper of praise, some form of affection, that she'd just...Oh, what was she thinking about? Her mind wandered something awful nowadays, always drifting somewhere between contented and despairing.

"It's about time. Don't you know I've got someplace to go?"

Kiara's mind was still buzzing. *Get it together girl.* She put her hands on her knees to catch her breath. Warm white fog froze in the air between them. "I've got your lunch."

Erik smirked. "What did you say?"

Kiara thought for a second, then smiled back. "F-o-o-d," she annunciated. Erik was always making fun of the brogue she added to her Norse.

He walked up to her. Close. Maybe too close. "Have you been crying?" He put his hand on the side of her face, and gently rubbed the side of her eye with his thumb.

She caught herself looking at him looking at her. Embarrassed, and still breathing too heavy, she grabbed his hand and pushed it away. She rubbed her eyes, "I haven't been crying." His hand was cold, but she felt warm, which made no sense. "I've been running." Her cheeks felt like they were cramping. She forced herself to stop smiling. Had she been smiling that whole time? His smile was infectious. That's what it was. He was the one smiling. "Why are you looking at me like that?"

"No reason." His smile widened. "I've just never known anyone to run as much as you. I mean, unless there's a troll chasing you or something?" He took the basket from her hand and pretended to hide behind her.

Erik was ridiculous. He reminded her of how she and her brother used to play when they were little. "All you talk about are trolls. Did you get whisked off to a trollheim or wherever they live, or something like that? You seem obsessed with them."

He looked a little shaken by her saying that, as if trolls had some hidden meaning to him. "Not me, I'm obsessed with your country, full of faeries and gnomes, which are really just nisse by the way. Same thing."

"They are not." She felt herself smiling again. Even though Kiara's cheeks were numb, she could tell, and she wanted to hit him for some reason. Maybe that would make her stop smiling. So, she hit him.

"Hey!" He laughed and pushed her way too hard. She fell.

"Hey!" Alright, she wasn't smiling now. She had stumbled over a pile of stacked staffs, about as big around as her arm. "What are these?"

"Sticks." Erik was looking in the basket at what she'd brought him for his lunch. He didn't even offer her a hand up. She grabbed a staff. They were carved down at one end, just a little too big around for her hand. She used it to push herself to her feet. "What are you doing out here. Your mother told me you were chopping wood."

"Stepmother, lass." His fake brogue was bad. She didn't

know whether he was trying to be funny or make fun of her. Since he didn't have the ability, or maybe the interest, to learn her language, she didn't think he had room to mock her or where she came from. At least she was trying.

He picked up one of the staffs by the narrow end. The narrow part was definitely a handle, which seemed obvious once he was holding it. "How could you think that cruel woman would be my mother?" He held the rod up like a sword or a club, like he was going to hit her with it. "Don't make me remind you again." Then he broke out with that impish smile again. "Go on, defend yourself. Tip up."

It took two hands for Kiara to raise the staff. It was heavy and awkward. "Don't you hit me." She wasn't sure what Erik considered to be fun half the time. Once, he bloodied her nose with a snowball packed so hard it might as well have been ice. Another time, he grabbed her and spun her until they were so dizzy they fell down in the snow. Well, she fell in the snow — he fell on her. That hurt.

Erik's games often spun out of control like that. From fun to not. She was thinking about taking him his lunch earlier and earlier, lately. Last week, she had it ready for him before he even left the house. She had to hide it from him so he wouldn't grab it on his way out the door.

Was the way he made her feel worth his antics? She knew the answer to that. Better to have a broken rib from someone trying to make you happy than a clean dress from someone who wants you to look presentable while you're cleaning their house — or feeding their animals — or cooking their meals. Erik always knew how to make her smile and helped her understand what koselig meant, after all.

She swung the staff right at his. He feigned to be surprised, then slapped his against hers. It made a crack. Is that what she'd been hearing the other day when she went to town with Runa? Runa said it was just someone chopping wood, but Kiara could tell it was something different. It would have had to be three or four people chopping together to make that much noise.

"Entertain me while I eat." He said it as if he were the king of all Norway.

"Put down that staff."

He put it down and looked at what she brought him. Kiara thought for a moment. "If I had my fife, I'd play you a song." Her mind traveled to happier times.

"Where is it?" he scoured the ground playfully.

"I lost it, sometime at sea. Or maybe it's in the belly of the Viking's ship." And, as quickly, Kiara felt the darkness of her situation again. She wiped her eyes with her sleeve, then her nose. "My father gave it to me. He'd been trying to teach me how to play..." Her mind wandered again. "He was really good."

"And you?"

"No. I didn't practice enough." How she wished she'd played with him more.

"Tell me another story, then." Erik said it as if curious why she'd even brought it up in the first place. "Tell me something good, something from your country, something with wide green pastures covered with sheep." He pointed an onion at her. "No goats." Then he held the little vegetable between his hands, closing his eyes as if its warmth were the best part of it. "Tell me something with magic. And the land of faeries, hidden in plain sight." He rummaged around some more, pulled out a skin and took a drink.

She knew he'd be cold, so she filled it with a hot tea she made with some herbs and dried berries from a basket Runa had hidden in the larder. Not enough that she'd notice, but just enough to add some sweetness to the water. He smiled after he drank it, then put the stopper back and put the warm skin under his shirt. "Tell me one with a hero like...What were their names?" He stood and knocked more snow from his seat atop an old stump. "Fionn? Was that it? Or Goll mac Morna, or Samson, the most powerful man who ever lived. I like that one. I haven't had my hair cut since you told me that one, did you notice?"

She just shook her head. He did have a way about him—even in this crystal land, where even some of the trees were white, and icicles as long as men made them bow to the ground like skinny priests in robes of snow. He made it feel like this could be a good place, despite her troubles.

As he ate his meager lunch—oh, how his stepmother neglected this boy—she told him a story.

"Have you ever heard of angels?"

"No," he replied. "Are they gods or men?"

"Neither." She thought for a moment.

"Real or made up?"

"Shut your mouth and I'll tell you. Go on, eat your terrible lunch." She caught a chill, so she stood up with the staff and started to walk to get her blood moving again. "The priest in my village told us one Sunday about a war in Heaven." That seemed to get Erik's attention. She knew he liked stories with fighting. "In the beginning, God created the heavens and the earth."

"Are we talking about Jesus here, or another God?"

"God and Jesus are the same thing. There is only one God."

"So why don't you just call him Jesus, so I don't get confused? And our story about how everything began is better, when the realm of fire collided with the realm of ice and there was a cow who licked the ice, because she was thirsty, and uncovered a giant who drank from her udders. And he birthed the first gods and giants from his armpit, and after the gods killed the giant the dwarfs came out of him like maggots, and four dwarfs hold his skull into the air even now, which made the sky, and-"

"Do you want to hear my story or not?" She couldn't believe she got him to stop mid-sentence.

"Ja, of course I want to hear it, but you're confusing me."

"You're confusing me. I've heard that story you were trying to tell, and something is wrong with the way you're telling it." Erik was a dreadful storyteller. He told them too fast and jumped all over the place. Kiara wondered if her stories were as confusing to him as his were to her. "All right, I'm starting again. Just so you know, for this story the Bible says God, the priest says God, and both of them say that Jesus was God, so I'm just going with the priest and calling him God for now, all right?"

Erik chewed his onion and waved for her to go on.

"All right." She had to remember what she was saying. This was usually when Toren would threaten Erik if he interrupted again, but he wasn't there. She didn't mind being alone with Erik, that wasn't it—even though she thought he liked irritating her. Pretty sure he did it to everyone. She started walking again. "Right. So, God created everything in Heaven, which is where he lives, and everything on earth."

"Which is the same as Midgard." Erik looked very proud of himself. "Where we live."

Kiara could feel a smile coming on, so she turned her back to him and started telling again, hoping he wouldn't interrupt her at least long enough for the smile to wear off.

"God created the angels to help him care for his creation. My priest says we each have our own guardian angel."

Erik acted like he was going to choke, but Kiara held up her finger to stop him. "Do you want me to tell the story or not?"

He shook his head and then gave her a look like a boy who was made to sit in the corner by his mother.

She had to turn her back on him again. No one else had ever bothered her the way he did. "One of the most famous angels, Lucifer, was the most beautiful of all God's creation. And he was jealous of humans."

"Why was he jealous of us?"

"Because we were special to God. He gave us souls and wanted us to be his children. For those of us that find him in this world, where he cannot be seen, he has prepared houses for us. And the angels, who are greater than us here, will be lesser than us there."

"If you're saying they'll be our servants in Heaven, then I don't blame them for being angry at us," said Erik.

"I'm not sure if they're angry at us, or at God." Kiara was stung by the irony of what he said. Should she hate Erik — or his stepmother, or father, or the village? Or just the Vikings? She was not always a servant, either. She pulled out her soul ring and looked at it. It was not pretty like Runa's. Only the priests covered theirs in gold or silver where she was from.

"I don't think the angels were jealous of us because they were going to be our servants in Heaven. I don't even know if that's how it works. I think they were jealous because God didn't give them souls — that they would never be his children, no matter what they did for him."

"Well, here having your soul ring just means you're old enough to vote at the village thing. It also means that you're a man." He looked at her and smiled. "Or a woman." She didn't know if he did it on purpose, but his eyebrows raised when he said it.

That, oddly enough, did not make her smile. "When do *you* become a man, then?"

His right eyebrow fell. "This year, when it's really cold." He cocked his head to one side, as if a chill went down his spine. "The gothi performs the ceremony every winter solstice." Then he tried to make his voice sound deep and serious. "The day the light defeats the darkness, and the days begin to get long again." His voice went back to normal, which was still pretty deep. "But I can never tell. It takes a long time before I notice the days getting longer again."

"After you get your ring, you'll be able to attend village assemblies?" she asked.

"Then, I'll be a man. With all the rights that come with it."

She tucked her soul back in her shirt. Kiara's freezing fingertips grazed her neck and goose bumps erupted down the length of her back. "Where I'm from you get your soul ring while you're still a baby." She started pacing back and forth.

Erik picked up one of the staffs and started swinging it like a sword. "What a terrible thing to do to a baby. They don't even know what's happening." He winced a little as he said it.

"They want to bless the baby early—in case it doesn't survive. Since a baby can't ask God for forgiveness of their sin, the parents ask the priests to bless their souls to make sure they go to Heaven if they die."

"I wouldn't let one of your priests near my children. That ring's got nothing to do with religion," Erik protested. "Children lose teeth, too, but I wouldn't ask a priest to pull one out before it was ready just because he says it'd make a god happy, would you? What kind of a place is Ireland, anyway?"

She could have said some things about how she felt about the place he's from, but she didn't have time for that conversation. "Someday I'll tell you what they do to baby boys," she smiled. "You really wouldn't like that." She handed him the staff she'd been holding, then pointed to the tip that he'd shaved down like a handle and raised her eyebrows.

His brow furrowed in confusion and maybe a little concern.

"I've got to go," she said. She didn't mind smiling at him now. "I'll tell you about circumcision another time."

"What about my angel story?" he asked as if he really wanted to know.

"There was a war in Heaven and God cast out a third of the angels to live here on earth until he cast them into the pit for all eternity. Now I've got to go. Runa doesn't give you enough food that it ought to take this long to eat. She's going to notice if her servant girl is gone too long." She could feel him watching her as she picked up the basket. "I thought you said you had somewhere to go," she reminded him. "Where is that?

Erik jumped to his feet, grabbed up the sticks, and rolled them into a horse blanket. He was so quick to leave, until a sword slid right out the back.

He turned to grab it, but his eyes met hers. Then they both stared at it.

"What are you doing with that?" Kiara's heart pounded in her chest. She hadn't seen a sword like that since they took her from Ireland. "You're planning to join them, aren't you?" She thought she was going to vomit. She started walking back toward the house. Where she was a slave to these heathens.

"Kiara!" Erik yelled, but he didn't follow.

She turned back once, but he was already gone. All the pain she'd thought she'd buried with her family welled back up, salting her eyes as tears. Alone in the woods, far, far away from home, Kiara sobbed. She wanted to be angry, but it hurt too much for that. She thought she'd cried all of this out already. How could she still feel all this pain after all this time? How could she have trusted that stupid boy. She hated herself for it, but as the tears slowed, she began to worry. She took the empty basket, turned it upside down, and gave it a shake. Crumbs fell to the snow. She could hardly believe there were birds that could survive in this cold place. And as Erik so proudly assured her, it would get worse before it got better. She shivered just thinking about it.

That stupid, stupid boy.

TRAINING VIKINGS

E rik was late. He arrived just in time to see Magnus run behind a tree. None of the boys liked getting hit with the stick, and Ubbi was about to remind them why. The Viking had that look again, the one that meant he was no longer training. He was fighting.

Ubbi was the opposite of Orri, more what a Viking was expected to look like. He was a berserker and a brute — thick chested and broad shouldered. Orri said the boys would be like that someday, after training and putting in their time at the oar. Erik figured it'd been a long time since fat Orri'd rowed a boat.

Ubbi hunched over, allowing his long black hair to fall heavily to one side to cover his face in hair and shadow. For the most part, the boys had little idea what he looked like, but when he fought, they could see the black tattoos running up his throat continued up into the shadows masking his face.

Crack! Erik winced as Ubbi's stick snapped across the flaking, spindly birch. Better the birch than Magnus's ribs.

"You win," Magnus pleaded.

Don't beg, you idiot. Attack. Hadn't he learned the Viking went berserk when he smelled fear? It was as if Ubbi hated weakness more than sticks. Erik hated standing there watching, but he couldn't look away. He thought about helping his friend, but how many times had Magnus laughed out loud when he retreated?

Ubbi jerked the staff Orri was leaning on out of his hands and came back at Magnus with something akin to a hardwood longsword. His eyes were as focused as a bull moose chasing a cow during the rut. Tor had taught him to stay clear of moose chasing a reluctant cow, and in the same way, he would stay clear of Ubbi chasing Magnus.

Orri the Fat, who usually couldn't stop running his mouth, turned out to have very little useful guidance for his young pupils. He wasn't completely useless. He would often explain Ubbi's beatings from the sidelines. And he'd keep the fire going, usually while cooking a chicken or eating his share of whatever Magnus or one of the other boys could steal them for lunch.

Between mouthfuls, he'd just wince along with the rest and tell the gawkers what he would do if he were the one taking the beating. He would lean in to say things like, "His knees are exposed," the grease surrounding his lips doing its part to renounce his authority in all things unrelated to food or spirits. "He should've ducked there," he would advise too late.

While the boys were fighting for their lives, they could hear him talking. They just didn't find any of his advice to be particularly helpful. And with all his talk, he didn't even try to convince Ubbi to slow down or show mercy.

At first, it sounded like a good idea when Orri made the offer. "If you're going to sail with us in the spring, I'll have to teach you how to fight like a Viking, turn you into warriors, and make you strong enough to pull an oar all the way to lands beyond the sea." So far, he hadn't done a thing except organize when and where to meet and who was bringing lunch. Ubbi did all the training.

Erik knew his father wouldn't approve, so it worked out well that he'd been off hunting in the mountains. If Tor had spent more time at home, maybe he'd have been the one to teach Erik how to swing a sword. No, he'd had plenty of time— he just didn't want to. It was like he didn't want Erik to have options — to know anything useful other than how to milk a goat. No, it was better this way. Erik and his friends were being trained by real Vikings now.

The boys guessed that Ubbi never listened to their cries for mercy because the men who cut out his tongue probably didn't listen to his. It was hard to imagine this man begging for anything, but at that time he must have, right? The thought of it sent a chill up Erik's spine. Or was that the cold? Hard to tell on a morning like this.

Ubbi made the boys use heavy wood for training. Orri called them sticks, but they were more like clubs. So thick, Orri had the boys trim down the handles so they could get their hands around them.

Orri explained, "They will make you warrior strong, which is different from farmer strong."

"Is that different than gut strong?" Erik whispered to the others. Lars laughed so hard snot bubbles came out of his nose.

"What was that?" Orri asked.

"I said Magnus is fighting like a girl," Erik elbowed Lars to get him to calm down.

Erik could feel Orri glaring. Had he heard?

"Warrior strong is more in the neck and shoulders," he continued. "When you get your hands on an iron sword, you'll need to be able to wield it against many men. You never get to fight just one in a real battle. Not if you're fighting Vikings, anyway."

Erik ignored Ovid's attempt to make eye contact. He felt a little sick at the prospect of upsetting Orri. He had a feeling that these Vikings knew how to hold a grudge. And how to get even.

Ubbi and Orri had been training Erik and Magnus to fight since they recovered from their swim. That's what Orri liked to call it. The swim. And as a reward for near drowning in the fjord? To get hit with sticks, repeatedly, by Ubbi. Ubbi did not know how to train boys, but he did know how to beat them. The ultimate lesson seemed to be—everyone gets hurt in a fight. Except Ubbi.

Three times a week for the past month, Ubbi had tried to break one of those sticks on every boy Erik and Magnus convinced to come out. They were glad that Ubbi hadn't figured out that after the first week the boys had carved a weak spot into every one of his handles, usually a well-placed knot would do the trick. It felt better sparring with Ubbi knowing that his stick was weaker than his stroke.

So far, Erik and Magnus had only recruited Bor's sons Ingjaldr and Ivar, and Thorfinn's sons Lars and Ovid. There would be more eventually, but for now, Orri wanted to start small. He only wanted boys who had no inheritance or land claim in the village. Boys like them.

During one of his teaching moments, Orri explained why. He planned to invite the older boys after he had a group of younger brothers competent enough to defeat them. He wanted them to want to fight, even if only to keep from getting pummelled with a stick by kids they'd been bullying all their lives. He meant to shame them into joining.

He also hoped that once the village saw how many of their sons were with the Vikings, anyone not on their side might reconsider. Ubbi always looked at Erik when Orri said things like that.

Even though these same boys had pretended to sword fight with sticks their entire lives, this was different. Ubbi was not a good teacher. He couldn't talk, for one, so his main way to correct a bad decision was to walk up and expose the weakness with a crack of a stick. Every lesson was learned with a bruise. Get off balance, and he would try to break a stick on the back of your leg. Overreach, and he would try his best to crack one of your ribs. Too light a grip, and with a quick snap he'd disarm you with a downward swing and then come back to get your forearm. He tried to avoid the face and fingers.

Orri didn't want anything that might be noticed at the dinner table. Mothers knew the boys horsed around and sometimes got hurt, but an eye swollen shut or a broken bone that may keep them from completing their chores might inspire unwanted attention. The Vikings were trying to win people over, and pissing off the mothers would not help the cause.

Magnus had hidden himself inside the limbs of a fallen pine.

"I yield!" he shouted again, but Ubbi still pursued. When Ubbi got like this, they'd all learned to run. He was strong, but he didn't have the lungs or the patience for a chase. He would get his shot in eventually, even if it was while they were taking a break by the fire. Better to be blindsided while resting than let the Viking get you while he was berserking.

Lucky for Magnus, today Erik showed up with a distraction. He unwrapped the bundle of sticks he'd brought to practice, and hidden at the bottom, he pulled out his father's sword. Tor would kill him if he knew.

"Ubbi!" Orri dropped his chicken leg. "Leave that boy alone and come take a look. Young Erik wasn't kidding. He's brought us a blade." Orri reached out to take the sword, but Erik stepped back. Instantly, he wondered what he was doing. It was as if seeing Orri take interest in something he'd clearly done to gain his attention ruined it somehow.

Why did he feel the need to impress these men? Was it to gain some favor? So far, nothing he'd done for them, including taking the swim, had done anything for him except gain him a lot of pain and bruising.

Ubbi had stopped his pacing around the fallen tree and made his way over. That just proved that the fat Viking could've said something to stop Ubbi's harassment. Now Erik really wondered what he was doing. Kiara was right, he shouldn't have brought it.

Magnus clambered to his feet but stayed near the

downed pine. The other boys came in close, but that only made Erik feel trapped. They were in an open forest and he was the only one holding a sword, yet somehow, he felt cornered. That was the moment he realized he was a long way from being a warrior. Erik's fingers felt numb around the hilt, as if he might drop it. "It was my grandfather's."

"All right," said Orri. "You've proved you weren't lying. Now give it 'ere. Let us 'ave a feel of it." Orri was speaking in his friendly voice—the fake one he used when he told the others what he wanted for the next practice's lunch. "That may be the only true sword in this entire village other than the ones you left to rust in the belly of our ship." Getting the treasure seemed like it should have been enough, but as soon as Orri had the gold and silver, he asked about the iron.

"What do you mean you didn't get the swords?" Orri'd acted as if they might as well have not gone into the ship at all. He didn't even mention it until they handed him the treasure. Then he acted like he was doing them a favor when he paid them their two gold pieces, as if they may owe him just because they didn't go back into the frigid water to rescue weapons they didn't even know were in there. Had he wanted the sail, too? How 'bout the oars? Having them would've been useful, come spring.

Ubbi stepped forward with an eye to take the sword. Erik reflexively raised it high, just as Ubbi had taught him. Maybe he wasn't such a bad teacher, after all.

With an upward thrust of his stick, Ubbi cracked Erik across the break of his wrists. Before he even felt the pain, he saw the sword fumble out of his dead hands. Ubbi dropped his stick and picked the sword up off the ground the way a boy skipping stones might trade a roundish stone for a skippier one. Erik's hands finally came back to life in a scream of agony that resonated from both wrists.

"Ehhhgh!" Erik groaned through clenched teeth. Sore muscles began to tense, elbows drew in, and a wave of pain climbed up his spine until it forced his eyes shut. His body had to process a reaction. By the time his legs gave way and he dropped to one knee, his eyes were ringing out tears like they were washcloths. For a second, he was embarrassed. Forgetting all else, he cursed himself for crying in front of the Vikings. And his friends.

"Come to me, son." Erik turned to see his father walking towards him with an axe in each hand, and he didn't look like he was there to fell trees. Behind him came Toren, then Kiara, almost hiding. Her eyes were trained on the Vikings, and she was crying as hard as he was, only hers were tears of fear.

Erik was getting the strength back in his fingers, and the pain gave way to a prickly burn. He sprang toward his father, trying to put some distance between himself and Ubbi, and that sword. He stumbled and fell. His mind raced through the hundreds of times someone had fallen while sparring and how Ubbi's response was to pounce. He could almost hear Orri say it; he'd said it so often. "A man off his feet is as good as dead." That would always be followed by a crack of the stick across exposed ribs, a painful lesson made worse by the fear of knowing the stick was coming back again. Expecting the worst, Erik scurried like a squirrel despite the pain in his wrists, falling toward his family until he slid face down at his father's feet, burying his tears in the snow.

"I'm sorry papa. I'm so sorry. I didn't think."

Toren cut him off. "Yes, you did. That's the problem. You always know exactly what you're doing. You're just lucky Kiara told us or who knows-"

"Toren, that's enough." Father put his hand on Toren's chest to get his attention.

Erik couldn't be mad at his older brother for hating him. Not now. He had left his pride with the tears he spilled at the Vikings feet. Toren was right. They shouldn't be there. This could lead to real problems for his family. If things went wrong here, the rest of the village may be forced to choose sides—the same villagers who he and his friends and some of their fathers had secretly been trying to ally with the Vikings. But his father was not a convert. Not yet. This could mess up everything.

But Erik had needed help—and his father had come. No matter what he had done he had always been there for him, and always would be.

"Stand up, now." His father lifted him to his feet, wiped the snow from his face, and hugged his son. "Are you alright?"

"Ja, papa." Erik felt ten. But he felt safe. He hadn't been hugged by his father in years. They didn't do that anymore. The last time he had cried at his father's feet was when the bear took his sister. And his father forgave him for that, too, even though he would never forgive himself.

Then, like a bear with her cubs, Tor put himself between his boys and the danger. This man had been a simple farmer as far back as Erik had memories. Still, he looked like he was ready to fight—probably for the first time in Erik's lifetime—armed with two axes made for chopping wood.

Ubbi the berserker, the breaker of sticks and maimer of boys, was holding their family sword in one hand and had picked up his staff again with the other. Statement enough that he was willing to fight if Tor was. The boys had learned to fear him with stick and fist What could he do with a sword? He looked eerily confident.

The other boys scurried back to where Magnus was hiding, but Magnus stepped forward, like he was claiming Tor as his champion, hoping he'd show Ubbi how it feels to have to beg for mercy.

Erik started thinking this through. Ubbi and Orri were outnumbered. Toren was nearly as big as Father. Even though he had never been trained to fight, they didn't know that. With Magnus, that made it four to two. But then there were the other boys, Ingjaldr and Ivar, and Lars and Ovid.

They were friends, but one of the reasons they were chosen to be trained was that their fathers wanted to ally with the Vikings. Had it been their fathers who came out to rescue them from a beating, would Erik have taken their side? Risk his future for loyalty. To what? A farmer who couldn't offer a future to his own sons, let alone him. No, they needed Orri as much as he did. He needed the Vikings, too. Suddenly, this felt like a big misunderstanding.

"Father, let's just go. It's not worth dying over. We'll get Orri to get it back for us later, after things settle down."

Orri put a hand on Ubbi's chest to calm him. But Erik had seen that look in Ubbi's eyes before. That was the look he gave when the berserker took over.

"Ubbi," Tor spoke calmly. "That was my father's sword before it was mine. And it will be my son's sword after I'm gone. Now put it down and walk away. You're done here."

Ubbi didn't put down the sword. He didn't walk away. Orri wiped his mouth and smiled. "I don't think he wants to give it back. There's something odd about walking around with nothing to defend yourself with other than sticks. It's not our way. You must remember how odd that felt, eh, Tor?"

Tor turned back to his sons. "I want you to go home." He looked at the others. "Boys, you too. You're done today."

Erik hung his head and started to turn.

"Father, I'm not leaving." Toren looked like he was trying too hard to look angry or mean or something. But really, he looked scared.

Tor put his hand on Toren's shoulder. "Your heart is right, but I need you to trust me. They will never disarm as long as they're outnumbered like this." The last bit he directed at Erik. "Go on now, we'll talk about this at supper." Kiara took Toren's arm and lead him back down the path. The others made their way down the trails that took them back to their houses, too, but it was a slow retreat. Erik looked to his older brother and thought about how he always managed to make him seem weak, or small. As he watched Kiara lead him down the path by his arm, Erik burned.

ALONE WITH VIKINGS

"Ubbi, you know you don't want to fight me," Tor reasoned.

Ubbi swung the sword back and forth as if getting a feel for its balance, then leaned on the staff defiantly.

Orri broke the silent stare shared between the two men. "Do you think you are the same Tor we all revered so many years ago, old man?"

"Why don't you stick to your chicken, Orri." Tor didn't take his eyes off Ubbi. "Save your snake tongue for farm boys and the villagers whose greed exceeds their intellect."

Ubbi and Orri were young Vikings when Tor was Olaf's second. He knew them before Orri had turned into a talking potato and Ubbi still had his tongue. Back then they were barely older than Erik, and their only value was pulling an oar. At that time, Tor would have been a god to them. They knew what he was capable of. Back then.

Tor took a step toward Ubbi, the mute raised the sword and stepped back. "Ubbi? You don't believe this serpent now do you? What would one sword do for you, anyway? There are hundreds of people in or around this village. What did Orri tell you? That if you made an army of boys then the rest would fall in line?"

"Don't mind him, Ubbi, his own son is on our side," Orri said smugly. Ubbi glanced at Orri, then down at the chicken burning on the spit.

"Sure." Tor kept trying to get into their heads. "Take comfort in knowing my fourteen-year-old son wanted to be a Viking. I'm sure that's the first time that's happened." That seemed to have gotten to them, which was dangerous for these two. They were leaderless, alone, and unsure of themselves — used to being part of a bigger army. "What has happened to you, Ubbi? You lose your young captain and think Orri is going to get you home? Why? Because he has a working tongue and was stupid enough to use it to send boys into a sinking ship to steal your master's treasure? You'd better hope that son of Olaf's doesn't wake up to see how you're spending his father's money." Tor laughed. "You can't even go home again. Not without him. I'd hate to see what Olaf would do to the two survivors who came back without his son. I think he'd make an ugly example out of you two for that."

"Ubbi. Do you remember this man?" argued Orri.

Ubbi nodded in a frustrated way, as if to say, *Of course.*

"He's the traitor, Tor Ovesen. Remember the cold nights we spent at the oar searching for this man? Don't you let him get to you. Can you imagine if Olaf found out we found his general and let him live?"

"Which son of Olaf's is that giant, anyway?" It was time for Tor to strike a bargain.

"Vidar," Orri said. "His youngest."

Tor couldn't believe it. He knew Vidar when he was just a little boy. "I tell you what you should do. We've got a harvest festival coming up, it's a big to-do in the hall. Everyone will be there. I'll get Elsa out of the house — you grab poor Vidar and drag him into the woods and end him there. Steal a few horses while you're at it, and all the food you can carry. The merchant's so rich he won't even notice. Cover him with stones, put a blade in his hand, a few coins on his eyes and send him on his way to Valhalla. Then take your money and go. Stay away from Jarl Olaf, and stay away from here. Everyone will assume Vidar woke up and you all ran off together. No charges, no outlawry, no nothing. Just the two of you with enough money to disappear and have a wonderful life. Let me tell you boys, the farming life ain't too bad."

Tor noticed Ubbi's grip on the sword had loosened, his shoulders had dropped. He had calmed, and he was listening.

Tor took a slow step forward. Ubbi raised the sword again. Tor shook his head. In his mind he kept reminding himself there were two of them, and they were younger than he was. Other than that, he wanted to slap Ubbi for his lack of respect. Fifteen years ago, he'd have had the fat one digging two graves by now. There was something telling about Orri though. He hadn't moved. No aggression, no nothing. Maybe he still saw the general of his youth.

Time to change tactics. "The next time you raise my father's sword against me you'd better be ready to use it. Last warning." Tor couldn't risk letting Ubbi regain his confidence. Well, it was a fifty-fifty shot and Tor was all out of ideas.

Like the snap of a twig Ubbi turned. Tor remembered Ubbi was a little unstable when he was younger. That's what caused him to lose his tongue.

It was his knuckles that gave him away. They turned white even before he threw his long black hair back over his shoulder. Those knuckles probably saved Tor's life.

Tor blocked the first blow with the handle of the axe in his left, then slammed the head of the axe upward to break Ubbi's jaw or cheek. That would be the quickest way to end the fight, confuse him with a blow to the face. The pain would confuse him enough to allow Tor to come back across with the oak handle and break his nose. If done properly, a broken nose would leave even an experienced warrior defenseless, too blinded with tears to see and choking on his own blood. It was amazing how quick a man goes down when he can't breathe.

Tor had no plans on killing Ubbi or Orri, that choice he'd leave to them. His right hand came across after the block but just missed the bridge of Ubbi's nose. He was quick, or Tor had gotten slow. Probably a little of both.

When Ubbi slipped the cross, he spun and caught Tor across his exposed side with his staff. Ribs cracked and Tor felt a stabbing pain as he gasped for his next breath. He shouldn't have had to breathe that deep. Tor fell backward to get some space but Ubbi came back with another stroke. Iron clanked iron as Tor barely got his axes head up in time to deflect the sword's downward stroke.

He grunted as he drove forward, shoulder first into Ubbi's stomach. Much as it pained him, he had to close the gap, or the stick would come next.

Ubbi was surprised by the attack and did not dodge, and the full weight of Tor put him down on his back, burying him deep into the snow. Tor wasn't sure if he cracked any of Ubbi's ribs, but he definitely heard the mute gasp as he at least knocked the wind out of him. Anything to slow the Viking down was a small victory.

Before he could be thrown off, Tor slapped his left axe down to pin Ubbi's sword hand to the ground, and jerked on the right axe's handle to bring its head skidding across the snow until the bottom of the blade caught Ubbi on the head. It landed with a dull thud. Not a death blow but still Ubbi's eyes looked dazed from the impact.

Tor smelled the rot of the Viking's breath as he watched the snow around his head dye red with fresh blood.

Tor pushed up off Ubbi and began to raise his right axe overhead. He wasn't sure if he was going to offer mercy or end him. He never got to make that choice.

Ubbi buried his sharp knee high up into Tor's groin, pinching one of his balls on its way to shoving the other up into his stomach.

Tor choked, but managed to make his fall forward, an attempt to try to smother the ugly, tongueless Viking. He knew this wasn't going to end him, but was hoping to buy himself enough time to find a way to breathe again. The knee had slowed his body but not his instincts, so as he buried his stomach into Ubbi's face to smother the brute, he turned to make sure Orri was keeping his distance. Then a sharp pain bit into his stomach. "Aayy!" The sound he made was a reaction, not a war cry.

Tor pushed off Ubbi's face with his hands, burying the man's bloody head deeper into the snow. With a quick punch he relieved himself of the new source of pain, and Ubbi of at least one tooth. Even so, the mute still managed to tear the fabric of Tor's outer coat as he jerked away.

A hard thump came across Tor's back as Ubbi rained down a blind and ineffective blow with his stick. Tor's attention immediately jumped to Ubbi's other hand. He had lost sight of the sword. Ubbi threw a right cross, narrowly missing Tor's jaw. Tor returned a right of his own. Dropping his full weight behind it he finally found Ubbi's nose.

He heard the crack as cartilage smeared against bone, and a new source of blood smeared crimson across Ubbi's face. Immediately, his eyes blackened, and he began to cough and spit out mouthfuls of pink and red froth.

Tor knew he felt like he was drowning and if he could hold Ubbi down like this it was possible he might die from choking on his own blood. But he did not need him dead, what he needed was to find that sword.

He rolled clear before another knee could find its way north. A man was never as dangerous as he was when he thought he might be facing death.

Tor fell away just in time to avoid a slow piercing thrust from the sword, which had made its way into Orri's hand. Tor remembered Orri, too. All mouth. He liked to start fights and then watch others finish them. That was lucky or one of those staffs could have ended this fight long ago.

The second thrust of the sword was faster but still slower

than Ubbi's worst, and Tor managed to deflect it with the head of the axe in his right. Sliding the head of the other behind the fat man's heel, Tor planted his forehead into Orri's soft, warm belly.

Orri tripped and fell as easy as a pine rotted from the inside, and without even trying to break his fall, landed on top of his champion. With only a whisper of a gasp, the last of the air was forced from Ubbi's lungs as Orri helped him finally find the frozen earth buried deep under the snow.

Tor put his boot on Orri's stomach as he picked up his father's blade. Then he coughed and spit. His too was pink with blood. No doubt the next time he relieved himself he'd find his urine to be tinted red to match.

"Take your coin and go, and forget this place exists. I'll even show you the way." Tor knew he should've killed them both as soon as he said it. What a ridiculous notion. But it had been too long. He had lost the stomach for killing anything that wouldn't help his family survive the winter. So, he continued with his warning.

"And if you come after me or my sons, I swear I'll fill your boots full of stones and sink you to the bottom of the fjord, where you can spend your next life as play things for the daughters of Ran. If you try to stay, I'll find you when you're alone, even if it's when your pants are down around your ankles."

He started to limp away, the pain from his cracked ribs making each step a reminder he was not the man he used to be. *Old man.* He thought about what Orri had called him.

Swinging his sword like it was a pruning shear, Tor cleared any branch that might force him to change his course and prayed to a God he hadn't spoken to since his wife died so many years ago. "Where is the freedom she promised, eh? Will I never have peace?"

CHECKING ON THE NEIGHBORS

Tor slipped through the woods. He winced every time he lifted his axe, just to push the snow-heavy limbs out of the trail. Had it had been so little-traveled these past years? When the children were younger, the trail had been wide and clear from wear. Besides their constant back and forth between houses, he and Pedar would host dinners for each other at least once a month. Had it been so long? Of course, with the engagement of Anja to Toren the families still came together. But it was so formal now. And taking horses down the road was so much easier.

They just kind of went their own ways. Pedar only wanted to talk about business. Toren and Erik liked to hunt and fish, but Pedar and Skadi coddled Ragi so much, the boy probably thought a great adventure was organizing inventory for his father's trading business.

Ah, there it is. Tor wasn't sure what he was going to do if they were home. He just had to see for himself.

"Tor?"

Tor's head jumped up like a mouse that heard meow. So much for spy work. He only made it thirteen feet out of the woods before getting caught by the maid.

"Hello Elsa," he nodded. "You startled me. I figured you'd be making preparations at the hall."

"The festival idn't till tomorrow." She looked even more perplexed than she had to see him popping his head out of the woods. "Anyway, I always do most of the cooking 'ere." She smiled an ugly, gap-toothed grin. "I have all I need between mine and Master Pedar's kitchens, you understand. The kitchen in the hall's good for keeping things warm, at's about it."

"Of course. That makes perfect sense." Tor couldn't believe he hadn't thought of that. He just wanted to see if Orri'd done the smart thing. If Vidar was gone. "So?"

Elsa stared at the axe in his hand, then she watched as he let it fall slowly to his side.

"Are you looking for Master Pedar?"

"Ja," Tor smiled back. That was as good as anything he could've come up with. And the obvious thing to say, too. He was always no good at making up stories, and his mind had drawn a complete blank the second he saw her.

"I'm afraid he's not here right now," she said. "I think he went looking for our guest."

Tor exhaled. "Mphh," his eyes closed in pain. It's amazing how bad cracked ribs can hurt over the littlest things. He inhaled slowly and tried to remember to keep his breaths shallow.

"Are you alright?" she asked.

"Fine," he smiled. The last thing he needed was her to force feed him one of her tonics. "Did you say Vidar's gone?"

"Vidar? Were you looking for him?" She looked back down at the axe. "He probably just took one of the horses to get some air. When he woke the other day, he seemed interested to see his ship. Are you sure you're alright, Tor? There's something odd about you, today."

"I'm fine, Elsa." He wasn't. He could feel the sweat on his brow as clear as the agony in his ribs. "You know if I don't find out details, Runa's going to be upset. Many were saying he wasn't likely to survive, and I know she'd been praying to the gods to heal him."

Elsa looked at Tor like he was the worst liar in the world. "I've got 'im back on his feet. You tell her that. He's as healthy as you and me. Not much of a talker, that one, but can he eat! And no wonder. Biggest man in the village, by far. A good head, maybe two heads taller 'an you."

This was a stupid idea. Tor just wanted to go home.

"Two heads?"

"You know," she held her hands up high. "One." then she reached even higher. "Two."

"Elsa," Tor just had to ask. "Were the other two with him?"

Now she looked at Tor like he did have two heads. "The Vikings? No—why?"

Tor waved with his right hand and turned back into the woods.

Tor had no idea what he was thinking. If Elsa told anyone... He looked down at the axe in his hand and wiped the sweat from his brow. Maybe he should've asked her for some tonic to help with the pain. Obviously, it was affecting his judgement.

He stopped to slow his breathing before he hurt himself. He watched as snow piled off the limbs hanging across the overgrown trail and suddenly felt a sense of peace. *Orri and Ubbi took the money and ran. And Vidar went with them.* He was sure of it. *Why would they stay?*

STICKS AND STONES

U bbi stepped out on the ice. He was less than four feet from shore, and the land fell straight down away from his feet.

"Come on." Orri was holding the other end of the stick. "It's too thick to crack that easy. Not without a little help, at least."

The ice was so clear it was as if there was nothing underfoot at all, but there were five heavy stones laying atop the frozen fjord to prove it was there, and thick. Thick enough to hold up those stones, at least. Still, it took a little mocking for Orri to get Ubbi to take the first steps, which are always the worst of them. And now that he was hovering over what looked like the edge of a cliff, the tongueless Viking looked like he was considering pulling himself back.

"It'll be fine," said Orri. And the fat man pushed his end of the stick, sending Ubbi sliding backward onto the fjord like an angry statue. He was either too afraid to move or too off balance. "See? I told you it was thick enough." Orri tried to be encouraging.

Ubbi's first movement was to motion something ashore with his hands, to express his appreciation for the boost. He probably felt the same gratitude a baby chick had after its big brother nudged it out of the nest. He snarled as he carefully shuffled his feet until he made it over the outline of the ship, where at least he wouldn't have to see how deep the water was anymore. The top rail wasn't too far below the surface, but the ship had slipped entirely under the ice except for the dragon's head, making it look as if it was taking a nice swim.

"Do you think it's safe?" asked a deep voice from over Orri's shoulder.

Orri spun faster than anyone would expect was possible for a man his size. A large hand caught the stick he was holding and jerked it out of his hand.

"Vidar!" Orri might as well have been staring death in the face. What did he know? What was he thinking? Orri had no idea, so he tried to sound cheery. "Thank the gods you're alright!" He might have hugged his captain to sell his love for him, but with Vidar that would've definitely gotten something broken.

Vidar's face looked like it was burning, even though it was getting colder every day. "What are you doing with my ship?" His voice took on a gravelly tone.

"Uh, we're here to see if we can get our swords," Orri realized he was still hanging on to the stick. He let Vidar have it. "Yours too. We've got no iron."

Ubbi started edging his way back to shore.

"Where do you think you're going, eh? You just stay out there for now." For someone who hadn't seen his crew since he thought he was slipping off to die at sea, Vidar wasn't acting very happy to see them. *What had he heard?*

"Swords?" Vidar flipped the stick in the air. His huge hand barely fit in the cut out the boys had made for a normal man's grip. "From the look of these sticks, somebody's been training. What happened to your head, Ubbi?"

Ubbi shrugged and gently put his hand to touch at his head. Then he pulled his long hair forward to cover the wound.

"Why didn't you get the swords when you sent those boys to take my treasure?" Vidar put the end of the staff into Orri's chest, pushing him backward onto the ice.

Orri froze and listened for cracking. Slowly he caught his

breath. "We weren't taking anything from you, Vidar. Believe me."

Vidar stepped out onto the ice. There was a crack. Orri was positive he heard a crack. Vidar put the staff back into his belly and pushed him farther back. Orri's hands went up, but his eyes went down. Thanks to the crystal ice underfoot, he could clearly see into the abyss. Orri's teeth chattered.

Vidar kept pushing.

"Come on, Orri. You've always got people doing your dirty work for you. First, that sweet talking tongue of yours got a couple of boys to nearly die trying to steal my gold and silver." He motioned to the mute. "I can't exactly blame Ubbi for convincing them to do it, can I?" Vidar slammed the stick down, pulverizing the ice where it landed.

Orri scanned the ice below his feet, and almost felt like he was going to start crying. "Please, Vidar. You were still asleep, and the fjord was starting to freeze, and we were afraid the ship might sink. Then where would we be?"

Vidar slammed the stick down again, and Orri may have whimpered.

"Why do you keep saying 'we'? Ubbi doesn't have a tongue. And even when he did, men like us convince with force, not forked tongues!" In his anger, his voice echoed off the steep mountain cliffs.

Vidar started walking back to shore, and without turning around, he held the stick back toward Orri and told him to keep walking until he got to that ship. "How exactly did you think you were going to get the weapons?"

Ubbi shrugged and pointed down as if he could see them right there.

"Well, if the ice was thin enough, I was going to see if we could break through it with his stick."

"What do you think about that plan, Ubbi?" Vidar seemed calmer now that there was some distance between him and Orri.

Ubbi shrugged, then cast an angry eye toward Orri.

"I think you're on the right track though, Orri. If we could break through the ice and get to those swords, I think that would be a good thing. Especially if some of the fathers start to realize that you were willing to let their sons die, just so you could get some gold for yourself. I mean, if they stopped to think how terrible the Vikings must be to ask their boys to take that chance. If I was them, I'd kill the ones responsible. Especially if there were only three of them — weak, rich and without weapons."

Orri started taking steps toward Vidar with his hands out. "That wasn't going to happen, because-"

"Shut your mouth before I have Ubbi cut your tongue out. You're not like us, Orri. I don't think you'd last a year without that mouth to get you out of trouble, and I'm not going to let it get you out of this."

"Vidar, let me explain." Orri sounded worried.

Vidar got a big smile on his face, as if a great idea just jumped into his head. "I tell you what, we'll let the gods decide if you should live or die. Since only the ravens know your heart, let Odin decide your fate just like you did with those boys. With my life, too really. Ubbi, you can come back here with me."

The more at peace Vidar seemed, the more concerned Orri got.

"I see those rocks you, eh, Ubbi threw out to test the ice. If you throw all of them down right on the spot you're standing at now, and the ice breaks, I'll let you swim down and get our swords. And just like those boys, I'll give you two gold pieces for your reward."

Orri started shaking.

"If it doesn't break, then I guess it was too thick after all and this was just another one of your bad ideas."

"Vidar please-"

"Come on, Orri, smile." Vidar's smile was actually genuine this time. "You never spar with us or play games

107

with us. You always just get things started. Smile, have some fun."

Orri chose the smallest of the stones first. He hoisted it up off the ice. It was so heavy, he just got it up over his belly—his heartbeat inside his chest like a hammer. He was sure this was going to drop right through the ice and bring him to the bottom along with it. He said a prayer to Thor, the god he prayed to whenever they had set out to sea or gone into battle. But he felt alone. Like no one was listening.

When he couldn't hold the stone any longer, he pushed it out, trying to get some distance between where he stood and where it would land. It pretty much fell straight down. Orri jumped a little when it hit, trying anything to keep from falling in. The stone crunched and slid, shattering the top layer of ice—but it didn't break through.

"That wasn't a good try. You'll never break through the ice that way. Next time I'd better see you get that rock on your shoulder at least. And I want to see you throw it down, not just drop it." Vidar seemed like he was having a good time watching. Orri was doing everything he could to keep from sobbing.

Orri, like most Vikings, was a man who followed rituals. You don't tempt fate. With each rock he pushed back to the ship, he said his little empty prayer to Thor, felt even more positive that no one was listening, and threw down the stone. If he didn't make the effort, Vidar and Ubbi would beat him to death with the training sticks.

Orri wasn't sure if he was afraid of drowning or afraid of heights. It only occurred to him when he had to get down on his knees and push that third stone back to the ship. He could see the steep slope of the mountain plummeting down into the eerie darkness hundreds of feet below. If the ice were to break now, Orri was sure the currents would drag him down like a rock. It would be like falling.

"Did you know that Tor Ovesen lives in this village?"

Orri tried to hide his smile. He stood, cracked his back,

and started in toward shore.

"Get back where you were." Vidar pointed with the stick. "I know you don't believe me, but a man can talk and break ice at the same time."

Orri wiped a tear from his cheek as he fell back to his knees in front of the third stone. The last ones were too heavy to carry to the spot, so Orri pushed his tormentors to the spot where he was going to die.

"Well?" asked Vidar. Ubbi had learned long ago not to even try. Trying to communicate without a tongue wasn't worth the effort, and usually lead to somebody getting killed. So he just stood next to Vidar, waiting to hear the answer.

"Ja, we saw him the other day."

"Did he recognize you?"

Orri got the stone to his shoulder first try. He realized that even if he could manage to swim, he'd never find the hole again. He said his prayer and threw down the stone. It bounced off the spot. Orri exhaled slowly and trudged back to stone four.

"Ja, he recognized us. We were younger then, maybe a little thinner, but we knew him."

"Thinner?" Vidar elbowed Ubbi.

Orri was getting angry just thinking about dying this way, after all the times he kissed up to Vidar — all the times his tongue had saved them a lot of bloodshed. He was just showing Orri what a terrible waste his life had been building up this man. Why? Because he was the big, stupid son of a jarl. He even got his size from his father. He didn't deserve that, either. He was the one who wouldn't last a year if he was just a regular man. If he wasn't the size of a bear — and twice as hairy.

Orri pushed the fourth stone back to the spot. He always knew he'd die some day, maybe in battle, or by the knife of some father whose daughter he'd defiled, but he didn't want to die in darkness, in the shadow of some mountain, undersea.

He grunted as he rolled the heavy stone up his belly, where it rested until he managed to catch his breath enough to...heft it up...the rest...of the way.

"Hit that same spot this time. I think this one has a chance."

Orri thought the same thing. After he said his prayer, he started to shake. He knew no one was hearing him now. It was just him and the stone. His knees felt weak from the stone, or fear, or cold; it made no difference. The stone crashed down, slamming hard into the spot, and stuck. With an unmistakable pop the ice cracked. It didn't run, it just appeared all at once, right between Orri's feet. And there was a little puddle of water filling the hole that the rocks had pounded into the ice.

Orri stared for a few seconds, petrified the ground would give way beneath his feet. Then he felt compelled to continue his story, maybe for the distraction—he couldn't say—but he felt it was important for some reason. "You see, Ubbi had taken a sword from the hands of Tor's son."

"What?" Now Vidar was interested in hearing Orri talk.

On his hands and knees Orri pushed the last stone back to the spot, talking between pushes. "We had been training boys to fight." He pushed it another two feet. "We were planning to raise a crew for our trip home." Another push, another deep breath, another sentence. "One of them was Tor's youngest."

Vidar looked at the thick training staff in his hand.

The more Vidar seemed to want to hear, the more determined Orri was to stop the telling in order to move that stone. The fifth and final one was by far the biggest, and heaviest. And it was all Orri could do not to fall on his belly while he shoved it along, foot by foot.

"When Tor showed up, he took the sword from Ubbi with a couple of woodsman's hatchets."

Vidar looked at the wound on Ubbi's head. The day after

he got it the area around the cut had already turned an ugly shade of yellow, and no amount of hair could hide that.

Orri knew that look on Ubbi's face. The one that said he would kill to be able to explain. That's what kept Orri and Ubbi so close. Somehow Orri always knew what Ubbi wanted to say, better than anyone else, at least. Usually, Orri would've put words to Ubbi's thoughts for him at that very moment, but he needed to play this to his advantage. He was the one still standing on cracked ice, after all. It wasn't easy being Ubbi's interpreter all these years. It took work. It meant he had been there to start fights and to stop them.

Maybe even Ubbi understood the manipulation, but it generally worked out well for both of them, because both, maybe especially these two men—the one with the golden tongue and the one with no tongue at all—knew that above all, everyone wanted to be understood. And the men that took Ubbi's tongue robbed him of expressing what he thought and what he felt ever again. Misunderstood men are the most dangerous men of all. And because of that, Orri could depend on Ubbi above all. Ubbi was as much Orri's man as he was Vidar's.

Orri was a gifted storyteller, that much Vidar had gotten right. He knew that slowing a story down made the hearer want to listen to it even more. He was depending on this little tale to save him from having to throw that last rock. Vidar kept listening and watching. Maybe he was too stupid to realize if the storyteller was to die, the story would go down with him. So, Orri leaked out a little more.

"The last thing Tor said was that he would kill us if we didn't take the treasure and leave. But we stayed." *Time to remind him of our allegiance.* "We would never leave you at the mercy of the man who betrayed your father. So instead of leaving as rich men, we came here for weapons—so we could protect you." Orri couldn't believe it himself, but somehow, he'd found a way to make his case. Stories were like that. Sometimes you just keep talking and out of nowhere you'll make your point.

Well, now he had to remind Vidar that his life was still in his hands. Vidar would stop this—he was sure of it. Orri leaned down, got his grip, exhaled for the lift, and-

"There you are, Vidar," someone else spoke.

It was Pedar and his beautiful wife, Skadi, with their young and possibly even more beautiful daughter, Anja. Well, by Vidar or any other, at least the game was over. And Orri won. He rubbed his back and stretched as he got back to his feet.

"Ja, you found me. Am I Elsa's prisoner, that I cannot get some fresh air with my men who I haven't even seen until today?" Vidar lifted Ubbi's hair to get a better look at the ugly wound, then let it fall. Orri he ignored, leaving him on the fjord standing over a rock like an imbecile. In a twisted kind of way, it was too bad it ended like this. Orri was kind of curious how long Vidar would have let him go before telling him to stop on his own. And in a twisted way, he wondered if the ice would've stood against the last stone.

"Don't say such a thing," said Skadi, almost flirting. "We have treated you very well. My daughter waited on you every day while you were asleep, didn't you Anja?"

Anja buried her head in her mother's fur.

"We didn't mean to interrupt anything," said Pedar.

Vidar scanned his men, then up to Skadi's pleading face. "Alright, we're pretty much done here." Then he started walking to the sleigh.

Orri hung his head and exhaled. Without a thought of thanking Thor, he started shuffling his feet back to shore.

"Actually, would you like to see something?" Vidar asked his host family.

Orri slid to a stop. He was involuntarily shaking, like the last leaf clinging to a branch in an autumn breeze.

Pedar just leaned forward.

"Orri is trying to see if the gods love him," explained

Vidar. "He's left something on the ship and wanted to see if he could break through the ice to get it."

"I'm not sure that's a good idea," whispered Pedar to Vidar. "He's likely to fall through if he succeeds."

"He thinks it's important to try. Don't you, Orri?" Vidar smiled. "Give it everything you've got this time; we're all watching."

Orri couldn't believe his luck—or the extent of Vidar's cruelty. Ubbi didn't even mumble a protest to help him, either. The crack at his feet had just had time to freeze over with an icy glaze. With a deep inhale, Orri worked the stone up until it rested onto his shoulder. He remembered Thor again, and prayed until he couldn't think of anything else to say. Well. This was it. Orri looked at the shattered glass floor, boosted the stone as high as he could manage, and slammed it down with everything he had left.

The only thing that last stone broke was Orri's delusions of importance. Vidar rode off with the family, leaving his men behind to make their own way home.

Pedar told Orri later, that while he was struggling to raise that last rock, Vidar was telling Ubbi that he didn't think a hundred rocks could've broken that ice, and that he expected to see them both at Elsa's in the morning, with his treasure.

Orri's wet feet froze to the ice with every step he made to shore. The gods had chosen his fate, or maybe it was luck, or maybe it was just that the ice was too thick in the first place. He was sure once Vidar had time to think about it, he'd realize Orri'd been doing the right thing for him all along. Maybe eventually he'd even reward him for it.

Orri's feet were too cold for such reflection. It was going to be a long walk home.

HARVEST FESTIVAL

Runa wanted to show off her new servant, Kiara, to her friends, so she made the whole family arrive early and help with the preparations of the hall.

Erik didn't mind. He'd sampled every meat and dish that walked through the door. Even Tor was there. He made the boys fill the troughs with firewood from the shed, and he didn't help at all, which was odd.

After the incident in the woods, he said he wasn't going hunting again for a few weeks, and he didn't. Instead, he stayed home and bossed Erik and Toren around — and caught up on his sleep.

The boys had never found out what happened that day. Their father had come home with the sword but refused to talk about how. When they asked about it, he said it was over. That meant it was not to come up again, unless he brought it up. It's the kind of thing Tor said when a big fish got away, or if one of them missed an easy bow shot. Erik figured he'd hear the story that night from Orri after one or two drinks. He wasn't the type to keep his mouth shut about anything.

The harvest festival was one of the few times the entire village, men and women, young and old, came together in the hall. There would be food and drink for everyone. Even the servants would join in.

It was a time for getting drunk with your neighbors, some of whom hadn't been seen since the soil thawed. And for some, this would be the last time they'd be seen until the ring ceremony, which wasn't for months, not until the winter solstice. The food for that was being delivered that night, too.

For everything brought in, half would be set aside for the solstice. Kind of a village tithe to ensure there would be something to look forward to, even when some families would already be rationing at home. Life was hard, and these celebrations were the only things most people had to look forward to all year long.

Erik was no exception. He loved seeing his father buy and sell and barter with the neighbors. He even liked to hear the women arranging marriages. It was a special time of music and songs and wonderful stories, stories of other times and worlds, of heroes and gods, and Elves and Dwarfs and Giants. And if they were lucky, Old Erik would tell one about dragons.

This was the last exciting thing before the gathering season, when the activities of the village moved indoors to wait out the long dark months ahead. Winter was difficult, even for the wealthy. It was a time of scarcity and darkness, when people hunkered down like animals in burrows until the sun's warmth beckoned them to come out again in the spring. It was a time to reap not what had been sown, but what had survived to bear fruit.

But tonight, was a celebration.

Ragi's family was late, as usual. Their servants had been there all day, of course. Elsa was pretty much running the kitchen. But Toren had been keeping an eye on the door for Anja, and Runa for Skadi, and for some reason Tor had been watching the door as well.

Erik hoped his father had worked out an arrangement with Orri since they'd had some time to talk. Orri said they'd be leaving in the spring, and Erik still planned to be with them. Ubbi could be a grouch, but the thought of staying one more year under Runa's oppression was too much to bear. The only thing she and Erik seemed to agree on lately was that it was time for Erik to find his own way. And the Vikings were the only ship out of town.

Knowing this might be his last harvest festival here made the fifteen-year-old feel a little nostalgic. He hoped the Vikings would stay long enough for Toren's wedding. Erik didn't really care, but he thought he would like to be there for that. Kind of one last family party before he set off.

The doors creaked open and the hall filled with noise. More from outside than within. As soon as Ragi poked his head through the door, Erik waved him over. Then came Anja, beautiful as always, dressed like a princess. Toren immediately went to greet her, and Runa wasn't far behind.

The excitement inside the hall grew with the new arrivals. It sounded like the entire village was right behind them, waiting impatiently outside. Finally, the party was about to begin.

"What took you so long?" Erik punched Ragi on the arm. He squinched his eyes as if he was hurt. *What a girl.* Pedar held the door open. Then came the surprise.

The giant Viking, Vidar, ducked in under the doorway.

As if a stopper had been pulled, the rest of the village poured in right behind. They must have been following the giant through town to get a first look at him out in the daylight. He was a spectacle. Unlike any man Erik had ever seen before. Broader than fat Orri, and a head taller than his father, Tor.

The behemoth was followed close behind by Orri and Ubbi, then their host families, then it seemed like the entire rest of the village.

Everyone piling in after the Vikings seemed to be looking for Tor, like they wanted to see them side by side or something. Tor's head shook and he scowled at the sight of the Vikings and the gawkers coming in behind.

Soon the hall was filled with the commotion of low talking families shuffling to their usual places between long benches and even longer tables.

Old Afi, the village gothi, or lawspeaker, rose from his unimpressive seat. His place was above everyone else's, on a raised platform at the head of the hall, next to the empty throne. He motioned for Vidar to come closer, his aged face uneasy, like a man who'd been offered a plate of rotten fish for breakfast.

Orri and Ubbi followed Vidar to the front of the hall. Vidar's gaze seemed to lock with Old Erik's mismatched eyes as he passed.

Old Erik was the gothi's younger, but still very old, brother. The two were relics. Runa said they arrived about the time Tor did, and she swore they hadn't changed in all those thirteen years.

Old Erik nodded slightly, like a teacher reassuring his pupil. Vidar glared back like he didn't need anyone's encouragement.

Erik was glad when a hush fell over the hall as Old Afi spoke quietly to the Viking.

"I am told you are Vidar, son of Olaf."

"I am." Vidar's gaze flicked between the elder and the empty throne. "I will speak to the jarl."

"They call me Old Afi. I am the gothi of this village. We are all farmers, save a few, and have no need for a jarl, here."

"No jarl?" He looked surprised. "Are you the leader, then?"

"We are governed by the law," said the gothi. "This is a village of free men."

"Are we not in Norway?" Vidar asked. "Who do you pay tribute to?"

With a slow and shaky hand, the elder sipped from a plain, wooden cup. "We are bound by the same laws as your father, the jarl, and that is what makes us free — not by the permission of any man."

Erik noticed Pedar raise his eyebrows to his father, Tor. As if to say, *I told you so.*

Vidar turned to Ubbi and Orri and his face began to turn

red, the way Ubbi looked whenever he went berzerk during training. Erik couldn't help but check to make sure none of the Vikings were carrying sticks. They weren't. Then, just the way he cut in on Ubbi to stop him from killing one of the boys, Orri put his hand on Vidar's shoulder.

"Then you lead these people?" Orri interjected. "An old man who wears the law for a crown? How convenient for the old man, wouldn't you say?"

Vidar looked at Orri like he might kill him on his way to sit on the empty throne.

Orri winked at Vidar, as if he knew what his captain was thinking. "Jarl Olaf always says, the gods allow men to have thrones to find out which among us are willing to lead — men with ambition, men who can give you opportunity — like Jarl-"

Vidar slapped his big mitt over Orri's face, one of his sausage fingers grazing along the fat man's teeth.

"What?" asked Tor. The room burst into a low mutter. "What was your man going to say? It sounded like he was about to claim our village for your father."

Vidar looked at Tor as if he was puzzled by the man.

Old Afi held up a hand toward Tor as if to ask him to stand down. Tor's shoulders relaxed, and so did the tension in the room. Then Old Afi decided to forego his usual long speeches and surprised everyone when he got right to the point. "Why are you here, Vidar?"

"That is a question my people only ask of old men like you." Vidar kept his eye on Tor as he spoke. "Men who live long, uneventful lives — who die in their beds rather than in the pursuit of glory."

Vidar looked like a man destined for glory. Erik sat up straight to try to catch his eye as the giant surveyed the field of men.

"Why am I here? Blame the gods!" Vidar filled an empty cup from a pitcher of mead and took a long draught, then stepped around Tor — ignoring him. "Maybe Odin finally answered the prayers of your hungry sons, or your lonely daughters. I don't know. Although this looks like a nice little village, I would prefer to be sitting at my father's table, to be hearing stories of his great adventures beyond the sea and news of my brother Egil's as well, not sitting here in this small hall that smells more of manure than mead, where men talk like slaves, mired in plans of growing crops and raising chickens and goats."

Tor watched Afi for a signal that never came. Instead, the old man smiled and signaled toward the kitchen. "Bring our guest food, and more to drink. He hungers. He thirsts. How can a man feel welcome when he has so many needs?" Then the elderleader turned his attention back to the Viking. "I want to hear more about your journey, and, more importantly, what we can do to help get you home to your father."

VIKING'S STORY

E rik loved feast days. He imagined he'd be eating like this every day, once he joined the Vikings. The smell of spit-fired venison, goat, chicken, and even beef permeated the hall. So much meat had been burned it had completely masked the scent of the fish. Dried fish, salted fish, fish stored in kegs and kept with lye—a food used in every meal in every kitchen and on every ship to flavor the water and to fill pots and pot bellies alike. And Erik was gorging himself on all of his favorites, and settling in for some good, Viking tales.

"Tell us, then," said one of the farmers. "Tell us of your journey."

"I'm no storyteller." Vidar scowled at him as if he'd hurt men for less.

"Come on, don't be modest. We don't have any Skalds here," said young Bjorn.

"We ain't got no stories worth telling," laughed his drunk father, Jan.

The hall fell silent, and all eyes were on Vidar. The Viking's face turned red, at first from embarrassment, then resentment. Just as he looked like he was going to hit someone, Orri put his hand on Vidar's shoulder and pushed himself to his feet.

"I'd be glad to tell the tale, Captain." The snakes on his bald head slithered when the fat man raised his eyebrows.

Vidar shifted his angry look to Orri, then nodded a tentative approval.

Orri took a quick bite off a chicken leg and washed it down with his drink. A sea of faces stared in waiting. Then he smiled, as if he was finally in his element, and began to tell their tale.

"Ours was one of just ten ships." Orri paused to fill his cup again. Erik leaned in, along with the rest of the hall. Orri smiled again. "Our captain's father, Jarl Olaf, had led us across the North Sea to the west. We visited many lands, met some strange people with even stranger customs. We had a profitable journey." He shrugged to Vidar, as if goading him for approval. Vidar nodded, as if he didn't appreciate being drug into Orri's show. Orri started nodding again, as if trying to remember where he left off. "Ja, that's right. We had run into some stubborn hosts on our way home, while in Ireland."

Erik watched as Kiara jumped up from their table and ran back into the kitchen. He must've been talking about her village.

"The trouble caused some of the ships, including ours, from returning home as early as we had planned. By the time we got our oars in the water, the early frost had already set in." He looked directly at Vidar as if for approval. Vidar gave him a stone face look, as if he was curious how the story would turn out. The people were drinking in every word. "Vidar, our captain, considered staying over the winter." Then he made quick eye contact with Tor and nodded as if looking for affirmation from someone who'd understand. "That would have been the sensible thing to do, ja?"

"But I am not always sensible," interrupted Vidar. He looked at Orri as if he would pay for telling this story. Vidar emptied his cup, then started to refill it. "I wanted to get home. The women were pretty enough, and the food was to my liking, but I just didn't like the smell of the place. And unlike you fine people, I don't think they liked me or my men being there very much, either."

Vidar laughed. Orri nervously laughed with him. Then, like a wave, laughter rolled across the room until everyone was laughing nervously along.

The villagers all started filling cups, steins, and horns and settling in for the rest of the story, interested in what happened next. Orri looked to Vidar, red-cheeked, as if for approval. Vidar motioned for him to continue. Everyone watched as Orri wiped sweat from his brow with a shaky hand. Erik was curious if the tattoos on his head would wipe off. They didn't. Orri began walking around the room as he continued, "But it proved to be too late. We got caught in bad seas and even worse weather. And even with our fearless leader manning the rudder, our ship was separated from the rest.

Vidar stood. "I don't know what happened to the others. My father, my brother, the ships that left before us, but we were out too long." Vidar stared into the drink in his cup. Erik looked into his own cup, too, curious what the giant might be seeing. The light of one hundred fires reflected off its calm surface. It must have reminded Vidar of the many nights he'd spent at sea.

When Vidar sat back down, Orri picked up where he left off. "Having lost our way, our means of navigation, and most of our sail in a storm that seemed to go on and on..." Orri cleared his throat. "Our navigator did the best he could, using the sun and stars, but soon we ran low on food. Then we ran low on-" His voice faded, then he smiled and cleared his throat again, and held up his cup.

"Many of our men are now sleeping with the daughters of Rán. We too..." He looked back at Vidar, who was still staring into his cup. "We too figured we'd be sharing her icy bed at the bottom of the sea." Orri took another drink. "Then we woke up here."

Vidar held up his cup and cut in again. "Here on this barrow atop Helgafjell, this holy mountain."

Erik had been watching. Vidar had drunk enough already to kill a normal man, but he barely slurred his words. "I wasn't even sure I was alive. I must have been fading in and out for a long time, But I remember seeing Anja who was caring for me. I thought she was a beautiful Valkyrie." A huge gap-toothed smile broke out across his face, and he raised his cup and winked at the girl.

Toren put his arm around her. His brows furrowed his eyes down to slits. What his big brother thought he might do to stop that giant from taking his girl, Erik would never know. But if looks could kill, his would've been arrows to the eyes.

"I thought I'd made it to Valhalla." Vidar nudged Pedar and winked, as if he'd appreciate the complement to his daughter. Pedar's cheeks turned red, and he just sat there, impotently staring into his cup while whistling and whooping erupted from some of the younger men in the crowd.

Kiara emerged from the kitchen and took her seat next to Erik. She pulled away when he put his hand on her arm. A misguided attempt to bring her comfort. He realized then, she had never talked about what happened in Ireland, or while they were at sea.

Old Afi stood. "You and your men are gifted storytellers."

Erik wondered if the old man realized one of them didn't even have a tongue.

Old Afi continued, "I don't think there are many skalds who could've captured the village's attention as well as you."

Erik looked at his father, and he did not look happy.

MUD IN THE EYE

"I have a question." Tor couldn't believe his neighbors were so simple. These men were admitting to raiding a village full of innocents, and maybe because it was people across the sea, his neighbors were acting as if their journey was harrowing for them. As if they were the victims. "What happened to your other men? Your crew?"

The giant's jaw tensed, then loosened. Then he nodded to his mouthpiece.

"The storm took our sail, and many of the men as well." Orri looked at Vidar for direction.

Vidar, never taking his eyes off Tor, whispered something to Ubbi. Ubbi nodded. Vidar nudged Orri on.

Tor recognized Vidar—he looked just like his mother. But he got his angry eyes from his father, Tor's best friend, Olaf. Well, that was many years ago. Olaf could cut a man down just with his eyes, too. But his son didn't realize it would take more than a harsh look to get to Tor Ovesen.

Orri continued, "After the sea calmed, while we were adrift, those that remained began to starve or thirst to death. That was much worse than the storm. That's no way for a Viking to die. Not many of us survived."

"But somehow you three made it. Didn't you, Orri?"

"What're you getting at?" Vidar growled.

The more anger Tor got from Vidar, the more he pushed. "My boys told me the men who rescued you didn't find any bodies, but I visited your ship. The ice was clear as glass.

There were some broken bones." Tor watched as Orri looked to Vidar, as if for once in his life he didn't know what to say. The room had fallen silent. Some of the women held their children close. "Whatever is there will still be there in the spring," Tor added. "As long the dragon doesn't sink as soon as the ice lets it go."

Vidar polished the meat off a chicken leg and kept watching Tor.

Orri never could stand silence. "We were at sea for a very long time. We nearly starved to death, all of us."

Vidar held up his hand to stop Orri from saying more. "Many of the men didn't make it, Tor. You know how it is. And those of us who did were lucky, indeed." Vidar punctuated his point by cracking the chicken leg with his teeth. Then he proceeded to suck the black marrow from the end of the fractured bone.

"Do these people know who you are Tor Ovesen?"

"You don't even know who I am, Vidar." Tor replied. "You were just a little boy when I left the Viking life."

Vidar's face began to boil. Vidar was so young, and so ready to fight, it would not be difficult to show him for what he was.

"I knew Tor," said Orri. "And Ubbi did, too. Did you tell them why you left? Does your family know?"

Tor expected to be outed by these men. He knew his reputation was done as soon as they arrived, but he had no idea what Orri was going to say next. He had done a lot of bad things in the past.

"He left, because he'd gotten a Christian slave pregnant, and then became a Christian, so they could be married in a church, somewhere over in Ireland."

That fat bastard. Was he out to ruin Tor's marriage or to destroy Toren and Erik?

The hall erupted. Runa ran to the kitchen, humiliated. She, of course, already knew. Runa was seventeen when her father took Tor and his young family in. But she hated anything that didn't make her life look perfect, especially in front of the neighbors. Toren and Erik just stared. Tor guessed they were wondering how it took this stranger trying to smear their father's reputation for them to find out the truth about their real mother.

Tor wished he could have told them. But it was better for them not to know. Runa would've been even worse to them if they'd ever let any of this slip around their friends. Kiara just shook her head as if she was disappointed. She knew he was Viking, everybody did. What did everyone think that meant—that Tor must have been one of the good ones?

"These Christians have probably kept this village from receiving the blessings of the gods," Vidar laughed.

Tor watched as Skadi, a very devout pagan, kicked her husband, Pedar, under the table as if he had something to do with Tor's choice in gods.

"I will not deny my past. And I'm done running from it." Tor announced. "I've lived here in peace for thirteen years, and I've tried to be a good neighbor to you all, but these men just arrived. They've done nothing but take—take our food, our beer," then Tor held his arms out wide, "and our hospitality. And yet, they've been secretly training our sons to be warriors. I didn't know about that. Did you, Bor? How about you, Thorfinn? Because Lars and Ovid were there."

Orri raised a cup as if appreciative of the food. Ubbi and Vidar kept eating as if there was nothing to be alarmed about.

The fathers of the boys gave them stern looks, but other than that, no one seemed concerned. How would they know what Vikings are capable of? Then Tor got an idea. "Alright, let me tell you the story about how Ubbi lost his tongue."

Ubbi cautiously pushed his long black hair over his shoulder. His face was hard and heavily tattooed, each indecipherable mark an attempt to cover or highlight thick scars that looked to have been slowly and painfully made. The scar unseen was the one across what was left of his tongue, and everyone looked like they wanted to hear how it happened.

Tor walked over toward the Vikings. He needed them to show these people what they were capable of. He would count on his neighbors to break up the fight before he was killed.

"All Vikings know the story of Ubbi the Tongueless."

Ubbi pushed himself back from his plate, just as he was about to put the lingonberries on his lefse.

"This man, who was much younger and prettier back then, was captured by the villagers he was planning to maim and kill. It was a failed raid."

Pedar, who was sitting next to Vidar, hid his face in his cup as if he wasn't paying attention. Orri looked at Vidar and Ubbi, as if wondering why they were letting him tell this story. Tor wondered the same thing.

"Before the daughters were taken from their cribs, or unarmed old men could be cut down from behind, and before any young boys could be abused or mistreated, they were stopped. The men of the village killed all of Ubbi's stupid friends before they could do any of those things. They didn't realize that seven Vikings and a Pictish Prince couldn't take an entire village of farmers who were willing to stand up to them." Tor cast and angry eye at Orri. "Like many here, Ubbi was a young man who wanted to play Viking, and it cost him his tongue. It should have cost him his life.

Ubbi threw his cup of beer at Tor. The cup missed but the beer doused his face.

Orri was unlucky because he was closest. Tor grabbed him by the ear and caught him across the nose with his fist. It was the second time he broke a Viking's nose that week, and the blood spattered when he followed through and smeared it again with his elbow.

Ubbi jumped across the table and tackled Tor, only this time it was Tor's knee that did the cracking when they both came crashing down. Ubbi let out a muted "Unggh," and fell easily off to one side. Before he could get up, Orri drove Tor toward the door. Tor wasn't sure if one of his neighbors opened the door, or what, but the sunlight temporarily blinded him when he found himself outside. Orri had gotten him down, but other than pinning him down on his back, he was still almost useless from that shot he took across the nose.

Tor smashed elbow after elbow against his head until the fat man let him go. They both staggered to their feet. Tor couldn't believe no one was helping him. They were watching as if two against one was a fair fight.

Ubbi pushed his way out into the sunlight before making a hard, limping stride toward Tor. The effect of the knee Ubbi'd taken to the groin gave Tor just enough time to turn Orri into a human shield. It worked, and Orri caught the brunt of Ubbi's shoulder in his kidneys. *Now he could try pissing blood, too.*

When Ubbi started limping toward Tor again, Erik and Toren put him to the ground. Then some of the neighbors started pulling them off, as if them joining the fight had finally taken things too far.

"Erik, stop biting-" Before Tor could get the words out of his mouth a massive hand grabbed him around the throat. Both his hands instinctively went to pull it off. He couldn't breathe. No air. Tor felt like his head was going to explode from the pressure. Then he was off his feet, dangling like a child's toy. It was as if Vidar was going to pull him in half; one hand had his throat, the other had his calf. Then, mercifully, he let go of his throat. He felt a push on his leg. Tor flipped downward.

The heavy traffic into the hall that day had turned the deep snow into deep mud. The first thing to hit the mud was the back of Tor's neck, then everything else followed. He didn't roll. It was as if his hip was racing the heels of his feet to see which could get to the ground first, but the winner was his ribs that found the stone base of the well, purposefully placed outside the hall for days just like this, when water would be needed for cooking and drinking and tending to the sick and dying.

Tor felt like he was dying.

He was glad to see some of his neighbors putting themselves between him and Vidar. The pain was agonizing, where the fight had moved inside him. From the choking Tor was dying for air, but with each gasp his ribs, already cracked and tender from the fight in the woods with Ubbi, punished him for every breath.

"Vidar, please. It's over." It was Pedar. Tor didn't expect him to be the one to step up to the Vikings. "Tor, are you alright?"

Tor nodded his head. It was a lie.

"Vidar, are you alright? Orri? Ubbi? Good. Come to my house. I'll get Elsa to take a look at that for you."

Tor coughed — the pain was excruciating. "That's alright, Runa will see to me."

"I'm glad," said Pedar. "But I was talking to Orri and Ubbi. On behalf of all of us, we are sorry if Tor caused you any embarrassment."

"What?" The sun was still hovering above the trees, and it was in Tor's eyes.

"Erik, Toren, you should help your father back to your house."

"Tor," it was Old Erik, "you were out of line with those men."

"Did you see what happened to me? Three against one? Vidar all but said he was going to take the throne, or gift it to his father."

"You were goading them." Old Erik nudged him with the butt of his walking stick. "You basically called them baby killers. What did you think was going to happen?" As he walked on, Tor could hear the old man reaching out. "Pedar, would you mind if Vidar rides with me back to my house. I'd like to talk to him, alone. See if there is something I can do to make all of this right. If you want to send someone out to fetch him in a couple of hours, I think I should be done with him before dark."

Tor couldn't believe what he was hearing. *They were apologizing for what he did to the Vikings?* The insults kept coming, too. As the throng piled back into the hall to continue celebrating, Tor was peppered with faceless jeers from voices coming from the crowd. He was accused of picking fights, of being Christian, and of embarrassing everyone in front of the jarl's son. The faces he did see didn't look like they were very sympathetic to his pain, either.

Runa was angry with him, too. "I hope you're proud of yourself. You decide to ruin our family's reputation during the second biggest celebration of the year. Are you drunk?"

Even his own sons added to his torture, insisting on helping their father to his feet, as if seeing him beaten embarrassed them. Tor didn't mind. He had been beaten before. Right now, he didn't care about his wife or his neighbors or his reputation. He just wanted to lie there a little while longer, in the ice-cold mud, the only thing bringing him comfort in his misery.

OLD ERIK

Vidar did not like Old Erik. His eyes were mismatched, and he looked at him as if he knew him. That old goat didn't know any more than the rest of the peasants. *Old Erik?* Didn't he know that even his name was an insult? Vidar had always told his men that if he ever lived long enough to get gray hair, just put a sword in his hand and put him out of his misery. And whether they liked the idea or not, he promised he'd do the same for them.

There were few things more annoying than an old man. They'd done everything, seen everything, and knew more about everything.

Vidar definitely didn't want to spend time alone with an old priest, any more than a trader or a farmer. But alone they were. The old man even drove the horses slow. It was like Vidar had been invited along to witness Old Erik's leisurely sledge to the graveyard.

Once they were far enough in the wood the old man started talking. "Do you miss your soul ring, Vidar?"

Uff-da. Priest talk. Might just kill him now, put them both out of their misery. "What do you know about that, you old goat?" Vidar ran his large fingers along the scar on his chest that his father had given him when he was just a boy. It was burning. *Never done that before.*

"I have it, you know," the old man said, his eyes drilling into him. One was blue and the other glowed an emerald green, the way a cat's eye reflected the light of a fire. Vidar couldn't look away.

"I think you're confused, old man." Vidar was afraid he wasn't, but kept on anyway. "I gave my soul to my father."

"Ja, ja. And in return he gave you that gold arm ring, the top one on your right arm, the one fashioned as Jörmungandr, the world serpent chasing its tail."

How could he know? The arm ring was hidden under layers of warm clothing.

Old Erik continued, "I'm sure you'd have given him anything for that arm ring. It meant he accepted you, as a son, and as one of his warriors. You wanted to make him proud that day, didn't you?" The old man smiled and looked like he was chewing his tongue or something. "Well, you didn't."

Old Erik's green eye seemed to quiver. He pushed the reins into Vidar's hands. Vidar considered wrapping them around the old bugger's throat.

He was right of course. Vidar had always known he'd been a disappointment to his father.

"He was proud of you that day, of course. But he was even more proud of himself. That's the thing about pride, it's always about..." The mismatched eyes held him in their unrelenting gaze. "It's always about *you*."

If he strangled him, the gothi, Old Erik's brother, would have him outlawed for murder. No, better to bring the horses up to speed and push him into a tree. A man as feeble as that could probably break his neck from climbing out of bed in the morning. Surely falling from a sled wouldn't be a surprise to anyone.

The old man touched Vidar's knee. He flinched.

"He was proud of himself for how cheaply he was able to get your soul. For the price of what? Acceptance? I was always impressed by your father for figuring that out. For that small gesture he got your allegiance, and your ring.

"You know, once he told me he'd have never bowed to his own father. He hated his father. I suppose he expected the same from you. Ironic, isn't it, the fact that you don't hate him may be what he hates about you the most."

Was this man insane?

"Of course, he loved you, too. All fathers love their children, at least while they're young. But it is very difficult to balance love and pride. Pride is a wolf, and love is a fawn. Pride preys on the innocent. It is a love killer."

The pupil on Erik's green eye was the size of a pinpoint. "Your brother Egil always favored Olaf more than you. You are more like your mother."

"My father would never give away my soul ring. Get a man to give you his soul and you have his loyalty and loyalty represents power. My father loves power."

"You're right, you're right, but I couldn't have taken it from him, now could I? Unfortunately, even I don't have that kind of power. You can't just take a soul. It must be given. And he gave it to me for the same reason you gave it to him—

"He wanted something."

"You'd better tell me who you are old man, and why I shouldn't cut you down." His hand reached for the hilt of a sword that wasn't there. Old Erik had him so vexed that he'd forgotten he was unarmed.

"Ah, pull up over there, put the horse in the barn, and meet me inside. I have something special for you."

WHO DO YOU THINK YOU ARE?

V idar burned inside. Put up the horse? What am I, the old man's slave? Still, he obeyed.

Too many years had passed since the house had been built. Whether by design or time it was hard to tell, but what was left of the structure was half buried, like its master should have been.

The only parts not covered in earth were the front and maybe half of the sides. A blanket of snow made it all blend seamlessly into the mountain. The roof was held up by two hazel posts that seemed to grow up through the wooden porch to hold up the earthen roof.

The door creaked like an old man's spine as Vidar ducked inside. With two hands Old Erik strained to pick up a cylindrical stone. Every house had one like it. They were heavy and used for grinding pine into flour.

The old man sat at a wooden table, rough-hewn but worn smooth from an eternity of use, and laid the grinding stone on an empty plate. When he pulled his hand away it wasn't the stone he left behind, but a loaf of fresh bread. Instantly the little room filled with the smell of it. It smelled delicious.

Vidar stiffened. "Magic?"

"Sit. Eat. You look thin. Once you gain your strength, you will be so much more useful. You're nothing compared to the types of giants I've seen."

Vidar wanted to leave but found himself sitting at the table across from the old man as directed. The old man filled his cup.

Vidar drank some mead, burped, and picked up the knife. It was a butter knife, but it was sharp enough. Again, he thought of the ways he could kill this man. Again, he couldn't figure out a way to do it. It was like he was as lost as a babe in the woods whenever he tried to act on his own free will.

Instead of cutting the magician, he slathered the end of the loaf with butter and bit into the crust. The bread was real, and it was good. Better than what was served at the festival feast.

"Who are you?" Vidar growled, mouth full. Crumbs flew out from it, but he didn't care. It was the only outward expression of his disdain for the old man he could manage.

"Like your father, I am a lord." Old Erik broke the bread, coated it with butter, and pushed the plate and the knife back in front of his guest.

I have many sons, many daughters.

They like to quarrel like you and your older brother, Egil.

And like you and your brother,

they too think they're ready to take my throne.

But I am more than your father.

My dominion is vast.

I am Pride, Ruler of All.

I feed Arrogance and Self, like carrion to ravens.

And after the bones are picked clean,

they look to me, never satisfied.

I know what it's like to want, so my way is easy.

Then Old Erik held up a flat, circular, hollow object. Vidar's jaw loosened. He recognized it immediately and wanted it. More than his treasure, more than any woman, more than freedom or power. It called to him, and he heard it as clearly as a mother hearing the cry of her own child.

"I know what you're feeling," Old Erik said. "Every being recognizes the sound of their own soul, when they only take the time to listen. This is probably the first time you've ever really seen it. It doesn't look so trivial in the hands of a stranger does it? Do you know what it is, Vidar?"

A chill ran up Vidar's spine, and he pulled the animal hide he was wearing tight to his shoulders.

Old Erik continued, "Your flesh is more than that massive physique that impresses men so much. It is an anchor to this world, as if you weren't meant to fly. And when you die, it will return to the earth, and all that will be left will be this ugly, stained, cracked little ring."

Vidar did see his ring, the way he saw it the day it was cut from his chest.

"But the experiences of the flesh that affect your mind, your gut, and your heart, those things that make you who you are, your soul ring binds to your spirit for all eternity."

Too big to fit on a finger, too small to fit on an arm, Vidar's ring, once coated in purest gold, was now exposed for what it was—cracked and stained, mottled with shades of brown and black.

Seeing his soul again was like finding something precious he hadn't even realized was lost.

"Of course, I had the gold your gothi had it dressed it in burned away. I find those adornments unnecessary, adding needless weight to something that's already a lot to bear."

Vidar yearned to hold what he'd so willingly and foolishly given to his father—never receiving the love and acceptance he believed his gift would bring in return.

The old man spun around on his heels, showing an unexpected agility. For the first time, he gave a half toothless smile, as if proud of his masquerade, before continuing to tell his story.

"I've eaten from the tree of the knowledge of good and evil.

"I've offered its fruit to men, and they have gorged on it—lowering themselves to that of the animals.

"There is a price to pay for such gifts. I gave my eye for wisdom, thinking it would bring me peace. Now, the same way you gave your ring to your father for acceptance, you will leave it with me in exchange for power!"

Old Erik pulled back his eyelid, and with knotted, calloused fingertips he tugged at the green eye until it snapped out of his head with a squishy vacuous pop — the gaping hole left behind, a window to distant constellations.

Eyes fixed on the emptiness, Vidar's throat tightened, and he felt a cold line of sweat run down his temple.

He hated this feeling. It was fear.

The old man kept talking as if pulling an eyeball out of his head was something people did every day.

"I drink the blood of Kvasir.

"I can be all, or I can be nothing. Either satisfies me.

"I am anything I need to be. I am the graven image.

"To some I am the world. To others I am nature, itself.

"I am the serpent. I am the wanderer."

Vidar only understood that the old man was a poet, and probably wasn't an old man at all. His attention had moved to the eye. The green thing had a stalking appendage coming out of the back like a black leech, probing until it found purchase. Latching onto the web of Old Erik's hand, between his thumb and forefinger, its pupil constricted as it focused on the giant from between Erik's fingertips.

Vidar had never been quick of mind, but that eye —

Odin!

Vidar dropped to one knee.

The old man flipped the green eyeball into his palm and lifted Vidar's chin with his open fingers until he was back on his feet. Vidar's vision blurred as his eyes locked onto the thing staring back at him from the old man's palm, now less than two inches from his nose.

"Stand up. You will show reverence for me later. We have much to discuss. Why are you here?"

"My ship got caught in a storm." Vidar didn't understand the question. "I would have said it was by your good favor, but now — well, I guess it was luck."

"Let me tell you a secret, Vidar. Nothing happens

without a purpose. Only a fool believes in luck." Old Erik pulled his hand away from Vidar's chin, dipped the eye in his cup like a teabag, and pushed it back into its empty socket. "Good or bad. You are here for a reason, and I will turn it to my own advantage."

"Excuse me, Lord. My ring?"

"What about it? Do you want it back? Do you still want it now that you know I'm not just an old fool?"

"It's just that, well, I can feel it," replied Vidar. "Ja. I want it back."

"Yes," Old Erik hissed, "I know you do. Not so insignificant to you now, is it? Worth more than your father's approval? How about a god's?" The green of Old Erik's eye strained to find its target, bumping around in its socket like a fish trying to escape a shallow pool. "What do you think he sold it to me for?"

"What?"

"You don't think your father just gave your ring to me without a price, do you? Do you think him that cold?"

Vidar's father was that cold. He was sure of that. Other than inheriting his large stature, being the son of Jarl Olaf hadn't granted Vidar many favors in life. He might've even been worse for it.

"Olaf included your ring as part of a sacrifice, over which he prayed that he would be able to build a great kingdom, that he would live a life worthy of being remembered, that he would receive a warrior's death, and a place at the table in Valhalla."

"A prayer worthy of a Viking lord," Vidar replied. His father always did have a way with words. Neither Vidar nor Egil had inherited that gift.

Old Erik slammed his fist on the table. "The same prayer every Viking who's ever whetted a blade, lord or common, prays—as if to blame all of their treachery on the religion *they chose*. I'll gladly accept the blood sacrifices of men on the battlefield, but they will be responsible for their own sins. If riches, power, and glory are what they wanted, then that will be their reward. But guilt is the cost, and that will be their debt to pay—not mine!" The old sorcerer's green eye twitched wildly as he sat back and emptied his cup. The drink did its work, and the old man seemed to calm.

"What made your father's sacrifice so interesting was when he gave me your ring, he asked that I grant your brother, Egil, and his sons after him, rule over his kingdom until Ragnarok come."

"He sacrificed my soul for the sake of my brother's line?" Vidar felt hollow inside.

"Surprising, yes? I agree. For we both know what's most important to your father is your father, and that if his line, by either son, continues to reign then he will never be forgotten. But he made his plea for your brother. I've seen fathers do worse for the sake of their first-born son."

An eerie calm set in, like the sea on a windless night. There was no feeling, no sound, no anything. Then a storm began to gather, and the emptiness began to churn. Olaf had not been a good father. He'd barely even been around until his sons were old enough to go a'Viking. He had often expressed his disappointment in them.

Now it was Vidar's turn.

It was like the man he respected the most had opened his chest and ripped his soul out again in this very spot. How could his father's treachery still have this kind of affect on him? He wasn't even here. Vidar hated him for that, too.

"Are you alright, Vidar?" Old Erik's face was solemn, but something in his mismatched eyes had turned wicked.

"You know, he barely ever mentioned the gods unless he was cursing or about to wield a sword in battle." He wanted to hurt his terrible father—and Old Erik, too. "Are you really Odin?"

The old man smiled. "You seemed so sure. Not what you expected?"

"You asked me why I'm here. Now I'm asking you why

you're here. I mean no disrespect, but I just woke up from a long nap, and I don't think I can solve a riddle right now. I need to hear it plainly. Are you Odin? And if you are, why are you here?"

Beer soaked into the old man's beard as he emptied his cup. It was the first thing he'd done the way Vidar pictured the old god would. "I'm here, because Old Afi has lost his way. I want a leader to take the throne and make these people yearn for a beautiful death. I want their souls."

"Why? There is no glory here. Does Asgard have farms that need tending?"

"I am a collector. I'm not the only one."

Vidar's eye's narrowed. "Why would you collect souls?"

"It's like a game," replied the old man. "Nothing to concern yourself with other than one thing: I'm keeping yours."

THE FLASK AND THE FLAGON

"Your soul was mine the very moment you gave this ring to your father. It was mine every time you killed a man for your own sake, every time you hated your brother or your father. You gave it to me every time you decided which of your men would live or die on your ship. All were sacrifices to me. Let me ask you, Vidar, did you recognize the flavor of the marrow Elsa puts in her broth?" Old Erik's green eye glimmered like a fire had been lit behind it.

"So, I'm keeping your soul, the one you gave to me more times than you'll ever know. But you are one of the fortunate ones, for I have bigger plans for you."

Vidar's gaze only left the ring when the old man put it in his pocket. As if a spell was broken, the longing lessened as soon as he lost sight of it.

Vidar looked around at the broken-down shack half buried in the mountain. It was nothing like how Valhalla was supposed to be. Maybe all fathers, even the Allfather, eventually disappoint their sons.

No, this was Odin, he assured himself. Odin, the great warrior, the father of the gods. And Valhalla was grand, with beautiful Valkyries and tables overflowing with food and drink. That place was reserved for his army of the glorious dead. Vidar would have to earn a seat at that table on the battlefield. Now was a time to watch. A time to learn from the god who gave an eye for wisdom. Still, both of Vidar's eyes lingered on the pocket that held the hole he now felt in his chest.

Old Erik used his forearm to clear a space on the table. Vidar just managed to save his mug of ale before the old man knocked it onto the floor along with the butter and bread.

Two ravens flitted down from nowhere to jockey for the scraps.

Old Erik licked his thin lips as he pulled out two containers, one red crystal flask, the other a blue glazed ceramic flagon.

The flagon had two red rings about the choke of its neck. He hummed to himself as he pulled the leather stopper out with his corrupted teeth and poured two small ceramic cups quarter full, before taking a swig directly from the jug.

"What are we drinking, Father?" Vidar asked.

Old Erik smiled—his green eye straying to peek down at the silver-colored beer.

"You will think of me as your father after you drink what I offer. This," he said, handing Vidar a cup, "is the blood of Kvasir. I offer you something many have sought, but few received."

"Why would you offer me such a gift?"

"Because I need you to lead for me. And right now, you are stupid, and that will never do."

Vidar's jaw tightened, but the old man touched his hand. Ice ran down his veins, colder than the winter gale that carried him to those very shores. Even the tears that old Erik's touch was ringing from his dry eyes refused to fall, like a maid trying to squeeze milk from a frozen goat's teat.

"How do you think your father got to be jarl?" the old man whispered.

He'd been eating onions.

"Do you think it's because he's so mighty? Hmmm? So good with an axe? Did you ever wonder why he was so terrible to you and your brother? It's because you reminded him of his own weakness—what he was before he sold me his soul. But since he doubts his bargain, I now offer the same terms to you. After all, a gift for the son is a gift for the father. Every good father would agree with that. Was your father a good father, Vidar?"

Vidar did not like this game. Olaf may have been a dreadful father, but it was his sword that made him jarl. Was this old goat going to try to claim all *his* successes, too? He wanted to flip the table—to remind Old Erik he was no ordinary man—but couldn't even blink his eyes.

"Calm down, Vidar," replied the old snake, smiling. "Your glory will remain your own. It's souls I'm after."

Did the old trickster know his thoughts, now? Vidar's veins thawed as Old Erik touched his hand again, and he managed to shiver. He could move but didn't dare try.

"No longer will you lead men because of your father's name, or because you are a brute. This drink, this mead of inspiration, will give you what you desperately lack—wit and the silk tongue of a skald. You will add generations of warriors to my army."

Vidar hated his father for selling his soul, but for Egil? With eyes locked on Old Erik's, he wrapped his fingers around the cup, slowly lifted it to his mouth—and drank. The mead was sour, and by the time he finished it his taste buds began to burn. His head felt dizzy as if he'd been drinking for hours. He cowered when the empty cup hit the table like a clap of thunder. He smelled the lye in the soap Elsa used to wash his beard, felt the dampness of the sweat breaking from every pore of his skin, from his forehead to the balls of his feet. The scents from the world outside overwhelmed him. Fish were curing in a distant barn. The chicken house almost turned his stomach. The stench of dung was so strong it was as if the cows were milling around in the old man's bedroom.

More sounds filled his head. The echo of a distant axe splitting wood had Vidar covering his ears. The fibers of the tree screaming as they splintered.

Every *plink* or *creak* hammered his senses. Every aroma made his stomach churn. Textures were like knives raking against his skin. The vibrancy of color crowded him, and the darkness of every shadow weighed him down. Old Erik smiled a toothless grin as he refilled Vidar's empty cup with a red liquid from the crystal flask.

Vidar gagged at the dried buttermilk on the old man's beard mixing with the fermented honey, malt, and yeast riding on every breath that passed through the gaps in the old man's foul teeth.

"What's wrong, Vidar? You look like you could use a drink." He motioned to the cup.

Vidar didn't dare shift in his seat for fear of stimulating his heightened senses. The drink swirled and the ripples reflected the fire, until Vidar imagined the cup too hot to touch. The liquid shone crimson like blood, though thin like water. It smelled of svovel, covered by a hint of cinnamon, which burned the tips of the hairs in Vidar's nostrils as if he'd been inhaling fire.

He thought he'd forgotten how to cry, and now the mere act of sitting, breathing, and listening roiled his senses and made such thoughts run through his head that he feared if he didn't he might die from the pressure welling up inside.

"The mead of inspiration will drive you mad and eventually kill you. Ironically, firewater is the only way to quench its burning." Erik pushed the cup closer. "This isn't that watered-down stuff your father's men got from some witch or the piss from some berserker. This was brewed from the finest virgin bloodweed, never having seen the sun's light, blood-fed and harvested from places barely known by living men."

Old Erik pressed the cup into Vidar's hand. His touch was ice. "It gets its heat from the dragon's breath."

Vidar looked at the cup as if he would vomit, not sure if his taste buds could handle more excruciating stimulation.

Old Erik pushed a knife in Vidar's other. Pain from the

edges of the handle rolled down his fingers.

"What is this?"

"A warning and a choice," the old demon smiled. "I tell you before you take part in this with me, you cannot undrink this. What is done can never be undone, nor can the power this decision may ever wield over you."

Sweat beaded on his brow, and he squinted his eyes against the unbearableness of everything.

"What have you done to me?" he cursed.

"Once you taste of it, especially under the influence of the mead of inspiration, you'll spend the rest of your life seeking its equal."

Vidar's brow furrowed and he leaned in closer. His leg started to jump. His breath was heavy as he tried to swallow down the urge to vomit.

Somewhere outside, footsteps were crashing through dry snow, each an avalanche of powder splashing down like the relentless tide in a sensation storm. "What choice do I have now, you old demon? I need to stop the pain."

"Why, Vidar," the old man crowed, "the choice is in your hands. Find your relief in the cup or the knife, it makes little difference to me. Your soul is already mine." Old Erik's icy grip burned as he pinned the knife down. "But I do hope you choose the cup."

Spittle dressed Vidar's beard as his shaking hands raised the firewater to his lips.

The taste was severe against the backdrop of his wailing senses. The scar on his chest caught fire, burning away the desire he'd felt to regain his soul from the old man. Then the heat hit his hands and feet, and the fire climbed until the flames licked at his spine, erupting like kindling in a wildfire, until they filled his head, blackening his brain.

The firewater had done its job. As the burning in his arteries smoldered, the pain and panic and fear faded into oblivion.

Relief.

Vidar exhaled, put his head in his hands, and his face down on the table. He rested in a pool of something wet and cool, and he didn't care.

Vidar embraced the numbness.

When he raised his head again, the world was noticeably different. The scents and sounds were sharp, but tolerable. His mind was clear, like a ship's hull after having the barnacles scraped off.

It was as if he had the capacity to understand for the first time in his life. He had clarity, and it felt good. Ambition coursed through his veins, and he thirsted for something new.

"Father?" He took the leather thong off of his neck and loosed all the rings he had on the table, save one. "What would you have me to do?"

Old Erik ignored the question and leaned over the offering as if trying to smell it. Ungodly he hovered, like a vulture over a battlefield searching for the ripest carrion. With a claw-like hand, the old man dragged the soul rings off of the table. The *plink*, *plink*, *plink* of the rings falling into his sack was sharp, but bearable.

There was a knock at the door. Vidar's nose told him it was Anja.

A WALK IN THE WOODS

"**M**y mother wanted me to fetch Vidar for dinner." Anja should've still been at the festival, eating, drinking— dancing with Toren. It was really Vidar's fault as much as anybody.

Why would he care that his stupid fight ruined her only chance to see her friends until the ring ceremony? And that was months away. With a huff, she blinded herself with cold fog. Only the pig saw — maybe he liked her new dress.

How long is that oaf going to take?

Why didn't her mother just let her stay? Worse, she sent her on this errand like a common servant. Couldn't she tell how upset she was? To make sure somebody did, Anja didn't even change out of her fine clothes. She looked around the porch. *Filthy old men. Hadn't they ever heard of a broom?*

She spun to see if the seat of her dress was already dirty. *Not yet.* She hoped to ruin it. Maybe they'd have to give it to Kiara. Her mother would be so upset. She wondered if she could break through the ice near the horse and mud the hem on her way out.

She loved the festivals and having a reason to dress like that. *Old Erik!* How long had he been standing there, looking at her like that. Vidar, too. Suddenly, she realized she hadn't thought this through. Her rebellion was meant for her parents, not to entice dirty old men.

What was she thinking? She had been sent to fetch a man,

no, a giant. Worse, a Viking, and she was dressed dangerously. Before she'd determined to ruin it, it had been her favorite. The dress was tight-spun, cream-colored, wool— flattering, form fit, and so long she only ever dared wear it in the winter for fear it might drag in the mud after the thaw. Over that she wore a new apron dyed blue as the evening sky, which she would burn before she would give away. Her apron was pinned over her shoulders with two gold brooches styled to match the rosemaling sewn to trim her outer cloak. Elsa had braided her long brown hair so tight that it still lay neatly over her left shoulder the same as it had been when they left for the festival.

"Just you?" The giant pushed the door wider. Vidar towered over the crooked old man's shoulder.

"Who would send a pretty girl like you out to gather a grown man by herself?" Old Erik's warbly tongue slipped in and out of holes left by his missing teeth.

Anja turned her eyes to her feet when she got caught watching the giant man pull on his coat. Suddenly, she felt very small, and very alone. Ragi should've been there. In her head she cursed her lazy brother.

"Is that for me, child?" As the village priest, Old Erik was used to getting meat from her mother and father. As Skadi always reminded Anja, her father's trade may have made the family wealthy, but it was her sacrifices that earned them the favor of the gods.

Anja handed the old priest the chicken her mother had personally tucked into the sack. Even with her mother, she hated coming to Old Erik's. Old people smelled of death. She preferred beautiful things.

"My mother knows how Old Afi likes eggs, so she wanted you to know this one's laying well. But when you make a sacrifice of it, she asked that you do it in Vidar's name, to any god he wants." She glanced up and caught Vidar staring. He was always so grouchy she didn't even think he'd noticed her before. She hated herself for not changing clothes. She handed Old Erik the chicken.

"Well, Vidar. Which god would you like to sacrifice her to?" The old man flashed a smile as crooked as his back.

Vidar ignored the question and ducked out onto the porch. They were both acting so weird. She wondered what they had been doing. Had they been talking about her?

A white owl flew out of the woods and landed in a snowy pine.

Vidar pulled himself between Anja and the edge of the porch. His touch was firm but gentle, not like the oafish way he'd plowed past her at her father's farm.

"It's just an owl, Vidar." She had to laugh. Such a big man protecting her from a bird. Ridiculous, but cute.

"Afi!" Anja waved as Old Erik's brother emerged from the same wood. She ducked under Vidar's outstretched arm to get a better look. She was relieved to see him, even though he was just another man. "Is the festival over, already?"

Old Afi stopped and stared. "It is for me."

"My mother sent over a chicken. Should get some eggs from her before she's-"

"She's not for you. She's for Odin." Old Erik twisted the chicken's head off. He held it by its feet as it flapped and kicked. Anja jumped off the porch, but it was too late, the corpse splashed blood across the men's trousers and Anja's favorite dress. Forgetting her plan to ruin it herself, she jumped into the snow and rubbed handfuls onto the drops of blood to try and catch it before it stained.

Old Erik ignored her. Holding the carcass high, the priest prayed in a foreign tongue as blood painted his arms a crimson red. When he was finished, he threw the bloody head toward the tree where the owl had lit.

As if from inside the little shack, two ravens swept in and pecked at the offering and each other. Taking to the air, they fought over the bloody head until disappearing beyond the dark edge of the wood.

"Get on home now, child." Old Afi helped Anja to her feet. "You'll need help to remove those stains."

She looked up to the porch in anger, only to see Old Erik dipping his hands in the neck blood and writing something in the palms of Vidar's hands, while whispering in his ear.

Vidar nodded, left the porch, and brought the sleigh around.

When Anja climbed aboard, he handed her the reins. "I don't know the way."

Anja's chest felt heavy, and her breathing labored under the weight of his gaze. "I wish you wouldn't look at me like that." She didn't know why she brought it up. She had been ogled by men, young and old, for the past three years.

"Are you frightened?" Vidar turned his attention to other things.

Nodding his head at every glade of trees, she heard him whispering to himself. He seemed fascinated by the most common things — like the scent of the wind or the vibrance of the snow, the quickness of the deer or the patience of the grouse, and the land, as if open pasture was suddenly of great importance to him. Before, all he seemed to care about was his ship and his men. Maybe he hit his head in the fight. Or maybe he was changed by something Old Erik said.

When he fell silent, she could feel his attention falling on her.

"Very few people ever get invited to that house," she said, an attempt to shift his attention elsewhere. "The old brothers keep to themselves, mostly. If my mother didn't insist we bring Old Erik animals for sacrifices, I'd only ever see them in the hall. It's not unusual for Old Erik to wander off for months at a time."

Vidar turned his attention fully on her, the way a wolf might watch an unprotected lamb. A lamb who'd strayed too far from home. Alone. *I can't believe my brother let me come here alone. If I survive this, I'm going to kill that little coward, if Toren doesn't get to him first. I can hear the women now. What a*

150

reckless girl you are! What happened out there? Did he hurt you?
She wasn't religious like her mother, but Anja found herself
praying to Freyja that a squirrel or a moose would steal
Vidar's attention, now.

QUESTION OF FAITH

K iara finished cleaning the plates, opened the door, and slung the bucket up to scatter the dishwater high into the air. She watched as it burst into a cloud and drifted slowly away. She liked to pretend she was a faerie princess being held prisoner in a dark land, forced to make clouds by the giants who'd locked her away. It was a small thing, but it was something to look forward to in the dark, cold place Norway had become.

She hardly ever left the house anymore, except for the few chores that required it, like bringing in firewood. And she tried to only do those things while the sun was peaking up over the edge of the world. It didn't stay long anymore, and Erik and Toren assured her it would slowly start to make its return after the ring ceremony, but that was another month away. Kiara wasn't sure she could take being held prisoner by the dark that long, not with a warden like Runa.

"I thought you said the hills were white with sheep in Ireland. So, what do you do with the wool?" Runa asked nastily.

"What do you mean?" asked Kiara.

"Well, you certainly don't know how to make yarn with it. Am I going to have to teach you how to tie knots, too?"

To pass the time, Tor, Toren, Erik, and even Runa took turns telling stories while they carved, wove, sewed, cooked, and anything else they could do to pass the time. Runa's favorite tale was about the battle between the gods and the frost giants that brought the seasons, and the long days, and the long nights, how the frost giants were strongest when it was cold, but the gods of the Vanir would drive them back each spring, because of the goddess Freyja's love of flowers. Runa prayed to her little idol of Freyja each night, asking her for a quick victory. She pined for the summer, reminding them all that every year there was a time when the sun would never set, when Sól would ride her chariot around the dome of the sky, proclaiming Freyja's victory over the frost giants and the long night. But now it was winter's turn, and everyone was hunkered down to wait it out.

"It's your turn, Kiara," said Erik.

She had told many stories to Tor's household. Some were like theirs, only with an Irish twist. But many they'd never heard before. It was cold, and she was missing home, so she decided to tell them the story of Christmas, for she knew enough to know they hadn't heard that one before. And she was pretty sure that as a Christian she was supposed to be telling it. "Where I'm from, this is called the good news. The birth, death, and resurrection of Jesus Christ, God's only son."

"Does it have dragons?" asked Erik.

"Hush now," said Kiara. "I don't want to be messing this one up on account of your interruptions." It was as if he thought it was his job to make her crazy.

"This is the story about how God came to save the world." She closed her eyes and started saying a little prayer. *Lord please don't let me mess this up. I know I'm no priest, but if it be your-*

"Before you doze off, I'd like some more dried berries." Runa held out her cup. "And some more to drink."

Kiara put her own cup down beside her on the floor, got up, took Runa's bowl out of her hand, and went into the kitchen. "Would you like me to heat up some water for you? Make you some tea?"

"No," Runa replied. "I'm drinking mead tonight." Her voice was slurred.

Kiara wondered how much she'd had. She didn't like it when Runa drank. She got mean when she drank. Meaner.

"Go on, tell your tale," urged Erik.

Kiara looked about to make sure everyone looked settled. All eyes were on her except Tor, who was always stirring the coals with a stick. So, she began again. "God created everything — the sky, the earth, the water, the plants, and the animals and people, too. I think I told you about Adam and Eve, right?"

"Ja," said Toren. "The woman was tempted by the snake and talked her husband Adam into eating the apple."

"They're the ones. Good, you remember. Well, eating that apple was disrespectful to God. He calls that sin. And for sin, he kicked them out of the garden, and they could never return again. And because of that, women would feel the pain of childbirth, and men would have to work, and they would have to start wearing clothes, and there would be weeds in their gardens and they would have to hunt, and many animals started hunting, too."

"That's not very fair," Erik protested. "I don't think I like your god very much."

"Neither do I," Runa licked the rim of her cup.

"Ja, I haven't ever tried an apple before, and still even the goats can barely keep the briars and weeds out of the yard."

"Well, just like we get our eye color from our parents, we get our sinful nature from Adam and Eve." Runa's eyes looked a little cross, but she said nothing. Then Kiara realized... *Stupid girl. Should be easy enough to remember they didn't inherit anything from her.* She waited for a stern word, but it never came. "The problem is, we can't fix sin. God was wronged and there's nothing we can do about it. My priest said everybody's sinned. It's not about apples. It's lust, lies, murder, idolatry, and some other things, too."

"What was that last one?" Runa leaned closer.

154

"What one?" Kiara's mind raced. Runa never talked to her unless she needed her to do something or to make her feel terrible. She didn't like her hair, her eyes, her clothes, how she talked—and when it came to insults, just like her stories, she didn't mind repeating herself.

"Lust?" Kiara didn't know why she cared, but she was determined to not repeat the last one.

"No." Runa leaned forward in her chair. "The last one."

Maybe if she pretended she couldn't remember, Runa would just call her stupid and let her finish her story.

"Idolatry," Tor said it as if he was sick of hearing Runa play her games.

"Ja, that's the one." She rubbed Tor on the shoulder. He shrugged her off and looked at her distrustingly. Everyone was tense, as if waiting to find out how bad things were going to get. "What does idolatry mean?" Runa sounded like she already didn't like the answer.

"It means not praying to-" Kiara stopped mid-sentence. She looked to Tor for help, but he just kept poking the fire, like he was trying to knock the orange out of the coals.

"Pray to what?" Runa's voice was calm, like a trap ready to spring.

Why didn't she just start with the baby in the manger? What did she know about sin, anyway? "To things," Kiara whispered.

"To little statues carved of wood, or stone, or cows, or mountains, or anything other than God." Tor sounded frustrated, like he didn't like where this was going but he wanted to get it over with.

Kiara would've preferred to try to avoid the subject a little longer.

"I pray to Freyja, so what does that say about me, eh? We make our sacrifices, and it's not to your god. What does that say about us?"

"She was just trying to tell us a story, Runa." Tor got up and filled his cup from the pitcher of mead.

"She wasn't just telling a story. She was calling us...sinners — whatever that means. Is that what you think of us, Kiara?" Runa's calm voice picked up an edge. "Tor, you were married to a Christian. The boys' mother was a Christian. Maybe I'm the only one who should be offended."

There was silence as the two boys turned to their father. Did they know anything about him at all? About their real mother? Kiara doubted it. And although she was interested in the story, she had a feeling Runa wasn't ready to change the subject. This was still about her, and it probably wouldn't end well. When Runa was drinking it never did.

"Well? Do you think I'm a sinner, Tor?" Icy blue veins began to bulge along Runa's long, pale throat.

"No," Kiara interrupted. Immediately she'd wished she hadn't. Tor didn't need her. He could defend himself.

"We're all sinners." Kiara thought for a second. "I'm not saying it right. I mean, nobody's good enough. And we could sell everything and give it to the priest. We could sacrifice a thousand goats, and it wouldn't change that. That's why God sent his son. He died in our place." She looked to Tor for help. "All those years you were Viking, did anyone take a sword for you? Or a spear?" Tor stared into the fire — his mind was somewhere else. "We all sin, but the price has been paid, so now we can live with God in Heaven when we die."

"I knew you were trouble, but how dare you try to turn us against our gods."

"I'm sorry. I've said something wrong." Kiara didn't know why Runa hated her so much. She thought back to her mother, and began to cry.

"Then — what are you saying?" Runa's voice cut like a knife. "Who do you think you are, a priestess? It's bad enough they're calling my husband a Christian — would you make us all outcasts among our neighbors?" Runa grabbed the little carving of Odin off the mantle and shook it in front of Kiara's face. "The Allfather's name is Odin. His son is Thor." She raised it up. Her eyes were fire. Kiara raised her hands to protect herself, but not in time. Kiara's world narrowed after Runa brought the idol down across her cheek. All thoughts of what was happening disappeared into the fog, and pain flared in her hip as she ploughed into the floor. She managed to cover her head before it hit. Her fingers smashed between the back of her head and the table leg. Pain increased as liquid poured onto her face from two wooden cups as they fell off the tabletop.

Kiara's first thought was that she needed to pick up the mess. Confused, she made it to her knees in time to see Runa standing over her, ready to strike down again. Erik jumped in between, grabbed Runa's arm and pried the idol out of her hand. In her rage, she smacked his ear with an open hand.

There was so much noise, even the walls seemed to be shouting. Kiara felt something patter over her calves and turned to see Jeger drop his little stick to add his ear-piercing yelps to the argument. Toren tackled Erik into the table before he could retaliate against their stepmother. Debris from the table rained down around her. The rattles of wooden plates and carved spoons added to the racket. As Kiara ducked to hide from the falling boys and utensils, she watched the graven image fracture against the stone fireplace.

Runa noticed. She cursed and started toward Erik like she meant to kick him while he was down, but Tor snatched her up off her feet with one arm and told her to calm down. Like a spoiled child she kicked and screamed for him to let her go, but instead of putting her down, he carried her outside into the cold. Without her goading, the room got eerily quiet except for Jeger, who was still growling toward the door, where Runa's screams trailed off toward the barn.

"You can let me go, now." Erik threw Toren's arm from

across his chest.

Toren pushed himself to his feet, and offered Kiara one hand, and Erik the other.

Kiara's hands were shaking wildly as she picked up cups and dishes from the floor. Erik gripped her by the shoulders, forcing her to stop. She fell into his chest and soaked his shirt with tears. "Ow." She pulled back and raised her fingers to try to very gently sooth her burning cheek.

"Erik, get me a cloth," Toren said. Erik looked at his older brother with the contempt of a younger brother who was sick of being bossed around.

Kiara pushed herself out of his arms and came back with a clean hand towel.

Toren opened the door and grabbed a handful of snow. The frigid night was quiet and still, and a chill crawled up Kiara's arms.

Toren put the snow in the cloth and gently guided it to an ache that throbbed with every heartbeat.

For the first time since she was taken, the cold felt good. Kiara pulled it away to see. There was blood on the towel.

"It's not that bad," Erik said. It must have been worse than she thought by the way he said it. She slumped down onto a chair. "Where do you think he took her?"

"Hopefully he buried her in the yard," Erik smiled. "She'll be in a better mood after she thaws in the spring."

"Why does she hate me so?"

"She doesn't hate you," Toren smiled. "She hates Erik."

Kiara laughed, and that made her cry. It burned so bad she thought it might melt her snow.

"Ja," Erik replied. "But not as much as Kiara's stupid stories." He picked up the little idol off the floor. Odin's head was broken off, along with half his spear.

Kiara felt the chill again, and Runa let the door slam in Tor's face as she shivered her way to the fire.

The three watched as she wrapped herself in a blanket.

Her face was so pale and cold it looked almost blue, like a winter moon.

The red came back to her cheeks when she saw what Erik was holding in his hand.

"Look what you've d-d-done!" her teeth chattered. Her walk in the freezing night air may have taken the fight out of her fists, but not her spirit.

Tor took the idol out of Erik's hand and threw the pieces into the fire.

Runa was heating up again. She glowered at Kiara. "You are a curse on this house. Everything has gotten worse since you arrived!" She pulled her blanket tight around her shoulders, wiped thawing tears from her angry eyes, and took deep breaths. Then she flattened her tousled hair and brushed off some of the snow still frozen to the bottom of her dress. With an eerily calm voice she whispered. "Your god may be dead, but I assure you mine are not."

"He's not." Kiara's cheek burned from the salt from her tears.

Runa cleared her throat. "When I die, I will go to Freyja's hall, where I will be reunited with my baby girl." Runa looked at Erik with disdain. She wiped her own tears from her eyes and calmly spoke to her husband. She didn't look mad at him, anymore, just disappointed. "Maybe you are a Christian. Maybe you and your sons will join their mother in Heaven when you die."

"I am not a Christian!" Erik looked like he wanted to hit her again.

Runa stepped back toward Tor for his protection.

"Remember, we are in Norway now, not Ireland or England." She looked up over her shoulder to catch the eye of her protector. "Your god has no power here. So, you'd better hope he can barter your soul out of Hel, because if you die a Christian here, that's where you'll end up."

GROW UP, THE TRUTH HURTS

D ark days passed.
No stories were being told.
Mostly everyone just whispered politely to each other.

"Pass the butter," they would say. "I'm going to check on the animals." There was a lot of that—preferring the cold and dark outside to the coolness within.

Runa, however, pretended everything was normal.

"The water's getting low," she would tell Kiara. "Your mother never taught you how to bake, did she?" she'd say if the bread wasn't to her liking. It rarely was.

Kiara thought speaking of her mother was an especially cruel thing to do, but she did not hate her for it. There was only pity.

The woman ran a dismal house, and everyone in it was miserable, and to have lost her little girl—that was the most tragic of all. It couldn't have always been this way. Runa must've been happy, once.

Toren said normally his father would have just gone hunting to avoid all the tension, but he was as snowbound as everybody else. So, Tor spent that month fixing things with the boys—from replacing slats of flooring in the barn loft to building new furniture for Toren's house.

The closer that house got to being finished, the more irreverent Erik became toward his stepmother and the state of her farm. More than once he'd confided in Kiara that Toren's house was like one big reminder—there was no place for him there.

"I made you another god for the mantle." Tor handed Runa a wooden figure he'd been carving by the fire.

"Hmph," scoffed Runa. "Looks like a stick carrying a stick."

Tor examined it, and just before he fed it to the fire, called the little house dog.

"Jeger. Here boy." Tor slid the spear out of Odin's hand and threw the idol to the floor.

The little Lundehund was the only thing with the power to relieve the tension in the house. He hopped out of Runa's lap, spun around three times at Tor's feet, and plopped down to gnaw on Odin's face.

"It's Fenrir, the great wolf," laughed Erik. "Kiara, help!" He sat on the stone hearth and started playing tug of war with the pup. "If he swallows Odin it'll ring in the end of the world."

Erik had already told her the story of the final battle of Ragnarok. Had they been alone, Kiara might've asked what happened to the souls of Odin's followers after he was eaten by the wolf—but not in front of Runa. Her face had just healed, and though the boys assured her it hadn't left a scar, they were wrong. She'd fought her religious battle and lost.

Tor had a talent for carving. Still, it took a few tries to get Runa a peace offering she'd accept. She said his second attempt looked like a troll. Everyone else thought that one was the best, but there was something about the nose she didn't like. Erik kept that one. Every now and again, Kiara saw him looking at it by the firelight.

After many more culls, the one Runa approved of was a robed figure as tall as Tor's index finger. It was light in details, more a shadow of the wandering god, complete with broad-brimmed hat and the spear disguised as a walking stick that Tor repurposed from his first attempt. She said it was the raven on his shoulder that made that one her favorite.

She knew exactly what she was wanted in her little gods. "Do you love me, Tor?" Runa had the most beautiful smile when it was genuine. She had made herself look nice that day. It had been a while.

Tor smiled. "I would do anything to make you happy." It seemed like he meant it, too.

"Do you want your son to be happy?"

"Of course, I do," Tor replied. "I want the best for them both."

"Then it's time we mended things with our neighbors. Will you let me make things right?"

"Of course."

"Because I have an idea that will let us get back to the business of Toren and Anja's marriage." Runa looked so happy — it was as if she was planning her own wedding. "But I need your permission to do what needs to be done."

He frowned. "We're already fixing the old house..."

Runa put her arms around his waist. "I'm not asking for money." She kissed his cheek.

Tor hesitated but smiled broadly back. "All right, let's get all of this settled already." He kissed the top of her head and hugged her tight. "But try to make it early summer. I don't think I can take any more of this."

Runa's smile burned away the rest of the icy fog that had been hanging in the air. When she was happy the house felt warm again.

"Why don't we go visit Pedar and Skadi," offered Tor.

"Now you're acting like the man I agreed to marry." Runa hugged him and his arms slid around her waist. It was easy to imagine how they might have been happy once. Runa laughed when Tor started rounding up the boys.

Within a week, the house was clean, the preparations were made, and Runa agreed she was finally ready to visit Skadi. She wore her nicest dress. It was black with red trim, layered with a cream apron. The brooches that pinned the apron straps over her shoulders were flowers made of fine silver, connected by a petite silver chain draped across her chest. She said the silver was her mother's. It brought everything together, and she looked beautiful.

Kiara wore one of the dresses that Anja gave her from her own closet. It was a brown work dress, but it was the best Kiara had. Runa was so pleased to be making a social call that she helped Kiara take it in to get a proper fit. She even let her borrow one of her nice rose-colored aprons to dress it up a bit.

Kiara was sure it had been red, once, but it was pretty, and she liked how soft it was from the wear. She couldn't believe how pleasant Runa could be when she was happy. She thought to herself how she would try hard to never upset her again.

Toren looked handsome, as always. His trousers were common but unstained, and Runa had made him new stockings and a tunic, both dyed a handsome blue. The gray wool jacket he got last year for his soul ring ceremony still looked new, and he made for a handsome suitor to call on Anja.

His gold-covered soul hung over his shirt, standing out nicely against the blue. Although he said he wasn't comfortable wearing it out like that, Runa insisted.

Erik and Tor were both clean and pressed.

"Can Kiara and I get the horse hooked up to the sleigh?" Erik had been ready to go for hours. "I'm burning up."

"Let's not take the sleigh." Tor rubbed Runa's back. "I thought we might cut through the woods, like we used to do when we were young."

Runa looked down at her dress, as if to say, *What are you thinking?* Kiara agreed with her, but watched as Runa took a deep breath and kissed Tor on the cheek.

"Sounds nice. But you'll have to carry. There are two bags in the bedroom and another in the kitchen."

Erik and Toren shook their heads as they put the bags near the door. "Are we visiting or moving in?"

"We're not going to call on our neighbors unannounced and empty handed." Runa's eyes gleamed. Getting Toren's marriage arranged was one of the things she seemed to want more than anything else.

"Erik," said Tor, "get a harness on Jakl and Sterkr and load the bags on the sledge. We're not carrying all of that."

The passage was narrow, and the snow was deep. Erik drove the dogs through first to flatten a path, then Toren used snowshoes to pack the snow more to make it passable, even in dresses, and Tor brought up the rear.

Kiara was excited. Even though it was freezing outside, there was something special about walking through the quiet stretch of woods with lanterns lit to make a surprise call on the neighbors. Toren reminisced about how he and Erik used to take this trail all the time to visit Anja and Ragi when they were children. Runa reminded them of all the wonderful parties Skadi and Pedar would throw at their house in seasons past.

"What is this?" Runa said as the trail opened up. There were many sledges parked along the road.

"They have so many houses." Kiara nervously clutched at her plain dress. "And such a grand hall."

Pedar's hall was smaller than the great hall in the village, but no less grand. It was crafted of layered yellow oak, and had the layered roofs been replaced by masts she'd have thought it was made to sail.

"Skadi made him build it," Erik grunted as he handed Toren one of the heavier bags. "She likes everyone to know they're rich."

"They only entertain in it once or twice a year. Most of the time it's dry storage for his trading business," said Toren. "Everyone's worked for him moving things in or out at one time or another."

"Did you know they were entertaining, tonight?" Tor eyed Runa.

She just shook her head.

Erik picked up one of the sacks and headed for the hall.

"Erik, wait!" Tor hissed.

Anja and Vidar were outside talking. She turned her head, then pushed him inside, doing a poor job pretending she hadn't seen them.

The first door led to a cloak room nearly half as large as Tor's entire house. Across the room the doors were much bigger, easily twice as large as the first.

"My father carved those designs," Erik told Kiara, proudly.

"They're beautiful." Kiara ran her hands along the relief. They reminded her of the cathedral in the city near her village back home. She wondered if the Vikings left it standing.

"I don't want to intrude. Just step to the side until I can talk to Pedar." Tor cracked the door, and the cloak room filled with the light from hundreds of whale oil lamps and wax candles — and the eyes of as many neighbors. There was no way to slip in without drawing attention.

Pedar's hall was made for grand entrances.

THE GREAT PRETENDERS

The air was warm and smelled of spiced gløgg and sweet mead, smoked fish and roasted lamb. Neighbors Tor'd known since he came to the tiny village stared at his family, confused, as if they didn't know whether to greet them or call for the host. Laughter dissolved like melting snow into low whispers. Finally, Pedar and Skadi pushed through to ease the tension.

"Tor! Runa!" Pedar said a bit too loud. "So glad you could make it."

"Is that right?" said Tor. "Because I don't remember getting an invitation."

Runa cut Tor off. "We just thought it was time to get the kids together. We didn't know you were having a party."

Kiara noticed Anja dragging Vidar into the kitchen. In the back of the room Ubbi and Orri stood with their backs to the wall, cups in hand. They didn't look any happier to see them than Vidar.

"We should go." Tor had an edge to his voice.

"Don't be ridiculous," said Skadi, taking Runa by the arm as if they were best of friends.

Kiara couldn't believe the insincerity.

Skadi gave Runa a pleading look and led the family to the banquet.

Toren and Erik explained to Kiara that the harvest festival was the last time many families would know the feeling of a full stomach until the ring ceremony. But that wasn't true for the people gathered there.

There was whole venison, lamb on a spit, smoked salmon, lutefisk, sugar cakes, and bowls and bowls of dried berries. At Erik's house, Runa reminded Kiara daily that berries wouldn't be coming in again until summer, and what she had was not for servants. But Skadi led them all straight to the table, and it was as if they got a second chance at the food they missed at the autumn festival.

Kiara recognized the investment on the table. These were the wealthiest people she'd ever met, in Norway or Ireland. No wonder Runa was so focused on arranging Toren's marriage to Anja.

"We brought you something." Runa motioned for Kiara to bring over her bag. They'd brought goat cheese and butter, a skin of wine, two jars of beer, and two butter cakes with a jar of sugared berries for topping. And Runa insisted Kiara make a traditional Irish fruit cake using her own family recipe, even though she had to substitute berries for the fruit they used at home. Kiara offered to make it before, but Runa had refused to let her. But for this visit, she insisted. Between the dress and the dessert, it was as if she was showing her off or something.

"That is so nice," Skadi said. "Kiara, I'm afraid we don't have room for any of that on the table. Will you bring it to Elsa in the kitchen? She'll put it out as soon as there's a place for it."

"And Kiara, dear, will you please get me a cup of gløgg?" Runa's tone was stern, but when she looked at Skadi, she wore a smile. "Can she get you anything, Skadi?" And in that moment, Kiara was reminded that she was not a guest, and this was not her party.

She looked for Erik for a comforting smile, but the boys were already off with Magnus, Ragi, and others their age. Kiara realized her night would be spent serving at the pleasure of Runa and Skadi, next to a table full of cakes she was sure she wouldn't be welcome to eat. Her only solace was that she knew Runa really wasn't welcome, either.

With a sack full of food that they could have used back home, Kiara made her way into the kitchen to ask some other slave what she should do with it. Should it be put in the corner for now or could she save them the trouble and just feed it to the pigs herself? Then she saw Vidar and Anja were still there. *Were they holding hands?* Kiara's stomach churned, like the time Erik tricked her into tasting lutefisk.

Anja pushed Vidar toward the door. He wore an easy, wry smile as he ambled past. Anja did not leave with him. Instead she paced like a confused bird, until she felt she could slip out unattached.

Kiara thought back to her little village back home. How poor Orlaith fell in love with one of the Vikings. When she ended up pregnant and her father complained... Well, it was terrible what they did to him. How men just like Vidar, who sometimes smiled when they passed in the street, burned Orlaith's house to the ground on their way to the ships.

They all seemed decent enough as long as they were getting what they wanted. But after they were finished, when the stories had been told, and the cups were empty, they became monsters. Maybe pretending not to be was the most human thing about them.

Kiara thought about how dangerous her voice could be, how everything bad that had happened to Tor started that day in the forest, when she told him that Erik had borrowed his sword. How Erik tried to keep it a secret, but she just had to tell. Why did she even care? She thought about how Tor's words had gotten him into fights with the Vikings. He seemed to think his neighbors wanted to hear the truth, but now they're having parties with Viking guests—and without him. She thought about how incensed Runa had become with her when she tried and failed to share the good news with her story.

Maybe she was finally understanding the world. Everything was better when people just let things be. So, she would be quiet, now. There was no way she would tell Toren what she saw. They had eyes. If they wanted, they would see it themselves. If there even was anything there to see. Kiara would pretend everything was fine, the way Skadi and Runa did. She looked around the kitchen, how all the servants busily did their jobs, so focused on making sure everyone was fed when they themselves probably hadn't eaten. Maybe everybody was pretending. Maybe truth was for children. Maybe it was time to grow up.

SINS OF THE FATHERS

The carving didn't look at all like a troll. It wasn't as tall as the other one, or as lanky, but the details were exquisite. "Kiara told me that back in Ireland, father would be paid well to make art like that," Erik smiled. Then his face turned red, and he began to snicker. "For the church." The gaggle of teenage boys erupted in laughter.

"She knows he was Viking, right?" asked Ingjaldr.

Ivar, his older brother, looked embarrassed. "That's what makes it funny, stupid," and he punched his brother in the arm.

"Ja, stupid." Fists and more laughter rained down on Ingjaldr's shoulders from the circle of friends until all the beer in his cup had been sloshed onto the floor.

"Stop!" Ingjaldr begged. "Now look what you've done."

Immediately cups poured in from all sides and filled his to the top with a combination of white beer, sweet mead, spicy glogg, and tart wine.

"So, your stepmother said this looked like Magnus?" Ragi grabbed the little carving out of Erik's hand.

"Like a troll," Erik corrected.

"Is there a difference?" As Ragi ran away from Magnus, Skadi grabbed the pursuer by the scruff of the neck.

"If you touch my son, I'll have you cleaning plates in the kitchen with your mother," she said. Then she moved on to whisper something in Vidar's ear.

Erik snatched the little idol from Ragi's hands. "Careful!"

he said. "My father made that." He stared at the little carving. "It may be the only thing I ever get from him."

"Don't be such a girl, Erik," said Toren. "If you keep breaking everything there won't be anything left for either of us."

"Speaking of girls, what was Vidar doing outside with Anja, eh?" Erik liked shaking his brother's overblown self-confidence whenever he got the chance, and he knew jealousy was a weakness he could exploit.

Erik, expecting his brother to throw a punch, pulled his little carving close to protect it. But Toren never did. He just looked up, and Erik felt a chill, as if someone had just walked in from outside. He turned, and there was Vidar. Orri and Ubbi were with him, too. He stumbled back into the table at the surprise, and thoughts of the fight filled his mind with grief. Vidar was by far the biggest, but it was Ubbi that had beat Erik senseless during those weeks of training. And it was Ubbi who he and Toren had attacked to defend their father at the festival. It was Ubbi he feared most.

"Well," Vidar asked, "aren't you going to show me what you've got?"

Erik looked down at his hand. At some point during all his fumbling, he'd wrapped his fingers tight around the little figure as if he was ready to throw a punch. Vidar seemed calm. Ubbi and Orri looked calm, and he wanted to be calm, too. He really did. With a drink from his cup, he swallowed hard to try to force his heart back down into his chest.

Orri filled the silence; he always did. "Don't worry, boys, we plan to make peace with your father. It's all been arranged. This one is Tor's youngest, the one we were training."

"Erik, right?" Vidar made a gap-toothed smile and clapped his cup against Erik's.

"And that one is Toren, his oldest. We got to see a little

bit of what he's made of back at the festival. Didn't we, Ubbi?"

Ubbi stood there like a statue. He didn't nod, raise a cup, nothing.

"I am betrothed to Anja, Ragi's sister." Toren put his hand on Ragi's shoulder and squeezed so hard he made Ragi wince and pull away. Erik thought he might need to calm down, so he filled his cup with the tart wine he was drinking.

The Vikings looked confused, but Vidar played along. "A little young to be settling down. I guess you plan to be a farmer, like your father, eh? Or do you want to be a Viking, too, like your little brother, here."

Toren stood so still, Erik thought he might be impersonating Ubbi.

Vidar cleared his throat. "I am Vidar Olafsen, captain of my own ship, leader of many men."

"You say you've made peace with my father," Erik said. "Does he know that?"

Vidar laughed. "Not everything you say is a lie, Orri," Vidar clapped him on the back. The fat man winced under the weight of it. "This one does have spirit. So, what have you got there? Are you also a follower of Odin?

"As much as any god, I guess." Erik opened his palm. "My father made it for me. He's very good with a blade, don't you think, Orri?" The drink, combined with knowing he was surrounded by family and friends, made Erik's mouth want to run, but not enough to insult Ubbi. Or Vidar.

Vidar laughed again. "I think I see what you saw in this boy, but his spirit would need to be broken if we were going to make a Viking out of him." Vidar winked at Ubbi. "I think your training just pissed him off." Vidar held his smile. Erik's eyes burned from the hall's dry, smoky air as he tried his best not to blink first.

"Erik's the one that brought in the others, the ones we're training–"

Vidar cupped his hand over the entire lower half of Orri's face. "I don't need you to speak for me, anymore," Vidar said sternly. "Orri's always been a talker." He lightened his tone. "I'm afraid I'm partly to blame for that. But if I need your help, I'll ask for it." The giant took his paw away from Orri's mouth. Orri looked so stunned his jowls quivered. "Have a drink, man." Vidar pushed the bottom of Orri's mug to his face, covering his gaping mouth, and kept pushing until it was empty.

"My men and I are satisfied with where your father stands," Vidar assured Erik. "He left the Viking life long ago, and we will not seek my father's vengeance. I guess some men prefer the smell of manure to sea water."

Toren looked like he needed to hit something.

Vidar ignored him and topped off Erik's cup. "You've done a great thing for us. You helped us gain the trust of your friends, and I won't let a misunderstanding rob you of your future." He leaned down to speak directly to Erik. "Listen, for this is a lesson I've already learned. Your father's decisions are not your own. I will not let my father's grudge against your father stand in the way of forging my own future. I want you to do the same." Vidar clicked his cup against Erik's and Toren's.

Without thinking, Erik raised his cup and joined Vidar. The drink was strong, and he felt strong drinking with this man. He wanted to hate him, but why? These men were only terrible to their foes. Shouldn't they only be hated by their enemies? And even through the fog of that drink, there was something Vidar said that resonated. His father's wife was not his mother. His father's farm was not his inheritance. So why should he let his father's past spoil his future?

PEACE OFFERING

"**I**'m glad you came, Tor, because we wanted to invite you. We really did," said Pedar. "But Skadi was worried about having you in the same room as Vidar after what happened at the festival." Pedar looked over Tor's shoulder, winced, then over to the women. "I think everything's going well, though. I'm sure you don't want any trouble after that fight."

"How are you feeling, anyway?" Bor asked.

"I'd feel better if my neighbors had helped a little," Tor replied.

Bor acted like he didn't hear him. "Was the worst fight I'd ever seen."

"Ja," said Thorfinn. "I can't believe you ever got out of bed again after that one." Tor tried not to show the pain he felt when his neighbor slapped him on the back.

He hadn't told his family, but part of the reason he had the dogs drag the sledge was to get out of having to carry any of the heavy bags. Just the walk over was like little knives stabbing at his cracked ribs. Even standing, talking to his neighbors, he felt it. The longer he stood, the more he needed to lean, and he was already looking for a place to sit. He hadn't slept through the night in weeks.

"Listen," Pedar assured him, "Old Erik had a long talk with Vidar right after that tussel."

"Tussel?"

"I swear, he's been a new man since then. Skadi noticed it, too." Pedar rolled his eyes upward as if looking for the right words. "He's nicer. That's the only way I can say it. Maybe you two just needed to work all that out, and now it's done."

"That would be good." Tor rubbed his back.

"I've talked to him about it," said Thorfinn.

"Me, too," said Bor. "And Pedar's right. I think he's a good man."

"Good man?" Tor asked. "Does the Viking's tongue turn spit into silver, now?"

"What's that supposed to mean?" Bor's attention faded as he looked over Tor's shoulder. They all looked.

Tor turned to see Vidar, Ubbi, and Orri in the middle of the boys, hovering over Erik.

Tor stared flames at his neighbors. "Were you going to tell me that the *good men* were talking to my sons?" He broke away and bulled his way toward Erik. Runa caught his eye, then she saw where he was heading and started shaking her head wildly to get him to stop. That woman wouldn't care if the hall was on fire; she didn't want anything to stop her from negotiating the particulars of that wedding.

The twinge in Tor's hip reminded him of how easily Vidar got him off his feet and what the fall had done to him. He focused on making easy strides. The goal was to not show weakness, or a limp.

The walk reminded Tor that he was in no shape to start problems today. For the sake of his sons and his marriage, he needed to keep the peace. The heat of the fires was stifling. As he mopped the sweat dripping into his eye, he found himself wishing someone would open a door. He could hear the bustle from the gaggle of men following close behind. That made him hotter, still—just that many more bodies between his family and the exit. Pedar, the host, ran ahead, putting himself between Tor and Vidar—a bent sapling separating two bull moose.

Vidar put his big hand on Pedar's shoulder. "Everyone calm down." His voice was low, and oddly soothing. "Don't

175

everyone get excited, now. Just some men getting to know each other."

"We're just talking," Erik told his father. "I'm fine."

Anja had sidled up between Toren and Vidar, and Toren put his arm around her waist and pulled her close. He did not look fine.

All eyes were on Tor. "I'm not here to cause trouble. Just checking on my sons."

"To show that everything from the festival is behind us, I'd like to buy your services." Vidar reached over and picked up a roasted chicken from the banquet table. "Anyone else?" He held it out. No one responded, so he grabbed it with his other hand and with bones crunching he pulled it in two. "My gods are still on the ship." Vidar began to devour the roasted bird from top to bottom. The shine of grease and mead covered his beard and hands as he stripped the bones clean. "Or at the bottom of the fjord, I don't know. But I don't feel I can properly sacrifice without them. I don't want Odin to think I've forgotten him, like the rest of your village." He broke off a leg, which was about the size of his finger, and used it to make his point.

Tor had no idea what Vidar was getting at, but curiosity had a way of easing tension, or maybe it was the spectacle of watching this man eat. For one reason or the other, his shoulders relaxed.

"Erik showed me one of your carvings," Vidar said. "I want you," — he pointed at Tor with the leg bone — "to make me some gods," — his face broke out in a wide smile — "like the one you carved for your son."

"I don't make idols anymore." Tor did not want to chat with this man. He wanted to get his sons and go home.

Vidar stopped trying to dislodge chicken from between his teeth. "Oh?" One of his eyes began to twitch. "But your son just showed me one you carved for him just this week."

Tor turned to his host. "Pedar, thank you for having us. You, your wife, and your children need to come by and visit—like we used to."

Vidar pulled a little leather sack from his coat pocket, dipped out a few gold and silver coins and put them on the table with thick, greasy fingers. "I'll pay you." Then he leaned in as if sharing a secret. "I know winter's hard on people relying on the land." Then he winked at Pedar. "You've got sons to feed, after all."

"No." Tor pushed the coins back toward Vidar, then wiped his hand on his pants. "I only made those to keep the peace. If you had a wife you'd understand."

"Tor-" Runa started, but he put up his hand.

"After you've made as many gods as I have," he added, "thrown the culls in the fire to heat your house because the person you made them for was looking for something a little different, a little more to their liking, you start to wonder, who made who?"

Vidar looked at Pedar as confused as if Tor had just tried to teach him how to braid hair. "I am also trying to keep the peace." Vidar slid the coins back toward Tor. "Do this for me and we'll talk about opportunities I may have for your sons."

Erik tugged on his father's coat. Tor winced at the sharp pain it brought to his ribs. Erik looked like his entire life hung in the balance. Tor's blood began to boil. Had this man gotten to his son so easily, too? He should've just walked away.

"My wife said one of my carving's looked like a troll. I can carve you one of those."

Vidar stared blankly at him, confused. "A troll?"

Pedar interrupted again. "Tor carves the most beautiful reliefs. Ships and waves and great serpents, and mountains and birds. Did you notice the door?"

"How about men dying in battles they could've avoided?" asked Vidar. The tone of his voice and the color of his face made it clear—the tension had returned.

"I like to carve trolls. Did you know, the worst inside

177

people can be shown on the outside of a troll?" — Tor took a drink of mead — "And that trolls and giants are supposed to be related? I can make a very good troll of you."

"For me?"

"Ja." Tor put the cup down on top of the coins, took Runa by the arm, and started edging his way through the crowd. "Toren, Erik, say your goodbyes."

He heard Pedar assuring Vidar. "I know a man — he is a very skilled wood carver, every bit as good as Tor. He will make idols, any god you want, any way you like them."

Tor heard Vidar shouting. "You think you are protecting your sons? You are putting them on the losing side!" Then the giant started talking to himself. "Just like my father. He never did anything to help his son's, either."

"Thank you, Skadi. We'll get together soon." Runa started pushing the slowing Tor toward the door.

"Wait! Let me go." It was Kiara. She had fallen behind.

"Skadi, it's alright," said Runa. "Let me talk to her. Tor, get the boys out of here before you start any more trouble."

Skadi let Kiara pass.

Runa spoke quietly, so Kiara knew it was special for her. "I want to be clear. You are not my daughter. You could never replace her." Runa wiped a tear from her eye. Then she wiped the tears from Kiara's eyes, too.

"I didn't mean to —" Kiara cried.

"Our house is too small, and the winter is too long for me, as it is." Runa pushed the hair out of Kiara's frightened face and tucked it gently behind her ear. "You are Vidar's property, and I'm giving you back." Runa's voice was calm and reassuring. Then she exhaled heavily. "You've turned our gods against us. Understand?"

"No." Kiara tried to pull away. "Tor!" she begged.

"Shhh, foolish girl. Because of you, our own village is against us." Runa looked coldly into his eyes. "My husband was too blind to see it, so it was up to me. It's always up to me."

Tor wanted to strangle her. He should've known Runa's peace came with a price. All eyes and ears were on them. Runa kissed Kiara gently on the forehead. "You could be such a pretty girl, if it wasn't for that red hair." Runa turned Kiara back toward Skadi. "Smile now. You want to look nice for your new mistress."

The only smile in the room was Vidar, who looked as if Runa had just given him an unexpected present.

PROPERTY DISPUTE

"Come child," Skadi said. "Get your bags and find Elsa."

"But I didn't know-" she wiped the tears from her eyes. "I didn't pack."

"Remember the sacks we brought over?" Runa's smile looked to be wearing thin. "I put your things in the brown ones, the ones that match your dress."

"See? Runa knew what she was doing." Skadi stroked the girls back the way she might have petted a dog with the mange. "Take your things to Elsa, and tell her she's to find you a place to sleep, but away from Magnus. Pregnant girls make terrible servants."

"I'd keep her away from Ragi, too, if I were you" Runa smiled.

Erik had made his way back to Kiara. "What's happening?"

Kiara stared at him, helpless and horrified.

"Father, she can't." Erik turned to see Tor just standing there, unsure.

"I did what needed to be done," Runa said defiantly. "The wedding is back on, and it didn't cost us a thing."

"No cost? Conjure up lies, woman, but don't expect me to play along." Tor ground his teeth to keep from breaking something he couldn't afford to replace. "Pedar, tell your wife to unhand the girl. You and I will talk about this tomorrow."

"But she's my property, isn't she?" Vidar's gapped teeth glowed yellow in the firelight.

Kiara crumpled down to the floor in a sobbing mess.

Pedar looked like he'd been asked to choose between cleaning the stalls or the kitchen, neither of which he'd likely ever done. Then he smiled, as if struck with a brilliant idea. His head jerked like chicken. "Where is Old Afi? We need a judgment."

"Just give her back and we'll talk about this later," Tor said more firmly.

"I've been trying to get through since I first heard the girl cry out." Old Afi tapped Bor's wife on the shoulder and nudged past, hobbling his way through the crowd one person at a time before making it over to Pedar. His brother, Old Erik, slithered through easily, ending up closer to Vidar.

"This doesn't concern you, old man," Vidar said.

"What I think my captain means is-" Orri stopped talking and cowered before Vidar could clap his huge mitt across his fat face, again.

"Father, don't let them," Erik pleaded.

Tor's heart wrenched. Erik looked so dependent on him. He hadn't seen that look in his eyes since he was a boy, since he'd lost their-

How could Runa be so cruel?

"I don't believe you should-" Old Afi started.

"Nobody cares what you believe. What I'd like to see, is justice." Vidar ignored Old Afi and spoke directly to the room. "Has there ever been any of that in this village?"

"This is why the girl has to go," Runa said calmly to Tor. "She has been nothing but a curse on our family since we took her in."

"Our *family*? Is that what we have?" Erik was quaking. "Who do you hate more, her, or me?"

"I am done caring about Tor's family's problems," interrupted Vidar. "Too much has been allowed to go on to protect them, already. It's time for justice. That girl is my property, and I'm taking her back."

"You said you'd found peace with my father," Erik reminded Vidar. "Well, this is not the way to keep it." Erik pulled Kiara to her feet, but before he could start toward the door, Ubbi grabbed his arm, nearly pulling him off his feet.

"Let go of my son," Tor's voice rang with authority. "Erik, let go of Kiara, and Ubbi will let go of you." His knee urged forward, but he resisted taking that step. The only way to win this was to not come across as the aggressor. "This is not the way to settle this," he said to Vidar. "Pedar, bring her to the hall tomorrow. We'll settle this then."

"Anja," Vidar commanded as if he was her husband, "get the girl out of here before my honor is offended, again."

Something must have snapped inside of Toren. Maybe it was the way Ubbi had grabbed his little brother, maybe it was the way his father was allowing it to happen, or maybe it was the way Anja came right to Vidar's side when he called her in such a familiar way. "Let go of him, Viking scum!" Toren slammed a wooden cup across Ubbi's forearm, breaking his grip, and hauled Erik and Kiara toward the door.

"Stop them!" yelled Vidar.

But the crowd looked confused and allowed the three clear passage toward the door.

"In the name of the gods, do not let them pass!" This time, it was Old Erik. The path narrowed but did not close, as if hearing an order from the village priest just added to the confusion.

In the center of the hall was Vidar, tall and commanding. At the end of the hall was Tor, standing near an open door, waiting on his sons to push their way to safety. Then Tor did the unexpected. He pulled the door to, and shut his family inside.

Tor loosed Erik's grip from the girl. His sons looked so bewildered, as if he'd sacrificed their bravery at the alter of his own fear. "I have taught you to live with honor," Tor said. "We are not thieves, and we will not run as if we are." His sons watched as he escorted the girl back to where Pedar and Old Afi stood. It must have seemed like the worst kind of betrayal.

THE MANY CUTS OF A SHARP TONGUE

"We will talk about this tomorrow," Tor said to Pedar. He nodded to Kiara as if to let her know everything was going to be alright.

But everything wasn't alright, thought Vidar. He could not allow Tor to dishonor him like this if he was to ever to become this village's chieftain. Did Tor really think this had anything to do with that slave girl? Had he just taken the girl outside this would be so easy, Vidar thought to himself. But did he really need to? His mind was weighing the possibilities. He nodded to Old Erik for giving him the potion that unlocked his mind, and for teaching him that a smart man with a sharp tongue can cut his enemy deeper than any sword.

And now, it was time to cut Tor.

"So, what are you going to do with them?" Vidar asked Old Afi.

"Who?" replied the gothi.

"Tor's sons. They tried to steal my treasure while I was yet asleep, and you did nothing. Now, in front of everyone, they try to steal my slave. Are your eyes too old to see?"

"They were not stealing from you." Old Afi laughed. He genuinely did not seem to understand what was happening. "They're just boys," he continued, a little less comfortably. "They meant no harm." Old Afi seemed to want to make Vidar look like a fool. He's the one who sat closest to the throne. Time to take him out of the way, as well.

"Who has done this? Who helps a stranger only to steal

from him?" Vidar asked the hall. He needed to see if they were willing to see things his way.

"Tor's wife has taken excellent care of the girl," Pedar said.

Vidar knew he'd have to make an example of Pedar to quell any other unrequested comments from the herd. "Are you justifying theft?" Vidar cocked his eyes toward Pedar, the interrupter, who visibly shrank under the rebuke.

Tor looked uneasy, like a man who could tell he had lost the advantage. Vidar picked up a cup of ale and pretended to drink to hide a smirk he could feel climbing across his face. He could not afford to look insincere, nor could he let drink cloud his mind—not until he'd won the day.

What a pleasant surprise Tor's uninvited arrival turned out to be.

"I have no idea why they would steal from me, but I expect there will be justice, for me and those who died to get me that girl, and my treasure."

"My sons helped your man rescue that treasure for promise of a reward. Do you think they dove into a frozen fjord for something they hadn't been told was there?" Vidar's eyes shifted quietly to Orri as Tor persisted. "As for your dead men, their need for wealth has passed. They will have to seek justice from Odin for their meaningless deaths, for my sons haven't wronged them, or you."

"Where I come from, we do not tolerate stealing—even from the children of the powerful." Vidar spoke directly to Tor. "But you already know how we would settle this under Jarl Olaf, don't you, Tor?"

Normally, Vidar would've turned over tables long before, but the drink Old Erik had given him opened his mind to more devious plans. The veins pulsing up Tor's left temple and the way the sinews along his jaw were rippling told Vidar he should keep pushing. "Old Afi, as gothi, I demand justice in this matter."

"My—my children have done nothing," Tor stammered.

"Afi, I want them brought in front of a council at a proper thing to let the law decide their guilt or innocence, not their father, who has proved he would drop an axe across a sleeping man's throat."

Tor leaned toward Vidar. "There will be no trial of my sons or anyone else in this village for the theft of a slave or a treasure. Do I need to remind everyone that this man still has all of these things in his possession?" Tor seemed so frustrated, Vidar thought he might throw a knife. Actually, he'd be easier to get rid of if he did.

HOW TO RETIRE A GOTHI

"You don't want a trial, Vidar," Old Afi tried to reason. "You are a stranger, with no family, and only two men to support you, here."

"Has anyone here still got faith in this old man?" asked Vidar.

Tor was grinding his teeth. It would take an axe to shut this man up right now. Until tonight, Vidar came across like an angry oaf, but now he was turning every argument back on itself like some troll lawyer.

"I demand justice, but I will not be part of a trial overseen by Old Afi. The man is incompetent."

Tor couldn't believe this man. Who would he come for next? And why was Old Erik smiling? It was his brother Vidar was verbally abusing.

"Well, we can't have a trial without a gothi," said Pedar. He looked relieved, as if it was all going to end over a technicality.

"Are you offering, Pedar?" asked Vidar. "I would accept your judgment."

"No." Pedar looked to Tor as if he needed forgiveness. "I am close to both of you."

"How about Old Erik?" offered Bor.

"That's what I was thinking." Thorfinn looked at Bor as if he'd stolen his idea. "Not to replace him brother indefinitely."

"And he honors the gods." Bor looked proud of his contribution, too stupid to realize his role in legitimizing

Vidar's claim.

All eyes moved to Old Erik.

"Ja, the priest is the right man," agreed Halfdan, the butcher. "Surely he knows the law as good as his brother." A quarter of Halfdan's business came from people giving meat to Old Erik for sacrifices.

The affirmations trickled in, slowly at first, but as Old Afi started to walk away, the votes came in quicker.

"Is this acceptable to everyone? That old Erik act as the law speaker for your trial?" Pedar asked.

As Vidar rallied for support, Tor's eyes were on his sons. As they voiced their approval, their faces said something different. They looked confused, and a little scared. Then they cast glances of disgust at their father. Tor harkened back to Vidar's warning.

You think you are protecting your sons? You are putting them on the losing side.

"Would you accept my ruling if I heard your claim?" Old Erik asked Vidar.

"Would you accept the ruling of a local jury?" Pedar added.

"By rights the thingmen and the gothi should be my father's men." Vidar looked around the room, ignoring Tor, and then did something peculiar. He smiled. Then he said to Old Erik, "Gothi, I would require some of my own men to serve as my thingmen."

"That is acceptable under the circumstances. Tor will be cut, which leaves one slot available for you."

"Let him have the mute!" blurted Thorfinn, the farmhand, and the hall exploded with laughter.

The giant stared at the joker, looking him up and down as if memorizing every feature. "First, I'll have my shipman, Orri. Unlike Ubbi, his tongue still works fine."

Why didn't Vidar push for more thingmen? Surely, he could've used Ubbi. You don't need a tongue to vote. Nothing he was doing made sense. Instead of going after

Tor, he went after his sons. Then he ousted the gothi in favor of the priest. And what did it matter? Old Erik would have to apply the law as it was written, same as Old Afi. But the girl was Vidar's slave. Tor wasn't sure if the law was on Toren and Erik's side.

He started running the numbers. Which of the men could he count on — and which could be bought. Even though his sons were to be tried, this was still about Vidar and Tor and who could sway the jury. Which men could he trust? The Viking's hoard could certainly buy favor among some of them.

Tor's mind began working this out. Bor would do anything for some coin. And even though Runa was good friends with Sigi, Karl had never gotten over their dog Jeger killing his chickens when he was a pup.

Pedar had his own money, so that was one. Bjorn was a good man, but he had a lot to gain by making friends with the Vikings. Many did. Jan, who knew? Arn would sell his own wife if the price was right. Thorir's wife liked to spend money, and he would do anything to make her happy. As Tor scanned the room of his neighbors, he realized he had never really fit in, there. Sure, they might favor him over Vidar, but over his coin? Had he been a good enough neighbor to these people? Had his wife? He wasn't sure he could depend on any of them.

It was a humbling thought.

THE CHALLENGE

Tor had options. He could counter sue the giant. But on what basis, sleeping through harvest? Besides, he had no money, which meant he couldn't afford a lawyer. Maybe Old Afi could represent his boys, he thought. No, terrible idea. The old man couldn't even defend himself. Tor might as well outlaw Toren and Erik himself if that was the plan. And he knew what slaves were worth. If his sons lost a trial, he didn't have enough to pay compensation. Without money, he couldn't buy allegiance, and considering who made up the jury, he was pretty sure he would need to. No, he couldn't chance a trial. He had to act before the new gothi called the thing.

Well — Tor couldn't believe what he was thinking — *time to pick a fight.*

"Son of Olaf," — Tor hated speeches, but he thought he might as well remind his neighbors as to who they were dealing with — "raider of innocents across the sea, enslaver of young girls, ouster of old men, and wielder of blood-stained axes that never touched a tree." It was the most hypocritical speech he'd ever made, but he needed Vidar to feel the insult like a knife twisting in his back.

"This old farmer is insane," the Viking laughed but his cheeks reddened, a mask to expose his fury. "First, he raises thieves for sons, and now he casts insults on me as if I have no recourse. Is your wife going to dishonor me, next? Your whole family will be outlawed, at this rate."

Tor had to go further. "We all see what kind of man you

are." He needed to grease Vidar's silver tongue with the bitter taste of pride. "First, you arrive on our shores with a little girl you stole from her mother's teat. Now you try to rob me of my sons in my old age." Tor had to make this personal. "Have things changed so much under your father's rule since I left? When Olaf and I were Viking, we challenged our enemies—not their children. Your father and I would've settled a dispute like this with shields—in the old way." The room simmered with excitement.

"You're trying to rob me, again," the giant said as if trying to win back the mob he'd roused in the first place. "This man knows his sons are guilty, and now he challenges me to a duel to escape their sentencing."

"After the ring ceremony. Three shields, your choice of weapon." Tor knew he had to be quick if he was going to set the rules. "Fight ends at first blood or three broken shields. Your choice of shield man. But he doesn't fight. He doesn't block. He just keeps it honest."

Vidar slowly exhaled, eyeing Tor, as if deciding if now was the time to pluck the noisy rooster's feathers for dinner. The blush left his cheeks, and a smirk slowly crept across his lips. Tor felt the weight of what he'd accomplished.

"Here are my terms. Agree to this and I will allow you to fight on behalf of your sons. Since I have no blade, I will use one of yours. Every weapon in the village will be brought to the hall, tomorrow. I will have first choice, and you can choose from whatever's left. And if I don't see the sword your son Erik showed my men, then the holmgang is off. It's probably the only blade that'll hold an edge, other than whatever you use to turn your fields."

Tor felt the blood rush out of his face. There went his advantage. "Alright," he nodded. What choice did he have?

Vidar wasn't finished. "If either of us run, they forfeit everything they have to the other. You, your farm to me, and me, my treasure to you."

Runa and Ubbi and Orri looked the most disturbed by

that concession.

"As is customary, three gold coins go to the winner. In addition, if you win, I will drop the charges against your sons, and after the thaw, we will leave, and my father will never know that I found you, or this village, not by my word, or that of my men."

Again, Tor nodded. That's all he needed. But he wasn't even sure if he had three gold coins at this point.

Vidar continued, "If I win, both of your sons will be indentured to me for seven years. That ought to be long enough for the sea to wash the stink of goats out of their hair."

"What about Kiara?" asked Erik.

"This is about your freedom," Vidar said sternly, "not hers." Then he looked on Erik and eased his tone. "You like the Christian slave girl, ja?"

Erik's face turned bright red.

"I guess the hatchet likes to split the same wood as the axe," Vidar laughed. The man was making jokes now, as if his future and fortune weren't on the line. "I tell you what, Erik. After you've won your first battle and you've earned some coin, I'll sell her to you, if you still want her." He looked at Erik with a kind of pity. "Had our fathers made a deal like that, maybe your Christian mother would still be alive, maybe you'd have already sailed on my crew, and maybe you'd have been the one who took the girl from Ireland in the first place."

TRAINING TOR

"**N**o. Hook the shield like this. Pull across, then counter." Tor pulled Toren's arm. "Go ahead. Pull. I need you both to learn what this feels like. It's time to stop pretending and start fighting. Time for you to stop breaking shields and learn how to get around them." Tor jerked Toren's axe from behind Erik's shield and pushed the two of them apart. "Again."

"Father?" Erik asked between breaths. Both boys had their heads down, hands on their knees. "If you're the one fighting Vidar in the Holmgang, why is it that Toren and I are the ones doing all the training?"

"Shield up, knave." Toren pushed his father out of the way with the face of his shield and lunged at his little brother. Erik hooked the shield with the beard of his axe and dragged him past, then drove his shield into his back and drove his brother into an oak support. Sliding his shield up he began gently punching Toren in the kidneys. Toren pushed off the post with his axe hand and spun around hard to put Erik on the dirt floor.

"All that training with Ubbi, and big brother still knows how to put you on the ground," Toren spat next to Erik's face.

"Get off me," Erik murmured, as if the weight of his brother was crushing the air out of his lungs.

Since the challenge, Tor had turned the barn into a training area. At least the animals could benefit from the heat of the fire they kept lit while they were training, and the slat walls provided some protection from the winter gales coming up the fjord and passing over the mountain. "Don't be too proud of yourself, Toren. You've got him by three years and outweigh him by two stone." His father was not much for encouragement. He wanted them to learn the reality of fighting, and he didn't have much time to teach it. "At your age, you won't be expected to fight many fourteen-year-olds. Besides, I wonder if you could've done so well when you were his age."

"In all my life this is the first time you've let me fight him," said Toren. "And he was trained, by the tongueless and the fat—remember?—when he was conspiring to run off with the Vikings." Toren shoved on his shield to drive the boss protecting his hand deep into his brother's ribs as he pushed off to get back on his feet.

"Besides, if we were really fighting, those little punches to the ribs would have been the blade of my axe instead of my fist." Erik was slow climbing to his feet. "You'd have been more concerned with pushing your bowels back in behind your separated ribs than coming back at me with that shield. It was like being attacked by a draugr when you turned on me, a dead man come back to life to get vengeance on his little brother for beating him again."

"That's enough. Toren, you will get this. But I need you to get it faster. I need you to carry a shield on your arm when you go out in the woods, and block every branch before it can cover you with snow, then counter against the pressure of it, severing it from its tree like an enemy's arm. If your axe is quick, you'll drop the branch. If the branch doesn't fall, then your axe is too slow. Fight the trees every time you're out gathering firewood. Practice your attacks and your shield work while you eat, when you feed the animals, and even while you sleep at night.

"Why are you training us, father? We're supposed to be training you."

"Toren, hand me your shield." Tor's eldest spun his shield in his hand and gave it to his father. Tor centered his grip behind the iron boss. "Don't just stand there. Pick up another shield. Always be ready with another shield." Toren picked up another. "There, Toren knows everything he needs to know to be a good shield man, and I am ready for Vidar."

"But we haven't even-" Erik started.

Tor slammed him up against the stall, shield to shield, then reached over the top and snatched the axe out of his youngest son's hand. Then he turned and began to wail down blows on Toren. Alternating, left-to-right, Toren's shield pivoted side-to-side with each blow until he was crouched down, axe on the ground, both arms lining the back of the shield to keep it in front of him.

Tor caught him off guard when he slid around him, flipped the axe, and swung the hammer-end hard at the back side of the shield, ripping the handle off as the disk flipped across the dirt floor, until it caught an edge and began to roll the length of the barn. Toren slid backward. His retreat was his last line of defense other than the long wooden handle he was still holding onto with both hands.

"Well, now you know what a real attack feels like, and you taught me a few things that I shouldn't do as well."

"Like cower under your shield like a turtle?" smirked Erik.

"I think he meant he shouldn't let Vidar pluck his axe out of his hand." Toren swung the handle at Erik's feet, but Erik skipped it like a jump rope. Toren looked wary of his father after feeling the real power of a man with an axe and shield.

Tor hoped they both remembered that feeling, too. Might get them serious about their training. "I'm going to have to talk to Magnus about these shields." Tor shook his head. "Vidar will kill me with my father's sword if that was to happen to me during the holmgang. Of all things, I'll be depending on my shields the most."

"I'll do better next time." Magnus picked up the shield and started examining where the handle came off. "How do you like the size of the boss this time? Did these fit your hand better?"

After Tor made the challenge, Magnus followed their family as they were walking home. Who knows how much pain he heard them throwing at each other, whether it was Erik's anger at Runa for betraying Kiara or Runa blaming Erik for refusing to let her go? Maybe he noticed what resonated with Tor—how Runa didn't blame Toren—probably for fear of upsetting the one person in the family who could better their circumstances just by marrying the right girl.

When Magnus caught up with them, he just wanted to know how he could help. Tor wondered if Runa noticed who *hadn't* come after them. Not Anja, the girl she so desperately wanted Toren to marry, nor anyone else from Pedar's family. None of the neighbors came to check on them, let alone offer them any support. None but the son of a slave. Vidar cried injustice, but it was Tor's sons who wouldn't have stood a chance had there been a trial. Tor had made the right decision, after all.

Without a thought, Tor put Magnus straight to work making shields. After spending only an hour talking to him about how they were constructed and why they were made the way they were, Magnus surprised Tor two days later with the first shield he'd ever made, the first he'd even seen. He always had the most natural gift for making things, which somehow Pedar never noticed. Pedar had him fixing things around his house, but it was as if, just because he was the maid's son, or maybe because he was only Ragi and Erik's age, that he didn't notice the boy's talent. Tor always wondered who the boy's father was, but Elsa wouldn't talk about it.

By his third shield Magnus had already improved the age-old design, making them lighter and stronger than any

Tor remembered using before.

"Tor," Magnus asked. "Can you train me to fight, too?"

Tor smiled widely. "I think I can show you a few things, Magnus, if you promise not to tell Vidar all my tricks.

"Father?" asked Erik. "You still know how to fight, and I'm glad for it. But why are you training me and Toren? And now Magnus?"

Tor leaned his shield against the wall, sank down beside it, and put his hand on his side. The sinew and bone still burned as if he was being branded with hot iron whenever he swung that axe. He didn't want to admit it, but Vidar hurt him at the harvest festival.

"I'm training you because if I lose, I need to know I haven't completely failed you as a father,—that I've prepared you the best I can to survive your first few weeks living with the Vikings—in hopes that I'll have bought you enough time to figure out how to live the rest of your lives the way you choose to live them."

REAL FRIENDS

"Fill that back up for me when you get the door," Skadi commanded. Kiara picked up the pot and made her way to the door. A woman was standing there.

"Runa?" Kiara was so surprised she dropped the pot. The cold broke into the warm house like an icy intruder.

"Kiara?" Runa waited for her to collect the pot spinning next to her new, tanned leather boots.

"I like your boots, ma'am." Kiara thought compliments might ease the tension. "Are those cowhide?" She thought it was interesting because she knew they didn't keep any cows.

"Never you mind my boots." Runa pushed inside and handed Kiara her soft hat and shook her shoulders until Kiara helped remove her green cloak. It was thick and soft and smelled nice like fresh pine. Kiara smelled of smoke and mud and worse, like things found on the ground in the yard. "Do people where you come from always leave their guests outside in the cold?"

Runa complained all the way to the dining room. "All those months you'd think I didn't teach you anything." Kiara hadn't seen Runa since the party. Seeing her here, in Skadi's house, reminded her how much smaller everything of hers had been.

"I thought I'd surprise you both by asking Kiara to help in the house today," Skadi purred. "Did I succeed?"

Runa sort of half-smiled her response.

"Please, sit." Skadi had a way about her that made people feel below her. Usually Kiara was bothered by it, but when she did it to Runa Kiara had to hide her smile. She still had snow to gather, anyway.

"She's a funny sort of girl. But sometimes I'm just not sure about her." Runa watched as Kiara left to fill the pot. "I had Elsa make some more of that salve for Tor."

"Thank you, Skadi. That's very thoughtful, although I don't know if he needs it."

"Keep it," Skadi insisted. "If not for now, then for after the holmgang. You know, he's not as young as he used to be. I mean, when's the last time he swung a sword?"

When Kiara came back, she put the pot of snow on an iron handle and swung it out over the fire. Then she added a few dry pieces of wood to feed the hungry coals. The fire popped, and sap sizzled like pork bacon.

"Come on, girl. You're being invited to tea. Or don't you do that where you're from?" Skadi put out a third cup on the table. Kiara was unsure, then dipped her finger in the hot water to try and clean a stain off her skirt before awkwardly taking a seat.

After an eternity of looking and smiling at each other, the snow in the pot finally melted, and the water began to bubble. Kiara had never been so happy to get up from a table in her life.

When she first started working in Runa's house, she was taught there were two things every woman in Norway needed to mind above all else: that the fire was always burning, and that there was always a pot of clean water simmering in the pot for drinking or cleaning or whatever else might come. Just keeping up with that had impressed Skadi enough to let her work directly under Elsa. So, Kiara had that—if only that—to thank Runa for. Else she might have been tending Skadi's cows.

"Sit, Kiara. We haven't really talked." Skadi pushed the bowl of dried berries toward the empty chair.

Runa pursed her lips, but followed Skadi's lead, pushing over the plate of crusty bread, brown goat cheese and dried fish.

Kiara stared down at the sharp knife lying on the plate, cut off a slice of bread, and buttered it, then bowed her head as she kissed the cracked, off-white ring hanging around her neck.

"Why do you pray to your god like that?" asked Runa. "Do you think he can hear your whispers all the way up in his heaven? Even from here?"

"Amen," Kiara whispered with a nod of her head. "If I've offended you, I can take my tea at the servants table." She pointed her cup toward the kitchen. Runa had seen her pray many, many times before, but never once wanted to talk about it. She had never talked to her much at all, unless she was telling her what needed to be done or complaining about something she'd done, or sometimes, it seemed, when she'd just wanted to make her feel bad.

"No. I just wonder. Did you pray before?" asked Runa. "I mean, back in your country?"

"Yes, ma'am, I did." Kiara was sure this time. Runa just wanted to make her feel bad. She must have missed that about her, at least.

"Even if your god could hear your whispers, what do you think he will do? Send his angels to save you?" Runa put her hand on Kiara's—her fingers were cold.

As if bored with Runa's needling, Skadi changed the subject. "Toren told Anja that you like Erik. Is that right?" Runa choked on her chunk of cheese. Kiara froze, but she felt the heat of embarrassment rising in her cheeks. It wasn't clear which one of them Skadi meant to cut, but it worked.

"I'd stay away from Erik, if I were you." Anja sashayed into the room with a smile on her face and a drink in her hand. "But as long as you stay away from Toren you won't get any grief from me." She was as well dressed and beautiful as if she was going to a party. "You know, I think

I may have another set of old clothes for you. You're so good with a needle; I'm sure you can make something of them."

Those were the first words Anja had spoken to Kiara since she was given over. Same for her mother. Just that morning, Skadi told Elsa she needed Kiara to come to the dining room to help with entertaining, and Kiara had been standing right in front of her.

Kiara nodded, unsure if the offer was real. "Thank you."

"Kiara is a nice girl." Runa also often spoke as if she wasn't in the room. "But she is a slave. And there wasn't, nor will there ever be, anything between her and Toren," — She glowered at Kiara—"or Erik."

"Now I'm curious," said Anja. "Vidar has talked to me. He's told me a lot about what happened in Ireland, poor thing."

Kiara's face burned. She raised the soul ring to her lips again and closed her wet eyes. She thought about her home, how they were convinced that if they allowed the Vikings to lodge over winter no one would be harmed. She remembered being woken from a deep sleep, the king's men, the screaming. *Aiden!* They had Aiden, too. The burning fires and the boats. The wading into the cold sea— it was no time to be on the water.

How would Vidar tell that story?

What did Anja think they did when they left—to the holy church, to the priests? God only knows what happened to her parents. She prayed for peace, every day. Inner peace. But she did not pray for the soul of Vidar, or his lying father, or any of them. She knew she was supposed to forgive them, but she couldn't. Not yet. And when she prayed for her family, she prayed for her brother, but most of all, she prayed for justice. She didn't know if it was right, but now she prayed for Tor, that God may use him to slay the giant, like David slayed Goliath. Maybe then she could forgive them. Maybe then she could know peace again. But for now, she would do as she was taught and just pretend.

"Is she praying again? I'm sorry, Skadi, but I just have to ask." Of course, it was Runa. "So, Kiara, if your god could not protect you in Ireland, where he has his churches and his priests, why do you think he can protect you here?"

"My God is everywhere, and he hears my prayers wherever I am. If I am here, it is because he wanted me here."

"Then he wants you to be a slave, or die." Runa pulled the dish of berries away from Kiara and moved it in front of Anja.

"Maybe he doesn't want you here, exactly." Anja reached across the table and pulled the bread and butter to her side of the table. "Kiara is still Vidar's, and in the spring he will either have her helping raise the ship or keep his house."

Runa grabbed Anja's arm. "Is he purchasing a house?"

"No." Anja said. "Whether he stays or not depends on your husband, I guess.

"Runa," asked Skadi, "has Tor taken Old Erik his sacrifice, yet? For luck?"

"You know how he feels about the gods, and Old Erik." Runa sipped on her tea. "Just last spring, after warming him up with a few horns of ale, I tried to talk him into making a sacrifice for the seed we'd sown, and he said to me, 'Why don't we keep our meat? The priest can keep his fortune-telling, and the gods can keep their blessings."

"Well," said Skadi, "I had Anja bring Old Erik a chicken just after what happened at the harvest festival and had her tell Old Erik to sacrifice it in your name."

Anja squirmed a little in her seat.

"I knew there'd be trouble after all of that happened," Skadi continued. "Do you need me to give you an animal to take?"

"No." Runa held her chin up high, then somehow managed to wriggle out a gracious smile. "Thank you. We've got plenty to sacrifice," she lied. "It's Tor," which was true.

"Well, you must do it for him. That's all." For having such a pretty nose, Skadi sure liked to stick it where it didn't belong. She could be the queen of condescending while doing it, too. "Do you think I wait for Pedar's permission to do anything around here? You wouldn't believe the sacrifices I've made. I'd sacrifice your children if I thought it would benefit my Anja."

"What?" Runa jumped to her feet.

That was a particularly stupid thing to say. Even Kiara knew what had happened to Runa's daughter. She doubted she'd have been so offended if Skadi had said Erik; that's for sure.

"I didn't mean anything. I mean, I-" Skadi put her hand on Runa's shoulder to calm her. "Stupid girl," — she spoke to Kiara as if she'd been the one who said it — "bring Runa a real drink. Bring us all some of that mead Halfdan brought over." Runa's chest was heaving. "You know what I meant, right?" Skadi pushed the bowl of berries back in front of Runa, and eased her back into her seat. "A mother's love knows no bounds."

Runa emptied two cups of mead before the color came back to her cheeks. The sound of falling snow broke the uneasy silence. "I blame Erik, you know. This whole thing is his fault." Runa tapped her cup on the table. Kiara had been well-trained. She jumped up and refilled all the cups. "Or maybe I should blame Kiara. Maybe she seduced him. I mean. Why else would Erik have risked our reputation to stop us from giving Kiara back?"

"He was defying you," Kiara whispered under her breath.

Runa cut her eyes to the girl. "Well, if I hadn't sent you back to Vidar before, I'd have had to send you to him now."

"Why is that, exactly?" Kiara hated to ask, but what worse could Runa do to her? She'd already been returned to her owner, like a lost dog she no longer wanted to feed.

It was Runa who was condescending now. "Oh dear, you don't know our way, do you? If fate smiles on my husband and by some error he kills Vidar in the holmgang, you will be buried at the Viking's side—no different than a weapon or bit of his coin. His men will see to that."

"What?" Kiara stiffened in shock.

"If Vidar has pleased the gods then he will go to Odin's Valhalla or to Freyja's field, Fólkvangr," continued Runa.

"But you are no warrior," Skadi said, as if Kiara should know what that had to do with anything. "You have done nothing to earn a glorious fate."

Anja put her hand on top of Kiara's. She must have mistaken her horror for curiosity. "In our culture, slaves accompany their owners into the afterlife, and if none of the gods want you, then you will go to Hel." Anja's touch was unnervingly soft and warm, which made her words that much colder.

Skadi smirked and lowered her brow, as if Kiara's repulsion was entertainment. "My dear, haven't you learned anything about our way? Our village may not be Viking, but our gods are still warriors. Do you think they would let your Christ save you here?" Runa seemed to always know just what to say to make Kiara feel worse. "And there will be no resurrection. Our dead stay buried. We lock the doors to their graves to make sure of it."

These women were preaching nightmares.

"Erik knows all of this, and so does Toren," said Runa. "And yet, they are still praying for victory for their father."

"We all are," added Anja.

Thank you mouthed Runa as she put her hand on Anja's forearm. "You're such a good girl." Then Runa turned to Kiara, a bright smile on her face, as if she hadn't been talking about her murder and damnation. "You think you're a good girl, too, don't you Kiara?" Runa pursed her lips like she wasn't so sure. "So, go on, sneak away to the woods, and talk and tell stories and laugh with my boys."

"I don't-" Kiara didn't know what to say.

"But know this." Runa apparently didn't want to hear excuses. "The best thing that can happen to you is that their father is killed by the Viking. Because my husband will surely kill Vidar if he gets the chance."

Kiara's head was spinning. Other than Skadi's burst of insanity, she couldn't stop thinking about Old Erik burying her with the Viking. So, did Erik assume she was praying for Vidar to kill his father? She hoped he knew her better than these women because she would rather God take her now than be the reason he saved Vidar.

"You see," Anja explained. "We're not like the men. We're not just smiling to make you smile, laughing to make you laugh."

"Real friends tell you the truth, even if the truth hurts."

Skadi mouthed the words *I'm sorry* to Runa.

Runa nodded to accept her apology. "In that case, we may be the best friends you have here." Then Runa gently tapped her empty cup on the table.

Obviously, the mead was doing its work on these beautiful hags. Kiara was still stiff. Her throat was still tight.

"Kiara dear, are you alright?" Skadi ran her claws along Kiara's back.

Kiara jumped back, away from the table. She didn't want to be touched, not by any of these black hearted crows. She really could use a true friend right now, someone sane to talk to.

Oh, Erik. What must he think of me?

"Are you alright, dear?" Skadi asked again.

Kiara took a deep breath. She wouldn't give these women the satisfaction of watching her break down again. She was done being their entertainment. "Yes, I think so. It's just a lot to take in."

"Ja," Skadi pouted her lips as if she understood. "Well, I just wanted to say, before I forget, after you fill our cups, I'll need you to get some more firewood for my bedroom."

Kiara pulled up the collar on her borrowed coat, then wiped a tear away from her eyes as she walked out into the cold yard. Behind her she heard the ladies at the table cackling, which reminded her she still had to feed the chickens.

COLLECTING SPICES

Sterkr barked in excitement, then started jumping up on Erik amongst all his spinning.

"Here to find out my father's secrets?" Erik held up both hatchets like he was ready for battle.

"Yes. The Viking's sent me to find out how your father collects his firewood." Kiara was nervous. She made jokes when she was nervous. Could Erik really hate her?

"Well, you can tell them it's no secret. He uses his sons." Erik smiled, and Kiara felt warm inside at the sight of it. "What are you doing here, lass?"

"I'm bringing you your lunch, like I used to." Kiara ran her fingers through Sterkr's thick fur. Then she reached into a wool sack and gave the dog a chicken wing.

"Whoa, look at all of this!" Erik started digging through what she brought. "Is Ragi coming to eat, too?"

"Ha. Ragi leaves more food on his plate after breakfast than this. Pedar's family will never miss it.

"Do they know where you are?" Erik put the axes down in exchange for a chicken leg.

"Of course," she said playfully. "I'm collecting spices. Plan to do it every day while the wee bit of sun you get around here still shines."

"With three feet of snow on the ground?" Erik looked like he was getting bigger, as if he'd changed somehow in just the last month.

"Pedar likes my cooking." Kiara missed her lunches with Erik. "He thinks it's exotic. So, I told him it's the special ingredients, that the Irish have a nose for 'em, and no amount of snow could hide what's needed from an Irish woman. So, he sent me out, just like that."

"What will you come back with — snow?"

"Ah, they've got more in that house to cook with than the Saturday market in my village. They just don't know what to do with half of it." She took a bite of a brownish cheese and shrugged. A little strong, but it was good enough to share with Sterkr. "Erik? Why do you and Toren always cut wood with hatchets instead of axes?"

"They're all axes, Kiara." Erik dropped a bone for Sterkr, picked the hatchets up, and cleared some limbs as big as his arms off a fallen tree with alternating strokes. Then he shrugged. "My father won't let us use a wood axe — I remember him insisting we do it this way since we were little."

She thought about the power in each of his downward strokes. Was he showing off for her? "Do you want any of this, or did I just walk out here to feed your dog?"

"If you give Sterkr all my lunch then you'll be stacking this wood for me tonight."

"If I go near your house, your mother will accuse me of spying, or worse." Kiara sat down and pulled out some dried fish and bread for them to share, much more than Runa ever fed him.

"Worse? What could be worse than helping Vidar?" Erik sent one of the hatchets fifteen feet, sticking it just below a knot in an old oak.

Sneaking off to have lunch with you. She couldn't bring herself to say it, so she changed the subject. She'd learned from her mother long ago that if you want to change the subject with a man, change it to something he knows he does well. They're never more than half listening, anyway.

"I didn't know you were left-handed."

Erik landed the second hatchet into the knot's center. "I'm not."

"Does your father train you to fight with axes or swords?"

Erik looked shocked as if she'd brought up something she wasn't supposed to know about. "My father's not training us, but we do spar him when he trains."

"Well, Vidar trains with a sword."

"Ja, I know. It's my father's — Ice Breaker. Remember?"

She pretended she might throw some bread at him, not sure if she was giving away how much she liked his sarcasm. "Well, did you know this? After Vidar practices with Ubbi, Ubbi and Orri still train the boys in the village. More of them now than when you were sneaking off."

"Are you trying to make me feel worse than I already do?" He stole away with a piece of fish. "Pedar has swords, too, but my father says they're just toys, not for real fighting. I was hoping Vidar would've chosen one of those. You should've seen Pedar's face when neither of them chose any of his shiny swords for the holmgang."

"So, you train with axes," she answered her own question. "Well, if Tor has always sent you out to cut firewood with two hatchets instead of a heavy, two-handed wood axe like every other man I've ever seen, then I think he's been training you to fight your entire life." Erik looked stunned. Then he just stared at his two hatchets, handles worn. They looked molded to fit his strong hands from years of heavy use. As he got his head around what now seemed obvious, Kiara interrupted his thoughts. "Teach me to do that?"

"I might be able to teach you to hit the side of the barn, as long as we were throwing from the inside." Erik's dimples showed when he smirked.

As he cleared snow off a log so he could eat his lunch, Kiara wrenched one of the hatchets from the tree, took aim, and stuck it into a fat pine ten feet away.

"I'd be impressed if I thought you weren't aiming for that birch over there." Erik was rummaging through the food. "You know, Skadi would probably kick you out of her house if she thought you could do that. Norse women aren't very trusting. Runa warned us you might have been planning to kill us all in our sleep when you lived with us."

"Are you thinking of telling her?" Kiara jerked on the handle of the second axe.

"There's a lot going on right now that's better kept from my stepmother." Erik watched Kiara struggle to retrieve the second axe, as if she were doing it for his entertainment. After trying unsuccessfully to pull it out, pry it out, and painfully kick it out, she picked up a piece of wood off the stack and smacked the hatchet's handle. It came out as easy as a nine-year-old's baby tooth.

This was their winter-long ritual. Kiara would bring Erik his lunch, and he would pretend not to look forward to it.

When Kiara was alone with Erik, he helped her work on her Norse or axe throwing, or anything else he was already better at than she was.

Sometimes, Toren was there, too, and they talked about more serious things. "How is Anja? Does she ask about me?"

"She doesn't know I come here," Kiara would remind him. "Promise you won't tell her?"

"When would I? That Viking has turned us into outcasts in our own village," Toren complained. "I never see her anymore."

"I'm sure things will change after the holmgang," she said. She wanted one of the boys to make her feel like everything would be alright, but they never did when she said things like that. They would always stuff their mouths with Pedar's food—or change the subject.

"Does Anja spend time with Vidar?"

"I don't know," she lied. Vidar seemed to have a power over people. He wasn't like that before. It was like watching the puppeteer who used to perform every year at her village's spring festival. He would push them away, and then he knew just what to say to bring them back to his side. Anja was his favorite puppet. "I'm just a servant," Kiara would remind them. "Anja doesn't come find me to tell me her secrets. I see her when I'm serving the meals, that's it."

"What can you tell us about Vidar? Anything we can pass along to our father?" Toren would always ask the same questions every time he was there.

For some reason, today Kiara was frustrated. "What do you want me to say?" —she let her guarded tongue run— "That he's injured? He isn't. He's getting stronger every day. Do you want to know the real reason I can sneak away with so much food every day? It's because of how much extra we're cooking to feed the man. Skadi's having us cook double to make sure he never goes to bed hungry. It's as if your future mother-in-law wants to help Vidar get stronger to beat your father, and it's working.

"Do you think your father can win?" Kiara asked.

Both boys looked like she'd put them back on their heels. Why couldn't she just keep her mouth shut?

The boys considered their answer. Erik confided in her that because of Vidar's silver tongue, their father had not only been training them how to wield axes and shields, but also words and diplomacy, something she needed to learn to do.

"My father will win," said Erik. "Don't you remember what he did to Ubbi and Orri?"

"Yes, I remember," said Kiara. Erik always had a way to make her feel better, but she'd obviously shaken his confidence.

"I don't know," admitted Toren. His words were measured, and heavy. "I used to think my father was so strong. But Vidar—well, now the Viking is using his own sword against him. It's as if Odin himself has set Vidar against him for trading his sword for a rake."

"And for marrying a Christian?" Kiara watched Erik bristle as she said it.

"Toren, you've been spending too much time around the house with Runa," said Erik. "The woman's so negative. It's like she's already planning his funeral."

"Is your father planning to kill Vidar?" Kiara was almost afraid to hear the answer.

"Go back to Vidar, Kiara." Toren said it as if scolding a little girl. "And don't come back here again." The sudden distrust in Toren's eye turned to rage as he slammed his hatchet into a log.

"She's not a spy, Toren." Erik stepped in front of Kiara and faced his older brother. "Of course, he will — if he can. If our father lets him live, Vidar leaves in the spring. And when Jarl Olaf finds out what happened, he'll seek revenge. His ships would be here by summer. Then father's dead anyway, isn't he?" It was as if he hadn't thought about it before. "Besides, Orri told me some things about Vidar. I think he wants this village for himself, not for his father." His voice trailed off as he put the pieces together like some grand puzzle. "Both father and Vidar are going to want to end this now rather than bring a Viking hoard to our shores."

"The only one who's ever wanted more Vikings is you, Erik," said Toren, "and your idiot friends, half of which are apparently still training so they can sail away with them now." Toren turned his fire toward Kiara. "What are you crying about?"

Kiara knew she shouldn't say anything — that Erik and Toren had too much to worry about already. But she did anyway. "Runa came by to discuss your marriage with Anja."

"Of course," said Erik. "That woman cares more about that than she does about my father."

"Shut up, Erik," said Toren. "Is everything still on?"

"I don't know. I guess so. They barely mentioned it while I was in the room." Kiara wiped tears from her cheek. "She said that if your father kills Vidar that they would bury me

212

alongside him."

Erik looked shaken.

"Don't worry about what Erik said. He doesn't know what he's talking about," said Toren. Kiara noticed he didn't deny that they might do it. "There are rules to the fight. We talk about them every night. No one is going to kill anyone, except Runa if I don't get back to work on my new house." He put on his skis and slipped off into the shadowy forest, toward his home.

That was the last time she saw Toren until the ring ceremony. As Erik would often sarcastically explain it, "As the heir, sometimes Toren was much too important to chop wood." He had to learn how to pluck his chickens or sweep the floors of the house that would one day be Anja's bridal gift—the girl who needed nothing.

Kiara was glad Toren had to work on his house because that meant there was never a day Erik wasn't chopping wood, never a day she couldn't meet him in the forest, the one place she didn't feel like a slave. She'd even learned to make peace with the cold. Erik was only there because the fires never stopped burning in Norway. She wondered how many fires Tor's sons had fed as their father secretly trained them for battles he prayed would never come. Who he prayed to, though, was anybody's guess.

THE BUTCHER

"I don't think I've ever done as much business with you as I have this year."

"Well, we've had a lot of unexpected expenses. With the girl, Erik's going away soon. So there's that. And the wedding."

Halfdan looked at her suspiciously, then lowered his eyes. "You haven't settled that, yet?" He pulled back the lips on the old bear's massive head and exposed the two-inch canines. "Remind me, Runa, is it Tor that has the death wish, or his dog?" The butcher shook his head as he unfolded the coarse black fur to see how well the hide had been cured.

"Well, the gods know I've tried to talk some sense into him." Runa watched as he fingered the sharp claws. She needed a good offer, more than Erik needed another layer between his blankets and the floor. Besides, somebody had to prepare him for the cold nights he was going to face at sea.

"You know, I'd pay better for a nice, fat red deer." Halfdan's brows knitted together.

Runa clenched her fingers into a fist. She'd known Halfdan all her life and disliked him just as long. "Make me an offer, please." She could hear the disdain in her own voice. That wouldn't do. She needed this man. She put her hand on top of his and tried not to pet the coarse hair, which was almost as thick as the bear's. She managed a smile. "Just do what you can."

"A little red meat for the pot?"

"No, I just need a little something for the gods." Runa looked down at his long, grimy fingernails as she spoke. "For Tor."

The butcher patted her hand and went to the back of the shop, which had become filthy ever since his wife died a few years back. At least the cold had killed the flies that normally swarmed the counter, which was nice.

Halfdan came back with the carcass of a yearling red deer and threw it on the counter, sending a flutter of brown hairs flying.

"The boys found it froze to death while gathering firewood. Don't worry," he smiled, "I wouldn't give anyone bad meat. This'll be a treat for Old Erik. He loves anything young. The younger the better." Halfdan had tall teeth and the kind of smile that made most people want to take a bath. "This poor thing must have gotten separated from its mother."

Fur flew as he deftly ran the knife down one side of the spine to expose the backstrap, which was the choicest meat. He clipped one end from the top of the neck, then started his knife down to separate the meat from the skin. When he got halfway down the back, he looked up at her, soured his face, and continued farther down and looked at her again.

"Don't worry about the color," he assured her. "This one's aged perfectly." He removed the long strap, blew along the table to clear it of loose fur—his breath being that of onions and pickled fish—and proceeded to lay the meat atop a pile of it anyway.

"That's good," she whispered. There was enough on the table to cut twenty nice-sized steaks.

"I think that ought to buy him the gods' favor, or at least Old Erik's." The butcher whistled as he ran the blade of his seax under the choice cut, put it into a hide sack for the lady, and pressed his long lips together in concentration. "You know, I have a great respect for you and your family. And even though I haven't always gotten on with your husband, I admire any man that earned the favor of your father."

"Ja. You know my father always appreciated you, Halfdan. And so does Tor," Runa added.

There was that suspicious look again, then he gave her a soft, almost genuine look. His long teeth only half-sticking out from under his upper lip. "It's because I loved your father, and because we always did good business together, he and I, that I want you to have this." He pressed two silver coins into the palm of her hand, holding it, looking into her eyes. "You know, Runa, I often worry about your husband, if he feels like he quite belongs here.

Runa pulled her hand back slowly; Halfdan refused to let go. His fingers were dirty with hair and old blood, and moist and hot.

"Ever since my wife died — well, you're still a beautiful woman, Runa." His lips couldn't manage to conceal his crookedly assuring grin. "If something happens to Tor in that holmgang, I want you to know, I'll never let you go hungry."

She stared down at the coins, bouncing them in her palm to get a general feeling for the weight. Every person she'd sold things to lately had been dealing in them. They were from Vidar's strongbox. The faces on the silver were of foreign rulers, usually with crowns on their heads, all of which she assumed had fallen to the Vikings. She wondered what the Vikings did with the crowns. Would Tor be wearing one, had he stayed? The features of the coins had been worn thin with use.

"How did you get these?"

"They're pure silver," Halfdan assured her. "They're good for trading. That's all you need to know."

She looked up into the butcher's face and mouthed *Thank you*. She forcibly removed her hands from his heavy grip and left him alone in his filthy little shop.

It was a good trade. The coin would go far in getting

Anja's bridal gift ready for spring. After waving goodbye to the attentive Halfdan, Runa wiped the lingering feeling of his damp hands off onto her linen gown.

Halfdan followed her with his eyes, petting the fur off the head of the bear with one hand while adjusting himself with the other. Runa spit twice. The man was disgusting, but like his shop, nothing a smart woman couldn't fix. And with Tor antagonizing the Vikings at every turn, and now the holmgang, she needed to keep all her options open.

SACRIFICE FOR THE GODS

Old Afi and Old Erik were ancient. No better or worse for the years that had passed. It was as if they were frozen in time like the fish that froze for the winter near the surface of the lake. Whose eyes stared up at her every time she and her sister Sigrid went skating when they were girls.

Runa shivered as she thought about those fish trapped in the ice. *It must have been so cold down there.*

At the caw of a crow, a little dog with a chicken bone in his mouth poked it's head out from under the covers bunched up over Runa's lap. As if still half asleep, he leaned back on his little haunches and stretched, then looked up to Runa with what appeared to be a smile on his face.

At just over three hands tall, Jeger was about half the size of a fox, but much cuter. The top of his curly tail and pointed ears barely made it to Vigi's shoulders. His coat was a light shade of brown, with a belly that was white all the way up to his cheeks as if stained by the snow while taking a nap. Jeger wasn't there for protection, unless it was from chickens. He was Runa's pet. Jeger was better company than Tor, who seemed to get grumpier every year, and the best gift he'd ever given her.

After taking his look around, Jeger nuzzled his chin down into the fur lining her thick coat and went back to his nap.

Runa wished she could be so warm and comfortable. She had been shivering since she started into the woods, from shade or nerves, she couldn't tell. And the shivers got worse the closer she got to Old Erik's—they always did.

The old hunting shack he shared with his brother made her skin prickle. Tucked back in a forgotten wood out behind Pedar's farm, it was a place lost to everything but the weather and the ravens. They must have liked that part of the wood, for they filled the trees like black leaves. Somehow, Jeger, the bird dog, had disappeared under the blanket again.

She knocked on the priest's moss-covered door, holding her sack of questionable meat in her hand. She almost hoped he wouldn't be home. For some reason, she always felt that way on this particular errand. She wished Tor would bring her, but he had never approved of her gods or her sacrifices.

The hinges creaked as the door eased open. "Old Afi?" she exhaled with relief. He was always the more approachable of the brothers. "How are you doing?"

"Alright for an unjust old man who no longer feels welcome in his own village, retired by his own brother." His words sounded bitter, but his face was kind. Could have just been his thick accent. She always struggled trying to place it. The brothers had somehow never revealed to anyone where they were from, keeping it one of the great mysteries of the village. "But, of course, you understand completely, don't you?"

Runa didn't like the sound of that. Why would she feel unwelcome? She was born and raised there.

Before she could reply, Old Erik brusquely pushed him aside. "Forget about us, child. We're fine. More importantly, how is Tor?"

"I-I don't mean to intrude," she stuttered, wishing he'd send her away and the gods would give her credit for trying.

Their eyes pierced her soul. That was the only place she could see a resemblance—like icy blue knives that cut through her — not the way Halfdan or other men undressed her with weak stares, but as if they could know her thoughts, her feelings.

"I — I only came to make an offering" — she tried to regain her command and shake off her sudden unease — "for my husband."

"A sacrifice?" Old Erik curled his lip and smiled as he cast his eye up toward his brother.

"It's red deer, young, but aged for flavor. I hope it suits you. I mean I hope it will be acceptable to the gods."

Old Erik licked his chops. He had a sour smell, his hair and beard oily, black, and wild. "I haven't seen red meat in the last month other than some goat Skadi brought over last week."

"Do you prefer goat?" she asked, pleased her husband wasn't here. Tor never liked the way she turned so needy around Old Erik.

Last year in the hall, during a celebration feast, after watching Old Erik cut the soul ring out of Toren's chest, a half-drunk Tor quieted the hall when he told Old Erik he'd thank the gods after they started bringing *him* the meat instead of the other way around.

Tor and Old Erik didn't talk much after that. The entire village remembered that speech every time their farm or family suffered any setbacks, including escaping goats.

"Pedar, keeps me in red meat all year round," Old Erik interrupted Runa's runaway thoughts. "His farm is always prosperous. Probably because he blesses his god's servant with regular sacrifices."

Runa tried to lighten the mood. "My husband often jokes that Odin opens our fences so our sacrifices can walk to his butcher directly." It didn't work.

Old Erik just frowned and began backing into the door, shaking his head as he weighed the bag in his left hand.

Runa placed her hand on the creaking door. Old Erik turned with a jerk gazing at her with his icy blue eye. She shrunk but did not give up her courage.

"I had hoped you would say a special prayer for us." The wooden slatted porch cracked underfoot, as if feeling her shift her weight toward the sleigh.

The old man's face curled from frown to smile. "What is it I can pray for, specifically? The gods are very busy, and they serve those best that serve them first." The old man weighed that package she'd given him in his left hand, again, making sure she noticed.

"The holmgang," she said. "Pray for victory. I'm not sure we can take another setback."

"Ja, I guess not." His face turned dire. "I hope you don't mind me asking, but the girl—did you send her away because she reminded you of Tor's wife, or your lost daughter?"

Old Erik's one blue eye cut into her as hot and sharp as the knife his brother used to extract the childrens' souls. Did he demand her to feel pain with her sacrifice?"

"Both." She felt hot tears freeze as they covered her cheeks. She thought of her lost daughter every minute of every day. It marked the moment she lost connection with her husband and began to feel truly alone. And now, since this girl arrived, the pain of those memories burned again, like a branding iron sizzling against her soul. "You know what I really want you to pray for?" After all these years of pretending, at that moment Runa burned with a mother's grief and didn't care what the priest or Old Afi or anyone else thought of her. "Pray that I will see her again. I just want to see my daughter again."

"I would've done that for you whether you asked me to or not. I know your husband's not a religious man, but the gods will accept your sacrifice on his behalf." The old man's smile broadened, and he stuck his tongue into the gap where his tooth had once been as if searching for something from yesterday's dinner. "After all, any sacrifice of yours is a sacrifice of his as well."

Old Afi pried the offering from Old Erik's claws and handed it back to Runa. "God doesn't need any more blood shed on his behalf. He already knows your husband, Runa." He looked at the gold-plated ring hanging around her neck. "I'll be praying for you."

Runa stood on the stoop, crying and holding her offering, not sure what to do next.

Old Erik pulled his brother inside, grabbed the sack back out of Runa's hand, and shut the door in her face.

She climbed up into her sleigh—confused, upset, and glad it was over. She thought about Kiara, looked down at her ring, and considered kissing it and saying a prayer the way the girl did. *Don't be stupid.*

Behind her, she heard the door creak open, but she didn't look back. She hurried the cart down the lane, her tracks already whitewashed and covered. Old Erik's voice carried through the winter air. He was arguing with his brother. She heard the words "filthy carrion!" and urged her horse on.

As if called to a feast, the black trees erupted as hundreds of ravens turned day into night. At the murder call, Jeger sprung to his feet, spinning and barking and drawing unwanted attention to Runa's escape. As the flock flew low over the road, she lurched in her seat and almost lost the reins. She urged the horse faster as if the river of black was intent on carrying her back.

Like a child's nightmare, Runa felt something coming up behind her. She dared not look back. She threw the blanket over the yipping dog's head to stop him from giving them away. She shuddered when she heard the priest's door slam shut, echoing out as loud as if she was still just outside the house.

Light. In the distance the woods opened up, and the sun's blinding rays reflected off the field like a diamond necklace against a black dress.

She drove the mare toward it, nearly tipping the sled.

Faster, faster. Her breath caught in her throat. Beams of sun hit her arms, and the cold fresh air never tasted so good.

As the sleigh redrew its tracks across the open field, Runa allowed the horse to slow, though her heart was still racing.

She finally allowed herself to turn around. The dark woods seemed less menacing, now that she was in the light. Jeger poked his head out from under the blanket again, confused and growling, ready to bark at the trees if they dared to follow.

Runa smiled as she ran her fingers down the little dog's back. His tail snapped back to curl high over his back when she finally let it go. *Stupid girl,* she thought to herself, *you've made your sacrifice. Nothing's going to hurt you now.*

CHOOSING SIDES

"I want to join Vidar," Erik said.

Tor looked at Magnus. "And you?"

"Ja," he replied, "I do, too."

"When Magnus and I join the Vikings Vidar will drop the charges against us." Erik looked at his father. "There will be no holmgang, and the two of you can make peace, before one of you gets killed."

Tor looked down at his fish as if he was considering Erik's proposal.

Toren had nothing to consider. "You can't go a'Viking! We need you here. What about your family obligations? What about the farm?"

"What about it? It's your birthright, not mine!" Erik loathed to remind him. "I'll be lucky if Runa lets me walk away with the cat."

Magnus almost spit his goat's milk into the fire. Even Toren smiled.

Tor held his hand up to silence the boys. Toren looked like he couldn't wait for his father to take his side. He was always the good son, already acting like a good farmer, like a man who had something to lose. But lately, their father hadn't been so safe-minded, had he? "I cannot allow you to join Vidar," Tor spoke soberly.

Erik wanted to smack the smile off Toren's privileged face.

"But I do think it's time you made your own way in this world," Tor surprised them. "It's time for you to go."

Erik was reminded of the shock he felt when the ice gave way beneath his feet, dropping him into the icy fjord. "Go where?"

"Father, if they go, how will we manage the farm? We can barely keep up with it now."

"Shut up, Toren. Everything will work out for you. Everybody wishes they had your problems."

"You shut up—you know nothing."

"Quiet," Tor hushed his sons. "I don't want to hear arguing. It's time for you to mature, now, and start living like the men you must...I mean, the men you have become." Erik peered into Tor's cold blue eyes nervously. This was a moment his stepmother had prepared him for his whole life; he needed to drink in everything his father had to say. "There's nothing for you here now, except trouble—no inheritance, no future. We need to prepare." He said it as if looking for the words in his cup. "No one can know what I am telling you now. If the Vikings find out your lives could be at stake." Somewhere deep inside Erik, a tear that had known this day was coming for his entire life welled up into his eye. He wiped it away before it made it to his cheek. Then as he swallowed the rest sank down into his chest and froze his heart like ice. He would not show weakness to his father, or his older brother.

"Father?" Toren asked, stoic as a soldier. "Is this because of the Viking?"

Tor scowled at the ceiling as if blaming the sunless sky. He put his powerful hand on Toren's shoulder. "You will leave in the spring."

"Not me, Father. I'm your shield man. I would never leave you or my home behind." Toren glared at his little brother as if he were acting so brave, as if marrying the most beautiful girl in town and inheriting the farm was a martyr's fate.

"I wish we'd never heard of that treasure," said Erik.

"This was never about you, or that chest. It is because

Vidar wants to take the empty throne to show his father what he is capable of. To do that, he needs me gone. He will try to kill me, holmgang or no. The Vikings will never leave here."

"Even more reason I will never leave," said Toren. "There are only three of them. We can protect our village until they leave in the spring — with or without Erik."

"There are more than three," said Magnus. "Even if we don't join Vidar, our friends already have. Just last month, the smith took on two new apprentices. He didn't do that to make more nails."

Erik eyed his brother. "Orri likes me. He used to tell me that if I joined them that I could be a great Viking. I think with his help I can influence Vidar."

Tor shook his head. "They will turn against you and me and anyone else who stands up to them."

"How do you know that, father?" asked Erik.

"Because it already happened! I have had to run from Olaf before, and when I did, my best friends hunted me like dogs after a red stag." Tor exhaled heavily. "Ragi's father has made arrangements with Jarl Adar. Apparently, he's been unifying the Sogn to fend off the Vikings. After the holmgang, no matter the outcome, you are all leaving to get his help. You too, Toren." Erik hated that he couldn't laugh in Toren's dour face. "You must keep this secret or we will all be dead before Erik and Magnus have the chance to see their souls." He looked at Toren. "That means you can't tell Anja." He turned to Magnus. "You can't tell Ragi." Then to Erik. "Not even Kiara. I'm not even telling your stepmother until just before the ceremony."

"I won't let you down, father," said Toren. "We will come back with ships and men and help unite the Sogn." Toren said it just like all the brave soldiers who'd never swung a sword. He'd never seen what a Viking like Ubbi could do with nothing more than a stick.

"No." said Tor. Erik enjoyed watching his brother cower

like a corrected pup. "None of you will make the same mistakes I did. After you return, you will sell this farm to Pedar or Jarl Adar and leave Norway. Whether Olaf or Adar is no matter, our gods have set this country on a path to war, and soon there will be no more villages left where men can be free from paying Valhalla's toll. It is the way of all things."

Somehow, witnessing Toren's fall made this day, which should have been the worst of Erik's life, a little brighter.

Toren just stared at his father with an eerie resolve. He was going to lose everything. The news should have broken him, but it didn't. He almost looked excited. Erik had seen him like that before when the roof on the barn had collapsed from the weight of snow. Erik and his father had cursed the old barn, and the cold. Erik even tried to convince his father to let it go until warmer weather. But not Toren. He just started working out all that needed to be done. Erik liked that look, and, in a way, felt better knowing his big brother was going to be with him on the trip he'd always figured he was destined to take alone.

Soon, Erik would get his soul and his father would face the giant. And win or lose, he'd be leaving the only home he'd ever known. Toren had the right look. There wasn't much time.

BLOOD AND SOULS

E rik looked at the sky to distract himself. It was just after noon on the winter solstice, the shortest day of the year, and although the stars still shone above in a sea of black, the mid-day sun was only offering a taste of its light as it skirted along the edge of the horizon. Erik winced as Magnus let out a loud whimper.

He did not turn to watch. Instead, he focused on the old owl that seemed to be looking back at him, too. Its head only turned once, toward the distant caw of a raven, then back, before preening the feathers under its wing. Erik's breathing quickened. It was his turn.

After seeing others receive their souls every year for as long as he could remember, he knew each step of the ceremony by heart. That's what they called it — receiving. Like he was to receive a gift, or a warm hug.

Knowing what was to come did not make it easier. Now that it was his turn, every step seemed excruciatingly precise, and slow, and his heart pounded with fear and excitement like a hammer against an anvil.

After emerging from the frozen snow for the third time, almost no blood remained on the sharp blade. Old Afi plunged the forearm-length seax back into the blue flames until a design hidden within the blackened iron emerged — its intricate pattern glowed orange as the coals.

Three times through the fire made the blade ceremonially clean. No one could remember why three times, but no one, especially those that felt its heat, ever forgot.

Erik looked toward his father, Tor and older brother, Toren, and receiving the nod, he quickly stripped off protective layers of cloak, coat, and shirt. His face grimaced like the others before him as the arctic wind bit him like a ravenous wolf. Goose bumps flew up his arms and down his neck until they covered his naked back and chest, his head snapping reflexively from the shock of the cold.

After a lifetime of his stepmother's nagging, never letting him leave the house without heavy constricting clothes to protect him from freezing to death even on the mildest Norwegian spring day, it seemed ironic now that she sanctioned a ceremony that forced boys and girls to strip to their bare backs on the day Winter's sting seemed to have the most bite.

For a fleeting moment, Erik pitied the girls also coming of age on this day. The Wind's invisible blade cut the thoughts of seeing them take off their shirts bitterly from his consciousness. Recently, he hadn't seemed able to think of anything else, his hyperactive imagination etching crude pictures of the moment in his brain while he slept.

He always woke up at the moment the girls pulled their undershirts up just above their belly buttons. Although ultimately unsatisfying, this distraction had been a good one. It was the only thing Erik had to counter his fear of the coming blade.

The girls, he thought, seemed to have no similar distraction. Every time a girl brought up her fear of the knife, one of the boys would repeat an old joke that was only clever to their hormone laden brains, usually something about this whole ritual just being a way for old men to see them with their shirts off. The girl's response was the more personal attack, often responding with the same old retort, that, if they had to take off their pants, Frost's bite would starve to death, or something like that.

All the jokes he had made to Anja about having her chest

exposed seemed childish now as the bite of an arctic breeze cut into him. As bad as it was for him to endure exposure to the subzero cold without a shirt, he assumed it must be much more painful for the girls. He actually pitied them.

Then, his attention found a singular focus. A new shiver clawed its way up his spine as he watched Afi pull the knife's glowing, orange blade from the fire. Long tongues of blue flame licked at it voraciously, as if afraid it was the last time it would taste its iron. It wasn't.

There weren't many of them this year. For five it was already over, Magnus among them. Erik looked back one last time at the others still in line, standing shoulder to shoulder, waiting their turn. Eleven would see their souls for the first time this year, this day. And all of them would prefer to leave them where they lay, hidden deep inside. First, he noticed Anja's chest. It was pumping in and out frantically with shallow breaths.

Forcing his gaze upward, he caught her beautiful eyes, only today they looked wild with anticipation, almost screaming. Next to her he saw her half-brother Ragi, his face frozen in fear and cold, eyes red and tearing. The others blurred. Erik cleared his eyes, the thin layer of water freezing on the back of his hand.

The elder was saying something, but his words were muted by the fear of that first cut. In his head he repeated phrases over and over. "Don't show fear. It'll be over soon. Stand strong." But his thoughts betrayed him, allowing fear and doubt to smash his mantra like a hammer crushing a chunk of ice.

At first, all he could feel was a surge of heat as he stared into the old man's cold, blue eyes.

Don't look down. Stay strong. Don't show fear.

Then, intense heat, intense pressure, intense pain.

Stay strong. Don't cry. Owwwch. Owww. Aaaahhhhgg. Don't cry. Don't cry.

The pain chased the thoughts around and around inside

Erik's head. His eyes welled with tears, but none fell, and he made no sound. Not a whimper. The old man nodded his head, and Erik put his hand up. Then the old man pushed it to his chest, stuck the tip of the hot blade into the wound, and *pop*, the thing fell into his palm.

It was over.

The old man held up the still sizzling blade, before starting the ritual cleaning all over again. Erik looked at the gory ornament in his blood-stained, shivering hand. His own soul ring freshly cut from his chest.

The elder stabbed the knife into the clean, white snow three times, staining it red with Erik's blood. Then he carefully laid the knife back into the fire, the flames immediately going to work, purifying the blade, coloring it a glowing orange once again. Somehow, Erik pried his eyes off his ring long enough to glance down the line, a weak attempt to assure his friends they'd be alright. But as he stared back at his soul, he shuddered. *Poor saps.*

The old man brought Erik back to himself. Looking him in the eye, he spoke to him—only to him, as was the custom.

This ring is the tether to your soul,
Yours and yours alone,
Neither flesh nor of bone,
The Maker's instrument,
Revealing the world and the heart,
Never taken, only given,
Ruined, but not destroyed,
Ring eternal. Protect it.
Place no liens against it.
Play it loud, and play it often,
May it never be a burden.
It is precious.

Like the others before him, Erik did not reply. He was lost in the ring, that thing that only blood and pain and scars could reveal.

"Aaaauuooww!" Erik howled, as the Elder drove the

glowing blade back against the cut, searing the wound it had just made shut. Out of instinct, he slammed a hand against the elder's arm to push the seax away, but Old Afi was surprisingly strong and had been ready with his other arm firmly around Erik's back.

Blood boiled. The wound smoldered and sizzled as fire seared it shut, stopping the flow of blood that had painted a crimson line down his front, even dripping into the bottom of his left boot. The sickly smell of his own burning flesh filled the air, overwhelming Erik's senses. Not sure if it was the pain or the smell, he felt like he was going to vomit, all pretense of keeping it together during the ceremony about to be spilled all over the elder's fur-lined boots.

While Erik struggled with pain and nausea, the elder flung the seax into the fresh snow between his left foot and the next victim's right. Then old Afi reached down and grabbed a handful of the snow stained red with Erik's own blood and slapped it onto his chest.

"Hmmph!" Erik let more pain slip out as the sting of the impact sent a chill up his spine and broke what remained of his self-induced hypnosis.

He didn't hear the rest of the ceremony, forgetting all about topless girls, the sound of vomit splashing on the snow, and the smell that followed.

He barely flinched when he heard the whimpers of fear and yelps of pain escaping from the others' hardened exteriors as the blade that had haunted his dreams for so long now escorted them into adulthood.

He'd hear about the details later. His older brother seemed to be enjoying every slice of the ceremony, empathizing for his friends with exaggerated winces and contrived cringes. He would fill them in on all the pitiful and hilarious details before they recovered, that was certain.

No, for now at least, Erik had lost interest in the ceremonial suffering. He just stood there staring at his new possession. A perfect circle taken from his chest. Too big to be worn on a finger but not big enough to fit on anything else, it would have to reside near where it was taken — on a string hanging close to his heart, the same place his parents and everyone else in the village kept theirs.

The only purpose this ornament had, that he could see, was that if he held it up close to his eye, his soul could put a frame around the entire world.

Erik had seen his older brother's ring a hundred times. He used to catch him staring at it all the time. The affect wore off though, and lately he'd kept it under his shirt like most of the other adults. Now, for the first time, he understood his brother's earlier obsession.

Somehow, although seeing it for the first time, he felt like he knew his own ring. It looked like everyone else's, but he recognized this one. It was his, and he was drawn to it, tethered to it by an unseen force. Looking at it now for the first time, his soul became more perplexing to him. He stared at that empty, peppered white frame and was entranced by what it could mean.

Why was it there?

"Here, put your shirt on before Runa pinches a hole in my arm." It was his father that broke the trance this time. "She's worried you'll freeze to death and won't leave me alone until you're clothed, so let's get on with it. That's right. Now this. Here, take this, too." After handing him undershirt and overshirt, he gave him a long leather braided loop. "Put this end through your ring and wear it around your neck for safe keeping. It'll hang near your heart, where we probably should have left it in the first place." Then Tor handed Erik his rabbit fur-lined long coat. "You can stare at it for the rest of your life, if you want, but for now, do me a favor, and put this on or I'll never hear the end of it."

Then he tossed a belt around Erik's waist and began to tie it tight. His father put his powerful hands on Erik's shoulders and looked at him solemnly.

"That ring signifies full rights as a man, and responsibilities." His eyes turned to wet pools, and his left one began to twitch. Then he smiled and put his arm around Erik. "I am proud of you. You have grown into a great young man, and the world is yours, now."

Time stopped for Erik as he inhaled his father's words. They were the highest and most important he'd ever received, from a man he'd nearly worshiped his entire life, a man not prone to showing sentiment toward his own.

"Now let's get over to the hall, ja? The smell of this morning's sacrifices cooking all day has me starving." Tor put his arm around Erik's shoulder, and they gathered the rest of the family and headed for the hall.

Like all others who went through the ceremony, this event changed Erik, and he would spend the rest of his life trying to comprehend what it, and the ring, was all about.

GETTING SOME REST

"Tor!" Pedar caught him sneaking out of the hall. "Leaving already?"

Tor looked back to check on his boys. "Do me a favor, and get Vidar as drunk as you can tonight."

Pedar seemed confused; then he caught on. "I'll tell Anja to keep his cup full. Hopefully he'll sleep through the holmgang tomorrow and everything will go back to normal."

"You mean Kiara."

"What?" This time Pedar was definitely confused.

"You said you'd have Anja keep his cup full. I'm not sure Toren would like that too much."

Pedar was slow to answer. "I think with the ring ceremony this afternoon and the holmgang tomorrow, I'm a little out of sorts."

"Alright, I've got some things to take care of; then I'm going to try to get some sleep." Tor started off again, then stopped. "Do me a favor, Pedar, and keep the boys out of trouble. I couldn't keep them in tonight, you understand. It being Erik's ring day and all."

Pedar nodded, but he did look out of sorts. "Are you planning to send your boys off to meet with Jarl Adar?"

Tor checked over Pedar's shoulder to ensure no one else could hear. "Do the Vikings know?" He sidled up close to Pedar, who smelled like he'd shampooed his beard with pine soap.

"No," said Pedar. "Not from me, anyway."

"Who told you?" Tor's mind raced. If Vidar knew that he was sending his sons off to form alliances, they would be in grave danger.

Pedar put his hand up, as if it would calm Tor's pounding heart. That kind of thing always made Tor more agitated. "Ragi saw Magnus coming home with a broken shield. He told me, but no one else," Pedar assured him. Then he sidled up to Tor as if he was scolding his maid. "How could you plan something like this without including me? I made the deal."

"Deal?" Tor stood up straighter. He liked having little Pedar stand up to him about as much as he liked the idea of sending his sons away in midwinter. "What did you do?"

"Nothing." Pedar puffed-out his chest and tried to inhale his belly. "I have no authority to do anything. But neither do you." He wiped beads of sweat and nerves from his bald head.

"Don't you think that things have changed now?" Tor asked. "Regardless of what happens tomorrow?"

"If you're sending your sons, then Ragi's going, too." Pedar started explaining. "He will represent my family's interests."

"Pedar," said Tor, "this isn't about that."

"Oh, come on, Tor," said Pedar. "This is about choosing our allies. It's about advantage and power, and I will not be left out of it." Pedar let his shoulders fall forward again as he focused on Tor's left eye, which Tor could sense had begun to twitch. Pedar took a deep breath and started again in a calm whisper. "Anyone who joins this village to the jarl will have a lot to gain, and I won't be left out—for my son's sake, or yours." It was Pedar's eyes that were twitching now.

"Alright." Tor took a deep, calming breath. "Toren leads, though. It will be dangerous. None of them have ever traveled so far this time of year. Have Ragi packed and ready to leave as soon as the holmgang is over."

"Ragi is already packed, and he will lead himself. I will not have him showing up at Jarl Adar's as a subordinate to Toren."

Tor did not have time for Pedar or his politics. "Fine. I have the boys packing light. Magnus can help Ragi get the weight down. Too much gear will just slow them. It's going to be dangerous enough just getting there this time of year." Cold air poured into the entry as Tor opened the outside door.

"What happens if you lose?" Pedar shuddered. "You promised your sons to Vidar."

"Regardless of how it ends — win or lose, live or die — we send the boys. My sons will not break their backs rowing Vidar's ships — or his father's." Tor plodded toward home with a sack full of food and a heavy heart. Today had been a big day for Erik. Tomorrow was a big day for everyone.

WEIGHT OF THE SOUL

V idar ambled through the hall as if the sacrifices that morning had been made for him. He nodded and raised a cup to each guest as he passed. Everything he did had become a spectacle, drawing attention like a fish jumping in a placid lake. With every step he made a splash, and a larger and larger ripple.

With a wide smile, he approached the table of young folk celebrating and put his cup down in front of Kiara. "Get me a refill, will you, dear?"

Erik sneered as he watched her shoulders fall, slinking away from the table to do as she was told. The sweet scent of mead wafted across the table on the giant's breath as he waited.

"Ragi said you might have something to say to me today, Erik, something that might be able to help you, and your father."

Toren glared at Erik, and Erik's eyes cut to Magnus, who shook his head toward Ragi.

"No," said Erik, "I'm not sure what you're talking about."

Vidar scowled at Orri, and Orri at Ragi.

Ragi looked like he might piss himself and hid his face in his cup of glogg, a woman's drink if there ever was one.

Vidar's attention slid back to Erik. "Didn't you want to be a Viking? I was told you would be offering me your ring."

Toren looked at his brother as if he was going to throw

his drink in his face if he didn't move this Viking along.

"No." Erik peered into his soul ring. "I just got it today, I don't think I know what I want to do with it just yet." Erik emptied his beer, put down his cup, and steadied his eyes on Vidar's, thinking he would just stare him away. Inside, he felt like he might lose the contents of his stomach onto the planked floor. No doubt that floor had been painted with beer soured in the stomachs of better men than he on their ring day. Someday — he burped — he was going to stab Ragi in the face with an icicle for this.

Vidar began to laugh to himself. "You'd be well served to consider giving it to me." As the smile wore off, Vidar spoke quieter, more thoughtfully. "If you did, we might be able to save your father from a lot of embarrassment tomorrow. Or worse."

"My father's honor is what's at stake tomorrow. There's only one way to repair that," said Toren.

Vidar kept his attention on Erik. "Forget about your father and your brother. Join me, like your friends." He pulled the leather thong full of soul rings from under his shirt. Some of them were stained with blood, cut fresh that morning.

Erik looked around the room for the other boys who'd received their rings that day.

Vidar stepped between him and the hall. "You know as well as I do that I'm the only one who can rescue you from your..." — pausing, he looked high and low around the hall as if searching for some redeeming quality that might temper his words — "your circumstances."

Toren tried to sound unimpressed. "How many of those rings belong to dead men?"

Vidar did not let Erik get distracted. "These men, and even some of your friends, pledged themselves to me because they knew I could make them more than they could become on their own. And I can do the same for you." Vidar shifted his gaze to Toren. "What is here for your younger brother? You are the eldest son—are you not?"

Erik's brother tried to keep his face as chiseled stone, not wanting Vidar to know he was speaking to his very soul.

Vidar smiled as if he knew he had found a weakness. "How could you understand? Everything your father has is yours. Your way is easy. But I do. I am the younger son, and so is Erik. He must make his own way in this world. He has no inheritance. Magnus is the same. He already has everything he'll ever get from his absent father. What wealth did your father leave you, young Magnus?"

Magnus looked down at his still blood-stained, hollow soul.

"It's easy for the eldest son to tell you what you should do. He has Anja, already a woman ready to wed." He looked at the girl, lingering. Toren began to stand. "Calm down, boy! You know what I say is true. You have a new house waiting for you. You don't need to adorn your dirty ring in gold to impress her." The giant cleared his brow of sweat with a quivering hand. "But these two have nothing to offer a woman. They will have to make something of themselves before they can marry. I've lived in Anja's house. The dowry she will bring to your marriage will be more than Erik or Magnus will ever know if they stay here."

The giant looked up to the ceiling. "Am I the only one telling these boys what they already know to be true?" Then he looked at Erik, and then Magnus, too. "You will have to make your own way. I'm sure your father has told you that much." He looked at their faces before going on. Without a blade he had still found a way to cut them. "My men live a life of adventure, not one of cleaning up after goats. With me a man can have more wealth by the time he is twenty than Toren will ever see from your father." He stared through Toren. "You may think you have everything figured out right now, eldest son, but you too should consider the Viking life as well. What your father has can easily be taken away before any of it comes to you."

Toren looked at Anja's worried face, then at Erik and Magnus to see past this man's silver tongue.

Vidar was visibly shaking. "Kiara! Where is that girl?" Then he reached in his coat and pulled out a flask and gripped it so hard his knuckles turned white. "Ever since I was left behind in England, ever since I found myself stranded on foreign soil without the support of my father, whom I would've followed to the ends of the earth, I realized I was on my own. He had nothing for me." He looked around frantically, "Kiara! Where have you been?" He grabbed the pitcher and the cup out of her shaking hands. She had been crying. "I think I'll make a gift of you to Orri. Maybe he can make some use of you."

Erik glanced at Kiara who looked like she might cry again, and he took her hand. Then he sternly shook his head to let her know that he would never let that happen.

With hands quaking, Vidar filled his cup and took a swallow of the mead, winced, then took a swig from the flask. After hiding it back into his coat, he filled his cup with mead and emptied it once more. "Again." He pushed the cup toward Kiara and turned his head down. His breathing slowed, and his hands steadied.

As soon as she pushed the cup his way, he grabbed it up and emptied it again. After a few seconds, he regained his composure. Then he smiled. The wide gap between Vidar's front teeth made the giant seem almost friendly. It was disarming—the power a genuine smile could have. But it didn't seem like it was for them. It looked like it was for a return to clarity—the smile was for Vidar.

Vidar exhaled heavily and continued as if everything was normal. Erik glanced over to see if Toren had noticed. He had.

"Anything I expected was my folly, not my father's." Vidar seemed to be talking to himself now. "He never promised me anything more than he promised to any of his men." He took another drink. "What's his is his, and if he's lucky enough to hold onto it then it will all pass to Egil.

Vidar raised his voice. "My elder brother slaves at my father's side, always fearful the old man will lose what isn't even his yet. And so did I. But no longer." He pushed his cup in front of Kiara to fill again. "Landing here has awakened my senses, and I see the world for what it truly is. I must learn from my father." Vidar's eyes had grown distant. "To be like him I must leave him." Vidar's eyes sharpened, and he lifted them from his drink. "When my father hears of my triumphs on the lips of his men, then he will respect his youngest son." He confided in Erik as if they had been just two farmers talking over a couple of cups of beer. "It's time I lift my sword for myself, not for my father, nor my brother's inheritance. It's time we live for ourselves."

LEG BREAKER

Maybe it was the familiarity he showed with Anja in front of his brother, maybe it was the beer, or maybe receiving his soul had also made his balls drop, but Erik reached up and tugged on Vidar's shirt.

"Vidar, your words are very touching, indeed." Erik smiled as he took another drink. "Before you leave," —he winked at Toren—"why don't you show me what my father is up against?"

Vidar turned to Erik, unamused. "Let me tell you boys something your father should have taught you long ago. Never touch a man to get his attention, unless of course, you are a woman." Vidar smiled a gap-toothed grin toward Anja. "Do you understand, farmer's son?"

Toren put his arm around her and squeezed tight. Though a noble gesture, Toren thinking he could protect Anja from Vidar was like a rooster pissing in front of a chicken coop to try to keep a wolf away.

"Vidar," Erik hugged Magnus wildly before raising his cup and taking another drink. "Come show us how strong you are."

The giant put his hands down on the table. "You wouldn't be the first one to try me, boy."

"I don't want to try you, sir." Erik removed the leather thong from around his neck, slipped his newly garnered soul onto the table and slapped his hand down to settle the ring before it took to rolling. "I will give it to you if you can pick it up." Erik had never known the limits of his own ego, and now he knew it did not end at eight feet tall. It was safe to say that he was pleased with himself, again.

Vidar clenched his jaw and his face turned a shade of red that caused Erik to sober and reconsider whether he should've had that last drink. Then Vidar started to laugh. "Ahh, you have spirit," he said. "You're going to make a good Viking—I swear to Odin you are. It must run in the family." Then he winked at Anja.

Toren had been sitting quietly, but at that last insult he started to stand. Anja pulled him in tight to mask any hint of an advance on the giant. She cast Erik an angry look, as if Vidar hadn't been the one who started all of this in the first place.

Who did she think she was anyway?

Everyone at the table leaned in closer. They knew that the weight of a soul cannot be borne by another unless it is freely given.

"I know you think you're testing me." Vidar furrowed his heavy brow. "But you're really testing yourself. And I like that. I can work with a man who is brave. You do not seem to fear me as the others do," — Vidar looked teasingly at Toren—"maybe as you should."

"You are right to not fear my fists, for I do not want to hurt you." He filled Erik's empty cup. "Fear me because of what I represent, a man who can open your eyes to so much more than you have in this place. I do not challenge your father—I challenge everything his beautiful little village symbolizes, an anchor far heavier than that soul you so foolishly put on the table as if it's a toy for a boy to play with. You do not respect its power, nor its worth. There are those that would have you dead that they might have that ring." Vidar looked at the young faces and exhaled as if wanting to start over. "I am merely a man trying to get my strength back and get home, where the world can be mine again."

Vidar smiled at Erik, then reached down to pick up the ring. It did not move. Somewhat dramatically, the goliath stuck out his tongue as he tried putting his thumbnail under it to pry it up off the table, but it did not shift.

Erik hated him for trying to make him feel small. It worked. *He's patronizing me.* He hoped his father would stick his axe between Vidar's big, gapped teeth.

"Well, now you know. I am just a man," Vidar smiled. "Like your father, I can never take your ring from you. But if you ever want to be free, just come find me. Put that ugly trinket in my hand, and I'll show you there's more to seek in this world than just gold and silver."

The giant leaned down and put his face in front of Erik's, so close Erik could smell the sweet mead on his breath. "I don't know what to do about you. You're brave, I'll give you that. Whether it's from being principled, stubborn or stupid, well, only time will tell. May not even matter."

Vidar put one of his large mitts on the tabletop next to the ring, then grabbed one of its legs with the other. Smiling, his face tensed, with a large crooked vein bulging along his temple, he gave a quick and mighty yank. Crack! The sound echoed through the hall as the thick leg snapped like a dry twig. With the power of his smile and a strong grip, the giant easily broke what had stood firm for generations.

Erik could only watch as the table crashed to the floor with a force that shook the hall's foundations. Cups flew, and beer spilled, and amidst the chaos, Erik's soul fell, first bouncing, then rolling along the floor toward the door. The ring seemed no different than one forged in fire rather than inside the kiln of Erik's chest.

Erik knocked Ragi and Magnus off the bench as he lunged and chased it down to the floor. He was single-minded, focused, forgetting all else for that brief moment. When he found his ring, he picked it up and held it to his heart, surprised at his own reaction to seeing it leave his reach.

To him it was not heavy. It was everything.

Erik lay there, belly in a pool of spit and beer and mead, elbow and jaw burning from a lunge to the floor he didn't remember making. He was soaked, embarrassed, and burning with a hatred for the Viking in a way he hadn't known before.

FIELD OF PLAY

T he lines had been drawn, the shields had been made, and the weapons were sharp enough to shear sheep. Vidar had chosen Ice Breaker, Tor's own sword, the one he had gotten from his father. That was the first cut.

The other weapon Vidar chose was a seax he got from his host, Pedar. The only time Pedar dulled that blade was to pull it from its sheath so he could use it as a mirror. Tor himself had honed it to a razor's edge the week Pedar came home with it. Though untested, it would be a fine cutter, but Tor doubted Vidar would use it. To choose it was a show of confidence, for even Pedar knew there was no honor in winning a holmgang with a seax.

Tor's bones felt very old lately, and he loosened them up by swinging his old two-handed wood axes from side to side. His cracked rib still bit his side with every stroke, as if the fight at the harvest festival had been just last week. After he realized his warm-up was not helping, he focused on something that could.

He prayed in whispers as he methodically ran cuttings of pine along the patterns he'd carved in the handles of his axes and shields. The pine was heated over the fire to draw out the frozen resin. Then he worked it in until the tack stitched his hands to the axe and shield handle's sweet spot for balance and power.

"What 'ave you there, Tor? Planning on cutting the wood for the fight's before the fight's even started?" scoffed

Halfdan the butcher. Tor noticed his soul ring was out on his coat like Erik or one of the other young ones that just got theirs cut out.

But there was something different that made Tor want to test the axe on his old friend. Halfdan's ring framed a shiny silver coin straight out of the giant's treasure box. Tor saw a lot of rings exposed and glimmering about his neighbors' necks and could only assume this audacious display meant they'd already been bought.

"I wonder, Halfdan," said Tor, "does that coin mean if I win today that you won't help me make the Vikings leave in the spring? Or does it mean you've sold Vidar that nice piece of land you've got down by the river so he can start building a summer home?"

Like a good dog, Halfdan huffed but took a good look around as he started back over to his master, Vidar. No doubt he was sent over to look at Tor's weapons. Tor hoped Vidar had paid him double for stabbing his neighbor of thirteen years in the back because there wasn't much for him to report. No one got what they paid for when dealing with Halfdan, unless they were asking for half the meat and twice the fat, or fish that was only half cured, or steaks cut from a horse that was already dead. What would he tell him, that Tor was using axes and shields?

Of the shields Magnus made, Tor picked his three specifically for their balance and weight. They were left unpainted and unadorned, except each were marked with coal dust, numbered 1, 2, and 3, heaviest to lightest. Tor figured if he made it to the third shield, he'd be too tired to carry the heavier, and hoped Vidar would be too tired to break it anyway.

He personally reworked the handles of the shields and axes and had Magnus reforge the heads to narrow the blade and draw out short beards so they would fare better at breaking shields and arms than their original purpose of cutting branches and downing trees. Magnus gave similar treatments to his own two-handed axe, and Toren and Erik's hatchets, in anticipation of having more trouble with men than trees after they left the village.

Ivar, the villages most talented carpenter, made Vidar's shields. Before the Viking arrived, Ivar had helped Tor work on Toren and Anja's house. Now he stood with the Vikings examining his handiwork, wearing a gold arm ring. Like Magnus, he had no experience making shields, but he was a master craftsman, and it looked like he had already become an expert in the craft. Tor could imagine that he'd already been consigned to help fix their ship.

Ubbi was leaning against two of Vidar's shields, and Orri had one strapped to his back, making him look like a turtle with that bald, tattooed head of his. Each was as big as a wagon wheel and painted red as blood with a black serpent around the iron boss. Shields that big would cut down on Tor's striking zone and be much different from what he faced when sparring with his sons. But there would still be plenty of Vidar to draw blood from. No shield could completely hide that monster.

At Pedar's house, Magnus heard Vidar brag that he had Ivar make over twenty before he got him exactly what he wanted.

Vidar was warming up against his boy army, the one Erik had helped raise and Ubbi had beaten and trained with his bloody sticks. Although some of those boys had just received their souls the day before alongside Erik, none had them displayed. Instead, they wore silver arm rings over the right arm of their new blood-red coats. Tor recognized the design of the arm rings — they were fashioned like the snake on the shield. It was Jörmungandr, the serpent that strangled the world while it chased its own tail. Vidar's father had the world serpent as his symbol, too — only his was a yellow serpent on a black field. The difference was a statement. Vidar had no intention of going back to serve in his father's army. He was starting his own, and he was starting it there.

This display was an organized effort, of course. It wasn't as if half the village randomly decided that the holmgang would be the appropriate time to show off their new wealth and allegiance. This was Vidar's way of showing he was already the new champion here. Regardless of the outcome of this duel, Vidar had already won.

As half the village polished their rings in public, like girls showing off new bridal gifts, some younger men who would be warriors, those who just a month before had barely proven their ability to properly use a rake, now bore their own new shields on their backs, looking less comfortable with the appendage than Orri the turtle wearing Vidar's wagon wheel.

250

THE HOLMGANG

Tor needed to get his head straight. He needed to protect his sons, and the gods knew he could use the three gold coins he would get for payment. Little as it was, the winner of the holmgang always received a payment. It was a formal way to show the honor debt had been paid and force the loser to publicly acknowledge he'd forfeited his right for revenge. If Tor won, he could give Toren, Erik, and Magnus one each as insurance on their journey. He hated to send the boys off without something, and Vidar's coin would spend well in the Sogn.

Tor's shield man was his oldest son, Toren. Tor spent little enough time training him for the job, but Toren knew what to do. He was to hand his father the next replacement shield for each one Vidar broke. First, shield one, then two, then three. That was it. The shield man was not to interfere beyond ensuring their man was armed and shielded between breaks in the fighting.

Instead of training himself, Tor spent most of his time focused on Toren, Erik, and even Magnus when he could make it. Tor had shown his boys how the sword fighting games they'd played with sticks their entire lives — the ones that cracked fingers, shoulders, and shins, combined with muscle memory they had honed following their father's seemingly ridiculous rule that they only use hatchets when chopping firewood — had done much to prepare them for actual combat.

Tor knew his family would never be safe as long as Vidar

was alive. He needed first blood to end the fight, and he planned to make it come from Vidar's shaggy throat. He had to kill the giant. He might have to kill Ubbi and Orri, too, depending on their response. But right now, he had to focus his energy on Vidar. He would do what should've been done the day the Vikings arrived.

All of Tor's shields were made of linden wood wrapped in goat rawhide and centrally mounted oak handles, very similar to the way his father taught him. Except for using goat. Their small hides cost his shields valuable size, but it was all he had.

Because of the power of Vidar, shield one was the thickest, and edge-wrapped with an iron band made from what was left over after Magnus made the bosses. The problem was Tor only had enough iron to make two. The third shield had a wooden boss, like the practice shields. The iron needed for those bosses alone cost his farm his best shovel and a garden rake. The plan was that if Vidar broke shield one, Magnus would rush to repurpose its boss onto shield three, hopefully before Vidar broke two. The shields were plain, but the axes were sharp and polished to a mirrored edge.

Ubbi hefted one of the red and black shields into Vidar's right hand, and the giant spun Ice Breaker with practice strokes that were long and strong — definitely shield splitters. If the giant got a clean shot Tor was likely to lose his shield with a single blow — if not his arm.

The fight would end on first blood, a common rule put in place to avoid holmgangs from being just a public way to murder a weaker man under the protection of the law. But that did not mean men did not die in these types of duels.

Bor Jonsen etched lines in the snow outlining the boundaries where the two would play at war. Bor drew a circle with a rake tied to a rope, the other end held by his son, Bjornie, in the center, who spun on his heels as his father walked the line.

There with their parents to see the spectacle, children at play held hands and spun each other around to carve out their own little arenas. The older ones held pushing contests to see who would be the last one standing inside. The biggest always won.

Tor bent down, picked up a handful of snow, and put some of it in his mouth, then ran the rest across his forehead and along the back of his neck. It was cold and dry, and steamed when it touched his fiery skin.

It was weird to see Old Erik standing in as the new village law-speaker, just one more reminder why Tor had to win. If the priest stayed gothi there would be more rituals, more sacrifices to the gods, and less meat for the table.

Old Erik stated the rules for all to hear. This was a required practice yet wholly unnecessary. The village had been rehashing the rules, even asking Old Afi for clarification, near every day since the challenge was made. Even though he had never seen one before, Bor had taken it upon himself to make sure everyone he met understood how this holmgang would work. He even visited Halfdan's shop in the village to correct the butcher, to keep him from continuing to spread gossip about rules that just didn't exist.

The rules were simple and clear and had not been changed since the initial agreement. Each man could bring three shields and their choice of two weapons. The duel ended at first blood or request for mercy. Shield men were there to help change broken shields and step in to protect the challengers from bloodlust or revenge blows after either man claimed mercy or victory. They did not fight, and until there was a claim, they stayed out of the circle for fear of disqualification. The holmgang could only be stopped by the gothi.

When Old Erik stepped out of the ring, Tor noticed something odd. Vidar's shield wasn't wrapped in rawhide, not even leather. Ivar the master carpenter must not have been able to get his head beyond the wood, and Vidar probably didn't think it mattered with the boat hull he was using for a shield.

Tor and Vidar stepped inside the circle.

From behind the massive shield, Vidar raised Ice Breaker high, it's iron edge sharp and glinting in the sun — and then he brought it smashing down. Had it not been for the iron ring wrapping the shield's edge, the very first stroke would've taken Tor's arm off on its way through. The giant rained down blows like he was hacking branches off a tree. Tor's plain shield splintered with every heavy impact.

Tor staggered back and propped his shield up with the length of his axe. This additional spine gave it added strength and Tor more control. He braced himself as Vidar once again brought down his sword. The shield absorbed and deflected the powerful blows that sounded like claps of thunder, each sending a ringing through Tor's arm and down his spine as if he were a clanging cymbal.

Vidar's face tightened in frustration, and he changed tactics, alternating blows from sword to shield. The first great slap from Vidar's shield sent Tor flying onto his back, sliding half his body outside of the circle.

"This man is truly a coward," scoffed Vidar. "Make him stay in the ring." The giant's breath was a white fog. The young boar was winded, not that he hadn't earned it, for he had sent a barrage of heavy blows down on Tor as hard and fast as he'd ever felt before.

That first shield and the initial flurry lasted less than a minute.

Tor looked at his shield — Vidar had turned it to pulp. When he raised his arm for a hand getting to his feet, half of shield one flopped to one side, hinged on its goat hide wrapping. That skin was the only thing that kept it, and his body, from being splintered into a hundred pieces in the snow. Tor swung his axe for the first time when he knocked his cramping hand free from the wilted shield's handle.

Toren quickly grabbed what was left of it and gave it to Magnus so he could start repurposing the boss. Tor's head was spinning, but he forced himself to focus. He had to figure this out.

The next two shields didn't have an iron ring protecting the edge. If he let Vidar drop blows down on the edges like that again then the second shield wouldn't last long enough for Magnus to get the iron boss onto shield three and it was going to be a quick day. Tor eased back to his feet. He shook the feeling back into his arm as he whispered to his son through a cloud of heavy smoke.

"Shield two."

As his son handed him his second shield, Tor exhaled slowly and steadily to calm his heart and breathing. He had to buy some time. "Fire the handle," he said. "I need a better grip."

Toren warmed the resin along the handle over the fire, then handed his father the second shield. "Aagghh!" Tor grimaced as he dropped his tormentor. The iron boss had roasted the knuckles on his left hand, and he punched the snow for relief. The ice cold was soothing, and the pain helped him focus. This was no time to roll over.

Vidar paced back and forth like a frothing, wild animal, glaring at Tor as if intimidation was in play. It wasn't. Tor would stick to his plan.

Tor tapped the inside of the boss with numb fingers. Ironically, it was there to protect his hand. Then he remembered, shield two's boss had been a tight fit. The whole shield was lighter, no iron wrap and not quite as thick as the first. It wouldn't last a barrage like the first one, but neither would he.

Toren began to whisper advice in his father's ear, but Tor pushed him aside and raged into an offensive.

Tor swung the axe hard across his body, aiming for Vidar's sword hand. The giant backed up and twisted to throw his shield to his weak side. Tor swung through and then back across to the underside of Vidar's shield, hoping to catch him in the leg.

Although he went in with aspirations of taking the giant's head, cutting off one of Vidar's toes would be first blood enough, at this point.

With a sweeping backhand, Vidar came across his chest with his heavy shield and planted it center mass across Tor's. The speed created a howling wind as if from a North Sea storm. Tor slipped but stayed on his feet, running in a wide circle toward Vidar's weak side. By the time he gained his footing, his back was turned. Quickly, he spun around. Sliding to one knee to decrease his exposure, Tor raised shield two just in time to absorb a hammer blow from the Viking's sword.

There was no deflection. The edge of shield two felt the full brunt of the giant's power. There was a loud *crack* as the sword made its cut. Tor saw daylight as shield two split.

The giant cried in anger as he tried to wrench the blade from where the boss had stopped its progress. The blade stopped just shy of stripping Tor of his fingers, its tip a handbreadth away from his left eye.

Tor did not hesitate. Taking his long-handled axe around the front of his shield, he hooked its beard across Vidar's blade, then cranked down hard on the handle. The action levered the tip of the sword skyward and away from his face before the giant thought to lean against its pommel and pierce Tor through to the back of his skull. When Tor cranked the sword tip up its handle wrenched down, slapping the giant's knuckles into the bottom of the shield and pulling him off balance and down to one knee. Vidar howled in anger and pain, then stood, pulling Tor to his feet.

Vidar's face contorted as he jerked back and forth to free his sword. Tor growled in pain as he clutched the shield's handle with a cramping hand, the inside of the iron boss raking his burned knuckles with every slip of his feet. At the mercy of the merciless, Tor skated back and forth across the circle until the snow turned to mud. With each yank the Viking made on his sword, the tip sawed closer and closer to Tor's head, but before it could make a cut, Tor dropped his full weight down on his axe, its beard an iron hook. Tor's full weight slid down Ice Breaker to the guard. Each time Vidar's knuckles rapped into the shield the sound echoed like an enemy pounding at the door.

Finally realizing what was happening, Vidar drove forward and dropped his full weight across Tor's shield, pinning him down into the snow. Tor heard something crack under Vidar's weight, but it wasn't any of his bones. He was helpless and blind. His shield covered his face like the lid of a casket. All Vidar had to do was pull out his seax and stab Tor's exposed legs.

To make sure Vidar kept his attention off the seax, Tor pushed up hard on his axe to try to catch the stubborn oaf across jaw. It was the only thing he could do.

Vidar screamed down defiantly at Tor through the shield's crack, then put his knee on it, crushing the air from Tor's lungs like water from a sponge as he struggled to get to his feet. Vidar slammed his heavy left boot down on shield two, pinning Tor deeper into the snow until his back found the frozen earth. With hard, downward thrusts Vidar's boot batted Tor against the cold ground like a child bouncing on his parents' bed.

Finally, Vidar slammed down his right foot on the shield as if jumping on a table, and with a jerk of the handle and a stomp of both feet the shield snapped in two. The giant raised the captive sword like Arthur freeing Excalibur from the stone, the king from one of Kiara's favorite stories.

With both feet, the giant surfed both pieces of Tor's shield down either side of his chest. As the weight left his chest, Tor managed to draw in enough breath.

"Shield!" He coughed out.

The giant growled and stood over Tor, as if considering

whether to drop his blade or his shield across his buried opponent's face. But at the word, Toren, the shield man, tripped and skated into the circle and fell against Vidar in his hurry, knocking the giant angrily aside. Magnus was still hammering away to attach the iron boss onto the third shield.

Vidar stared at the boy, and Tor's heart stopped. He could read those thoughts. Vidar was considering whether he should drop his cold blade through both their necks, starting with the son. Ubbi ran inside, but the giant stopped him cold, planting his lightly scratched wagon wheel of a shield in the tongueless Vikings chest.

"Is there no justice in this village? His man is not allowed to interfere!" Vidar huffed. The struggle had taken a lot out of him.

Then Old Erik stepped up to Vidar. "This needs to be done the right way. Show yourself the bigger man."

Vidar scanned the onlookers for support, but the field was quietly watching as Toren helped his father flounder to dig himself out.

Tor heard "Mercy!" murmuring through the crowd. "This needs to stop," came from others.

Vidar dropped his shield and stabbed the tip of his sword into the icy ground. Both hands went to his knees. His breathing was labored, and every inhale sounded like a winter gale whistling through the slat walls of a curing barn.

"Orri!" Vidar coughed and spit. "Get me my drink."

Orri shuffled through Vidar's things. Halfdan handed Vidar a cup, but he knocked it to the ground.

"In my coat you worthless pig!"

Orri shook the coat up and down and started lifting and tossing everything in the pile as if to let Vidar see there was nothing there.

Toren finally helped his father find his feet. Toren started over toward Magnus to steal away number three when his father held him back. Magnus held up a finger, kept his head down, and continued to work with his hammer and file. Behind Magnus stood Erik, looking as proud as a dog chewing on a dead squirrel. Then he flashed a smile and a glimpse of the red flask before hiding it back into his coat.

"Erik!" Vidar yelled frantically.

Erik jerked his head up like a boy caught stealing chickens, when Old Erik entered the circle. Tor watched his son breathe again, then slink back and toss the evidence behind a tree.

"It's all back at my cabin," Old Erik whispered to Vidar. "If you can't win this, then I chose the wrong man, and you get nothing." Then Old Erik looked at Tor as if he didn't care what he heard. "So, do what your father couldn't, and end this now."

As Old Erik left the circle Vidar snarled at Orri like an angry dog. He pulled out his seax and scowled at his quivering hand. Then he took up Ice Breaker with his shield hand and swung the two in tandem to get the feel of this lighter, quicker setup.

"Give that anchor to the turtle," Vidar panted, "and keep your eyes on the sons." Ubbi nodded and rolled the heavy shield away.

Tor calmed his breath and looked down. There was an outline of his body imprinted in the snow, and the arena was littered with chips and slivers of his first two shields. Orri the turtle cowered behind Vidar's abandoned shield like a whipped dog. It had hardly been scratched.

"Call for mercy," Kiara pleaded with Erik from outside the line.

"Watch what you say, girl." Vidar coughed and spit something green into the white, powdery snow. "Remember to whom you belong."

Tor shook out his shield arm while his eldest son collected the shield numbered three from Magnus. Magnus reluctantly gave it up after quickly slapping it two more times with his hammer.

Shield three was Tor's last and his lightest. Half as thick as the first.

"If either of your two sons steps foot inside this circle," Vidar said to Tor between heavy breaths, "by rights I will take their heads immediately after taking yours, coward."

"Toren," Tor said, "don't let Ubbi or Orri interfere." Tor's elbow raged from the abuse it'd taken on the back of the shields. But there was no blood, and he was glad for the ease with which he could raise the lighter shield.

Tor took a step forward, and so did the giant. Vidar moved differently without the protection or weight of his shield. Tor focused on his chest, no longer looking for a death blow, just an opening.

All I need is first blood, he reminded himself. He could deal with the rest of the Viking once Toren and Erik were safely gone.

The giant's eyes narrowed and filled with murder. Vidar raised the sword in his weak hand. Tor faked right, then stepped toward Vidar's weak side, circling. The giant looked exhausted and tripped on his feet.

Tor pounced at the opening. Using his axe, he slapped the giant's sword tip down and charged his off-balance opponent with his shield while rolling the long-handled axe around to get ready for a downward swing.

Vidar stabbed with the seax, but Tor turned the lighter shield, glancing the blade off to the side. The point stuck deep into the handle of Tor's axe. Vidar pulled and Tor twisted, and the tug of war ended with a *ping* as the tip of the borrowed seax snapped off.

The giant planted his foot to slide to his strong side and mount another attack, but his ankle turned, and he stumbled when he stepped in a Tor-shaped hole in the snow.

Tor saw the stumble and drove hard into Vidar with his shield once more. Tor rode the giant down, sword and axe tangled, and Vidar cursed Tor as they fell.

They broke through the top layer of snow with a crunch, planting down hard where they landed.

Tor yanked hard on his axe, liberating it from its trap between Vidar and the shield.

Vidar screamed in anguish, his eyes wide and white as he tried and failed to throw Tor off. Tor choked up on the handle, and raised the axe high above his head, ready to slam it down onto his pinned opponent.

The white snow turned red.

"First blood!" the crowd yelled. "Stop the fight!"

Flustered, Old Erik hooked Tor's axe by the beard with his staff and called the fight. "Hold your weapons!" The blood crawled into the snow like wine spilled on a white shirt. "Get these men up from there. Shield men, get them separated."

Strong arms and fresh hands pulled the two to their feet. Both men were getting the snow slapped off their backs, and everyone was trying to see who cut who, and where.

Erik pushed his father back outside the ring to clear him away from the giant's grasp as Toren put himself between his father and the Vikings.

Blood was on both men, but where was it from? As they stripped the clothing back, Tor could hear Vidar cursing. Old Erik pulled a bloody piece of sharpened steel out of the giant's hip.

"Aaaugh!" he yelled as the old man pushed a handful of snow into his hand.

Old Erik shook his head like a disappointed father. "Hold this where it's bleeding." Blood melted the cold compress and pulsed from between Vidar's fingers with each beat of his bitter heart.

"That doesn't count," argued the giant. "The blood was drawn from a piece of my own blade!" Ubbi thrust his head under Vidar's arm to help him balance on his turned ankle.

Ice and freezing mud crunched underfoot as Tor pushed his way through the crowd to the center of the circle, axe in one hand, cracked shield in the other.

Old Erik used the tip that broke off Vidar's seax to trace up Tor's axe handle to a fissure in the wood surrounded by a splatter of drying blood.

"Tor's weapon drew first blood," announced Old Erik, "Pedar, have your sledge brought around to help Vidar back to his bed. That's as much blood as I want to see in this field for a while."

Vidar looked at the broken blade, then glared at Pedar before throwing the borrowed seax down at his feet.

Old Erik pulled Vidar's hand from his hip and shook his head in disgust. The wound was still pulsing blood.

"Choke on some humility—you earned it." Old Erik glared at Vidar as he slapped another handful of snow on his bloody wound. "Save your revenge for tomorrow."

RACING THE WOLF

S terkr was the first to notice. His thick curled tail
wagged high over his lower back. Erik rubbed his
neck to calm him down. "Easy boy. Stay," he
whispered.

From atop the hill, Magnus broke out of the wood on skis
towing a packed sled. Putting a cupped hand to the side of
his mouth, he let out three short, high pitched calls, as if
announcing his arrival.

"Whoop, Whoop, Whoop!"

It was a big day. For the first time, the boys were leaving
the village on their own.

Sterkr whimpered at Erik's feet, waiting for the signal
that would turn him loose.

As Magnus descended, he repeated the call even louder,
his deepening voice cracking either from the cold air or
what it was doing to his manhood. "Whoo-wup, Whoo-wip,
Whoo-wip!" Magnus covered Erik and Toren in snow as he
slid past.

"Are you trying to wake the dead?!" Toren's face was
stern like the captain waiting for his crew.

Erik didn't know about Magnus or Ragi, but he wasn't
about to take orders from his brother. As he knocked the
snow from his pants, he noticed Kiara for the first time. His
heart pounded a little harder. She was making her way
down the hill on foot, knee deep in Magnus's path. It was
as if the cold had frozen the smile on his face.

Sterkr's eyes never left the wood line, his small ears erect, tweaking left and right as if cataloguing distant noises. Erik followed his eyes beyond Kiara, into the dark forest. The dog's vision was clouded by excitement and clouds of his own warm breath. There was something there, movement from the west.

Snow blasted from the trees as a wolf the color of smoke bore down toward the clueless girl. Its body was long, like the shadows cast by the low hanging sun.

"Kiara!" Erik yelled.

She waved back, ignorant of what was bearing down on her from above.

With a tug on Sterkr's collar, Erik sent the Elkhoud running. He blew through a wall of snow to find the trail, tearing up the hill in a blur of white powder. Square and compact, strong and sleek, Sterkr looked like a younger version of his father, Vigi.

With long, loping strides the wolf maneuvered noiselessly through the deep snow. It noticed Sterkr and picked up speed.

Kiara stopped and put out her arms to welcome the dog, but Sterkr raced past her, disappearing into a wall of white.

The wolf leapt onto the spot, and with a yip, Sterkr's curly tail disappeared under its shadow. Growls and barks echoed skyward on a white cloud. The wolf stabbed its head downward, then reared up on its hind legs. Sterkr buried his head up into its fur, jawing at the nape of the larger animal's neck. The wolf reared up and dropped down again, pinning Sterkr down and out of sight again.

A second later, Sterk's tail raised up above the path, giving away his position. As he retreated back to the boys, the wolf nipped his heels. Sterkr slid around behind Erik, but the wolf barreled past, knocking him to the ground. Its growl was menacing, but only half as much as the long, white fangs exposed and gnawing at the thick black fur along the back of Sterkr's neck. Sterkr bared his teeth and growled a response but could not turn enough to find purchase. He was pinned.

"Sterkr, I hope you don't try bringing me a bear if that's the way you bring me a wolf." Erik grabbed Sterkr's front paws and pulled.

"Garmr's no wolf." Magnus grabbed the big animal by the scruff of the neck and pulled the other direction.

"He's at least half," Erik jerked. "Look at him."

"Garmr." Magnus spoke like a mother talking to a child not playing nice with his friends. "Let the little dog go. I know you haven't seen him for a while."

After the boys pulled them apart, the dogs acted calm. But as soon as they were released, they started playing again. Sterkr jumped high in the air, and Garmr raised up on his back feet.

"Do you think they know we're leaving today?" As Erik watched them play and yip and bark and spin around in tight circles, he couldn't help but smile. Somewhere in the pit of his stomach, he felt the same way.

SPEAKING OF MARRIAGE

"Hello, Kiara," Toren practiced his Irish. "Are your feet...warm? Do you need..." he scratched his chin, then scrunched up his face as he tried to find the words, "dry mittens?"

"Very good," Kiara laughed. "Somebody's been practicing." It was the first time she'd been back on their farm since the party.

Magnus looked at Erik, confused. "What did he say?"

Erik shrugged. "He's speaking Kiara." Then Erik bowed to her. "Good marnin', wee lass." He spoke slowly, with a mocking Irish accent. "Mae fa-der has been tae-ching us how ta kill giants. Now mae bru-der thinks we are going to Ireland. I think ya should run away while ya can."

Erik was right, Kiara's eyes sparkled when she laughed. But they weren't nearly as beautiful as Anja's, which were a kind of solemn brown.

"You boys look as sharp as your father's axe." Kiara laughed, though her cheeks were wet with tears.

"You look nice today." Erik looked as if he hadn't realized he was talking out loud.

"Thank you." Kiara did a little spin. "Anja gave me one of her old dresses. And the scarf is new, a gift from Skadi."

"Are you friends now?" asked Toren, a little too interested.

"No," she replied. "It was all kind of abrupt, now that I think about it." She looked confused as she played with a green circle embroidered into one end of the scarf. "Hey," she perked up, "if you do ever go to Ireland, take me with you, and I promise I'll wear the dress for you."

"I promise," replied Erik, "as soon as I get back."

"Don't be cruel, Erik. I think Vidar may have something to say about that." Toren perked up as a horse-drawn sledge approached, but it was only Skadi. She looked cold and drove past the gathering and on to the house.

"Are you sure you and Anja even want to marry each other? Even Kiara came to see us off." Erik was just upset with Toren for questioning him. They both knew he'd never come back here. But Erik wouldn't let it go. "You forget, brother, Runa's not telling me where I'm going to live. Maybe I will take Kiara home someday. She's got me wanting to see this island of green pastures and rainbows and faeries she's bragged so much about."

"Get serious." Toren hit him with a snowball. *Always playing.* Toren's path may have been set, but recently he had never felt so lost. Ever since his father said he was to leave, that's all he could think about. Somehow the village had gotten smaller. His inheritance, the birthright Runa had prepared him to bear his entire life, had started to feel heavy, like a cloak in the summer.

Toren fought hard to fill his mind with the house and the farm and the problem of the Vikings—anything but the question Erik so flippantly asked. Of course he wanted to marry Anja. Who wouldn't? Why would he even say that?

Toren looked at his father, who kept his head down, sharpening his axe. Surely *he* wanted Toren to live the life he chose for himself, right? It occurred to Toren that they'd never talked about it. His father was always so busy with the farm and providing for them. He spent all his time hunting just to make sure they had meat on the table and something worth trading.

That was the life he chose and had to be the life he wished for his oldest son. *He would've told him if he thought he shouldn't marry Anja, right?* A chill ran up Toren's spine and raised the hairs on his head. He still had to talk to his father about what he said about selling the farm. That must've been the stress of the holmgang talking, but he would like to get that settled before he left. Anja was here to see him off. Probably wouldn't be able to talk about it with her family around. Might make them think he wasn't committed. Maybe it'd be best to wait until he got back, and let his father figure things out a bit now that the holmgang was over—now that they were making alliances with Jarl Adar. He must know that Anja would never leave the village. She'd never leave her family.

What did Erik know of responsibility? He had nothing. Ragi understood. He was the only one who could. Toren hated the way the question whirled around in his head like a black fly. No, they all just wished they had his luck. Anja was the most beautiful girl in the village. She was the right girl for him. Always had been.

Things were easier before he'd gotten his ring and the women started negotiating—it's Runa and Skadi, and all these wedding plans. Everything would be better after the wedding, and they could put all of that behind them.

"Take some wood to the shed." Tor had a way of keeping his sons from focusing too much on their feelings. "Kiara, you can go too. I told Runa you'd be coming. And I told her to be nice." He cut off another branch. "Boys, after you say your goodbyes, come see me with your things. I want to talk to you before you go."

Tor always said chopping wood helped him think. That never made sense to Toren, as chopping wood was about as far from thinking as you could get. From the looks of things, he'd been doing a lot of thinking that morning.

SINCERE INSINCERITY

Nearing the house, they walked past the small barn and animal pens and the fenced yard that was under siege by the trees and weeds and forest vines. Tor's farm had chickens, pigs, and horses, but what he had more than anything was goats, not necessarily because he wanted goats or loved goats, but because it was goats that seemed to thrive under his general lack of interest, care, or attention.

The boys piled the firewood they'd been carrying on top of one of the large drying stacks against the storehouse. Stooping to fit through the low entry, they led Kiara into the house that they'd grown up in, and out of.

Although there was still room for the family, somehow the walls had grown in on Erik as he grew older. But now that he was about to leave, the familiarity of it felt like safe harbor for a ship made to sail, longing to take its maiden voyage into the open sea.

The air was filled with the smells of baking bread and boiling berry and pine tea and all those things that make a person feel warm and welcome in their own home. At the detriment of caring for an aching Tor, Runa had been preparing for Skadi's visit since she found out Ragi would be leaving with the boys. Erik didn't think Skadi felt much more love for Ragi than Runa did for him, but he also figured out that neither of them would be outdone in their pretense of love for their stepchildren.

Erik was going to enjoy this.

Before they could remove their layers, Runa came over and smothered Toren and Erik with hugs and kisses in a very motherly way, as if she loved them.

Erik wanted to hate her petty act, but he liked it. He often wished she could love him. He thought she might have once, before he lost his sister.

He didn't blame her. It may have been the one thing they had in common. He wasn't sure he'd ever forgive himself, either.

But if she was going to be insincere for the sake of the neighbors, he was going to take full advantage of it.

"Skadi, I couldn't help but remember, the last time Kiara got a new dress Runa gave her away," Erik smiled. "Are you here to give her back?"

Runa looked at him as if she was about to hit him with her spoon.

"No, I just thought she ought to look decent on a day like today. Runa, is there anything she can do for you while she's here?"

Erik and Runa both turned to Kiara, Erik apologetic, Runa stern.

"Go feed the chickens, girl. You remember how to do that, don't you?"

Kiara quickly hugged each of the boys around the neck and blessed their journey. "I'll be praying for you." She pulled out the chain around her neck and kissed her soul.

"Go on, girl," Runa said sternly. "And don't let the dogs into the barn."

Erik furrowed his brow as he watched Kiara leave. She hadn't even had time to warm her hands.

"I brought something for all of you, too. And I want all of you to wear it on your journey."

"Skadi?" Runa opened the bag and pulled out three wool scarves, each died red as blood. She passed one to Erik and the other to Toren. They were well made and would be warm. Erik liked that they matched the one Kiara was wearing. As Runa started passing the third to Magnus, Skadi stopped her.

"That one's for you." Skadi draped it over Runa's shoulders.

Magnus looked back as if there might be another, but the bag was empty.

Runa looked annoyed, like she didn't trust Skadi's sudden act of kindness any more than Erik did. The only generosity she'd ever shown in the past was to draw unequal favors. Even when she went to Old Erik's for sacrifices, she would offer the gods a goat in exchange for the health of a barn full of newborn piglets.

WARM HOUSE, COLD GOODBYE

Erik was feeling like being a little difficult, now that Kiara had been sent away, and even a little more after seeing Magnus's face when he realized he hadn't warranted a lousy scarf from his mother's master. "Is Ragi coming sometime today?"

"Or Anja?" Toren stared out the cracked door, looking like he might slam it shut.

"Ragi is on his way." Skadi was as cold as the air Toren let inside. "But Anja was too upset to come. She knew you wouldn't want to make her cry. And Elsa stayed back to console her."

Magnus just shook his head.

"He'd better get here soon." Toren's mood mirrored Erik's. "We've got to go."

Runa seemed to be particularly cheery this morning, and not just pretending for the neighbor, even to the point of doing what good mothers do when their boys are going away. She put food on the table, and Erik was going to get as much of it as he could manage.

There was røkt laks and tørrfisk, gjetost and fresh bread. And of course, there was butter. There was always butter.

Still wiping the kiss from his cheek, Toren, the favored son, grabbed some bread off the table and handed it to Erik. Runa scowled at the youngest as he nabbed a slice of cheese, too.

"Mother?" Erik couldn't help but smile at how ridiculous that sounded. "This is quite a lot of food. Were you expecting Skadi to come visiting today?"

Runa did not scowl. "Not at all. This is for your last meal, Erik." Runa's smile looked genuine. "You are a man now. Who knows if you will ever return?"

"I was hoping to catch Ragi before he left," said Skadi. "I found a few more things that I thought he might need." It was hard to tell which woman disliked her stepson more.

"I'll make sure he gets it," Magnus offered.

Erik was surprised Magnus could bear to look at the woman. She wasn't good to him or his mother. Magnus was freeborn, but she'd let him act like her servant as long as he'd allow it. It reminded Erik of how he used to lick Runa's boots until she slapped him with the epiphany that it wasn't going to fix anything. Then he resented her even more for allowing him to try so hard for so long.

"Whatever she's brought, it's for her son, Magnus. Not you. You didn't bring anything for Magnus did you, Skadi?" Erik didn't know why, but something inside him made him want to pick a fight. The faster they got out of there, the better.

Magnus's face turned red. Then, as if Erik was the problem, he threw a piece of dried fish at him, which Erik caught and popped into his mouth.

Runa eyed Erik as if he was stealing food from the cupboard while she picked up little Jeger off the floor and gave him a piece of cheese.

Whenever his father was away, she'd always found her reasons to keep Erik from filling his stomach, and she did it in a way so that it was just their little secret. It was always for the sake of the family — to make sure there was enough food to last the winter. Ever since he was little, she figured out a way to ignore the growling of his stomach, the way she ignored a dog when it scratched at the door to come in from the cold. Any dog but Jeger. He was hers.

So, Erik was particularly pleased to have Skadi here to shield him from Runa's excuses about not having enough food. The lies were worse than the hunger. He hadn't eaten this well since the last time Kiara snuck him lunch in the woods. Tricks like that, along with stealing the porridge Runa'd been leaving in the barn for the nisse, kept him from starving to death altogether.

"Can I get you anything else, boys?" Runa's lips were stretched thin, but nothing could get her to break character in front of Skadi.

Erik put his arm around his stepmother. "What else have we got?" He liked this game. Today he was leaving, and Runa had no tomorrow to rob him of his portion.

"You're already taking my heart." Runa held up her little Lundehund. "I don't know why your father insists on sending him."

But Erik and Toren understood. Tor had brought Jeger home as a gift for Runa after coming back from the one and only time he spent the summer away helping Pedar with his trading up the coast. Jeger was to be a companion for Runa while Tor was away on hunting trips, and he did that job very well. She loved that mischievous little dog, often letting him live inside the house during the frigid winter months.

And although Jeger's skills weren't immediately appreciated by the boys, they soon learned he had one that made their stepmother very happy. He was a natural bird dog. After they finally trained him to stop raiding the neighbors' chicken coops, his positives quickly outweighed his negatives. In one evening, all by himself, that little dog could bring home enough wild pheasant to feed the whole family. He would have stripped the whole mountain had the boys not continued to work with him until he was pretty well trained to only hunt on command. By the third year, he'd wiped the pheasant from their side of the mountain, but occasionally he'd still come home with a bird, ignorant of the range of his territory.

"Ragi said the only good Jeger would be on this trip

would be to be used as bait," laughed Magnus.

Both Skadi and Runa stared at him with knives coming out of their eyes until he joined Toren to help watch the falling snow.

Even though most of the troupe felt the little Lundehund would be more useful than Ragi in all practicalities, Erik was glad Ragi was going. He might not have been able to pull his own weight, but his horse could, and his father would make sure it was packed with enough food for all of them.

When the boys were younger, Tor took them on a two-night hunting trip. Pedar made sure Ragi's pack was full, and it was more food than they could eat in a week. Erik stole enough food from him that week that both their packs were still half full when they got home. He had a stash in the barn that kept him fed for weeks—for the nights Runa would make up reasons to send him to bed without supper.

Erik grabbed more of the rich, caramel-colored goat cheese and raised it toward Skadi, as if to toast her for being so wonderful.

"Runa?" said Skadi, "why aren't your boys taking horses again? If it's a matter of money, I could've let them have some of ours. Worst case, Ragi could offer them as gifts to Jarl Adar if Erik and Magnus don't come back." Skadi looked at Erik as if she understood why Runa was so happy to see him go.

"Tor was worried as soon as they got hungry the boys might eat them." Runa smiled.

"Hungry? Why would they go hungry?" Skadi asked. "More bread, Erik?"

"Thank you," Erik replied, as he cut half the loaf and stuffed it into his sack.

Toren opened the door and looked outside again, pretending to look for Ragi—more likely hoping for Anja.

"We've got to get going," Toren said sharply, as if the women's hen-pecking was suddenly upsetting him.

"You're right, Toren." Erik kept talking to buy time to survey what he hadn't already pilfered off the table. "It's already mid-morning."—he grabbed the bread—"the days are still short,"—he filled a scrip with dried cod—"and we probably need to get moving if we're going to make it to where we're going to camp tonight before sunset. Would you pass me the cheese, mother?" Erik cut the brick in two and smiled at Runa as he stuffed it in his scrip.

"Where are you planning to stay tonight again?" Skadi asked.

"We haven't decided yet. Father wanted to keep it close."

"Here, Erik, you look thin." Skadi put another sack on the table. "Surely you know, though, right?"

"What is that?" asked Runa.

"It's what I was saving for Ragi. Just some cakes Elsa made with some berries she preserved last year. I just wanted to make sure there was enough." Skadi sounded a little agitated. "I'd like to know that you know where you're going if I'm going to allow Ragi to go with you."

"Don't let him go then." Erik took the other half of the block of cheese.

Runa was not smiling. "Toren, here, have some cake before Erik and Magnus eat it all."

"We've got to go if we're ever going to get back." It was clear that Toren's mind had turned a corner. What wasn't clear was if it was because of Anja's absence or the fact that he was about to lead such a goofy bunch of boys on a trip around the fjord before the first blade of green pierced the snow. "It's starting to snow harder now." What had started as a simple agitation was quickly snowballing. He closed the door and started putting on his layers.

Erik and Magnus started grabbing their gear and layering up.

"If Ragi shows up, tell him if we're not out at the woodpile in the woods then he's on his own." The sound of heavy hoofs stopped him short.

"It's about time," Erik said as he grabbed the remaining pieces of the bread and cheese and stuffed them into scrips.

"He must have been saying goodbye to the entire village," said Magnus.

"My father will kill him if he did," replied Erik. "This was supposed to be a secret."

"Vidar knows nothing we don't want him to know." Skadi put some cakes in another scrip. "Which direction are you going?" she badgered on. "Tell me that, at least."

Erik grabbed the little sacks from her hand. He was running out of places to put them.

"Hurry," Toren said. "If he gets off that horse we'll never get to the bald before dark."

"Which bald?" Skadi was being drowned out by the scuffle.

The boys cinched on their heavy packs. The women were having some sort of race. Skadi was trying to fill small scrips with whatever food she could gather faster than Runa could stow it back in the cupboard.

Runa slipped in one last lie. "There will be a time when you miss my cooking. Don't go feeding any of that to your dogs." The boys ran out the door, spinning each other around to make sure they hadn't forgotten anything.

Erik slipped off into the barn. "I brought you something."

Kiara put down the pitchfork and ran over to hug Erik around the neck. Sacks of food fell to the ground as she wet his cheeks with her tears. "I can't believe you're leaving me." She hugged his neck so tight he had to pry her arms apart to breathe.

Erik suddenly felt like he wanted to tell her everything, how excited he was, how scared he was, how sorry he was—for the first time in his life, he had no reason to hide.

"I'm not even sure exactly where we're going. To the sea and take a right is all I can remember."

"Take me to the sea and then let's keep going until we

get to Ireland, away from all this ice and snow. I promise it'll be the greenest place you've ever seen."

Kiara's eyes looked even more like emeralds when her cheeks were red from the cold.

Had she not blinked, he'd have lost himself in those eyes. "I-I made this for you." *Why did he feel so nervous?*

She looked down and started to cry when she saw his gift. "Father helped me carve it," he explained. "I know it's not as nice as your father's, but-"

She jumped in his arms, grabbed him around the neck, and kissed him hard on the lips, like she would never let him go. It was his first kiss. Scrips of food fell to the ground.

She tasted like sweet berries and spruce. Her warmth filled his empty soul, driving shivers of cold down into his boots, leaving behind a heat that made him want to take off his coat.

When she loosed her grip, he realized it was he that was holding on to her. Erik put her gently down. Flustered, and unsure, he backed up to the door. "I'll come back for you. I promise."

"Erik!" He could hear Toren yelling.

Erik didn't know what to do, but he didn't want to leave.

She came close again, put her arms up, and tucked his new scarf into his warm coat. Erik shivered at the touch of her cold fingers against the back of his neck. "Sorry," he said. He didn't know why.

Her smile made him feel like everything was going to be alright. "It's the nicest gift I've received in a long, long time." She pulled him close and he met her halfway, kissing her this time. This time was different. Their lips grazed each other's, gently at first, then deeper. For the eternity of that kiss, Erik forgot why he ever wanted to leave—why he could ever leave this girl. It was the first time he'd ever felt love, and for some reason he was leaving her behind.

"I didn't know if I'd see you again." She eased herself back. "Will you come back for me?"

"I will. I promise I will."

She started laughing as she pushed hard against his chest. His hands refused to let go, sliding along her cold coat.

"You won't forget me?" she asked, wiping tears away from her smiling eyes.

He felt like the smile was frozen to his face. "How could I?"

She pushed him toward the door.

He didn't know why, but he let her. It was the only way he could leave. When the door closed between them, Erik waited for second, hoping she'd open it again and drag him inside.

"Erik! Let's go."

The door didn't open. Erik hesitantly turned. He could feel his cheeks almost cramping from the smile that refused to let go.

It was mid-morning, one of those perfect days in early spring when the air was cold and the sun was warm.

Ragi looked down from his horse as if he'd been waiting on them all morning.

"Is that for me?" he asked, eyeing the scrip of food Erik held between his hands and teeth. Three went flying. One missed, another hit his horse, and he just managed to catch the third before it hit him in the face. Ragi frowned as he looked inside.

"Dried cod for my going-away breakfast?"

A gaggle of dogs surrounded him as if waiting for scraps.

"I'll give you anything you want if you promise to stay here," replied Erik.

As Ragi smirked defiantly, he began to empty the scrip to the dogs from his perch, like a king throwing coppers to his subjects. Runa hurried to save little Jeger from being trampled in the feeding frenzy. Shaking her head, she stole the scrip out of Ragi's hand and implored the boys as she hand-fed her little pup.

"Take care of my Jeger, now, alright? You take care of my dog." Jeger tilted his head with a look that was almost as if he understood. Then he licked her nose. When Runa put him down, she wiped her face. As the little dog trotted over and climbed onto Erik's sled, it wasn't clear if Runa was wiping off Jeger's goodbye kiss or her own tears.

"Are you alright?" Ragi kicked at Erik.

"Ja. Why?"

"I can't tell if you're sad, or what."

"No." Erik looked past the tears of his stepmother to the emerald eyes peeking from the shadows behind the barn door. "I've been waiting to leave this place my entire life."

Runa watched Skadi take the scrips out of Erik's hand and tie them onto his sled. She looked like she was witnessing a robbery.

WEAPONS CHECK

Tor had been dreading his sons leaving even more than the holmgang. Things were changing so fast. In a way, he felt better knowing Toren would be there with Erik, for awhile at least. Had it not been for the Vikings, Erik would've been leaving on his own—if not this year, then next. *Maybe it was better this way.* Before Tor could see them, he could hear the chaos driving up the trail.

First to arrive was Sterkr, who drove Erik's sled through heavy powder to shortcut a path to Vigi and Tor. Little Jeger's tongue flapped to one side as he rode high on Erik's gear while Erik hung on to catch a tow. Ragi trotted up next on Gardrofa, followed by Toren and Magnus on skis, each pulling their own sleds and gear.

"Don't get Vigi too excited boys. He's not going anywhere today." Tor motioned for Ragi to get down from his horse.

"Take off your packs. I want to take a look."

The boys started taking their bows and arrows off their packs, then their packs off their sleds.

Ragi dismounted with an unpleasant look on his face as if being asked to do something very difficult, like waking up in the morning, or opening a door. He waved Tor off. "My father and I packed my things and we've got it balanced just the right way."

"You're going to have to take it off eventually," said Tor. "You can't leave it on all night."

"I know that."

Tor wasn't sure that he did. He shrugged and started with the others. "I want to see everything down to your fire kit."

"How did you keep your leaving a secret from Vidar?" Erik asked Ragi as he emptied his pack.

"He never paid me much attention," Ragi shrugged. "If Anja was leaving, he'd have noticed."

"What's that supposed to mean?" Toren threw his bag on a downed tree.

"Calm down Toren. I'm sure she's not interested in him. I'm just saying he has never cared what I was doing. Plus, he's been gone a lot training for the duel."

"That was a waste of time," Erik laughed.

Tor looked hard at his youngest son. "I got him tired and angry and he made a mistake, that's all. Vidar will rest and he will heal, but he will never forget. And he will seek revenge. That is our way." Tor walked over to the horse and petted her nose. "If I had won, if I had done what I set out to do, none of you would be leaving home—not on this task, and never at this time of year."

Tor needed to calm down. He wasn't feeling very good about any of this. "What's her name?" Tor scratched her thick, shaggy winter coat.

"Gardrofa," Ragi replied. "My father said she was always breaking free from her pen."

"Did you make that pen, father?" Erik laughed mischievously, like he did when he was little.

Tor hadn't seen that smile in a long time. He tapped the tree. "Where's your fire-starting kit?"

Erik looked, then raised his shoulders. "Guess I left it at home."

Tor glared at Erik, dug into his pack, and threw his own fire kit into his son's gear. Every Norse male over the age of nine carried the basics to start a fire. It was wet country, summer or winter, and the ability to fire a spark into some dry tinder could mean the difference between life or death.

"That's a bad start, Erik. I need you to grow up now. It's not Toren's job to take care of you." Then Tor shook his head. He didn't want to state the obvious, but what choice did he have? "Toren, take care of your brother." Tor started wondering if there was any other way. Exhaling heavily, he walked slowly around Ragi's old mare to collect his thoughts.

"She is strong and smart." Ragi's cheeks were pink.

"What?" Then Tor realized he was talking about the horse. "No offense to your father, Ragi, but I don't think a horse packing your burden for you is the best way to get where you want to go. Still, she will be useful." She was a healthy old mare, likely seventeen, only a year or two older than her rider. She was a typical farm horse, just under fourteen hands, brown dun in color, with a near white mane and tail—better kept than any horse on Tor's farm.

Ragi decided to ignore Tor and pet the dog. If any of his sons had shown that disrespect—well, he wasn't, that was obvious, and this trip would either make him or break him.

Tor rummaged through his boy's packs, removing some items from each. "You can't carry everything. Sometimes, having too much will weigh on you like an anchor."

As he rummaged through Magnus's pack, he gave him a look. "Yours is a little heavy for my taste," Tor held on to it before letting Magnus take it back. "But I think they're all as light as can be expected. You've got to be smart. Replenish your stores as you go. That's the way men travel or they'd never leave the villages around the fjord." Tor looked at Ragi, who was still ignoring him. He picked up each pack with one hand to test their weight.

"Show me your weapons." Tor stood tall over Ragi. "You too, Ragi. And I will not ask you again."

Magnus and Erik laid out short- and long-handled axes while Toren retrieved his grandfather's sword, the one Vidar used in the holmgang. Next came hunting slings and finally the seaxes from the scabbards hung across their waists. Quickly, a downed tree was covered in weapons of wood, bone, antler, leather, and iron.

Tor picked up his father's sword, and with a mix of power, grace, and speed he dismembered several wrist-sized limbs off a medium pine. Then he ran his thumbnail up the blade to test for rolls and clear away the sap. Swinging that sword was like reacquainting himself with an old friend. He put the sheath around his own waist and holstered the sword. Then he handed Toren one of the axes he'd used in the holmgang. He gave the other to Erik, who broke out in a proud smile. It was probably more than he'd expected to get of his father's.

Toren looked confused. "A sword for an axe? But father, I-"

"It is the mark of a warrior to carry a sword," Tor explained. "It can get you into trouble faster than it can get you out of it."

"But father," Toren tried to explain, "what if we-"

Tor raised his hand, and his eldest son fell silent. "I hope you don't need any of this, 'cept bows for hunting and axes for firewood. If you need a sword, you'll have to earn it with your axe. You're all good with axes. Takes time to master the sword." Toren, Erik, and Magnus had spent countless hours of their lives cutting wood with their axes. The fires that heated their homes were the forges that turned their growing bodies to iron.

"But what about Ragi?"

Ragi scrunched his face up at Magnus as if he had committed the greatest betrayal.

"Look at him like he's your servant and I'll show you how your horse runs on three legs." Erik raised his new axe.

"Erik," Tor grabbed the axe out of his youngest son's hand, "I'm glad to see you defend the honor of a friend, but you've got to leave your attitude here now. If you pick fights where you're going, you'll be risking everyone's lives. I hesitated to allow you to go at all, the way you've been acting. But you can't stay here." Tor slowly handed his son the axe but didn't let it go. "Can I trust you?"

"Ja, father." Erik pulled on the handle, but Tor didn't let it go.

"Can they trust you?"

Erik loosed his grip and made eye contact with each of the others. "Ja, father," he said solemnly. Tor let go of the axe, and Erik eased it back.

"Don't blame Magnus, Ragi. I noticed the sword when I met your horse."

After removing several small scrips of food, Ragi found and awkwardly removed the sword given him by his father.

"Have you ever swung it?"

Ragi shrugged. "Enough."

Tor inspected the blade. "If you insist on taking the horse, I will say this" — he turned to Toren — "none of you will fight to save this animal, whether from thief or bear or Viking or troll, you will not fight to save this horse."

"Ja," they nodded. Ragi's jaw hung loose.

Tor focused back on Ragi. "You heard what I said to Toren. A sword is a warrior's weapon and will only bring you trouble if you carry it." Tor looked back to the others. "None of you will fight to save that sword, whether by thief or warrior, let it go if it draws a challenge. You know how to wield axes, and you know how to shoot bows. You will only wield swords if you take it off an enemy's corpse."

"Ja." They all looked at Ragi. Ragi looked betrayed.

"It'll probably break, like that seax your father gave Vidar." Tor held up a third axe to see if Ragi would trade, not as pretty as the bearded ones he gave his sons, but functional for its purpose.

Ragi put the sword back in its sheath on the side of the horse.

Even though the other boys winced in anticipation, Tor did not scold him. "Keep it hidden but always at the ready.

Never wear it unless you plan to use it. And you're going to want to put an edge on it, too, before you run into anyone who cares." Tor looked to his oldest. "Toren, you can help him with that if he needs it—or anything else for that matter. You have each other and that's all you have, so be smart." He looked at Erik. "Be careful." He looked at Ragi. "Take care of one another." He looked at Toren. "And above all else, come home." He looked at Magnus.

"I think you've got everything," said Tor. "Not enough. It's never enough. But you'll find the rest along the way."

Tor pulled Erik's scarf aside and looked at the soul ring hanging from a double leather thong around his neck. The once pearl-colored ring was already beginning to mar with gray and yellow stain.

"Such a simple little trinket. Maybe this trip will help you find out what it's all about."

Tor picked up his axe. The boys stood staring as if there was more to say.

"Go," said Tor. "Take care of one another, and help each other stay on the path. There are a lot of benefits to traveling while the ground is still frozen. Speed. If you leave now you may still have time to make it down to the balds before dark."

Tor made a couple of short calls. "Sssst, sssst."

All of the dogs—except Garmr, who was off by himself watching from a distance, as usual—began sniffing and circling each other as a small chorus of high-pitched whimpers, low barks, and a kind of talking dogs do arose from the lot of them as they said their goodbyes. Tor then broke it up with a quick call.

"Vigi, Vigi, Vigi! Come! Come on, old man." Vigi ran over and sat down next to him. The dogs were used to being split up this way, but it was as if they sensed this time was different. Erik, Toren, and Magnus sensed this, too and ran over for a quick wrestle with Vigi one last time before leaving. When they were done, Tor picked up his axe and an arm full of wood and began his walk home.

Then Tor stopped and turned back toward the boys.

"Throughout your lives you've heard legends and stories told as we'd sit around the fires of the great hall, or at home, or while on hunting trips, stories about the evils that live beyond our borders and in dark places, of giants and trolls, of sea serpents and dragons, of the fierce battles waged between the light and the darkness." For a moment there was only the sound of falling snow as the boys stared at him.

"The myths, they were not all just scary tales meant to entertain old men or keep little boys from getting a good night's sleep. There is truth in them."

Relieved of a burden he'd been carrying for some time, Tor turned and started his walk back to the farm. He knew he should be worried, but now that they were off, he felt excited for his sons. Erik's distant whistle and the barking of the dogs let him know they were safely on their way, all quickly absorbed by the calm of falling snow.

As Tor made his way through the quiet wood, he heard his name.

"Tor!" It was Anja, running and short of breath. "They've got Runa!"

DUPLICITY

Tor's heart pounded hard in his chest. He knew how bad this could be. He wanted to go faster, but that was a fool's strategy. He would be outnumbered. He had to be smart.

Tor's vision was clouded by the fog of his own breath. Although he held Anja and Vigi to a steady pace, his mind was racing. Twisted memories from his own past fed his imagination, painting pictures of Runa's horror. He knew what could be happening. The woods were quiet, but from the shadows of his mind he thought he could hear her crying out to him.

Anja was leading him toward the old burial mounds where, in a more religious time, his neighbors put locked doors atop the stone barrows to keep the dead from coming back to right past wrongs. How bitter the draugr must be to carry their grudges beyond the grave. For the first time, Tor thought he could understand why. Although he could only guess what he was about to run into, he was sure he would die trying to make it right.

His mind was on Runa, but it was more than that. It was the same terror he felt the day they'd lost Gefn. How helpless he felt that day—stumbling around the forest screaming his daughter's name. He would not pretend he could go on living if something happened to another that was in his care. If they hurt his wife, they'd better put a lock on the door above his pile of stones, for he would do everything in his power to come back for them. As Tor pushed on, he felt as if he was living the nightmare that tormented him for years. But in his dreams, he always woke when she screamed. How she must have cried out for him. Why hadn't he been there for her?

The smell of smoke mingled with the air—then Tor caught a glimpse of a fire. He began to trot ahead of Anja, moving from tree to tree. Only Vigi could outpace him now, and Tor snapped his finger to remind his old friend to stay close. Tor held them up behind the girth of a large, leafless oak. He needed to know what he was up against—and catch his breath.

It was only a small fire. Old Erik was there, and he had Skadi. They were talking.

"Your mother." Tor pointed around the tree. Anja just shook her head. Vigi growled. "Easy boy." Tor ran his fingers through the thick fur around his neck. Vigi whimpered and stamped his front feet, begging to be turned loose. Then Tor noticed the source of his agitation.

It was Kiara, laid out on her back along the mass of a dead log. A man with a hood pulled over his head sat next to her outstretched body, his face blurred by smoke and fire.

"What are they doing?" Tor whispered.

Like an idiot, Anja waved to her mother before Tor could pin her back behind the tree. Tor slowly peered out, only to see Old Erik pointing a long bony finger in their direction. Tor threw his back against the tree and scowled at the girl. She had wasted the only advantage he had.

"Did you see Runa?" he asked.

She shook her head, so he carefully took another peek. The sitting man pushed off the prone slave's chest to help find his feet. He turned, removed his hood, and revealed a clean-shaven, heavily tattooed bald head.

Orri? None of this made sense. Where was Runa?

Tor looked over to Anja, confused. Vigi was growling like he was facing a pack of wolves.

Orri carefully knocked an arrow into his bow, leaned it

into the fire until it lit, and took aim in their direction.

Hearing Orri slothfully exhaust before taking the shot was like hearing bellows empty onto a smith's forge. Then followed the twang of the fat man releasing the string. Tor shoved Anja back and ducked behind the oak again.

The impact sounded like someone had slapped the opposite side of the tree with their hand. When the barb pierced the bark, fire splashed like water, showering the surrounding snow with flaming embers and pieces of oil-soaked cloth. It looked like snowflakes were catching fire as they fell all around where Tor and Anja hid.

"Viking trick. He's marking our location. Stay here." Tor withdrew the seax from across his belt and handed it to Anja. Like a flipped coin, Anja's confused look was replaced with stoic determination.

Tor scanned their surroundings. Nothing moved among the trees except an icy fog rising slowly from the snow-mantled forest floor. He had his father's sword but decided to leave it sheathed. He would start with the axe. If Orri drew his bow on him again he might need something to throw.

Anja was eyeing the knife, its finely etched handle worn flat in places from years of constant use.

"If something goes wrong, make sure my sword goes to Toren and that seax goes to Erik."

Why was she smiling? But before he could ask, she rolled out from the shelter of the tree and started running toward her mother.

"Anja, stop!" called Tor. Vigi scampered after her. Tor leaned out to stop her, only to see an arrow pass through his best friend. "Vigi!" he cried.

Anja stopped and stared at the dog. Vigi lay helpless, whimpering, trying to work his way back to his feet. Tor plucked the arrow out of the ground. No greasy fat, no foam—just blood. "Stay down, boy. Stay down."

Anja ran her fingers along the old dog's wilting ears.

"I'm so sorry." Tears filled her eyes as she looked back, horrified. She started running again.

While the fat Viking knocked another arrow, Tor dragged his old friend back behind the tree. Vigi bared his teeth as Tor examined the wound. It looked clean — away from the heart, and not a lot of blood.

"You'll be alright, boy." Tor buried his face in Vigi's fur. "I think you're going to be okay." His heart filled with pain as he ran his thumb gently down Vigi's cheek. Tears fell from eyes Tor thought had run dry long ago. "I'll come back. Just stay here." His heart began to burn.

As he broke cover, another flaming arrow clipped the tree near his shoulder. Fire splashed, igniting his left side. The pain of a thousand embers burned through layers of clothing like molten fire. Tor dove into the deep snow off the side of the path and rolled into the thicker trees, dousing flames from burning clothes and cooling sizzling flesh. The pain fed his anger and brought him clarity.

Old Erik had betrayed them all. Tor had told Runa a hundred times he was evil. Now the old snake had Kiara and Skadi, and if he didn't do something now, he was going to have Anja, too. Runa would never forgive him if he let something happen to that girl.

The trees provided cover from flaming arrows while Tor drew fire away from Anja. She was running at her assailants like a true warrior, but Tor was faster.

The distance closed quickly, and he emerged from the woods to tackle Orri before Anja could finish closing the gap.

Arrows snapped under Orri's weight after Tor put a shoulder into his abdomen, dropping the fat Viking like a falling tree. Somewhere in the impact he'd also managed to end Orri's struggle when the hilt of his axe found the bald man's temple.

The unconscious man got his revenge when he puked in his mouth and burped unceremoniously into Tor's face, proving he was not yet dead. Tor got another face full as he pushed off Orri's round belly to find his feet. The fat Viking had eaten fish for breakfast.

Tor squared up to Old Erik. His knuckles cracked as he choked the handle of his axe. Kiara wasn't moving. Orri gurgled as he breathed like a man with a mouth full of sausages. Tor kicked him in the face.

"That's for Vigi, you fat goblin."

"Skadi, are you alright?"

Tor followed Skadi's gaze as it turned fearfully to the ground, her heavy breathing filling the air with clouds of warm smoke as if she were half dragon.

Tor put his boot on the side of Orri's gurgling head and turned his gaze back to Old Erik. "Which one of you should I kill first, serpent?"

Then Vidar stepped out from behind one of the naked masts. "I think your wife should be first." The giant yanked Runa onto her toes by the hair, a knife parted her new scarf and lay tight against her throat.

She was choking on a scream.

Tor felt the weight of his missing soul. He and Runa hadn't known love for a long time, but these were ghosts of *his* past, not hers. He needed to shame Vidar into coming after him.

"I never got a chance to ask your father, Vidar, when we were as close as brothers. Were you born of a woman, or do they pluck giants from the dirt like cabbages?"

Vidar growled as he let Runa drop to her feet.

Tor continued picking the scab. "You know, in all our years, your father never left me behind. Ever. He wouldn't even let me go when I tried to leave." Tor began resurrecting the berserker he'd tried so hard to bury with his past. He panted hard like a wolf to light the inner fire he'd extinguished long ago. "Why hasn't he sent his Vikings searching for you?" Tor needed to kill this man. It was the only way he could save his wife. Then he bit his tongue, restrained by the trickle of blood rolling down Runa's long pale throat.

Tor raised his gaze to his wife's begging eyes. Maybe Vidar needed him to spell it out for him. "I tell you what, let her go and have a go at me, ja? I promise you won't win any favors with your father if you hurt my wife."

Vidar dropped Runa a little more, until her feet settled flatly on the ground.

Tor unsheathed Ice Breaker and threw it at Vidar's feet.

Vidar leaned down and picked up the sword. An icy fog poured out from between the gaps in his teeth. Then he jerked Runa back up again.

"Erik!" Tor pleaded. "If you have any sway here then call him off." Tor noticed Skadi wouldn't look him in the eye. Her hands weren't even bound. Anja looked guilty, too, like a child who'd just let a weasel into her neighbor's hen house.

They're in on it. Tor exhaled slowly and tried to gather his thoughts. He'd been lured into the trap like a winter fox. How could he have been so blind?

His mind switched to his sons. They'd be hunted and killed. Or worse, they'd be lied to, and Toren would still marry this treacherous girl. Tor stared a hole in Anja's pretty face. If given the chance he would cut her down like a spindly tree. Vikings were Vikings, but a pretty, ambitious girl could bring down an empire. Knowing that parasite had been removed from affecting his family would help Tor rest while the ravens carried his soul to whichever god would still have him.

Tor's mind focused on who to kill first if Vidar killed Runa.

Start with the biggest threats and go as far as these blades will take me.

"Vidar, this is between us. Let the women go." *First it will be Anja.* He could end the idea of that marriage without losing a step. *No, first Vidar.* He had to be smart about this.

Tor's eyes scanned the perpetrators. *Next, the old snake, then Skadi, and if he's not already dead, I'll crush fat Orri's round skull.* Anja would be last. She would know fear before tasting death.

'Who to Kill First?' was just a game helpless men played. Tor knew he'd be lucky to get to Vidar before one of the others put a knife in his back.

"Skadi, please!" Runa begged.

Tor remembered an old saying from his father.

Deceit is a blade, and its cuts never heal.

Runa's eyes widened, as if she could sense the pain coming.

Tor heard the sound of Ubbi rushing in, and then the lights went out.

CONFESSION

"Shhh," Skadi whispered.

Runa just stared in horror as her long-time neighbor gently kissed the little circle she'd embroidered into the scarf, then used it to wipe the blood off her neck. Runa jerked as the pain of agitating the fresh wound ran down her spine, but she couldn't fight back. They'd tied her to two saplings by her middle fingers, her arms spread out above her head. Ubbi was busy tying one of Tor's middle fingers to a sapling up the hill.

"That's not enough." Old Erik grabbed Tor's seax out of Anja's hand, and pushed Skadi away. "Here, let me show you."

Runa tried to scream, but the old man began stuffing her new scarf into her mouth. The more she tried to spit it out, the farther he pushed it in. His green eye bulged out of his head as if it might fall out onto Runa's cheek as he made his first cut.

"It wasn't long ago that you offered me the butcher's carrion as a sacrifice. Do you remember that?" Old Erik jabbed her wound. Then, as if satisfied, he crammed his gnarled finger tipped in her blood into his mouth, pulled it out clean, and wiped it dry on her shoulder.

Runa could feel a warm, wet flow of blood pulse down until it soaked the collar of her coat.

"There must be blood at a sacrifice." He held his hand out to Skadi so she could help him to his feet. Then his attention went back to Runa. "You said you prayed for your husband to defeat that brute over there." He gestured the quaking finger toward Vidar. "But as long as I've known you, your constant prayer has been that you'd see your daughter, Gefn, again. Hasn't it?"

Runa cried the pain of that memory into the scarf. Her throat burned outside and in, from the blade and her muffled screams. Through all the confusion of that moment, nothing could make her bleed more than that. *What kind of torture was this?*

Old Erik ran his fingers through Skadi's long, dark hair. "Skadi's prayers have always been a little selfish. Many years ago, when Anja was sick—do you remember that?"

Runa remembered. Skadi and Pedar thought they might lose her. They were all so close back then.

Erik continued, "Skadi offered sacrifices to Freyja to save little Anja, but it wasn't enough to get the goddess's attention, was it, Skadi? But I knew her heart." Old Erik pulled some of Skadi's thick hair into his face and breathed in deeply. "She prayed for her daughter, but she was thinking only of herself. She was afraid she'd look like a failed mother if something happened to her little girl. You understand that feeling, don't you?"

Runa felt like she was choking. The embroidered circle at the end of that scarf was cutting into her tongue. But it was only half as harsh as his words. Skadi looked like she was also feeling the sting.

"Not too long ago—last summer, in fact—she prayed for her son, Ragnall. By that time, she'd learned to come to me." Old Erik sucked on his teeth. "She prayed that he wouldn't become an embarrassment, really. And that's why I brought Vidar here." Old Erik pointed his long nose, wet around the nostrils, into Skadi's ear, and sniffed. "That cost you Toren."

"But Vidar was shipwrecked." Anja looked to her mother for answers Skadi didn't seem to have.

"Shush!" Old Erik ordered.

The old priest is delusional. Runa tried to make sense of it all. *Does he know the daughters of Rán that he can influence the sea?* She cut her eyes to see Ubbi still struggling to get a knot tied to Tor's other middle finger. *He must still be alive.*

"You see, the things Skadi prays for cost more than a goat or a cow. A heart wants what it wants and will make deals the mind would never agree to. A soul for a soul, as the saying goes." Then he let Skadi go. "Go make your offering."

Tears streaked Skadi's face as she knelt beside Runa, put her finger to her lips — a sign that she should keep quiet — and pulled the scarf gently out of Runa's mouth.

Runa gagged and nearly vomited as it came out. She wanted Skadi to explain. She tried to plea with her with her eyes. *Please!*

Skadi picked up some white snow and put it to Runa's lips. It was icy cold, like the night, but it helped with the thirst, and for that, Runa was grateful.

Skadi fingered Runa's scarf in the weak light of the rising moon until she found the little embroidered circle. Then she dragged it across Runa's throat. Runa winced but tried to stay quiet. She couldn't bear the thought of being gagged again. At first it felt like Skadi was rubbing sand across the open wound, then she dabbed at Runa's throat as gently as a nurse.

"Runa, I know this must be a little confusing," Old Erik explained, "but bear with us. You see, Skadi's an apprentice of mine. She's just learning." Old Erik pushed up on Skadi's elbow and nodded. "You are being offered as a sacrifice for her to become a priestess. Now that I'm gothi, I won't have time for it all." Skadi kissed the scarf, leaving a bloody stamp of the embroidered circle about the center of her lips. Then she wiped blood from the scarf across the backs of both of her hands.

Runa felt a chill colder than ice climb up her spine.

"Your husband Tor is Vidar's sacrifice — a blessing for Anja, that she will not die bearing his children as his mother did when he was born. The Christian girl is a gift for Hel." The old man didn't even bother to look at Kiara when he said it.

"Skadi, don't do this! Not to me," Runa begged. Her heart was beating so heavily she thought she might faint. Then she thought to appeal to her as a friend. "I do remember when Anja was sick. Remember how I stayed with you to help?" Runa's mind raced. Even Skadi couldn't be this cruel. But Skadi was trying to ignore her, as if she hadn't known her at all. "What price did you pay to save Anja?"

Skadi looked away, but Old Erik gave her a scowl, his mismatched eyes gleaming, unholy in the waning light. "Go ahead. You can tell her."

Skadi was in tears. "It was the only way to save her."

"What was the cost?" Runa felt a shiver down her spine once more.

"A soul for a soul," Skadi cried as she ran off into the darkness.

Old Erik hobbled over to Runa and started laughing. "You prayed so many times to see your little Gefn again. Well, my dear, your sacrifice was acceptable. Here is your answer to that prayer." Then the old demon cracked the butt of his staff across her cheek.

VALHALLA'S TOLL

T or awoke to the clean, crisp smell of winter mingling with the earthy scent of red clay and frozen leaf. His legs were painfully bound at the ankles. He was lying on his back next to a large hollow at the base of a massive fallen oak, its roots standing high in the air like they were drinking from the green river of light dancing amid the twinkling stars. A small hawthorne stood to gain from the large tree's falling, its trunk crooked like an old man's back from years of seeking light inside the oak's shadow. It was twilight, the sun was down, and the moon was on the rise, its dim, cold light filling the forest.

Frozen leaves and snow slid up Tor's back as Ubbi dragged him down into the hollow and tied his feet to a vine.

"Aaaugh," Ubbi grumbled unintelligibly as he used his nub of a tongue to lick blood from a fiercely bleeding finger. Tor's eyes widened as the vine seemed to react to the taste of Ubbi, its thorns digging into his ankles as it slowly retracted, the thick fur insulation and tough reindeer hide of his boots stopping the vine's sharp talons short of piercing his feet.

Tor tried to grab something, but someone had tied the tips of his middle fingers to two saplings while he was unconscious. The vine loosened, then tugged at Tor as if something underground was fishing and thought they may have had a nibble. He ceased his struggle, not wanting to let whatever had him know he was still on the line. With each slow tug of the vine, Tor's feet sank deeper down into the recess of the earth until disappearing into the shadow of the massive roots of the downed tree. The tugging stopped.

The old man held a ring up against the backdrop of the rising moon and took a better look with his left eye, the mismatched, oversized one that would be better hid behind a patch. The green of it lit up in the darkness, even as the western sky sucked the rest of the color out of the world. So far, this had not been a good day, but it was getting much worse as the greedy Sun took both light and hope away on its nightly stroll over the horizon.

A whopping and flitting sound filled the air as two ravens, blacker than a moonless night, landed on the branches of the twisted hawthorne, nipping and nudging each other as if vying for a better seat.

Old Erik smiled and began to work his jaw, as if chewing on his tongue. Then he drew out a sharp seax. It was Tor's.

Tor's head was still in a fog. *Where's Runa?* Twisting left and right, he looked frantically for his wife. *There she is.* She was prostrate, splayed out, and unmoving. Her throat was bleeding heavily from Vidar the oaf's lack of delicacy, but he hadn't opened it. Whether unconscious or dead, he could not tell. Kiara was tied up beside him.

Old Erik hobbled over to Tor and whispered in his ear.

"When is the last time you made a proper sacrifice to your god?"

The fog was still there, and Tor's tongue tasted blood. He spat, then lifted his head toward the old snake. "If I wanted a god I'd carve one." Then he smiled. "And it would care more about how I lived than how I met death."

Old Erik's brow furrowed, piercing Tor with his eye's icy gaze. "You never wanted a god. You wanted a jinni in a bottle. Here's one of yours, I believe." The old man held up a carving of the goddess Freyja.

"That's my wife's."

"Not the same care you put into your other carvings." He

held it next to the handle of Tor's seax, its blade dangling precariously close to the tip of Tor's nose. The old man looked at the two as if comparing fine art. "She lacks a little something, doesn't she? I don't think you gave her any soul." His jaw hung loosely as he examined the knife. "Hmmph. Not like you gave this weapon. I think you put your whole heart into this one."

Both had certain features nearly worn away from years of handling. Both were used most whenever Tor had been away from home.

Tor turned to his wife; she was still unconscious. His pride drained from him, and he tried to conceal the fire burning inside.

"Let her go, Erik. Please, let her go."

"I couldn't do this to you." Old Erik acted like his feelings were hurt. "Vidar made this sacrifice—and Skadi and Anja. But, so did Runa."

Tor lunged, but the vines just got tighter. "There's nothing more evil than a wayward priest."

"Is that really all you think I am?" Old Erik's green eye contorted like it wanted to climb out of its socket. "Imagine how surprised I was when she asked that I make a sacrifice to the goddess for the safe travels of your sons. You sacrificed them—for what? You sent them out before the thaw because of mistakes you made in your past." The old man pretended to be sincere. He wasn't much better at it than Tor. "Your wife was right. It's time there was a proper sacrifice. You know the kind, Tor, don't you?"

"No." Tor gritted his teeth as he lied. He tried to stay focused on his wife.

"Now, if your sons survive, they will be able to make their own decisions, of who they will follow, and who will get their souls."

"You really did have a talent." Old Erik smiled as he looked at Tor's seax. Then he dragged the blade across the front of Tor's shirt. Tor grunted as the knife slipped into the cutting board of his chest. Saplings flexed as he drew his limbs in and stretched him back as soon as he quit.

The slice Erik put on Tor stung but was not deep, splitting open his shirt and only the top layers of skin underneath with no damage to muscle or bone. His chest and stomach became warm and sticky wet as blood drew into his shirt before coloring the surrounding snow.

Old Erik leaned in close to whisper directly into Tor's ear. "Tonight, you will escort your wife to her goddess." His breath stank of onion and cod and teeth rotting from a neglect.

He winked at Tor with his green eye, which started twitching almost violently as his face turned stern and angry.

Old Erik hung the little idol around Tor's neck. Blood from the bubbling wound climbed into the dry wood like wax up the wick of a candle.

Old Erik placed the ring on Tor's chest on the scar where his own soul had been cut out long ago. Tor gasped for air under its weight. It wasn't his, and it locked him to the earth, an immovable burden holding him firmly to the ground.

The ravens chirped and cawed.

A reanimated Orri lunged toward Tor and stared down at him. Dried blood coated the right side of his face like a black mask from where the blunt side of Tor's axe put him down.

"Is that my soul ring?"

"Yes." Old Erik hissed. "Had you been better with your bow we wouldn't need it." The tension left his face. "Don't worry, Orri, soon it will have you back."

Tor couldn't move. The weight of Orri's soul was stifling. He'd never felt pressure like that before.

Vidar appeared and grabbed the bloody seax out of Old Erik's hand, and pushed the blade deep into the fat of Orri's back.

BITTER

At first it looked like Orri had been hit in the back with a hammer, not a knife. Orri's jaw dropped, but he didn't scream. Instead, he whimpered, the way Vigi had before taking his last breath. His eyes closed painfully tight like he was burning on the inside, and tears froze to his jowls as his cheeks drained of all color. When he opened his eyes, trembling and wet with fear, they fixated on his ring, still crushing down on Tor's bloody chest.

Orri lost his legs, and with a quiet thump he fell across the vine tied to Tor's feet. The fat Viking slid headfirst down into the dark shadow, into the hollow left by the uprooted base of the tree, dragging Tor down as he painted the pure white snow a crimson red. The dying man looked up to Vidar, confused.

"Why?" he uttered with shallow breath.

"You betrayed me," said Vidar, as he wiped the blade off on Tor's shirt. Orri's reaction was only one of confusion, as his blood soaked down into the surrounding earth and snow. "Did you think you could just send those boys to take that chest? Did you think I wouldn't find out, or that I wasn't strong as you and wouldn't be waking up?" Then his demeanor changed to that of a man speaking to a dying friend. "I wanted to forgive you, Orri. But what kind of man would that make me?" The giant stood. He cast a glance at Ubbi as if he needed someone to understand. "I had a right to my revenge—for my honor."

As Vidar was talking, something moved in the shadows, slithering into the blood and disappearing under Orri's back. Vidar didn't seem to notice. He laid Tor's sword on Orri's chest and pressed the fat fingers of the dying Viking's right hand around its hilt, then placed a small silver coin in his left.

Orri stared at Vidar, the light flickering in his eyes. "My soul," he whispered. "Please."

Vidar shook his head as if arguing with himself. "You did this." He took a drink from his flask with a shaking hand, then dripped some into Orri's loose lips. "I do not suspect the Valkyries will be coming for you, my old friend, but if they do, I will see you in Valhalla. And we will drink mead and firewater, and you can tell me your stories, and we can laugh together once again."

Something was definitely moving under Orri. A horror seemed to reanimate his dimming eyes. As if whatever was wriggling along the small of his back was pulling itself inside.

Vidar started shaking in anger. "You did this!" The still, cold air ate his words. He left his old friend behind as he climbed out of the pit and settled with Old Erik. "Do your worst to the others, but have mercy on Orri. I've had my revenge, and it tastes bitter." He spat toward Tor. "Orri was a good man, and his debt to me is paid." He looked down at him. "Your fate is in the gods' hands now."

The black ravens began to caw ferociously, jumping down to the feet of Old Erik as a great white owl swooped in and landed on Kiara's chest. The owl jumped down onto the ground and chased the two ravens, screaming, splitting them, and sending them into the trees. The owl clawed back onto its perch on the still unconscious girl, like a white knight from one of her stories, a savior on a dark night.

BLOOD WEEDS

B lood was sprinkled over Orri, Runa, Tor, and Kiara. Handfuls of dirt were tossed over them. Prayers to the gods were spoken. Then there was nothing.

The night air was still. Snow began to fall on Tor's face, and all he could hear was the sound of his own breath and the falling snow.

"Runa?!" he grunted in pain.

She did not move, but he could see her breath.

"Orri?" Tor saw movement. If he was still living, he could thank that thick layer of blubber he'd been piling on like a bear preparing for a ten-year hibernation.

Orri groaned a reply.

"Can you get up? Can you cut me free?"

No reply.

He looked into the forest, but Old Erik was nowhere to be seen. They were all gone. Despite the pain, Tor pulled at the vines with everything he had.

"Nnnjaah!" he groaned. The saplings seemed to resist more the more he struggled.

Then he felt it—a strong tug at his feet, then another. Then the vine around his ankles pulled his feet down toward Orri until he was stretched out in three directions between the tugging and the two saplings.

Something was moving in the blackest part of the shadow below Orri's lifeless form. Tor stopped struggling. He stared into the black. Nothing. Quieting his breathing, Tor listened, the way he did when Vigi alerted during a hunt. He listened past Orri's shallow breaths, and then he heard it. It was like a slither. Something was there, but he couldn't see what it was. It was getting bolder now, rustling damp leaves, shifting under the snow. *There.* Something on the surface moved. Blood-red snow shifted near Orri's ear. Orri didn't move. Tor wanted to call his name, but he dared not make a sound. When he forced himself to breathe again, the warm air in his lungs clouded his vision.

He shifted his head back toward the forest. Nothing. No Old Erik, no Anja, no light. Before the fog cleared from his last breath, he was staring back down toward Orri, scanning left and right, trying to pick up the sound again, the movement — any clue to what was there. Nothing. Runa lay still but breathing.

Tor's neck ached from holding his head up. He gave in and laid it down on the cold ground. He watched as the moon continued its rise high above, its light quickly erasing the shadow of the downed oak's roots. The outline of it reached up like a massive claw waiting to drag them into the earth.

Owwww. A wolf howled in the distance.

Aaaowwwww, came a faint reply. *Had the wolves picked up the scent of blood or heard the struggle?* He wondered what the old devil would do when he returned.

It wouldn't matter soon — it was a clear night, and the cold had long ago settled into Tor's bones. Even if Old Erik didn't come back, even if the wolves didn't discover them and tear them apart, they would all be frozen by morning — an odd way to sacrifice to Odin, or Freyja. Maybe the tribute was to Loki. The trickster might find this an amusing tribute since his mother was an ice giant.

That must be it. He was freezing to death. When had Tor stopped shivering?

He heard a growl. This was it.

Vigi limped out of the shadows and dropped down

beside him. He was warm and he smelled bad. He licked at his side, then raised his head, growling. Then, as if satisfied with that defense, nuzzled his head in close to his master.

Tor's mind wandered as he drifted in and out of consciousness. What would happen to his sons? They were out on their own tonight as well. Had they made it to the fields? Were they safe, warm? He imagined them huddled around a fire, telling scary stories, making sure Ragi did not sleep at all. Worse could be happening, but he tried not to think about it.

Vigi jumped to his feet and growled into the leaves at his feet, his bared fangs crimson with blood. He yipped and jumped back, fur standing high along his neck and shoulders.

"What's wrong, boy?"

Tor He stretched his head down. Nothing. Then back to look into the forest. Still no light. No sign of Old Erik.

Vigi barked insanely, backing away.

"Shush now," he was killing Tor's ears. "There's nothing there — "

A serpent struck out from under the leaves and hit Vigi in the side, knocking him off his feet. The snake was gone. Tor could see the fog of Vigi's breath.

"Vigi? You all right, boy? Vigi — Aaaaauuhhhh!" A sharp stick dragged the length of the cut across Tor's chest. He pulled his arms to knock it out of the way, but practically dislocated his middle fingers as the saplings backlashed. Arms spread wide, lying on his back, helpless, he saw them, two black, hollow eyes.

He shifted his head and pulled again, this time with quick, jerky motions, trying to pop at least one of his restraints. No luck. His slashing, spinning gyrations were all stopped short, pulled back in every direction except where he wanted his limbs to go. He helplessly turned back toward the source of his pain.

The two empty eyes were set into what appeared to be

an elongated face made of slipping, writhing, thorny vines.

"Vigi! Wake up!" Tor turned his head wildly but Vigi was out cold. He turned back to his tormentor, and in his terror he saw that it wasn't a stick scraping into the wound on his chest. It was the creature's tongue.

The long, dry instrument probed and prodded at his cut, each lick sending sharp strokes of pain ringing the length of his spine.

"Get away from me!" He struggled. No reaction.

The figure was in the crude shape of a man made by a thousand thorny snakes trying to keep hold of one another. Only they were not snakes. They were vines, or maybe just one long vine—one long, writhing, dry vine with a sharp tongue scraping agony out of Tor's freshly reopened wound. Its tip wetted, the vine sipped on Tor's crimson blood, and Tor could feel the excess bleeding seeping warmth down his side.

The vine was dressed in splashes of glowing foxfire, which cast an eerie, death-blue light with each heavy beat of Tor's raging heart.

The creature looked down at the heavy ring holding Tor's chest solidly to the ground and poked at it, sliding it easily along the blood-soaked path with its barky tongue, apparently unaffected by its weight.

Tor hoped it would lift the burden off him, but something else got its attention.

The head turned to watch another vine, now two, emerge from the bottom of the pit. They slithered like snakes, pushing and prodding each other as they went. They moved tentatively at first, like dogs sniffing to find a trail. But then they made contact with the blood-trail Orri's wound had pumped into the snow and immediately began to writhe as if jockeying for position.

One of the vines slipped along up the hill while the second rolled and twisted until its end joined its beginning. A head raised out of the pile of prickly rope, then two crude hands lead two long arms up toward the stars. When the hands pushed off the ground they linked to the head with makeshift shoulders, and the whole of a legless torso was pushed out of the pile. One of the hands grabbed the other snake wriggling along the trail of blood and began to pull at it, throwing it into a pile at the bottom of the pit.

The snake turned back on the body, wrapping itself around its assailant. The two were indistinguishable from each other, the snake coiling around and amongst the other's chest and head, the hands of the first trying to pull the other out of its chest. A third arm grabbed the first by the neck from within the twisting, sliding core. Then a second head appeared.

The whole thing was easier for the immobilized Tor to follow as the second body emerged. Only this one was shaped like a woman, who slithered up onto legs and stood over the man who still looked as if buried to his waist in a pool of quicksand made up of his own vines.

Her long fingers were tipped with sharp thorn talons now gripping at his neck, which collapsed, then reformed, slipping in and out of her grip until she found what she was grasping for. The man-shape stopped as soon as she pulled a hidden gold medallion from the heart of his slithering chest. The creature had a soul!

She carried it as she slinked over to Orri. The male figure stopped resisting, instead giving her line so she could saunter freely to her target.

Tor's eyes turned to the creature crouching next to him, its finger pinning Orri's ring to his bleeding chest. There, he could see it, something reflecting in the moonlight as its vine slithered and jockeyed for position to maintain its form. Deep in its chest, his tormentor also bore a beautifully adorned soul ring. Its owner must have been wealthy, for it was not only dipped in gold, but there were glimmers of red ruby and green emerald, too.

Tor gasped. How easily this creature was able to

maneuver Orri's soul on his chest, so heavy to him that he felt he could barely breathe under its weight.

The female creature threw the other's soul to the ground as she got to Orri, who lay there quiet and still. Her arm turned back into a vine and slithered over his body until it found his waist. Then it slipped underneath the fat of his belly until emerging again on the opposite hip, in the shape of a hand, holding a small flask.

She pulled the wooden stopper with wriggling, excited tentacles. Patches of pale blue luminesced rapidly with excitement as she held the flask to her face and poured the drink into the cavity where her mouth would have been, sending the red liquid tumbling over layers of dry, brown, twisting bark until it spilt into the snow at her feet.

The creature next to Tor transformed, the tongue now playing the role of a finger as the vines of the face spiraled into a hand, the eyes disappearing into the mess until the old arm turned into a neck and head rightly atop the creature's shoulders, the onyx colored eyes emerging in the spot on the face where they belonged. Tor's companion's face gave little interest to the frenzy, a passing glance, before turning his head upward. Those black, lifeless eyes cast skyward, reflecting the light of the moon that sailed the undulating river of green and purple now coloring the breadth of the cloudless sky.

The female was oblivious as she turned the flask up to drain it of every last drop before letting it fall, only to be joined by the other, both dropping to the ground to frantically try to lick up what had tainted the snow with tongues of root probing the earth like a couple of blind snakes.

Tor's tormentor's eyes looked longingly at the beauty of the heavenly show while the others dropped their masculine and feminine facades and melted into one large, swirling, slithering mass around the site of the spill.

They looked like two thirsty serpents, but with no real

mouths, no throats, no stomachs — no way to get satisfaction. Tor knew Orri, and thought it likely the flask had been firewater, making the weeds no better than a couple of sots fighting over a drink they had no way to taste. The male raised a head from the swirl as if catching a scent, and began to slither over to Kiara. Just as it was climbing up onto Kiara's chest, the owl returned and dug its talons into the serpent, causing it to draw back, slithering away from her soul to its pulsing coil nesting in the shadows.

The owl screeched at the vine as if in warning, then took its sharp beak and started biting at the Christian's ring. It was as if everything in these haunted woods were after men's souls. But the owl stopped short of taking it, turning back to screech again at the vines, who drew back in respect of the white bird.

A cold breeze blew, and Kiara's soul began to sing as new pinpoint holes in its fractured exterior acted as key holes on a flute. The owl took another dig at the ring, unbreakable by any means of men, and the pitch changed again, invisible bellows playing a new song for all manner of creature lurking in the cold, dark forest that night.

ENTER DARKNESS

The feminine vine left Orri and slithered over to Tor. Around his ankle she slipped, encircling his calf, then up his thigh.

"Get away from me!" The words were ripped from his throat. She ignored Tor's rebuke, and the creature sitting next to him ignored her. Instead, its blank eyes continued to stare at the beautiful night sky. Tor wasn't sure if he should be happier his tormentor was ignoring the oncoming snake or whether he wanted it to fight her for him. Then he recognized something in the creature. It was looking at the night sky the way a boy would on his first night sleeping out under the stars.

Was it in awe? Could they feel at all? Just because it chose to take on the form of man did not make it like him, but there was something, something eerily recognizable in the way those two fought over Orri's flask, and now the way this thing stared at the moon and stars.

They were made of vines, like roots, or weeds, but it was as if there was something more, something recognizable, not like some mindless thieves who'd scavenged bright trinkets. It was as if the souls they carried could be their own. Could these be draugar? Their bodies returned to dust but their souls living on, if such an existence could be called living at all. It was more like living a nightmare. These things seemed to be yearning for things they couldn't have, unless they wanted sacrifices of flesh and bone and a few fresh souls.

Large swaths of green bands danced above the trees, turning purple then back to green again, and the draugr stared on. It seemed to be looking for something, affected the same way his cohorts were when they deeply wanted a taste of Orri's flask.

The vine climbing his leg seemed to be sniffing around his belt, prodding and probing. Tor hoped she was just looking for firewater.

"Get off me, you blood weed!" He pulled his hands in, just unable to reach the snake as it slithered over his stomach and up to the ring on his chest. The vine slipped through Orri's soul and lifted it up off of Tor's blood-soaked chest as easily as if it were just a simple gold ring. Tor threw his head back, coughed, and breathed deeply again, finally relieved of the unbearable weight of it.

As she passed through the ring, the vine spiraled up into her female form again and sauntered back to Orri, his soul rolling along the length of vine making up the cracked, barky fingers of her left hand.

She didn't slow as her right hand dropped into a lagging vine before slithering over to wrap around Orri's thick ankles. As she walked, she slinked her form down to that of a serpent, then slid down into a shadowed opening at the bottom of the pit where the dead roots once lived. She dragged the barely conscious Orri, too drained of life and blood to cry out, down into the darkness, like she was plucking him from this world to be her bridegroom in the next.

A marriage arranged as a sacrifice to the gods he spent his life chattering about, but never actually worshiped.

"So, this is it?" Tor shouted angrily. "This is what I get for sacrificing my soul? It's not what the old gods promised!" As he looked at his still unconscious wife, his heart sunk, and his anger grew. Mustering the power of the wolf, he went as berzerk as his strength would allow and started jerking wildly to try to free himself one last time.

After he'd exhausted himself, he looked up and laughed.

All the trees he'd fallen in his life, and he was being held captive by two spindly little saplings. As his head fell back into the snow, Tor started laughing hysterically through cold tears.

"Are these your Valkyries, you old demon?!" he screamed into the beautiful night sky. The vines did not seem to care.

With a final burst of energy, Orri managed to turn his head back toward Tor before he was tugged through the small black passage to the underworld, the opening stretched wider by the fat of his belly.

Tor's tormentor pulled back his thorny finger that had been tapping the blood flowing from the cut across his chest. Sweet relief. He took a moment and breathed a sigh of brief respite.

The sky that fascinated the stone-faced weed at his side — was brilliant. The sound of Kiara's soul changed pitch again amidst the sound of dragging.

Tor watched as his guardian began its decent into the pit but it wasn't finished tormenting. Its thorny finger slithered around his neck and began to clamp down as if to punish him for his insults. But the pain of the thorns digging into his throat was quickly superseded by the need for air.

Only silence came as Tor tried to lash out, and by the time he felt his hands were free from their bonds he had to ignore his want to grab something to keep from being dragged down into the pit for his overwhelming need to breathe. The palms of his hands were pierced by thorns as he pulled and struggled against the vine around his throat, but he was no match for it.

The white owl, their only champion, screeched, rolled its head and ruffled its feathers in protest before being forced to give up its post, as the third vine began dragging Runa and Kiara into the pit.

The last thing he remembered of the light was the

silhouette of his own bloody hands grasping at the mouth of the world that would swallow him whole. The moon faded as Tor slipped into unconsciousness. Then there was only darkness.

ENEMY OF MY ENEMIES

T or spat twice, waking to the taste of blood and dirt in his mouth. His hands were free, and he could breathe, so that was an improvement. His head hurt—neck stiff. Eyes open wide, he tried to find light, a change, something.

Am I blind? No, keep calm. I'm alive. He felt his waist. *Nothing.* Then he remembered; he'd given his fire kit to Erik.

The smell was dank but clear of the foul, decaying smell of the draugr. He ran his fingers along a rough-hewn wall of stone. Cool earth settled under his fingernails.

"Runa?" The sound of his whisper was hollow, empty. Something moved in the darkness. Thoughts of the vines filled his head. He felt around for a weapon, a rock, anything.

"Unnngph."

Tor stayed silent. Still no rock.

"Who's there?" The words were Irish.

"Kiara?" Tor exhaled.

"Tor." The voice shook with terror. "Help me."

"Have you seen my wife? Is Runa with you?"

"I can't see anything. Wait," whispered Kiara. "Something's here."

Tor felt a chill run the length of his spine. "What is it?" Boyish nightmares raced through his mind.

"It's sniffing my leg."

"Have you got a knife — anything sharp?" Tor had to be strong — for Runa and Kiara. Neither of them deserved this fate. "I think they're just vines."

"They're not just vines," she sobbed. "It's in my pocket."

"A knife?" Tor's heart jumped.

"No," Kiara's voice was filled with terror. "It."

A high-pitched note played through the darkness.

"Shhhh! Are you crazy? Put your ring away." Tor couldn't believe this girl.

"I'm scared. I always play when I'm — what do I do?"

"Maybe you can slap that ring over its slithering head."

"I'm scared," she moaned.

Tor gritted his teeth and frantically scoured the area for a weapon. Whatever those things were, he'd be next. "Runa!" he whispered harshly. His hand ran over something. *Pebbles?* He picked up a handful. *No good.* They crumbled in his grip — soft, and a little wet. He dropped them and continued running his hands along the ground. There had to be something. Then he felt *it.* Like a huff. Like breath. He froze. He was on all fours, no weapon, and something was there, close to his head. It had just sniffed in his ear.

Tor thought of the creatures — like people, but able to shift, like snakes. No reason to strike at it. That would be like punching a thorn bush. He would have to grab it. Nothing else made sense.

"Unghh." A new sound from the other side. Was it Orri? He didn't dare think about what the creatures were doing to him.

"Tor?" said Kiara. "Are you still there?"

"Shhh!" he grunted. Slowly he pulled his hand in his sleeve to protect it from the barbs. Sitting perfectly still, he waited for his chance. He would not go down like the girl, not without a fight. As he strained to sense motion — hear something, feel something — his body tensed. The flex before the fight reminded him of his wound as his chest burned. He felt the wetness from a trickle of blood slowly pulsing down the length of his stomach.

"Maaaahhhm!" A sound echoed out through the dark chamber.

He fell backward and hit his head against the wall as the piercing wail rang in his ears. He clenched his stinging skull.

A rush of air that smelled of dirt, onions, and rotten cabbage blew in his face with a huff.

"Maaahhhm!" Another scream, louder than before.

"What was that? Tor, is that you? Are you alright?" Kiara sounded as if she were near tears. "What's it doing to you?"

Tor sat there, leaning against the wall and rubbing the back of his head, burning sharply from being slapped against a rocky wall. He wiped the other hand against the ground, scrubbing the remnants of the crumbly pebbles from between his fingers, all the while shaking his aching head.

Another huff of stale breath filled his face. He put his hand out and felt the dull tip of a long horn. His hands ran the length of it, curving and broadening until it landed on overgrown, matted, scratchy fur. He took his other hand and cupped the pulsating muscle along the jaw of his new tormentor.

It was familiar, and a wave of irony struck him.

"Maaaahhhm!"

Tor flinched as it screamed into his face again. His hand ran under the jaw to stroke the bearded chin. Then he grabbed a curvy horn, put his other hand on the coarse, wiry hair along the back, and used the beast to pull himself up to his feet.

"Tor?" He could hear Kiara crying. "It's biting at my pocket."

"Pet it," Tor replied as he ran his stinging hands and his useless eyes up the wall. No sky. No way to climb. He scratched his chin, his fingers smelled like dung. "Hmmmf."

"What?" the girl replied.

"Pet it." He couldn't help but laugh. "It's a goat."

THIRST

"It's a goat?!" cried Kiara. "It's just a goat! It's eating some of that rotten vine—I think the goats eat the vines!" Relief poured from her still shaking voice.

"Yes." The one Tor was petting had a collar. It had a ring on it. "They're mine," he laughed. "So, this is where you wander off to, saving the world from the evil dead. How'd you get down here, eh?" He petted his little hero. Then he helped Kiara to her feet. "If your feet are tied, push its nose to your ankles and it'll eat through the vines. Just stop it before it gets to your boots."

"Where are we?" Kiara sounded as lost as Tor felt.

"Underground if we're lucky—the underworld if we're not. Can Christians go to Hell?" He was trying to lighten the mood, but that last word echoed hollowly.

"Tor?" another voice cried out.

"Runa!" He dropped to all fours and rummaged around among the goats, crawling toward her confused, tired voice.

Kiara shuffled behind with one hand cinched to his coat. He followed the shallow breathing until his fingers grazed a prostrate body.

"Runa!" Tor pulled her tight and felt like he could breathe again. It was as if the weight of that ring had been lifted off his chest for the second time. "Are you all right?"

"Ja, I think so. Can you help me up?"

He hugged and kissed her neck. Tasting blood, he ran his hand along the cut.

"Owww! Be gentle. It hurts." She punched Tor's sliced

chest.

Tor ignored the pain and grabbed her up in his arms, glad to know she had some life in her.

"Have you got any water?" Runa gasped.

"Here." Kiara pushed a skin into Tor's back.

Tor kissed Runa's cheek as he gave her the skin.

"Over here," said a weak voice from the blackness.

Tor exhaled slowly. "Be glad I can't see you, Orri, or I'd kill you with my bare hands."

"You almost did," Orri coughed, "about your dog. Well, I was after you—you know that, right?"

"You really do want to die today, don't you?"

"Aaugh!" Orri cried out like he still had a knife in his back.

"What? What is it?" Kiara whimpered.

"Get away from me, you stinkin' goat," Orri coughed again, then hacked for a few seconds. "Tor, my flask is missing. You got anything to drink?"

"You mean firewater? No, I don't touch it anymore." Tor's mouth suddenly felt very dry.

"Too bad." Orri sounded like that was the worst thing that had happened to him all day. "If you did, I'd force some down that little girl's throat, just to shut her up."

A little taste would take the edge off about now. Tor hated agreeing with the dog-murdering goblin, but the thirst was something all Vikings understood. Gods, most people who'd survived their share of long winters probably did, whether for firewater or some other soul-withering vice, which was why people covered their souls in silver or gold, if they could afford to.

Before Tor ever tried firewater they'd warned him—once he tasted it, he'd thirst for it the rest of his life. He'd done a lot of things when he was young that he'd been warned he shouldn't do. In fact, he had been famous for doing them all.

"I-I have water," Kiara said hesitantly.

"Bring it to me," Orri begged. "I'm not sure I can walk."

Kiara didn't let go of Tor's coat as she edged toward the voice.

"Aiyyy!" she screamed. "Let go of me!"

Tor heard her hit the ground and scoot away like a frightened pup.

Orri's weak laughter turned to chokes and coughs. "Don't worry, I'm not going to hurt you as long as you may be of some use. Fat men have to be smart to make it in this world."

"How much use is a bleeding, crippled fat man?" Tor would've kicked Orri if he could've seen him.

"Don't be like that, Tor." Orri pretended to find his humility. "I didn't want to kill you — either of you."

"Me?" asked Kiara.

"No," Orri replied. "I'd have sent you to your heaven without blinking an eye. I'm talking to Tor now, and his lovely wife."

"She was lovelier before she got that scar down her throat," Tor seethed.

"That was Vidar; you know that." Orri spoke like a true victim of circumstance. "You know how it is. Remember our first raids? We didn't have to kill those people. Those monks were as weak and pathetic as this slave girl. But it had its purpose, didn't it? The more we killed early, the less we had to kill later on."

"It's not the same," said Tor.

"No. I guess not," agreed Orri. "Come on, lass. Where's that water?"

COLD REVENGE

On all fours, like a dog, Kiara cautiously felt around to find Orri again. She'd prayed for his death so many times, and now she was giving him her water. Who knew if they would ever see water again? Her hand brushed against something, and she reflexed back. Her heart pounded in her chest as she eased her hand out and found it again. Its outline was cold and hard.

"What was that?" asked Tor. "I heard something scraping."

"Nothing," said Kiara. "A rock." It was Ice Breaker, the sword Vidar had laid on Orri's fat, wheezing chest. Her mind raced. What should she do?

"Alright, you found me. Now on with the water," Orri complained. "I'm dyin' o' thirst."

Kiara pushed the skin toward the voice until it touched his leg, then pulled back. She never wanted to be grabbed by him again. "There it is."

Kiara stood up, and as quietly as she could, she lifted the sword. It was lighter than she expected. "What are we going to do now?" She stalled for time. Kiara held the blade out toward Orri, her fingers tightening around its grip. One swing, even a blind one, and she could end this villain — this man who speaks so callously about all he'd done, what he'd been a part of doing to her family, and what he'd done to her. He'd have killed her on that tree had it not been for the grace of God — and Tor. She tightened her grip and raised the sword high. All she had to do was let it fall.

The intent must have added to its weight. Kiara's hand began to shake. Lowering the sword, she took a deep breath, then raised it again, staring blindly toward the sound of Orri's shallow breaths. She could strike toward the sound of the drinking. There's no way she could miss.

God forgive me. Kiara eased the sword down. She couldn't do it. She shrugged her shoulder to mop the cold sweat from her forehead.

She stared up into the blackness, looking for something—a sign, a light—anything. *Pathetic.* She wiped new tears from her face. *Lord, please forgive me, and help me do what you would have me do.* She prayed silently, putting her soul to her lips. *Your will be done Lord. Not mine. Amen.*

A splash. "Echh! That's terrible." Orri wretched and spit, then Kiara felt him grab for her leg. She jerked away and fell back, hitting her head against a wall.

"Assassin!" The fat Viking wretched again. "She's trying to kill me! This poison's making me thirstier." Orri spit again and again. "Get away from me you, stupid goat!"

"Give it to me," said Tor.

"It was just water, the same I gave you. I don't know what's wrong." Kiara could hear Tor's heavy hand hit Orri.

"Aaagh!" Tor yelped. "Something stung me. Will somebody figure out how we can get some light?" Tor kicked around until he found Kiara's leg, barely missing the blade. Then he dropped the skin on her lap. "Drink," he said sternly.

"It's the same water I gave you."

"Drink! And if you poisoned him, I'll leave you here to die alone."

Kiara drank, the icy water refreshing. She didn't realize how thirsty she was. For proof, she gargled and swallowed with a gulp. "It's good—believe me." She pushed it back at Tor.

Tor sniffed it, sipped it, then drank. "It's just water." The edge was off his voice.

"Keep it away," said Orri. "It's stinks to me."

"I wouldn't blame her for killing you if she could," Tor kicked again.

"Oww." Orri sounded weaker.

"Lest you forget, you're the reason we're here."

"Old Erik wanted her dead." Orri sounded like a dying man making his last confession. "He told Vidar she was a curse on this land, and the only way to fix it would be to sacrifice her to Hella."

There must have been a lot of goats, because with bleats sounding the charge a herd of padded hoofs faded from earshot like a rain passing in the night.

"Something spooked the hungry grubbers." Tor sounded worried. "How we coming with that light, Orri?"

"Maybe we should follow the sound." Hairs bristled up Kiara's neck. "They might lead us out, or at least to where we can see."

Then an unfamiliar, gravelly voice echoed from the darkness. "Don't worry love. They's everywhere."

"Yes-s-s," agreed another heavier voice that whistled with each 's'. "Goats eats the vines, and they's everywhere."

SVINDL AND SVIKAR

"Does you have to repeat everything I say?"
"Shut up, Svik," whistled the other. "It's my turn to talk."
"Who's there?" Kiara pulled herself behind Tor and away from the voices. She was shaking like the last leaf in autumn.

"I'm Svindl," graveled the first, "and this is me brother, Svikar."

"Are you brothers?" Tor thought of his own sons. Maybe these two would understand. "We're lost." He had to try something. "Can you help us find our way home? I have two sons, and they need me."

"You're lost?" it cackled. "No, friend, you're exactly where you deserve to be, I'd say."

"Shut up, Svin."

"What? I'm allowed to answer a question, same as you."

"If you'll just get us a light," Tor knew how boys could get distracted, "maybe when we can see better, we can find our own way out." Tor thought if he could just get them talking, maybe they'd come around.

"Just let me talk, 'right?" Svindl asked. "Your whistlin's hurting my ear."

Whistling? Tor thought, before he realized he wasn't talking to him.

"I smelled 'em first. Just let me handle this."

"If anyfing, they smelled you first."

"He's a big one, isn't he? For a man, I mean."

Svikar was right. Svindl's whistling was tough to take.

"You can 'ave the little 'un. She's as skinny as Hella's stick."

Tor pulled Runa behind him and backed into the women until they were up against the wall. He squinted in the dark. No improvement. "Try to find me a rock—anything," he whispered.

"The little 'un stinks the worst. Never smelled one like that before," graveled Svikar.

The air was indeed foul, but the stench came from the direction of the disembodied voices.

"She'd be better to stuff under a rock for a while. Let the vines flavor 'er up first."

"We could stuff 'er wif goat meat or somefin."

"Aw, I've had enough goat for a lifetime. Anyfin' but that." Then, with the sound of two flags flapping in a hurricane, he broke wind.

"Oh, come on, Svindl!" graveled Svikar. "Keep it together, eh?"

"Feels much better though, don't it?"

"I suppose," laughed the other.

Tor tasted death and rotten eggs.

"It smells like something died over there," Orri gagged.

"Was that supposed to be funny?" whistled Svindl.

Tor was wondering the same thing. *Good.* If anyone could bring these two around, it was Orri. Time he put that silver tongue of his to use.

"It does smell pretty rank now, doesn't it?" Svik laughed. "Even for us."

"What about 'im? The fat one?" Svikar sucked his teeth.

"Oh, he's the one, all right. The vines have 'im seasoned good right now. He's a boiler, that one is."

Tor cringed as Kiara started praying softly. "Please Lord, help this heathen protect your servant and kill your enemy."

Tor felt something hard bump against his elbow. He

reached back, and in the darkness, found a reason to smile. He let his fingers walk up the cold iron, and he was filled with hope when he took Ice Breaker by the hilt.

"Stay down," he whispered to Runa as he reached back. She was already crouched. "Orri," whispered Tor, "you'd better get me some light before these two drag one of us off for dinner."

"Oh, I don't like the light much," said Svindl.

"Don't need it," added Svikar. "But sometimes we do go into the light, into your world, at night and all."

"Ja, we go to hunt sometimes, when we're sick of goat or what we can't pluck out of the burrow."

"You mean barrow?"

"That's what I said, when we's sick of plucking what we can from down 'ere, we go up top to get somefin' a little fresher.

"Grave robbers," whispered Orri weakly.

"More than once," Svindl whistled. "But thanks to the gods, sometimes we get delivery."

"Did you say thanks to the gods?" Svikar sounded unamused.

"I know," Svindl howled in laughter. "I couldn't help myself."

Svikar cut his brother off. "We've taken some time to look up at your moon too—like a couple of forlorn draugar. It's not bad, really—your world."

"I don't like it—I just like to get what we're after and get back. That much light gives me the creeps-s-s," said Svindl, whistling a long time as if unable to escape the last word.

"Lookee there, Svin." Svikar's voice dropped low, almost growling.

The air stood quiet and still. Tor stepped forward, and raised the sword defensively, blind eyes squinting in the blackness. "Orri, how's that light coming?"

"Hey, I don't know what you plan to do with that pig-sticker, big man, but best you put it away before somebody gets hurt."

"Ja," said Svindl, "there's no need for violence 'ere."

"Besides, you're as likely to cut your friend's head off as ours."

Tor heard the grind of earth move under heavy feet and lifted the sword up high, ready to strike.

"Easy now, fella," whispered Svikar heavily, attempting to sound reassuring.

With a crack, a flash of light filled the space, then everything went back to black.

"What the—" came two heavy voices.

Orri had finally fired a spark. In that moment the lost caught a glimpse of their surroundings for the first time.

"Again!" Tor was shaking. "Orri, can you make fire?"

"I can't find anything to burn, just dirt and stone."

"Use your shirt if you have to. I need light." Hope filled Tor's heart even though what he glimpsed in the flash filled his mind with dread. What he saw was large. Very large. A hulk of a figure lurked in the darkness not three paces away. The room they were in was a stone cavern that ate the light of the spark before it could make an impression.

"Break his arm off," whispered Svindl. Tor shifted toward the voice, holding the blade up even higher now.

"Shush. He can hear you, idiot," said the deeper voice of Svikar. "I'm not losing a hand over it. You can bite his arms off if you're so tough. See if you come back with both your eyes."

Another flash. "Help!" Orri cried. The spark caught something dry and formed an ember. When compared to absolute black, even that tiny light cast a shadow. "It's got me!" The voice was Orri's, but the figure wasn't.

From the back, Tor saw the silhouette of what must have been two huge figures hovered over the source of light.

"It's biting me!" Orri screamed. Tor stepped forward. Experiences from long ago reared up inside and Tor's muscles knew what needed to be done. He let the blade sing.

It tore through flesh and bone. Lethal and deadly.

"Aaaaagh!" Something rolled across the floor, but the hulking figure didn't fall. "Svikar!"

The silhouette turned, lifting Orri off the ground by one of his arms as if the fat Viking were just a child's toy.

A small flame was coming from Orri's stomach, illuminating the gory scene like a single candle in a dark cathedral. The giant figure turned toward Tor.

"You cut his head off!" squealed Svindl. Orri looked small and insignificant in the hand of the goliath.

The light was poor, but Tor caught fleeting glimpses of the creature's ugly face. It looked to be in shock. Ice Breaker had bathed in its blood. Tor retched from the stench of the stuff that had an oily blue sheen.

"Over 'ere, Svin! He got me wif his sticker!" a deep, angry cry shouted from across the room. Tor turned but saw nothing, so he squared up against the giant still standing before him.

"Put that thing down before you hurt someone," whistled Svindl. Then he tossed Orri into the air, caught him by one of his legs, and slung him at Tor like a club. The small fire exploded across Orri's chest as Svindl whipped him back and forth like a little boy taunting his sister with her favorite doll.

One of Orri's hands slapped Tor across the top of his head knocking him to the ground. Runa helped him back to his feet while Kiara cowered in the corner, blowing into her soul with her eyes wired shut.

"You cut me deep, big man." Svindl sneered, his eyes glowing green in the light of Orri's flaming chest. Orri hung lifeless, upside down at the troll's side.

"Svindl!" Svikar's voice came from across the room, but Tor forced his focus up to the enemy he could see.

"Keep an eye out for his brother!" Tor shouted.

"I don't see anything." Runa near broke his eardrum

with her screams.

Tor peered into the shadows for movement but found it hard to concentrate with the spectacle of the giant troll dangling fiery Orri around by his legs.

"Leave 'im be and come get me before you lose *your* head, you idiot!" yelled an angry Svikar from the darkness.

The massive troll, Svindl, at least twice as tall as Tor, huffed and turned his head. Tor saw his chance to free the Viking, and swung the blade as hard as he could, cutting the creature's arm off at the elbow. Orri and the fire fell with it.

"Aaaaaayyyyeee!" Svindl howled, like a dozen pigs trapped between two mountains scraping together. It was terrible.

"My arm! Can't you do nothing right, Svindl? You let 'im cut off me best arm!"

"Your arm?" squealed the angry Svindl. Orri's flaming stomach lit the scene better now that he was so still. The troll looked fierce, more angry than in pain. Its disembodied arm lay between Tor and the knobbly toes of its left foot — the massive paw still gripping Orri tight.

"Come get me, you big oaf. Then I'll show you who's arm that was!" Svikar shouted from the darkness.

"I've 'ad about enough of hearing from you." Svindl craned his neck toward the darkness but with one eye still bent toward Tor and the sword. "I tell you what, Svik, you can 'ave the arm and the men, and I'll keep the rest! I'm sick of hearing your voice ringing in my head all the time, anyway. Two hundred years I've... Well, good luck wif this lot. Now you can ask them anyfing you want."

With that, the troll kicked the dismembered forearm, with Orri still in its clutches, into the darkness toward his brother's hiding place.

Tor watched Orri and the light of the fire skid away, and suddenly, he could see nothing of the monster standing overhead.

"Don't you dare leave me 'ere Svindl, or I'll..." came the voice from the shadows.

"You?" Svindl cut his brother off before he could finish. "You'll do nothing but give these buggers your eyeballs. That's all you'll do. Your skull might make a nice table for Frickel or one of the dwarf lords." For a moment there was only the sound of heavy, labored breathing overhead.

"You wouldn't leave me 'ere, would you, Svin? Not your older brother?" Svikar's voice was more amicable now.

Svindl's labored breaths gave way to stone grinding underfoot as the beast seemed to pivot away but then stopped.

All was black except where Orri lay burning, some fifty steps away. Tor tensed as the beast corrupted the air with every foul exhalation. Tor raised the sword higher as he eased back next to his wife. He recoiled and pinned Runa against the wall when he heard a splash. The Troll's oily, wet spittle bathed his feet as it soaked through boot and sock.

Incredibly quiet for such a massive beast, Svindl slipped off in the other direction, allowing Tor to breathe again.

"Don't you leave me 'ere!" Svikar sounded like he could've been crying. "You need me!" The stone walls drank the hollow ring of his voice the way a river drinks raindrops. "If you do this you will no longer be my brother, Svindl! Come back." He sniffed, and his voice got quiet. "Stupid oaf."

CANDLE STICK

Tor did not lower his blade. The other troll was still somewhere near Orri.

"I've got to get Orri." Tor started forward, but Runa grabbed his arm.

"No," she said.

Tor was resolute. "I don't want to, but I have to. I can't leave him behind. Not with things like that running around."

"I agree with Runa," said Kiara. "It's too dangerous."

Runa ignored her. "Forget Orri, but we do need his fire. Kiara should get it."

"What?" Kiara wanted to run, but there was nowhere to go.

"We're not sending Kiara." Tor focused on the darkness surrounding Orri.

"Look, Tor," Runa slapped his shoulder, "you always take everyone's side except mine! It's time you started putting your wife's needs ahead of everyone else's!" Runa grabbed his chin and made him look at her. "You are smart enough to realize that Kiara's the reason we're down here, right?"

Kiara's face burned. Then her heart stopped when Tor put his sword in his torch hand and drew back like he might slap Runa back to reason. Instead he dropped his shoulders, exhaling almost sadly.

His aggression scared Kiara, but it didn't stop Runa. She wasn't done sowing her poison. "That girl's the reason you had to fight Vidar—you'll have to admit that at least. Everything's gone wrong since she showed up, and still you protect her over me?"

"I'm not putting her before you," he assured her. "I'm just not willing to make a sacrifice of her to prove myself to you."

Then she put her arms around his waist. "Tor, when we married, you said you'd take care of me. You made a promise."

"And I'm going to." He looked down to her. "Of course I will."

Runa put her head against his chest. Her eyes reflected fire, and her burning stare made her feelings clear—that everything bad that had happened to her family since the Vikings arrived had been Kiara's fault.

"Husband?" Runa sweetened her tone. "Can I tell you something that will help us both."

"What's that?" he asked.

"Don't start pretending you're still a Viking now. It's too late for that. I need you to be smart, like a farmer. If something happens to you, then what? Can this little prayer warrior save me?" She smiled as she crushed his soul. "No. We all die. Not just me, but Orri and...and the girl, too." She could barely get the words out.

Kiara felt Runa's words as deep as any cut, but she had a point. If something happened to Tor, then all was lost. She straightened her back, and even though her body began to shiver uncontrollably, she spoke as bravely as she could.

"I'll get the fire—you keep an eye out for the troll." She ducked under Tor's raised sword and ran forward toward the light. After she got close to Orri, she slowed, like a mouse stealing cheese from the cat's dish. The light blinded her to whatever might have been lurking in the shadows. Orri's chest moved with a ragged breath. "He's still alive."

"The troll or the Viking?" asked Runa.

"Both, I'm afraid."

Runa followed Tor, who approached cautiously with his sword and eyes up. Orri lay there, a vine penetrating his abdomen burning with orange and yellow flame. Orri was stirring, still in the troll's severed grip.

"We need to get him free, then get out of here." Tor turned back to the darkness he'd left behind.

"He's burning," said Kiara.

"*It's* burning," Runa corrected. "He's got one of those vines coming out of him."

"Should we put it out?"

"Leave it," said Tor.

"It's a gift from Freyja that we've light at all in this miserable place." Runa gave her thanks.

"A gift from Freyja?" Tor and Kiara both rolled their eyes.

"I don't know how that vine is staying lit, but leave it be. If not for his might, Orri may still be of some use as a candlestick," Runa said.

The fire reflected off Ice Breaker, highlighting streaks of blood where it had done its work. "We need to get away from here." Tor tried to peer past the flickering shadows. "An injured beast is more dangerous than one that is whole. Who knows what the smell of trolls' blood might attract?"

The girl kicked at the hand. She'd never seen anything so frightening. It was disproportionately large, even for the size of the beast it was emancipated from.

"Hurry," whispered Tor. "Let's get him free." His eyes and sword still pointed outward.

The smell of it was terrible. The large digits were gross, with a thick layer of filth built up under cracked, broken nails that looked like they'd been chewed short by crooked teeth—blunted from prying the heads off of helpless victims.

Kiara cringed as she sunk her fingers into it and pulled back on one of the nails. The finger she had chosen was about as big as one of Orri's legs, and the more she pulled the more it seemed to tighten on the poor man, as if still alive.

"This is disgusting," whispered Kiara. "Is there anything agreeable about a troll?"

Orri groaned as the hand closed around him, but when the fingertips touched the flame spewing out of the Viking's stomach, they jerked back spastically, knocking Kiara onto her back. Tor quickly grabbed one of Orri's feet and dragged him from the palm of the monster's dismembered paw, keeping a wary eye on the rest of the fingers as if they were a set trap.

"Pitiful." Runa's face had grown an edge. She was not nearly as beautiful in this light, wearing disdain the way most women wore braids. She watched as Tor helped Kiara up off the stone floor.

Kiara ignored her. She was done trying to make friends with this woman.

"Look at the way it burns," said Runa. "What's happening to him?"

Kiara reached down to try to pull the vine out but stopped short when she saw the sharp barbs. It writhed at her approach like it was looking for someone to bite.

Lowering the sword, Tor cut the head off the flaming snake close to Orri's stomach, making Runa a nice little torch. More vine crawled out to take its place, growing slowly but steadily from the wound. He cut the head off the snake again, shaved the thorns, and lit it—another torch, and yet the vine kept coming.

He passed the next one to Kiara.

"Help me keep an eye out for the other troll. If we're lucky it slunk back off to its hole to die."

"Maaaaaa!" cried a little brown and white goat, pushing past Tor to nibble on the snake.

Runa shoved it away.

"Maaaaa!" it cried again, then started making a meal of the barbs and scrap Tor had sent to the ground.

"Tor," Runa kicked the goat aside, "you really are the worst farmer. It's no wonder your sons were always hungry when most of our flock avoided the stew pot by hiding down here. Think of how much time you wasted in the woods searching for the little devils while they were lurking right under your feet."

"Is that what you really think?" A gravelly voice echoed from the shadows. "You reckon you can just climb up a wall until you break through to the other side? Sorry love, but that ain't the way it works. Come closer. I won't hurt you. Not now, anyways."

They turned as one toward the voice. It was a head. As if resting on the ground, two large green eyes glimmered sideways from the shadows, not much farther apart than a man's.

"Stay back." Tor's knuckles cracked as his grip tightened around Icebreaker's hilt. "I am capable of defending myself."

"That is an understatement, Norseman." The troll ground its teeth.

"I don't think it can hurt us," said Kiara.

"Stupid girl," scolded Runa. "Its brother was twenty feet tall."

"It won't hurt us 'cause it can't. It's been there the whole time, watching us." Kiara let her torch lead the way as she eased toward the green eyes.

"If it likes the taste of Christians, as I suspect it does, don't expect my husband to come save you." Runa seemed so proud, refusing to accept that they were all in the same sinking ship.

Kiara wondered if Tor was ever going to get sick of her nonsense. She turned her focus toward Svikar. That beast said he'd seen the moon. He'd hunted atop the barrows. If they couldn't just climb out, then he was the only one who'd know how to get them home.

As she approached, the light of Kiara's torch illuminated

a long nose and heavy brow. Svikar was exactly the way Erik had described trolls in his stories. But its exaggerated features were more like a child's drawing of an old man than of a dangerous eater of the weak.

How it was alive she could not say—much less how it managed to talk. This troll had lost the battle. Tor had reduced it to its mind, with a big ugly mouth to tell you what it was thinking. What it could smell with that long, crooked nose, what it could hear with those long, pointy ears, and what it could see with its bulbous, reflective, green eyes was anyone's guess.

"I can still bite." The head clicked its teeth together playfully. "Come back. It was just a joke. I'm sorry to disappoint your mother, but I've never eaten a Christian. And by the smell of you, I'm interested in starting now."

"I'm not her mother!" Runa corrected.

"I figured," laughed the head.

Tor circled it, poking a yellow tooth with his sword. "You are Svikar, then?"

"If I were still wearing my shoulders I bet you'd remember."

"Stay away from its mouth," Runa advised from a distance.

"Umph, owww." Orri shifted, his stomach still alight.

"How is he alive?" asked Kiara. "He's been on fire for half an hour."

"Even if you put that fire in his belly out, he's never going to stop burning," said Svikar.

"Shut up, troll," said Tor. "You'll be dead long before he is."

"Oh, I don't know 'bout that. The weeds 'ave got 'im pretty well done already," said Svikar. "Did you put that hole in him?"

"No." Tor looked as confused as his wife that he was having this conversation.

"Can't even blame whoever did that to 'im, either." The

troll seemed to like to talk.

"This wasn't fate or coincidence or bad luck. No, it was all the fat man's doing. I can smell it. His soul was coming 'ere sooner or later. You all always get what you wanted in the end." Svikar looked over to Runa. "You are on your own, love. And you won't be making it out of 'ere, either."

"Come on, girl," ordered Runa. "Make yourself useful and see if you can find some wood—anything to make a sled out of. Maybe we can make something to get these goats to drag Orri for us."

"Heh, heh. You won't be finding any sticks down 'ere," said the disembodied head, "only blood vines. And they'll be finding you, not the other way around, if you know my meaning."

Tor looked worried, like he knew Svikar's meaning exactly.

SNAKE TONGUE

"**O**rri, you fat slob. You got us down here, so if this hurts blame yourself. And be glad we don't leave you to that."

"'That?'" Svikar sounded offended. "Be nice now. I'm not a 'that.' I'm an 'im. I've got a heart, you know."

"You don't even have a neck," said Tor. "Come on, Kiara, grab an arm."

Runa nodded as if giving Kiara the order herself.

Kiara hesitantly did as she was told. They dragged Orri down what looked to be a wide corridor. With each step the glow of the torches exposed etchings cut into the high stone walls. Images of tall things, short things, and swords, hammers, axes, and rings, and chained up beasts. Pictures of men and serpents and vines and flames. The goats followed, nibbling at the bases of the torches they carried.

"Do you know where you're going?" asked the gravelly voice. "'Cause I do."

Kiara looked at Tor, who did not turn but instead gave Orri's arm an extra tug as if signaling to ignore the troll and keep pulling.

"You don't want to go that way this time of night," said the troll.

"Night, day, how can you tell?" Tor gave Orri's fat wrist another tug.

"Wait," Orri's voice was fading.

"Christian," Svikar pleaded. "You wouldn't let 'im leave

me 'ere like this? His wife hates you more than I ever could, she does. I saw the whole thing. And you heard his vow. He'll never take your side over hers. Trust me on that—you need me."

Kiara looked over at Tor again.

Tor kept pulling, one strong arm gripping Orri's, the other holding the sword ready at his side. "Ignore him."

"Yes," Kiara growled, "because it is evil—a lying son of the devil himself."

"No." Tor looked at Kiara as if she had just eaten a bug. "Ignore him because he knows nothing."

"Oh, that's where you're wrong. I know lots of things." The croaking voice echoed from the ever-darkening shadows behind them. "I'm the only one other than the goats that knows where you're heading right now. Keep walking and you'll be no better off than your fat friend. You'll be fertilizer before that torch you're holding snuffs out."

"Wait," said Orri.

"Orri, I could use some help here." Tor said it with an odd desperation. "I'm going to need you to walk if you don't want to get left behind."

"So thirsty," he mumbled.

"Thirsty?" Svikar sneered. "There's more to worry about down 'ere than where you'll get your next drink, that's for sure."

Tor stopped dragging and turned toward the darkness. "Ja?"

"Come on," said the head. "I'll make a bargain wif ya. I'll help you find your way if you don't leave me 'ere. Keep you alive, I will. Help you find your water."

Tor looked down at Orri. The fat man lay still, eyes half open, lips cracked.

"It's too late." Kiara crouched down and put her cheek on Orri's face. "He's gone."

"Tor," Runa sounded frustrated. "Give me that sword."

Tor gave it to his wife. "Sons of Odin!" He slammed his hand against the wall. A hollow echo mocked them all. Runa took the sword and sliced Orri mid-belly, letting out a putrid stench.

"What are you doing?" Kiara gagged and fell back toward the wall.

"I'm collecting more of the vine. These torches are burning fast."

"You're defiling him."

"He's already dead." Runa backed away from the odor. She looked like she was going to vomit. "We don't know how much longer this vine'll grow." Runa smothered the flame on Orri's stomach.

Without the appetite of the fire, the vine grew wickedly fast. At first, it was like she was cutting the head off a snake before it could get out of its den. Then Runa let it grow longer, long enough to start to shape into arms or other appendages, like the draugr that fought over them in the moonlight.

Tor watched closely as she attended to her work. "Be careful, Runa."

"Just let me be, Tor. My torch is right here, and I'll set fire to this thing if it gets out of hand." Runa stayed focused on the task, cutting and then deburring each piece. "I think we could use some rope, ja?" As she got more comfortable working with the vine, she started allowing it to grow more and more before making the cut. The longer the vine, the more it seemed to organize. They watched in a trance as it shaped itself into an arm.

"Cut it off, Runa."

She waited until it began to form a head, looking eerily like a man trying to climb out of Orri's stomach.

"Now!" barked Tor.

She cut it off, and it fell into a pile on the ground.

She deburred the length of it as a new weed began to grow. This time it came a little slower.

It formed a head first, allowing the rest to gather into a pile beside the dead man. As Runa raised the sword to make the cut the pile drew up into an arm and tried to grab it from her hand, only to be dismembered by her quick, sharp stroke.

Tor took his torch and lit the vine at Orri's stomach again. The new growth wrenched from side to side in protest but never made it far enough to form a recognizable shape before burning away like a candle wick.

"Kiara's right. You shouldn't be doing that," Tor said to his wife.

"That girl knows nothing," she replied. "Would she have us leave without something to burn or a piece of rope? Perhaps she can say a prayer? Which is about all she's good for."

"You'd be wise to take the soul ring off the dead man's chest and protect it from that vine." Svikar sounded bored of the bickering.

"It is up to God to determine the fate of his soul. To remove it would be sacrilege." *Anything that head said must be a lie.* Kiara was sure of it.

"Your god has no power here! He is Odin's now," Runa huffed. "When my own father died, our priest collected his soul. That's our way, Christian."

"Old Erik took it?" Kiara wondered if the irony was lost on the woman.

"I doubt you know what your priests do with your dead." Runa wouldn't let it go.

Kiara scowled. "I've seen a lot of death, thanks to that fat Viking, and Vidar, and the rest of your savage countrymen and women."

"Well, I've never killed anyone." Runa cut the fiery head off the snake and started deburring and pulling it out of Orri's dead body as unfeeling as if she were weeding a garden.

Had these people gone mad? Kiara couldn't bear to look at

Runa.

"Why should we take Orri's soul?" Tor turned toward the troll.

"Oh, now Svikar may have some wisdom, eh?" Tor held the torch up to the tip of its nose, and the troll started talking. "To keep the weed from getting to it." Svikar puffed at the torch like a child trying to blow out a candle. "If it does you'll have another problem."

Kiara looked at Tor, his stoic face hard as stone. "What kind of problem?" she asked.

"Your soul's a manacle." He spoke to Kiara as if she were seven. "Who you are is bound to it, and you'll be bound to whoever ends up with it after you die—whether be God or some lying snake. Once this life ends, your will'll be your master's will, and the master will call its lost souls home."

"But Orri doesn't have his soul," Kiara remembered. "Old Erik put it on Tor, and then—"

"Then one of the vines took it. Runa!" yelled Tor. "Get away from that body."

"As always, the husband talks and the wife prepares," Runa complained to herself like a mother cleaning up after her grown children. "If it weren't for me we'd never eat. No one would make the sacrifices. No rope. No light—"

The hall fell silent as if Runa was satisfied she'd finally gotten in the last word.

Runa's light snuffed out. The goats started bleating wildly.

Tor held his torch into the black. "Runa?" He started running toward the sound of screaming goats. "Runa!"

By the time his fire lit the scene, Runa was in Orri's arms. The vine from his stomach had wrapped itself tightly around her throat, and she'd lost all color in her face.

Tor raised his sword to kill Orri for the second time in one night. Runa was kicking Orri's legs and punching at his face. She was not helpless, for his cheek was peeling back at the eye socket with each vicious blow. His dirty fingers were inside Runa's lips, pulling her mouth apart by the teeth, and a tongue of vine stretched from his mouth into hers.

Kiara heard the crunch of Orri's teeth as Tor slammed his left elbow into his face. Orri's jaw snapped and dislocated, leaving the lower half of his face swinging open to one side—but the thing didn't fall, didn't react, didn't show pain. Tor tried to pull fat Orri off his wife, but he couldn't overpower him, as if the draugr had the power of ten men.

Kiara hovered just outside the fight. Not knowing what to do, she prayed aloud and grabbed Runa around the waist and pulled. Jerking and pushing, she didn't have the strength to move the pile of bodies.

Runa's eyes were wide, and tears streamed down her cheeks as she watched a golden soul ring ride the vine from Orri's mouth into her own. As she clutched at the vine, trying to pull it out of her throat, blood ran from her grip and down her wrists from thorns strewn the length of the serpentine tongue.

"Find the sword!" Tor yelled over the sound of the struggle and the bleating. The draugr was killing his wife before his eyes.

He shoved his torch into Orri's slack jaw, but the prickly tongue continued to slowly work its way down Runa's throat.

Kiara saw Ice Breaker, and this time she did not hesitate. The first cut severed the leg off the draugr, bringing the whole group down hard onto the stone floor. Goats scattered to avoid being crushed in the melee, but Orri was not slowed. Kiara sawed at the vine coming out of Orri's open gut, leaving the end noosed around Runa's neck loose and snapping like an angry whip. She cut at it again, this time closer to Runa's throat, dropping the length of it down to be finished off by any goat hungry enough to claim it.

In the struggle, the vine in Orri's face had caught fire. The smell of burning hair mixed with roasting flesh as it climbed his beard and rolled yellow flames over his bald, tattooed head. Tor grabbed the sword out of Kiara's hands and cut his flaming head off.

When Orri's dismembered body fell over it toppled onto Kiara, pinning her under what now felt like a sack full of vipers. The fiery, stinking head dangled by its tongue as the stubborn vine kept trying to climb into Runa's face. Tor started pulling, the sharp thorns coating his palms in blood. Desperate for air, Runa grabbed the blade from her husband's hand and cut the vine off near her lips. Tor dropped to the floor with the second head he'd cut off that night.

Runa swallowed, gagged, and coughed as the remainder of that prickly vine disappeared down her throat. Coughing turned to sobbing as she drank the air in, then threw up.

Tor didn't stop chopping at Orri's body until no fingers, toes, or vines dared to twitch. The only sign of life was a thick, red sap oozing from the ends of the severed vines. The shredded remains of Orri's sack of a carcass did not bleed.

INFECTION

Runa threw up again.

"Can we just cut it out?" asked Kiara.

"Kill that girl." Runa spit what looked to be blood, but the aftertaste was sweet. "Kill her before she starts the dissection."

Tor gave Runa a hard look. "We need to get it out of you somehow, before you end up like Orri."

"If you do she'll die," said Svikar. "You might as well ask if you can cut out her heart. It's feeding on her, and it's waiting for her to get tired."

"You don't have a heart, troll, and yet your mouth will not die." Tor looked at Svikar as if he was responsible for all of this.

Runa slunk to her knees and sobbed. "Freyja help me!"

"It'll be alright, Runa." Tor sat beside her and rubbed her back as she vomited. "We're going to get the weed out." He tried to sound reassuring.

"Ha!" laughed the head. "It'll take more than a goat to pull that weed."

Tor's eyes burned a hole into the troll until Svikar used his big ugly mouth to say something more helpful. "As she weakens, her soul will become a burden. When her body can't carry it anymore, she'll let it go and take up the vine. Then she'll be like old Orri over there.

Orri was hardly recognizable now that Tor had had his way, just a pile of scraps and bone.

"Don't listen to him, Runa. He's a liar." Tor turned his

back to the troll.

"When the blood vine has her soul ring, you'll call her draugr. Her body will fade but not her spirit. You can't kill the spirit." Svikar seemed to be thinking of some distant memory.

"Runa, I know you don't like me, but you need to listen to me now." Kiara took a deep breath—her heart was pounding. "Look, I'm no priest. All I know is that if you give your soul to Jesus, and you ask, he will forgive your sins, and he will save you. If not in this life, then forever after." *Why was that so hard?* she wondered.

"Shut 'er up with all of that," said the troll.

"I'm just trying to give her peace."

Runa put the torch in Svikar's face to shut it up. "Have you given your soul to your God?" Runa stood up straight and knocked the dust from her dress.

"Of course I have." Kiara kissed her own tattered soul. *Dear God, could you have put me here to save this woman?*

Runa wiped the water out of her eyes. "You are in the underworld with a dying woman, a Norseman with a sword, and the head of a troll, far away from your homeland that you will never put your eyes on again. Are you at peace right now?"

Something inside Kiara snapped. The woman was as bad as the troll.

"That's enough of that," said Tor. "Svikar, what can we do? How can we save my wife?"

"There is someone who may help her. Her soul will guide the way, but you'll need me if you want to get there alive. You gotta take me with you."

"Take you with us?" Kiara's hand shook as she dropped her ring back in her shirt. "How exactly are we supposed to manage that?"

HARNESSING THE TROLL

"**A**ren't you good at anything, Christian?" Runa seemed to have renewed her zest for treating Kiara like her slave.

"I don't want to get anywhere near them— not the vine or the troll." Kiara couldn't hide her panic.

"You know that when a creature with a soul is dying, its soul gets heavier? To it, I mean," said Svikar. "How's yours feeling, Runa?"

"You must not have one, then," said Tor, "or much of a brain, either, 'cause your head is light."

"You taking my neck may have had a little to do wif dat, Viking." Svikar's ugly features twisted. "Too tight," he huffed.

"Would you rather stay here, with the goats?" Tor threatened.

"It's not the goats that worry me." Svikar furrowed his thick brow. "And I wish you'd tame that tongue of yours, Viking, since our fates are tied as tight as that weed."

"Are you sure this is safe?" Kiara thought about Orri as they pulled the harness off the troll."

"Perfectly safe," Svikar winked.

Kiara froze. *What was that supposed to mean?* She didn't like the troll. Didn't trust it. And the thought of being tied to it was making the bile rise in her throat.

"If we just had a dwarf," Svikar never seemed to run out of things to say to make things worse, "they'd make a harness so nice you wouldn't believe it. Clever little things those dwarfs are. The only creature worse than men for making up things to do is dwarfs."

"Dwarfs?" Kiara held her torch into the darkness.

"Concentrate, girl," scolded Runa. "I've almost got it."

"Are you really asking the head of a troll if dwarfs is real?" asked Svikar. "Suppose you don't believe in goblins, neither?"

"Goblins?"

Svikar seemed to like scaring the wits out of Kiara. He sniffed with that big nose. "No worries. I ain't detecting any been 'round 'ere in a while. It was the dwarfs who built these passages. Wouldn't be much here at all without 'em."

"There isn't much here now." Runa sounded sick. Or maybe the troll was getting under her skin, too.

"Oh, dwarfs is always making things better, always planning. If we do this, then next we'll have that. Then we can build one of those." Svikar had a talent for mocking.

"Are they dangerous?" Runa kept tying her knots.

The troll raised his eyebrows, considered his words, and spit. "A dwarf with nothing to do might get to thinking — and that could be dangerous. No, we can't have that. Keep 'em busy. Keep 'em busy. That's what we says." Svikar winked at Kiara again dubiously.

"Take this." Runa pushed her torch into Kiara's hands and slipped the new harness over Kiara's shoulders. "Watch it, girl. If you light it afire, then I promise I'll leave the thorns on the next one. Tor, help me get Handsome here into the sling."

Tor and Runa lifted Svikar's head and dropped it into the harness, nose out. Fear coiled in Kiara's belly. The harness was made of a piece of the same vine that had overpowered Tor and forced itself down Runa's throat.

The head was surprisingly light for its size, but the stench of his oily hair and dank breath made Kiara's eyes water.

"Do all Christian's stink like this one?" Svikar's protest

woke Kiara from her scent-induced trance.

Runa touched the filthy troll on purpose without retching, as if none of this bothered her. She wrenched the troll sideways by its pointy ears.

"Maybe I'd be better off with the goblins!" he cried in pain.

Runa ignored him. "Svikar, your eyes go out in front, so you can see for us, and so my husband can cut them out if you give us any trouble."

Svikar whispered up to Kiara. "The more the vine takes, the more her true self will come out. Sweet gal you married there, Viking."

Tor scowled at the head. "Alright, Runa, we've been still too long."

Runa may have looked sick, but her grip was strong. When she jerked the harness, Kiara stumbled forward into the darkness.

She tried to think of better things, of fresh air and blue skies, as she carried their untrustworthy guide like a bridled horse.

"Well, Mister Svikar with the big mouth," Runa gave mocking a try, "two heads, one set of arms, and one set of legs. Just like when we met you."

"Only shorter," snarled Svikar.

"Now take me to my goddess," Runa cackled. "I can feel her calling."

VIKING LOST

After hours of winding and climbing and twisting and turning, their two-faced guide stopped them again. Svikar's long nose snorted and sniffed. He'd done it so often that Runa stopped worrying about it. She wasn't feeling much at all, actually.

"Strange," Svikar sniffed. "Can't be. A little faster, Christian, I know a place we get out of this passage up here."

"Why?" asked Tor. "What do you smell?"

"It's a shortcut," Svikar grinned. "And we need to get out of this passage."

Kiara arched her back to stretch. "Why are we trusting him? 'Cause it feels like he's leading us straight to the gates of Hell."

"Don't think I ain't thought about it." Svikar looked nervous.

Runa didn't care. "You know, I've heard enough of that girl's complaining."

"I wasn't-"

"Every time you adjust that harness or rub your back or ask to take a rest, I know what you're implying—that we're only following the troll because of me."

"Runa, we're all tired." Tor tried to calm her.

"Still taking her side?" Runa was sick of all of this. Sick of walking, sick of the girl, sick of the dark, and sick to her stomach. She just wanted to crawl up into a tight crack in the wall and get some rest. But she couldn't let up or they'd leave her. "Tor, you know she wants to leave me here to die—she wants to take you for herself."

"You're not feeling well. I think we all need some rest." Tor talking in that calming tone made Runa want to hit him with a rock.

"We can't stop now." Svikar cast his eyes back down the hall. "Something's caught our scent."

"You know she wants to take you from me." Runa didn't care about the weeds, the troll, or whatever was following them. "The girl wants you Tor. She thinks she can just leave me for dead to get eaten by the weed and the troll and have you all to herself.

Tor gave Runa a look.

"Save that look for the goats, farmer," Runa yawned. *Why is he looking at me like that?* She slid to the ground. The dirt on the floor felt warm and welcoming. "The troll's right. Kiara does stink." She laughed at the nerve of what she was saying. She couldn't exactly smell her—it was some other sense, more like a feeling. But she didn't like it, and she didn't mind saying so. "I wish my husband had cut you into pieces along with that pig, Orri, a bit of Odin's justice for daring to spew your Christianity in the cathedral of our gods." She grabbed at Kiara's foot.

"Watch it!" growled the troll. "She falls, I fall. And you need me, remember?"

"What was that?" Runa sensed something coming up behind them.

"Get her up, Viking," said the troll. "Just a little further and we can throw her off our scent."

"W-what is it?" Kiara stumbled.

"Don't worry. Just keep moving."

Tor grabbed Runa by the arm and dragged her to a trot.

"Can't you hear that, Tor?" *Stupid man always was oblivious.* Runa just wanted to sit down. Just for a bit. "It's still a ways off, but it's gaining."

"What is it?" Tor held his sword and torch up behind

them.

"If you can't hear that then don't bother looking," laughed Runa. *He used to be so strong.*

"Slow down, girl. We made it to the cut with time to spare." Svikar sounded relieved.

"You want us to go in there?" Tor stared at the narrow slit in the stone wall as if he was going to be sick.

"Through there," Svikar explained. "Shine your torch over to the right, ja? You may have to twist to squeeze through. Go on now, Viking. You first."

Runa could sense Tor's blood pressure rising. The space was going to be tight, even for her.

Torch first, Tor flipped up and into the high crevice and used his elbows to crawl inside. Before his feet disappeared, he stopped short. "Mmph." His voice was muted. He started squirming back out.

"Viking!" Svikar shouted. "Kiara, we don't have time for this. Push him back in or something.

Did my husband just scream? Runa laughed.

Tor kicked and squirmed, and there was no way Kiara could stop him from coming back. He fell to his knees trying to catch his breath.

"I can't fit," he gasped.

The sound was getting louder. It was hard to tell from the echoes, but it sounded like howling.

"Tor! Stop cowering like a child afraid of the dark. You said you'd be there for me!" Her anger echoed a response to the howling.

Svikar's eyes followed the sound. He looked nervous.

Runa smacked her husband across the ear.

"Aagh!" The Viking raged to his feet, his fist shaking over Runa like a hammer ready to drop. As if scared of his own anger, he relented, opened his hand, and wiped at his ear. His hand came back covered in blood.

"Out of the way." Runa pushed him aside and climbed into the crevice. Just as she was worming her way in, a strong hand grabbed her ankle and dragged her back out.

"There has to be another way." Tor was staring back into the darkness. Even he could hear the howling now.

From along the walls and up from the floor the herd of goats flooded the spot, nipping and bleating as they poured into the crack like water through a funnel.

"There's nothing on the other side, just a bottomless pit." Tor's face turned as red as the blood on his ear when he blurted it out.

"Din' you look down? There's a ledge you can—" The troll smiled a gap-toothed grin. "Well, that explains a bit."

"Scared of heights?" Runa's chortling was buried in the sound of a stampede of soft hoofs. "That's the man my father chose for me to marry." She felt so tired. "No farmer, no merchant, no butcher." Her voice faded with one last cut. "A Viking lost."

LEAVING A MARK

Sleep had tamed Runa's angry tongue, and she snored in her place on the dirty floor. But she had no peace. Her soul clutched in one hand, she mumbled to herself as if suffering a nightmare.

For the first time, Tor was glad for the weak light of the torches, so he could hide his shame. "There has to be another way." Tor's knees felt weak from the thought of the narrow ledge on the other side.

The goats' bleating faded as the last of them disappeared into the cut.

"They's no other way," said Svikar. "Do you want to save your wife or not?"

Tor grabbed the troll's ear, dragging it and the unfortunate harness bearer up against the cold, stone wall.

"Hey!" Kiara barely let out a cry before her momentum stopped with a crunch, her full weight finding Svikar's head.

"It's too late," yelped Svikar.

The darkness growled.

"She's already here."

A hulking shadow broke through the dull light, its retreat sounding like it was dragging a corpse.

"Tor!" Runa's voice was weak and confused and trailing away.

Tor spun around to see the light of Runa's torch bouncing off into the darkness. The only sign of her abductor was the foul, lingering stench of wet fur, like a dog coming in from the rain.

"Runa!" Tor's heart sank as he felt the heat of his dying torch lick at his fingers. He forgot about heights, about insults and fear, but he couldn't ignore the fact that he couldn't see. He looked for more vine, but the passing goats had raided their supply. He turned to Kiara. "Follow me. I'm going to need your light."

As soon as Tor got to speed the fire bit his hand and his nub of a torch fell to the ground. His only light was Runa's, and it was quickly disappearing around a bend.

Then her light was gone. He looked back. Nothing. Alone in complete darkness, he kept going. His only companion was the wall. He was thankful for it, and found himself praying Runa's light hadn't snuffed out. To whom he prayed he was not sure. With every stumble he blamed himself. After a lifetime of living in the mountains, it was the underworld that made him face his fear of heights. Maybe the girl was right. Maybe the troll had been taking them to Hell. He pushed forward.

By sheer will he'd managed an awkward trot. In the black it felt like the tunnel began to twist, and he bounced off the wall in his struggle to stay upright.

The only thing worse than leaving their only source of light was to split up—and he had done both. Even the horrid howl of the beast would've been a comfort. At least he'd know he wasn't completely lost. As he pressed on, he thought of Vigi and all the times he depended on a distant bark to help him find his way.

Tor was struggling.

He stopped to scratch the hilt of his sword against the stone wall, too blind to see if he had even left his mark. *Who did he think would find it?*

Tor was giving in to hopelessness. Beaten, tired, and lost, he was drowning in the blackness of his thoughts. *Can't stop.* This was no time for despair. All he could do was keep going—and pray.

PETTING THE PUPPY

R una regained consciousness. She was groggy and could barely focus, but she could tell she was being dragged.

"Tor?" she reached up her hand and instead of an arm she felt fur, thick and coarse. Everything was so slow to her, like she'd had too much to drink. Her head swam. "Are we almost there? I don't think we have much time." Her words were slow and slurring.

She sunk her hand deep into its coat and scratched like she would Vigi or Jeger. A piercing yip rang in her ears and she jerked her hand away. When she brought her fingers back, they were wet with blood. In a fog, instead of wiping them off, she stuck them in her mouth. It had no taste, but felt like a drop of color in a world of gray, something added to the emptiness. She wanted more.

Runa reached back again. Again it growled. Its teeth were big and sharp, and they gripped down hard on her coat. "It's all right," she heard herself say as she sunk her hand deep into its fur. It felt good to sink her nails in.

It growled and then yelped and ran away. *My scarf.* It tore her new scarf from her neck. She focused on the yelp. All that pain and emotion released into the world like a spark of life, like the time she threw a rock at Magnus's dog and hit it on the head. *That got it out of the barn.* She felt a smile creep across her face as she remembered it.

She was feeling almost human again. With a touch of energy, she turned over onto her stomach and pushed herself to her knees. She heard Tor clamoring about somewhere behind her — but didn't care. She wanted to pet the dog. Petting it made her feel something. Like warmth.

She held her smoldering light out toward the whimpering. "Here, puppy," she slurred. "Come here, pup." She put the torch down on the ground beside her. *Not doing much good, anyway.* She licked her fingertips, running her tongue down the length of each and every one. *Dry.* She tried to put on her best smile. "Come on, girl. Come close so I can take a look at you."

The whimpering got closer, then stopped. Out of the darkness, a girl appeared with her hand to her face. She was about Erik's age, maybe fourteen. She tucked her short brown hair behind one ear, exposing swollen scratches and fresh blood running down her cheek. Runa forgot about the dog and leaned forward.

"Are you hurt? Let me see," Runa said as a soft heartbeat rang in her ear. Not hers. It belonged to the girl. The metallic scent of blood filled the air. "It's not that bad. Come. Let me take a look."

"Where'd you get the scarf?" asked the girl. Fear rippled off her like a tangible color, all purple with shades of blue.

"You know, I can't remember where I got it. I think I heard your dog back there. I hope she didn't pee on it." Runa was feeling fuzzy again. "I have a little dog, you know." Something stirred inside her. "His name is Jeger, and he's away with my stepsons now, all alone. Probably cold."

"I bet he's alright. Dogs are smart."

Runa inhaled as she felt a drop of blood splash against the stone floor. "Can I pet your dog again?"

"That scarf was marked," said the girl. "It's why the troll was bringing you to her. What's your name?"

The girl was nosy, and she wasn't making any sense. "Come closer and I'll tell you." Runa spoke sweetly. She could almost taste the blood pulsing down the girl's face.

"You and your dog here all by yourselves?"

"You smell familiar, somehow," said the curious girl. "Can you hold the light up so I can see your face?"

"Of course." Runa tried to pick up the torch, but the fire bit her skin. She hissed at its heat. "I think I know you, too," she lied.

"Runa?" Tor was getting closer.

"Not now," she grumbled as more pounding rang in her ears. Tor's heartbeat. *Was he still afraid?* She didn't understand.

The girl came closer. She was young and pretty.

"Are you all right?" It was Tor again. "Who are you talking to?"

Runa could hear him bumbling his way closer in the dark.

"Dear girl, you're shaking like a leaf. Why are you crying?" Runa licked her dry lips as she opened her arms widely. "What's your name, child?"

"We're coming!" Kiara sounded scared.

She was still a ways back, and Runa had sensed her shuffling up the passage with that troll minutes before. *When had they all become so clumsy?*

The girl let her hand drop from her face. The blood had thickened around four deep scratches. Her eyes. There was something about her eyes.

Runa might have known her once, but she couldn't think about that, not now. The child's pulse was racing. Runa didn't know how, but she could tell.

"Don't go through the gates," the girl wept as she came in to nestle her head against Runa's bosom.

The girl hugged her tight, like she was hugging her own mother. Runa could not feel the warmth of her embrace, but the girl's heart pounded faster. She closed her arms around her, in a slow, tight embrace. The girl cried out as if in pain, but she accepted Runa's affection.

"Poor thing." Runa must have needed a hug, too,

because she was feeling much better.

The girl whimpered.

Runa pulled back. "Why, you're bleeding all over me now, aren't you?" Tears ran down and into those scratches. Runa felt empty without her; she pulled her back in, tighter this time. She couldn't look away from the pocks of fresh blood bubbling from the girl's shoulder.

Runa's tongue reached out like a snake. It seemed natural; she needed to clean it off—to taste it. Before the tongue landed, a wave of new energy filled her. Runa's fingers and arms were dipping into the girl's power, too, like dry roots after a rain. She pulled the girl in tighter. Everything was better this way, like she was borrowing strength from this child. The energy helped her find her focus.

"What did you say your name was again?" Runa pulled back, just for a second. Something like an echo in her mind urged her to look at the girl. To really see her.

The girl shuddered as she pulled away. "Gefn."

Some of the fog in Runa's mind cleared, and a memory formed of her tiny daughter, playing with the baby goats and little Erik. What had Runa done to him? All the pain and anger and shame burned in her soul, and it gave her focus. She could finally see.

"Gefn?" Runa stared at the girl through dry eyes. She ached inside, but the tears wouldn't fall. "It's you? It's really you? I knew the gods heard my prayers."

Her daughter cried out when she pulled her close, kissing her brown, beautiful hair. "I'm sorry. I'm so sorry! My sweet, sweet girl." The taste of blood sent Runa's head spinning.

TRUST ISSUES

Tor noticed his own shadow shifting against the cave wall. "Kiara, get up here with that light. She's up here."

"Don't go to her, she'll never let you go," someone said. It sounded like a young girl.

"I'm coming, Runa," Tor said as Kiara finally caught up. Light flooded the cavern, and he could see a young girl kneeling over his wife.

"Hold on." He grabbed the torch from Kiara and rushed forward.

"Aaagh!" The young voice screamed in pain.

"Get away from there," Svikar yelled. "Kill it, Viking, before it rips her to shreds!"

"No!" The figure of a young girl jerked her arm from Runa's grasp and stumbled back into the darkness.

"Gefn!" Runa screamed. When Tor got to her, his wife was alone, clawing desperately at nothing. "Don't leave me again!"

Tor reached down to help her to her feet, but she slapped at his torch hand, raking his skin with nails as sharp as thorns.

"Who were you talking to?" He sucked at the scratches on his hand, warm with blood.

"It was our daughter, Gefn. Freyja be praised, she came back to me." Runa put her fingers to her mouth.

"Wha-a?" For the first time since they'd met him, the troll sounded speechless.

She's hallucinating. Tor swung the waning torch into the darkness. The light reflected off a set of soft eyes — the color of Runa's when she was young.

Could it be?

He lowered his sword. "Don't be afraid." For the first time in years, Tor allowed himself to hope.

"Get me up there," the troll barked at Kiara. "Look, Viking, I still got two good eyes and they can see everything you can't. An' that ain't nothin' you'd want any part of unless you're looking to lose an arm."

"Shut up, troll." Tor edged forward.

"Get back or you'll suffer for it," Svikar shouted at the darkness. "Back away, Viking. Sword up. Everyone, let's just back away."

Tor took a step farther out. "I want to see who Runa was talking to."

Kiara ignored Svikar's order and followed Tor. Svikar slapped his tongue around the torch and almost jerked it out of Tor's hand, until it illuminated his ugly face.

The soft eyes in the darkness shifted to a savage malice, followed by a deep gutteral growl that echoed through the hall until it sounded like a pack of wolves. Tor raised his sword.

Svikar's tone turned unusually soft. "Your wife's delirious. The vine's gotten into her head, and maybe your's, too, from the way you're acting. We've got to get her away from here or she'll die — whether by that bleeding devil or the vine."

"It's Gefn — I swear to Freyja," Runa mumbled. "Her pup peed on my scarf."

Tor looked down at his bleeding hand, then at his addled wife. Runa was licking her fingers like a child after eating a piece of cake. Tor shifted his attention, and his fire, to Svikar's reprehensible face.

"Careful, Viking," whispered the troll. "'Tis what you can't see that wants to hurt you, not me." The troll's gaze never left the darkness, his bulging green eyes reflecting the torch's last gasps. "I'll get Runa to her goddess." His forked tongue moistened lips stained red from chewing blood weed. "You 'ave my word."

Tor didn't trust the troll—but did trust its fear of his sword. "Svikar, lead us back. I'll cover the rear."

FACING THE ABYSS

"**A**ll right, love, shouldn't be much farther now." Svikar tried to keep up morale. "Ja, now we're getting somewhere. Just keep walking — up around the bend 'ere."

The troll led the way, and Tor made sure whatever was growling stayed behind them. When they reached the crack, Tor's vision blurred as he thought about what they had to do next.

"Christian, you scared of heights?" asked the troll.

Kiara shook her head.

"Then take off the harness, and give me to the big man. Viking, you give your torch to her. 'At's it." Svikar's tone was calm and soothing, for a troll.

"Now, Viking, if you don't stop shaking, you're gonna collapse the tunnel. Cut off one of the shoulder pieces of this harness, and light it wif that torch so you can have a little light once she climbs through," said Svikar. "While you're at it, cut a bit off about as big as your thumb and split it wif me."

"What?"

"It'll give you courage," Svikar winked. "Go on. If it ain't swiggling on its own, it can't hurt you. Do it for your wife."

Svikar's eyes were nearly bulging out of his head when Tor's sword hand stuttered while cutting the vine next to his ear. After the troll's long tongue stabbed the short piece out of Tor's fingers and he coaxed Tor on with a chew and a smile, Tor bit off the tail end of his torch. He figured dying of poison would be better than going through that crack.

"Now, Christian, you climb through first." The troll smiled a red-stained grin.

Kiara shifted from foot to foot.

"You feeling left out?" said Svikar. "You want a taste of blood weed to calm your nerves?"

Kiara shook her head.

"Get on wif it then. And don' worry love. Maybe your God'll be waiting on the other side," the troll laughed, "wif the goats."

Kiara looked anxious to get through—even if it was just to get away from the troll—and disappeared as quickly as one of the goats.

Runa was back to her blank stares again. She slithered through next without being asked.

"Feelin' better?" Svikar asked.

Tor nodded. He wasn't feeling much of anything, really. The chaw of weed had done what a day of drinking beer could not.

"I bet you never had anything like 'at before, eh? Now after you pass me through, don't think too much. Just squeeze on in behind, 'cause I may be the only thing keeping that thing in the shadows from killing you right now. And if *you're* dead, we're probably all dead. I think your wife was right about that much."

Tor pushed the troll up and started inside. The thought of what he was doing flooded back into his mind, only he didn't care quite so much as before. Just climbing blindly into such a tight space was a lot to ask.

"You're not going to fit." Tor was a little slow, but unlike being drunk, he still had his wits.

"Go on, push! Trolls is incredibly squishy when need be. You'd be amazed at where we can hide. Christian? Get ready to catch me, eh? This baby's coming out."

Tor pushed it and squeezed it, and sure enough, Kiara was able to tug it through.

"Come on, farmer," Runa mocked. "The Christian is here, and she wants to save you, too." Her cackling sounded tired.

Tor thought about that growling thing nipping at his heels and turned to lay the fiery torch at the entrance of the crack before elbowing his way in. Quickly he nudged on — but considered turning back when he arrived at the window of his nightmares. It was a little hole about the size of his head. Last time it greeted him with cool moving air and a glimpse at something that caused his testicles to retreat before the rest of him did the same. It was a view from Hel; it was a bottomless pit.

"I've seen bigger things than you get through smaller 'an that. Believe me." The troll tried to sound encouraging. "Now make the turn. Come on. There's no going back now."

Svikar was wrong about that, for Tor had shimmied away from that same sight not a half hour before. He had promised to keep Runa safe, and an irrational fear he'd had half his life nearly cost her hers. *Not this time.* His inner voice tried to sound convincing.

Torchlight moved to another spot past a tight bend. "Come to the flames."

Tor took a deep breath and focused on the light. Turning onto his shoulder, he had to suck in to wiggle into the turn. That got him halfway. He let his arms fall to his sides to try to narrow his wide shoulders. He made it further, still. The light got closer, but the space had gotten tighter. Every time he inhaled, his torso was pinned to stone.

The tighter the passage gripped him, the more the heart in his chest felt like a hammer beating against a prison wall. The harder it pounded, the harder it was to catch a breath. Each shallow pant was poisoned by his torch, insignificant and smoky, warm and thick. He wanted out. And because he'd made that turn, forward was the only way.

Tor wanted to scream but only managed a cough. In his

panic, he nudged and kicked, and kicked some more. He pushed with everything he could manage, from clawing fingertips to toes bound by soft leather boots, but found no relief. In his panic, he lunged forward spastically with everything he had left. Finally, leaning on his chin to help with the pulling, he found a way to progress.

"Help me!" The first words he managed to get out exposed him, wholly humble and afraid. With every snap of a fingernail, the crack loosened its grip. "Can't breathe!"

He was in the Christian Hell, and the only way out was to face the abyss. But filling his lungs was of bigger concern, and he used everything he had left to keep edging toward the light.

All at once, the gap widened, and Tor caught his first deep breath since the turn.

Kiara pulled Tor's arm to try to help him along. Even so, he clawed and scratched until his fingers grasped the cool stone edge. Finally free, he laid his head down and devoured the cool, fresh air.

When he looked into the chasm, he almost pissed himself and had to look away. The goats were everywhere, chewing their cud on invisible imperfections as comfortably as if they were on the farm back home. He could even hear their chomping down below, though he dared not lean out over the edge to see. The shelf the others stood on was a generous one-pace deep at its widest, but to either side it became harrowingly narrow, and at some places it seemed to have been shorn off completely.

If it had been made with a purpose, its caretaker had done about as good a job with its upkeep as Tor had maintaining his goats' pens—although he had begun to wonder if underworldly saboteurs might have had a role in those escapes.

"I need another piece of the weed."

"Where's his sword?" Svikar's face was a handbreadth away. Kiara was right; his breath was disgusting.

"Under me, beside me." Tor dragged the sword up by the pommel. After Kiara made the cut, she checked the weed for signs of life, then pushed it into Tor's quivering hand. The weed crunched when he chewed it, sucking the moisture from his tongue. It tasted like burnt sap. It eventually condensed into a warm, sickly-sweet pulp that made Tor gag. He coughed and spit until he felt a cool calm rinse all feeling away, like a cold stream on a hot summer day.

"You all right?" Svikar asked.

Tor felt beaten, but he nodded and pushed the troll's head out of his face.

"Once you're through, it's only a little drop."

Tor elbowed his way forward until the crack opened wide enough for him to swing his legs around. The weed had done its work. For the first time in his adult life, the heights did not make him queasy. He sat in that opening, suspended over a narrow ledge, and beyond that, the world was hollow.

As he eased his way down, he put his back hard against the wall. The blood weed may have numbed his fears, but it still hadn't made him stupid.

Once he found the security of the wall, he could see there was more.

The chasm had a sort of heartbeat, details in its endless depths that were highlighted by dangling, swaying vines. The depth and shape of it pulsed a phosphorescent blue.

"Well, darlin'?" Svikar eyed Runa. "Which way is it gonna be?"

Runa looked perplexed. "How would I know?" She sounded a bit sharp. "Anywhere but down, I suppose."

Svikar spit out into the abyss. "I told you I'd get you where you needed to go, but it's you that has to tell me where that'll be."

Runa nearly pushed a long-horned billy off the edge as she plopped down and swung her legs over the abyss.

"Throw him over."

"Wait, that's just the vine talkin'." Svikar sounded like he thought Kiara might do it. "Listen to your soul. It'll tell you where you're headin'. Once you tell us the way, I'll make sure we get there in one piece."

"One piece?" The irony wasn't lost on Tor. He watched the head swinging slowly in its sack of vines.

Svikar ignored him. "It's up to you, pretty lady. When you feel it, just let me know."

Runa drew the braided leather around her neck until she had her ring in her hand.

"Don't worry, love," said Svikar. "If it gets too heavy for you, just give it to me. I'll carry it for you."

Runa looked tired. "It would be nice to let someone else carry it. Just for a while."

"Don't listen to it, Runa." Tor grabbed her hand in his. They were usually so warm. "Just point the way. We'll get that vine out of you and get you better."

Runa stared into the chasm. Along some of the shelves were tunnels, a series of angular passages spiraling into the stone walls like spokes on a tilted wheel.

Tor was just about to ask Svikar for a recommendation when Runa pointed her finger straight out, then hinged at the shoulder until her arm aimed down to the left toward a passage of stone leading away from the abyss.

Tor exhaled in relief. He couldn't see any other path that looked more welcoming. More like a hall than a tunnel, the opening was easily twice as big as the others. The space was cloaked with a veil of long, shimmering blood vines that stretched down like a waterfall as far as Tor dared to look. "Well, there's no way to get stuck in there."

"Hmm," said Svikar. "I figured that would be the way."

"We're going to have to go down a bit." Kiara hung her torch over the edge. The mouth of the abyss swallowed light. Even with Runa's torch it only shone down to the next step. "Who would cut ledges as high as this into the side of a cliff?" asked Kiara. "Are these stairs?"

"Humans are such clever creatures." Apparently trolls were skilled at sarcasm. "Not the dwarf's best work is it?"

"I thought dwarfs were short," said Tor.

"Who said it was made for them?" said Svikar. "To a few, these may be stairs, but for us they'll be more of a ladder. Better get at it or the Viking'll chew his way through what's left of my sling trying to get past this next part. All right, Runa, take this sling apart and see if you can make a proper rope."

"I can't go over that." Tor couldn't breathe.

"Would you rather go back into the crack?" Svikar smiled.

Tor grabbed the sling out of Kiara's hand, and with one hand pressed firmly against the wall for balance, he swung the troll's head out over the abyss.

Svikar let red spit dribble off his lower lip until the sap's string finally snapped and disappeared into the black.

"Does this seem like a game to you, troll? I've lost my friends and my home, and my sons are all alone." His sons. If they came back to the village and Tor wasn't there to protect them, Vidar would sacrifice them, too, either at the oar or to the underworld.

He had to get back home.

He looked at his wife—her lifeless eyes and her hollow face. Tor thought about what his boys might be facing. They were smart, and they were prepared. He had gotten them away, and that was enough, for now.

"Look. I will not lose my wife, too."

"She's hanging on better than that fat Viking, I'll give her that," said Svikar.

Tor shook the troll, using all his restraint not to bash it into the stone and send the broken thing flying.

"Find another way."

"Where is my husband—killer of bears, defeater of giants, beheader of trolls?" Runa's eyes flashed red in the firelight.

The troll eyed Tor as if he saw him in a new light. "I don't know this man—haven't recognized him since he lost our daughter!" The vine had exposed Runa's true feelings, and they were as ugly as the troll.

Tor thought of all he'd put up with over the years—how much of himself he'd sacrificed for this woman—and for the first time he realized it could've never been enough.

"Give it." Runa put out her hand. Tor reluctantly gave her the troll. "And your father's sword." He did. "This coward has become too afraid of his own shadow to save his wife." She started taking the sling apart. "We don't need him anymore. Just leave him."

Tor was shaking wildly, but he couldn't tell if it was from fear or anger or disappointment. "Weed." He reached out his hand.

Kiara wept.

"You can stay, too, for all I care. Doubt you'll be of much use to us, anymore." Runa handed Tor a long piece. "That ought to be enough for a while." She looked at the troll's expectant eyes, dropped another piece on the ground, and lowered Svikar's sling so he could nab it with his tongue.

As the calm of the vine washed over him, Tor sifted through his options. "Wait. Don't cut that harness. There, where the path is broken, I think we can use part of the rubble as a step."

With an entourage of goats, they walked the ledge around the chasm until they came to the spot. Kiara handed Svikar to Tor and scampered down like a child at play.

Neither Tor nor Runa had scampered in years. The descent to the broken step was still a decent drop, probably almost as far as Runa was tall. Tor put the head down, took his wife by the hand, and lowered her down. As he let go of her wrists, she raked his arms with her nails and drew new blood.

"Mphh!" Tor winced in anger and pain.

"Drop our guide down to the girl," Runa laughed as she licked the blood off her fingertips.

Tor wondered if it would kill his wife if he knocked her unconscious and just carried her the rest of the way.

He dropped the troll down, and slowly — very slowly — eased himself over the edge. Before his arms straightened, his feet found the stone. It was then he realized the strange power of the weed. With every taste he'd lost more of his inhibitions. It reminded him of the firewater he used to drink before raids. He gave away his soul for it. Only this was purer and didn't fog his brain. The memory of getting off the water made him shudder. In his heart, however, he knew this was going to be worse.

"Give me to 'im!" Svikar grumbled at Kiara. "Viking, I hope you've got better hands than the Christian. The girl can't catch. I nearly rolled into the pit."

"You swipe that tongue at me again and I may give you a little kick next time, Svikar." Kiara snapped back. The closer they got to where they were headed, the more on edge everyone seemed to be.

"All right, now. Back this way."

"But there it is, not a quarter mile up ahead."

"Can't go that way," said Svikar. "Those vines ain't hanging there for decoration — well, not completely. They'll eat you quicker than that thing is eatin' — that thing ate Orri."

"That thing inside of me?" Runa sounded stronger. "Tor, you're bleeding?" She didn't sound surprised.

Tor pulled away from her outreached hand. "Just lead the way, Svikar. Whatever it takes."

GATEWAY TO THE FALLEN

Not far in the wrong direction, Svikar lead them off the narrow ledge. Tor was too weary to argue, so when the troll said push the stone wall—he pushed. A hidden door swung open on a hinge so perfectly crafted, Tor wished he had one half as good on his own front door. Even with all they'd seen, it was the first time he'd contemplated little dwarfs running around with their pickaxes, maybe a gold tooth or two, just like in the old tales of his childhood. And that gave him hope. Maybe there was magic there. Maybe his wife would meet her goddess and everything would be made all right again.

The tunnel out was short, about as tall as Tor's shoulders and equally as wide. But compared to the crack they came in through, it was spacious. And compared to creeping along the edge of an abyss, the confined space felt like a warm blanket of protection.

Crawling through was relatively painless, thanks to a fresh bite of blood weed. Besides, it wasn't long before they emerged in another corridor. The walls were cleaner, like they'd found some hidden entrance into a palatial hall, albeit a poorly lit one. It was not roughhewn, like the mine they'd first woken up in. They were finally getting somewhere.

"How you feelin', Runa?" Svikar asked. "This is the way you're being called, idn't it?"

She nodded and pushed on.

Her attention was eerily focused on the blood dressing

his torch hand. Her tongue working feverishly inside her mouth, like she was trying to free a piece of meat stuck between her teeth.

But there was a new problem—the same as the old one. They were running low on light again. Thanks to Runa leaving a rope's length of the harness up at the crack and Tor and the troll's appetite for the stuff, there wasn't enough of the weed left to light.

"Don' worry 'bout the torchlight," Svikar assured them before anyone mentioned it. "We won' need 'em much longer."

For a time, they walked with two torches, and a hundred steps later they were down to one. As the last one fizzled out, a glow shone up ahead to take its place. It turned out it was easier to walk toward a light than by one. They kept one shoulder to the wall as they rounded a long bend, and when they came out of it, it was like the world opened up—big and bright.

The walls turned polished obsidian and were aflame with columns of burning blood weed, a proper fire that was warm and welcoming. The flaming weeds wriggled and writhed, as if wanting to slither back where they came from, but couldn't—being forced out by another weed wanting its turn to see the light. Tor could relate to the feeling. The very light that had attracted them might soon be using them for kindling, too.

"The weed," said Kiara, "has Runa beaten it?"

Runa looked alert for the first time since the attack. The only thing giving her away were her eyes. Once the color of the sea, they now favored dark clouds.

"No, it's just loosed its grip," said Svikar. "It's afraid to show itself here, so it's borrowing her eyes—sees what she sees now."

"It's afraid?" Tor raised his eyes and his sword to see what the troll was staring at.

"Don' run," Svikar whispered. "Forget all thoughts of

turning back."

Out in front of two towering wooden doors were two hulking sentries — trolls, one head each, twenty feet tall if an inch. Their fat bellies were covered in black, shiny mail. Long noses protruded from under dust-covered, black helms that matched the obsidian walls. Skulking heads rested on broad shoulders covered in matching black plate. Green reflections from beady eyes shone from the shadows under each helm like polished emeralds. Of these eyes, one troll had two, the other only one.

Each wore a heavy iron collar, married to a thick black chain that spilled onto the floor before passing through holes cut into each door. Each chain was made of enough iron to outfit an entire army.

"Steady, everyone," whispered Svikar. "These be mountain trolls, prone to hiding in the hills. Still as stone, their whispers carry on the wind."

"They didn't even turn to look at us. They're covered in dust." Kiara's mouth hung open, as if by being very still she could better see them move. They didn't. "Are they statues?"

Dear God, Tor thought, or maybe he was praying; even he couldn't tell. But he hoped Kiara was right. If these two were warnings, they'd succeeded.

Like the crash of falling trees, synchronized knocks came from the other side of those doors.

"Weed," Tor whispered. When none came, he looked down to see Svikar crunching down the last piece. *Trolls!* He had to bite his cheek to keep from slapping the beast. That's when Tor noticed the tails. Each coarse-haired whip had been hidden among the chains. Each were tipped with balls of black iron.

The first proof they were alive was when the mountain trolls swung those devastating maces to rap the doors. The sound echoed so loud that Kiara hit her head against the wall. If the draugar were remnants of the dead, the trolls had just woken them all up.

Other than the mountains themselves, in all his years of hunting, Tor had never seen anything stand so still. It was as if God had breathed life into stone when the creatures picked up their chains and started walking their way.

"We will not die without you," Tor whispered as he pinched one of the Svikar's pointy ears. "If you've betrayed us, I'm going to cut your head into pieces until I find that soul of yours. Then I'll offer it to those weeds burning high up on the wall."

"You should thank me, Viking," —Svikar spit red sauce onto the floor— "because I'm the only one here willing to give your poor wife what she's been praying for." Then Svikar got serious. "Besides, it's not those poor fellas you've got to worry about."

Svikar wasn't lying. The chains stopped the trolls ten feet short of where they cowered. A mere two steps for those monsters. They looked sullen and uninterested, except for a one-eyed glance at a wayward goat.

With a deep click, the doors unlatched from the other side, and the two brutes took a knee. With disproportionately long arms, they pushed forward on their chains, and the doors opened.

On the other side were two more trolls, kneeling sentries equal in size and dress to their mates.

A warm glow filled the hall as a beautiful woman sauntered into the doorway. "Glad to see you made it alright, Svikar." Her voice was soft and calm.

"Some of me, anyway," replied the head. Svikar's face lurched forward on Kiara's chest, as if trying to will her to bow.

THE GODDESS

She was beautiful. Her glory filled the room like the sun. In her presence, the flaming weeds that had been lighting the hall were now bright and green, reminding Kiara of Ireland on a summer afternoon. The mountain trolls were no longer. Instead, black pillars held up decorated ceilings where they'd knelt. And the once ominous doors now shown—inviting, white, and grand, inlaid with a pattern that matched the lady's white flowing gown, which sparkled as if embroidered with diamond thread.

Before Tor could stop her, Runa was leading the way to the lady. On the approach, Kiara's eyes squinted to adjust to this new light, the first good light she'd seen since...since she'd said goodbye to Erik. *How long ago had that been?* What had seemed so dark, deep, and heavy a place was now bright and airy. Transformed. She hoped Erik was safe.

Runa looked strong again and knelt before her. The lady took her hand and whispered something in her ear.

"An-an angel," Kiara stammered and stared.

"Kneel before her," came a whisper.

Kiara turned, fully expecting the two mountain trolls to be hovering over her, breathing down the back of her neck. Nothing.

"Goddess." Tor kneeled. He tried to force Kiara down, but she pulled away.

"Kneel or see death." A more ominous whisper floated into her other ear, more of a feeling than a sound.

Kiara turned to the other pillar.

"Kneel, fool," said Svikar. "If not for your head, do it for mine."

"Are you here to save her?" Kiara stared at the beautiful woman. She had never seen such eyes, green, like the sea, calm, and still, yet deep in a way that made her afraid.

The woman approached and lifted Kiara's soul ring as easily as if it were her own. "So, this is what I've been hearing. These halls have not heard those sour notes before. At first it shook me to hear them again. Will you play it for me?" she asked.

"Is this a test, lady?"

"Yes." Her eyes softened, and she caressed Kiara's cheek. Her touch was cold. "You played it for God, and as a reward he sent you here. Play for me, and see that I will treat you better."

"I would ask that you play to our Lord for both of us, lady, for your notes would no doubt be sweeter. Where is your instrument?"

The lady looked startled at the request. A sadness overshadowed her arrogance. Then her eyes narrowed, and her melancholy twisted into a defiant pride as she reached a hand into her bosom, unconcealed like the rest of her by her sheer flowing gown.

She withdrew a ring much the same as Kiara's, except it was covered in the finest gold, like a rich man or a priest might wear. But that was only the first.

Slowly the angel teased out another, then another, each more beautiful than the last. As they piled up at her feet, each was bright and polished as if she'd given this jewelry as much attention as she might have given her own perfectly coiffed hair, or a mirror.

Where it came from, Kiara could not tell, but came it did. By the time the lady pulled out her soul, she was standing ankle-deep in a pile of gold chain so beautiful that no Viking or king — or even the Pope — had likely ever seen a treasure its equal.

Kiara felt embarrassed by her dry, cracked soul and found herself tucking it back into her shirt.

A length of white ribbon looped through the lady's own soul, making it the first and most beautiful link in the necklace. The ribbon disappeared through a small hole in the second most beautiful ring she wore, a dazzling yellow gold choker resting tightly around her throat.

Both her choker and her soul were adorned with precious gems that painted her aura with many hues of reds, blues, and greens. The gems were set atop what looked to have been an inscription where Kiara's soul had only cracks and fissures. The rest of the priestly rings paled in comparison. As the lady admired her ring, for it was impossible not to, Kiara noticed the center had been filled, and inside was the sparkling graven image of a dragon.

Startled by the likeness, Kiara withdrew. Her priest taught that the dragon was symbolic of Satan himself.

As if she were reading her mind, the lady's glory dimmed along with her façade. Suddenly, Kiara was reminded of the cave's dark stone walls that the woman covered with her magic like a clean rug thrown over a dirty floor.

"I haven't played since before time began, or so it seems," the mistress purred. "Yet, unlike yours, the sound mine made was beautiful." Her light shone brighter, and the room slipped back to reflect only beauty and light again. "I don't think I could bring myself to play it now." Her eyes looked wet and beautiful as she lost herself. Then her voice turned cooler.

"Would you like me to play for you?" Kiara asked.

"To me?" she asked.

"To God," Kiara clarified.

The lady dropped her ring into her blouse, and her necklace sounded like thunder as it was dragged back to invisibility. The lady's eyes became a rousing storm.

"Why are you here?"

"Beautiful lady," — Tor bowed his head — "my wife was attacked by a draugr, and I think she might be dying."

"I can see that." The lady turned her attention back to Kiara. "But why are you here?"

Kiara stood up straight. "I have been wronged, lady — dragged from my home by Vikings. This man and his family protected me." Kiara looked at Runa and thought about how much she should say. "The Vikings had us sacrificed. Now we are lost, lead here by this troll. He said you could help her."

Svikar winced as the lady pinched his ear with the tips of her sharp nails and waved his ugly head in Kiara's face. "Do you believe you're here because of a troll — or them?" She pointed a long finger toward Tor and Runa. "Are you so blind that you cannot see? Or are you just a liar?" She lifted the ring dangling around Kiara's neck. "This is why you are here! Look at your soul." Her splendor turned dark, like an inglorious shadow, even as Kiara's ring shone brighter, highlighting its every flaw. "It's because of this filthy little instrument. Each crack, each blemish, is of your own doing. Maybe there is finally justice in Heaven! The truth is you are not worthy, and I am your reward!"

"My soul is filthy, lady, but at least it still serves its purpose."

"Are you speaking down to me?"

"No," said Kiara. "I'm agreeing with you." Kiara put her soul to her lips, closed her eyes, and began to play. Assuming her life was about to end, she wanted to die worshiping her God.

Any splendor left in the room faded, along with the lady's beauty and allure. For a moment, it was as if the truth overpowered her. The smoky, gray light of the burning weeds became visible once more, and the stark reality of the underworld that she'd been masking reemerged.

The lady took Svikar by the hair and swung him at Kiara,

using his squishy head to knock her ring out of her hands. That stopped the playing, and Kiara focused on wiping the greasy residue from her face with her sleeve.

"Thank you," said the lady. "That noise is giving us all a headache."

Runa's face had fallen to the floor, but Tor had been watching when reality temporarily slipped through.

"Bow your head in my presence!"

Tor moved his head down but kept his eyes up, and Kiara noticed him shift his hand to the hilt of his sword. The lady turned the head around to berate the troll, who now looked meek and frightened.

"Why would you bring her here?"

"Svin and I were just going out to the graveyard, mum. Thinking of taking in some air — maybe grabbing a bite."

"Does she look dead to you?" She held the head up to face the Christian. Then down to Tor. "Does he?" Svikar cringed as she flailed him by his ear. "You're the one who looks dead to me, Svikar."

"Please, mum. The weeds got one. Then they got 'er, too." He craned a bulging eye down at Runa, who held perfectly still in her reverence. "'Twas 'er soul that lead us here. Ask 'er."

"It looks like this girl used you to get to me, not the other way around, Svikar. Where is your brother Svindl?"

There was no more snark left in the troll. "Is he not here? I was hoping you would —"

"Hoping? Speak to me again as if I'm here to grant wishes and I'll feed that forked tongue of yours to the others. I should give your eyes to your sisters! Even in their blindness, they've managed to hold onto their heads." She looked beyond them into the darkness from which they had come.

"Lady, I —" Svikar started, but the lady cut him off again.

"This must be one of *his* tricks." Her eyes calmed again, and a chill filled the hall, as it did when the world turned to bury the sun under the horizon.

"They were marked, mum. I smelled Old Erik on their scarfs," said Svikar. "Thought he might have meant 'em for you."

"Old Erik? Is that what he calls himself? I thought the *Allfather* liked the titles. I rot down here in this prison while he plays charades with filthy humans!"

"It's not fair, mum." Svikar's ugly face relaxed as she cradled his gourdish head in her arm and ran her sharp looking nails through his thin, grimy hair. She held the head close, the way a distracted mother might carry her baby. One of Svikar's bulging, green eyes squished tight against the side of her bosom.

"We made a bargain, and that old demon owes me rings!" She pulled Svikar's long nose up to hers. "Instead, he sends me a dead woman, a slave, and a warrior—and you probably can't even tell me which is which."

She dropped the head down to her side and ambled over to Tor.

"Lady." He feigned a bow.

"Shhhhh," she whispered as she looked down at Runa, who looked like she was bowing—until she snored. "Your beautiful wife is dying, and her soul was right to lead her to me." The lady stooped to lift Runa's ring and frowned when she saw the image of Freyja stamped onto a silver coin bound inside—like a little picture frame. "I will be her goddess. And I will set her free."

Runa woke as the lady dropped Svikar's head next to hers—probably because of the smell.

"I see you brought me a gift," said the lady to Runa. She circled Tor the way a dog circled a spot to find the right place to pee. Her eyes followed her fingers as she dug them up into his graying, blond hair, then traced them down onto his broad shoulder and along a strong arm. As she circled, she edged closer, inhaling him as her fingers ran up his abdomen. Careful to avoid his wounds, her fingers traced around the cut across his chest. "Maybe you are right, Svikar. Perhaps this was meant to be a gift for me after all."

"She's only here because of me," said Tor. "We came with nothing, but if you save her, I will do anything you want."

She ran her finger around the scar on Tor's chest where he'd had his soul taken. "Who'd you give it to? Did you trade it for an arm ring?" She smiled as she traced his triceps with her sharp nails. "Or did you drop it into the sea as a gift to Rán to save you from a storm?"

Runa looked up at her husband, drained and confused.

"Can you help her?" he asked.

The lady allowed the edges of her down-turned lips to climb into a smile. "You will give me a blood sacrifice."

"Ja." Tor looked around for a goat. He couldn't believe it—not one.

"We'll figure that out later, Viking." She gave his bicep a squeeze.

Like rolling thunder, two hairy tails swung until their iron tips cracked together like a shutting gate.

"My name is Hella. Follow me."

THE OFFER

Beyond the gate, everything was better. The walls gave way and the ceiling opened up. Even the air was fresher. It was a new world. And there was something else — no goats.

The lady led Tor by the arm next to a river. Runa followed close behind, and Kiara stumbled forward with Svikar in hand, splitting her attention between what lay ahead and the massive columns she knew to be mountain trolls in disguise behind.

There was no clear path. Lush green vines covered more columns, the only markers of distance and space. Dressed as stone trees, their branches reached high overhead to hold up a rising ceiling.

The transformation was incredible — even beautiful — but Kiara didn't trust any of it. For all she knew, they were being led into a pantry for hungry giants and their beautiful guide was just the bait. She'd gotten her hooks into Tor quickly enough.

It wasn't long before the ceiling rose so high it disappeared altogether, replaced by a twinkling, almost starry expanse.

She looked around, trying to figure out a way back for when this dreamy place inevitably turned back into a nightmare. The light in the distance gave off a cool glow. Had it not been for the circumstances, it would've reminded her of a nice, warm evening stroll, like the kind her family used to take back home in Ireland.

Home. Salty tears trickled down her cheeks. She wondered if she'd ever stop grieving for everything she'd lost and left behind.

Runa didn't seem to notice the sky or the scenery, but she kept up well enough. The twinkling light was barely enough to cast shadows, but was enough to highlight a rolling landscape.

Hella lead them through a gate, almost exactly the same as the one on the goat pen at Tor's farm. Tor pulled his arm away from the lady as soon as it slammed shut.

On the other side, a long table had been set—five places, even one for Svikar, the head. Kiara's stomach growled at the site of it. She hadn't eaten since the morning Erik left, and she'd lost track of time long ago. *A day? A week?* Without a sun, who could tell in that place?

Hella sashayed toward a curtain of pulsing blue vines and took her seat on a gold and silver throne at the head of the table. A warm, dry breeze swept through Kiara's hair as it poured in from behind the throne. She didn't have to ask what was behind the curtain. She remembered Runa pointing the way from the ledge overlooking the abyss. Tor must've remembered, too, because he winced when the lady took her seat.

Her throne was massive and beautiful. It was made of small, intricate repeating patterns—soul rings inlaid with gemstones of every kind—circles of gold and silver woven with a rainbow.

After her necklace, the bedazzled throne was a testament to how many people of means gave their souls to this woman. When she sat on it, magnificent as it was, Kiara could only see Hella's eyes. The beautiful emeralds had withered in deference to whites that looked like polished pearls.

Two maidens appeared from the shadows to seat Tor and Runa across from each other, next to Hella. Tor pulled his chair away from the lady, and the ledge, before he sat.

Runa's face was drained, like she needed to rest. The maidens sat Kiara next to Tor. Then, as if seating a troll's head was a perfectly normal thing to do, plopped Svikar right on the table next to Runa.

Runa emptied her cup.

"That's what she needed. I told you I'd take you to someone who could help." Svikar smiled a cautious, toothy grin. "Are you sure you want me here, mum?"

Hella ignored the troll. Runa refilled her cup, fumbling the pitcher and spilling some of the red liquid on the table. Svikar extended his forked tongue and licked at the pool like a dog cleaning an empty plate.

After Tor took a sip and quickly put it down again, Kiara sniffed her cup. Foreign and strong, it burned her nose. The drink clung to the sides, red and thick as blood. She put it down without taking a sip. "Do you have any water?"

"Is my wife going to be alright, lady?" asked Tor.

"She's definitely stronger, but only a shell of her former self. Wouldn't you say, Svikar?" Hella smiled.

The troll looked up from shining the table with his tongue. "Yes, mum. I think she needed a drink. Just a bit o' the thirst is all. I'm a little thirsty myself."

The lady looked at Svikar as if what he wanted was about as interesting as his bathing advice.

Done waiting for assistance, the troll's tongue slid up and over the edge of his cup like a serpent, and he managed to tilt it to where it cradled awkwardly between his long nose and quivering lower lip. Somehow, he managed to get most of the red liquid to spill down his face and into his mouth.

Between Runa and Svikar, it was hard to tell who was more responsible for wetting the table.

"I can see you all are famished." Hella snapped her fingers, then put her hand on Tor's thigh as she leaned toward Kiara. "You are a pretty little thing, aren't you, girl?" She tilted her head back to look her over like a prized pig. "Well, you could be if you did something with yourself."

Kiara reflexively pushed her hair behind her ear. "Do you want me to bless the food, ma'am?" Kiara lowered her eyes and waited.

The troll slowed his awkward attempt at drinking to raise a confused eyebrow at their hostess.

"Are you praying now?" asked Hella.

"No, ma'am. I was just—"

"Let me be clear, little girl." Hella turned a ghostly white. "When you sit at my table, the only being you will give thanks to will be me."

Tor lifted the lady's hand from his leg and reached across the table.

"Runa, how are you feeling? Better?"

Runa shook his hand away and continued to empty another cup.

Kiara put her ring to her lips and began to breathe a silent prayer.

Hella rolled her eyes, then sharply slapped her hand on the table.

Kiara almost fell back in her chair.

Plates clanked as three different, uglier girls brought the food and refilled the cups. One held a heavy tray as the others dished out what appeared to be mutton with stewed vines mixed with onions and something else Kiara didn't recognize.

Hella aggressively waved her hand at Kiara. "Keep going. It's been so long since I've heard those sour notes. I'm actually feeling nostalgic."

I wasn't doing it for you. Kiara dropped her ring back in her shirt. She looked down at her plate and pulled a long, black hair from atop the meat. She was so hungry she wasn't sure she cared. She reached out to tug on one of the girl's apron strings to get her attention.

"Can I get some water, please?" She nearly choked when

a tail slipped out from under the girl's dress. Before the girl tucked it away again, Kiara had seen every coarse, brown hair and doubted she'd ever forget its black, tufted tip.

That broke whatever was left of the enchantment. Kiara dropped the black tail hair back where she found it and pushed the plate away. She'd be better off starving.

"That's not mutton." Tor pushed his plate away after tasting the first bite. "Lady," —he wiped his tongue on his sleeve—"I need you to help my wife. Look at her."

Runa continued to guzzle the draft, as if her thirst had no end, and Svikar obliviously lapped up the drink he'd spilt on the table to wash down whatever his tongue had managed to drag off his plate.

"We're here for your help, not—whatever this is."

Hella put her hand on Tor's arm and smiled. "I like you, Viking."

"I'm not a Viking." Tor pulled his arm away. "And that is my wife."

"I'm sorry. Did my touching your husband offend you, Runa?" the lady mocked.

Runa was too busy stealing Tor's cup to notice.

"I'm sorry to you, too, Tor." She put her hand back on his arm and smiled again. "I guess I didn't understand. Are you not Tor, son of Ove?" Hella turned a mocking grin. "And you brought Runa to me because she wanted me specifically—not Freyja. And you love her because she is a wonderful wife and mother to your two boys—Toren and Erik."

Maybe she was a goddess, thought Kiara. No. Maybe a witch—or a demon.

Tor looked like he'd been called out for trying to teach a butcher how to sharpen a knife.

Hella wasn't done. "And you aren't at all interested in me." As she ran her fingers through his thick hair, he looked lost, but he didn't pull away. Her voice sharpened. "You did not lose a daughter to a troll."

Both Tor and Hella turned their attention to Svikar. The troll's tongue caught halfway out of his mouth while inhaling a piece of stewed vine.

"You didn't stand by while that saint of a woman blamed your son all these years—an eight-year-old boy, for not doing a good enough job of taking care of *her* child!"

Tor started to stand up to leave, but Hella pushed him back down in his chair like he was a little child.

"I will give you a choice then, Tor," Hella whispered in his ear, then licked his cheek. "You said you were just a farmer, yet you carry a sword. Well, use it. Sacrifice the Christian to me, and I'll save your wife."

Kiara's fingers tightened around her soul as the room went silent. Her pounding heart racked in her chest. All this way, and now she was going to die.

She had to escape. Tor would catch her if she went for the gate. Hella and a curtain of blood vines were between her and the ledge—beyond them, the abyss.

For the first time since they filled the cups, Runa stopped drinking. Even the troll stopped gorging himself. Stares criss-crossed the table.

When Hella let go of Tor's shoulder, he bolted to his feet, knocking his chair over as he backed away from the table and the throne, his sword drawn.

"Well?" Hella sat down, looked at her plate, and pushed it away in disgust. "Runa or Kiara? It's your decision."

Then her cold pearl eyes cut like knives toward the gate. It swung open, and two dwarfs clunked across the room.

Kiara drew her cup close. It was all she had.

Both were short, about as tall as her shoulders. She thought about Erik's stories. *Did dwarfs like humans?* She doubted it mattered.

The first dwarf was thin. His shirt was white and pressed, and his boots were dainty. They looked new, clean, and shined to a gloss with thick soles and tall heels that added two unearned inches.

The one who followed was thicker, harder, redder, and hairier than the first. His shirt was not white, not anymore, anyway. His boots had metal toes, heavy and thick with dust. He carried a hammer, and it clunked against the floor as he landed it at Hella's feet. He used it as a prop to lower himself, bones cracking, to one knee.

What chance would a hammer stand against a sword?

The former stood up straight, trying to be tall in his own way, and he brushed his strawberry-blond beard with his thick fingers. A gold tooth centered with a yellow jewel glimmered with its unfortunate color choice. Kiara was reminded it had been a while since she'd cleaned her teeth.

He placed a furry, orange sack on the table in front of Hella. Bile rose in Kiara's throat. The fur looked like it came from a cat.

The dwarf swelled with pride as Hella peered into the sack, showing off another ugly gold tooth just under the first, this one emblazoned with a very red ruby.

If this was what Kiara could expect from dwarfs, Tor would be scraping their gold teeth from the bottom of his boots while Icebreaker cleaved her in two.

That was it. She was going to die today.

SACRIFICE TO THE GODDESS

"Rotinn, you little maggot! You dare barge into my—" Hella stopped, took a deep breath, and let her face return to its unnaturally cool pallor. "No. Actually, I could use a little adoration right now." She smirked at Tor. "Pay attention, Viking— this dwarf is about to show you something you can do to make me happy."

The young dwarf stuck out his white-shirted belly and rocked back and forth on his tall heels. The elder stayed low and kept still.

Hella's eyes sparkled as she poured the contents of the sack onto the table. Her lips pursed as her thin fingers pushed one, two, then three rings back toward the dwarf.

"Nice jewelry, eh lady?"

Hella's palms scattered the gold- and silver-coated souls around the table where she sat. "Did you bring nothing for me, Rotinn?" she asked glumly.

He looked at the rings, his left eye twitching. Then he smiled, picked up a gold one inlaid with a gold coin, and shined it against his jacket. With a thick, calloused finger, he pushed it back toward the lady. "Did you not see this one, lady? It's as fine as half the rings I've ever brought you."

She picked it up and smiled. Then shoved it in his face— nearly knocking him off his treacherously high heels. "Whose likeness is carved into this coin, Rotinn?"

"It's Freyja, mum. But it is finely made—for the work of

a man, anyway. Many a dwarf would be proud to have made that one — many of these, in fact."

"Let me see your hammer, Slegge," she demanded.

The rougher, older dwarf looked at Rotinn, unsure.

"Well? Give her your hammer," said Rotinn.

With a calloused hand, an "Umph," and a crack of his knees, he leaned on the hilt of his hammer and pushed himself to his feet. The little brick of a dwarf removed his long, knitted cap and used it to wipe fresh sweat and stale soot from his face and balding head. Then he crossed his arms in front of his belly, his hat and hammer hanging from thick hands, his heavy shoulders rolled slightly forward.

"Ma'am?"

"Put it right here on the table."

"Come on, then. You heard her. Chop, chop! Put it on the table!" Rotinn squawked.

Slegge eased the heavy sledge down on its iron head with both hands firmly on the handle. The room cringed when the table shook under the power of it.

"Rotinn," said Hella, "you're the second living soul today to bring me a ring bearing the picture of Freyja as tribute." She sneered at Runa, a mere shell. "Does your ring have a likeness of that angel, too, Slegge?"

"N-n-no." His long, bushy brow climbed high on his crinkled forehead.

"I want to see it."

"Ma'am?"

She took the dwarf's hand in hers and smiled. "Please show me your ring. I want to look at it."

She guided his hand to the hammer's base. Slegge's eyes drooped as his fingers gave a quick twist to loosen the thick, golden collar before lifting it up off the handle. He stared at it as if seeing it for the first time, or perhaps the last. Hella used her forearms to clear a space in front of her, leaving a lonely hole amid the array of silver and gold. The dwarf pushed his ring toward the center. The lady's eyes tilted and urged him on, and he gave it another nudge.

"Now this is beautiful." Hella examined the soul, picking it up as easily as if it were a common arm ring. "The details are exquisite." And they were. Tor remembered the stories of dwarfs being able to work magic at the forge. And Slegge's ring was steeped in it. Both white and yellow gold seemed to swim along the surface of the ring to play at forming dwarfish words and runes. Hella smiled at the old dwarf. "This is your best work, Slegge?"

"I think so." Her eyes pierced his. Then he stood up straight. "Yes. I've worked it over and over again my whole life. I can't do better with what I know. Well," he looked at it hard, "perhaps a few things." He lifted his hand as if to take it back, but she just drew it closer.

Tor remembered that feeling. When he gave up his ring, he knew he'd made a bad trade, like everything he thought he wanted seemed hollow. He knew the yearning to get it back. He looked around the table, hoping to find another piece of that weed to calm his nerves. No luck.

"You can have these." Hella pushed the gold and silver rings toward Slegge. "This is the one I want."

"Lady..." The older dwarf took a step forward but stopped when Hella's eyes turned to flame. "Ma'am, there's ten feet here, maybe twelve. My ring'll get you an inch."

Rotinn looked worried. "Mum, without his ring my father's hammer is all but useless to you."

"To me, Rotinn? You mean to you, don't you?" With eyes as callous as Slegge's hands, she stared at the white-shirted pretender. "Let me see your ring, Rotinn."

"Mum?"

Hella put Slegge's ring down on the table and held out her hand. Rotinn pulled a gem-encrusted ring from his hollow chest. It hung on a thick, gold-weaved necklace. "Very colorful. And big. I can hardly see your ring at all in there." She took Rotinn's wrist and ran her nails to the charm. His hands looked supple and smooth. "Is this your work, Rotinn?"

He scratched the floor with the heel of his boot. "I designed it." then he stood up straight. "I'm too busy managing our mines and bartering for rings to work the hammer or the forge."

"I'm sure your father is thrilled."

Rotinn's frown hid those bejeweled and tinseled teeth of his. "My father would have me break stone all my life." The dainty dwarf caught the glare of the elder and softened his tone. "No, ma'am. My father dressed my ring for me."

"You are skilled with the hammer, Slegge." She nodded to the red dwarf. Slegge took his eyes off his son.

"Lady." Slegge leaned forward but stopped short of reaching for his ring. "We did not mean to offend you." He bowed his head, then picked up a handful of the rings she'd rejected. "These can still help you extend your reach. I can add these at the bottom of your necklace if you'd like — where the images of Freyja will melt back into the world by the fires of Svartalfheim's forge — you'll never see them again."

Even Tor was sweating from watching her give them a silent stare.

"There might even be fifteen feet here, ya think? You'll never see them. Maybe eighteen, eh boy?"

"If you want my father's ring." — Rotinn turned his shoulder to shrug off the elder's hand — "it's yours, of course, lady."

Slegge's wild red eyebrows bent hard as he glared at his son.

"Why, thank you, Rotinn." Hella smiled, and the air grew warm again.

The fancy dwarf sighed, lowered his eyes, and tried to withdraw his outstretched hand along with his gaudy ring — but she tightened her grip on his wrist.

"Eeeahhh!" The dainty dwarf winced.

"But I like yours, too, Rotinn," she whined. "It's tiny and

garish, but charming—like you. You know, your father does have magnificent skill with the hammer and forge. You should show him more respect. He's a credit to all dwarfs."

Slegge snatched at his ring, but the lady's supple hand was quick as a serpent, and she locked her grip around his thick forearm.

Tor jumped back from the table and started making his way toward Runa.

"Aaagh!" Slegge grabbed his hammer and swung it to break Hella's arm. Her soft, pearl skin spiraled into a mass of wild, ice-blue vines that caught its iron head like a fisher's net.

With a snap, the hammer came back at Slegge, hitting him in the chest. He barreled backward, knocking Svikar off the table before cracking his bald head against the stone floor.

Tor grabbed Runa's arm and jerked her away from the table. She cradled her cup as if it were a baby. Tor looked inside. It was empty.

An icy tremor ran up Tor's spine.

Everything had shifted, as if a veil had been torn away. The throne and the table stayed the same, but they were no longer under the stars. They were inside a great stone hall— and the simple gate was gone. Tor looked down to make sure he was, in truth, still holding Ice Breaker and not some prop of a magic trick.

Still there. His heart started beating again. *There had to be a door along that back wall.* The only other way out was the wall of vines behind Hella's throne. *Could that be an illusion, too?* But before the thought passed, the terror of the abyss took his breath away. *We've got to find that door.*

Hella wasn't finished with the dwarf. Each finger of the hand that held Rotinn lengthened, becoming its own blue, spindly vine. One tied up his wrist before snaking its way to his throat. The others slithered down the table to slip on some of the gold and silver rings, until they looked like the fingers of some rich widow. Before retracting back into a hand, she dribbled the rejected rings down into Rotinn's shirt and wrapped him up tight.

Tor dragged the half-conscious Runa away from the table as the white-shirted dwarf struggled to breathe.

The rest of the lady remained unaltered, petite and beautiful. Ignoring Rotinn's struggle, she gently rolled his jewel-encrusted ring between her other hand's pretty, perfect fingers.

"You really have been a greedy little dwarf, haven't you, Rotinn? Whoever takes your place may be less refined on the outside, but not as filthy on the inside. I promise you that." Her arm of vines pulled him close, swinging the dwarf around as easily as she might a cup of wine. "Maybe he will be a she, actually." Rotinn's eyes were bulging out of their sockets—out of fear or pressure, it was impossible to tell. "Whoever they are, they will know better than to offer me the seconds after picking the best of the rings for themselves."

"Mmmmmph! Mmmmph!" Rotinn couldn't manage a word. Her fingers were squeezing his chest and head like he'd fallen into a nest of serpents.

As Rotinn's father came to, he used Svikar's sideways head for balance as he worked his way back to his feet.

"Rotinn, I'm going to have your ring added to my necklace, right here, near my heart, where I can admire it." Her pearl-like eye turned to a prism of colors when she tried to look through the tasteless trinket. "All will be reminded of how Rotinn the coward offered me his father's soul. How will the story end, though? Will it be that Slegge used his hammer to add his thieving son's ring to Hella's necklace?" She swung Rotinn into his father, slapping the old dwarf back into the wall. "Or that Slegge died trying to avenge his little boot-licking disappointment."

"Hold this for me, will you dear? I'll send some friends for it later." Hella stuffed Rotinn's ring down his throat with two of her grotesquely long fingers. "You'll be famous, Rotinn." She spoke tenderly to the fancy dwarf, as he coughed and gagged and gasped for air. She winked at Slegge. "Isn't that what all mortals want? Man and dwarf alike?"

With a flick of her tentacles, Hella tossed the dainty dwarf out into the curtain of thick vines. They came alive before he could pass through, which seemed like mercy, until they began fighting over him. There was a gold and silver splash as they ripped off his pressed white shirt with cutting barbs, spilling the rings Hella had hidden inside. After stripping him of his pride, and some of his skin, the weeds rolled him down like a broken yo-yo that would not be coming back.

Tor thought about the stories—how Hel was the spawn of Loki. Even the gods feared her, so much that Odin condemned her to Hel, a place where she would rule over a portion of the dead—the souls of the unclaimed.

Hella arose from her throne and walked to the curtain, grabbed one of the vines, and cut it free with a swipe of a finger. She winced a smile as she squeezed it, seeming to enjoy the sensation of tiny barbs piercing her hand. The vine's dry husk drank what dripped from the bottom of her grip. The taste of her brought it to life, and like a pet, the rest slithered up from the pit and coiled up at her feet.

She sifted through the remaining soul rings, picked one, and slipped it over the end of her new slithery pet, like she was putting a collar on an eel. Drawing up from the coil at the lady's feet, the vine slithered through the soul and twisted itself into the form of a tall, skinny man.

Hella gave it a squeeze. "Gather the rest. After we're done here, I want you to find Rotinn the thief and bring me his soul." She handed the draugr the bag the dwarf used to deliver the rings. A makeshift tongue came out of its mouth and licked at the orange tabby fur. Then it ingested it. It looked like a cat got stuck in a bird cage.

The tall figure bowed and made its way to the table. While rifling through empty vessels looking for traces of firewater, its free hand began its work, uncoiling like a worm and sniffing out the rings scattered on the table.

Each time the vine slipped through another ring, a new draugr would form, drawing vine from the one before it. This went on and on until all the rings were gone. The forming of the draugar from this single weed was like a continuous line drawing, where the artist never lifted pen from paper.

What made the assembly most amazing was that each draugr maintained their own bodily form, never giving more vine than they were taking.

Soon there were six men and four women. Three of each were short like dwarfs, the rest taller like men. The last one to form rolled up into shape of a woman, then immediately collapsed to her knees as if crying. It must have been a reflex, a reaction from what she had been in life, because it had no lungs, no real mouth, and was incapable of crying out, or even shedding a tear.

She crawled over to Hella as if begging. The lady bent down as if she might be empathizing with the creature, then with a swipe she cut off what would have been the draugr's head and threw the vine on the floor near Svikar.

The troll stabbed the weed with his tongue and chewed it like tobacco.

The headless vine did not die, it just snaked more vine through the chain of draugr until she had built another headpiece. The desperate looking draugr slapped the stone floor with her new face and crawled toward the edge of the pit. She rubbed the part of the vine anchoring her to the rest against the ledge until she cut herself free. Like a teary woman, with her hands over her face, the draugr stepped off the ledge and disappeared into the darkness.

Other than that suicide, which seemed temporary at best, the only free-will common among the group was that each spent time rummaging the table, pretending to search for rings that were long gone while really looking for any drink that might still be at the bottom of the overturned cups they could use to wet their dry, barky tongues.

Tor thought about Runa emptying cup after cup. Even now, as he watched this harrowing procession unfold, he couldn't help but salivate as he watched Svikar chew his blood weed.

Glimpses of the old stories came flooding back, and Tor remembered a few things about Hel. Her food was served on a dish called Hunger, and the curtains she dressed her rooms with were called Glimmering Misfortune.

RUNA

R una watched as the vines did their work, feeling jealous as the draugar took their turns ravaging the table in search of firewater. She held her empty cup close, repeatedly turning it up against her parched lips.

So thirsty.

"Kiara was right, Runa," whispered Tor. "This woman is no goddess. She's a demon!"

The moment the dwarfs started causing trouble, Tor pulled Runa away from the table. She expected his hand would be warm, but it wasn't. His firm grip gave her no comfort. Indifferent to his purposes, Runa felt empty and confused as her husband felt his way along the wall, looking for the door like a blind mouse. She knew where it was.

It stood out to her, the way all the cracks in the wall did, the way the hanging vines were so different from the ones wearing soul rings, and the way the drink stood out from the table or the floor. She couldn't see these things, but she could feel them.

They were hollow, frustrating feelings, like lost memories hanging just beyond recollection. She clung to them, though, because everything else was slipping into a sort of gray — imperceptible to old and new senses alike. She felt like she was sleepwalking and lost, on the cusp of finding that wonderful dream again, damned to seek but never find.

Every good thing she could sense this way — the lady, the

rings, the firewater. Fresh blood glowed brightest, then the soft earth, which seemed to call her like a warm blanket on a cold morning. But her husband was not as clear.

He, the troll, and the girl were blending more and more with the rock walls. Had it not been for the odd pressure she could feel from every beat of their pulsing hearts, they may have been completely lost to her.

I'm freezing.

Runa hated to be cold, above all else, but it was the one sensation that not only remained but was growing in intensity. Out of habit, she pulled her wrap tightly over her shoulders, but winter clothes brought her no more warmth than her husband's touch. Her own skin was just another useless layer, a cloak of cold flesh.

She stepped toward the fire before shying away. It sent spikes of fear into her belly. She began to pity the vines that burned to light the place. Now the cold was the only feeling she knew — and she knew no remedy.

So hungry. So thirsty. "Hella wants my ring," she muttered. "She's coming for them all."

"Well, she's not getting them." Tor shoved the tip of his sword into a crack in the wall and began to pry, a full two stones away from the hidden door.

Her husband's lack of competence would normally have shaken her, but she felt nothing for him now, nothing for anybody, except her own intensifying thirst.

She lifted the ring up from her chest but could no longer feel its texture. Why is it so heavy? She could no longer see its expensive gold covering. She no longer cared about the valuable gold coin she'd taken from her family.

Death's toll.

Everyone knew that's what they were, but in the village no one had the guts to call them that, — not out loud, at least.

How worthless money seemed in a place like this. The lady had just rejected more gold than Runa could ever have offered. But the ring, the thing she had covered and ignored — that seemed important. She felt the urge to protect it.

With the tip of her finger, as easily as Hella had cut the vine, Runa sliced through the leather thong that held it around her neck. Then she put her ring into her mouth and swallowed it. This did not seem odd to her. Tor didn't notice. He was too busy scratching at every crack in the stone wall, looking for an opening he'd already passed twice.

The chaos faded, and the room grew quiet. Runa only knew her own thoughts. She felt alone. Lost.

So dark. So empty. Trapped.

She clung to her husband, cutting his arm, trying to hold on to anything to keep from slipping.

She barely heard Tor howl in pain as her nails dug in, scraping down the length of his arm, then only echoes of him calling her name, yelling at her to come back to him.

She didn't feel his angry tears fall onto her face. She didn't feel her legs give way as her body crumpled into a heap on the floor. She wanted to talk to him one last time. She wanted to say she was scared. She wanted to tell him she loved him — once. She tried to hang on.

WEIGHT OF THE SOUL

"**G**et the hammer," Svikar yelled to Kiara. "You don't want to see what happens if that vine gets into me!"

Tor couldn't leave. Even if he found the door, Hella was the only chance Runa had. He saw Kiara cowering on her chair and thought about the lady's offer.

Kill the girl. Save my wife.

When he was twenty, he would've cut her in half on a bet—but not now. There had to be another way.

He broke out in a sweat as he lifted Runa off the floor and approached Hella, knowing this might be the end of them both. On his way, he did them all a favor and kicked Svikar away from the draugr. He deserved the boot after leading them to this demon. Besides, he was right. Nobody wanted to see what would happen if the vines got to a troll. Tor laid Runa on the table in front of Hella, trying to ignore the vines and the draugr and the girl he would not kill.

"Can you save her?"

"You will be her final sacrifice. Do you know that, Viking?"

The blood raged in his veins. "Enough of your games, woman. This is my wife. Help her!" He was angry that they were there. Angry she was dying. Angry at his own helplessness.

"I have authority over the dead—but I can't give life. Nor can I take it." Hella leaned forward on her throne. "I think

God enjoys his ironies."

"You can't just let her die."

Tor glanced toward Kiara. She looked scared—of the draugr, of the lady, and of him.

Hella continued her rant. "If I healed your wife, what would she do to ensure her soul wouldn't be back in ten-twenty years? If it's just about timing, why not just get it over with?" Hella wasn't really asking. "Death is a devourer, a wolf that preys on all mortal souls. It culls the unfortunate and the weak, and I thank God for it. It's the only justice I get. Ask this one, Viking. She understands." She pointed to Kiara, as if to tempt him again to strike her down. "That girl knows how unjust the Lord can be."

"I tell you again, I am not a Viking." Tor unsheathed his sword. "Show me your power and heal my wife or show me your weakness, witch."

Hella just laughed. "Mankind is all alike. You kill, you steal, you lust, and when you grow too old and weak to do those things, you have the gall to count it morality. Well, you cannot erase your past. You will always be Viking, still guilty of murder and still a pillaging thief. No matter what you think you've done right, it could never outweigh everything you've done wrong. You, above all, deserve to be here."

Maybe she's just so used to talking to plants that she doesn't know when to shut up.

Her pale hand slipped back into icey blue vines, the way a lady might slip on glove. Then Hella took Runa by the ankle.

"No!" Tor sliced down onto the tentacle, but the lady pulled back—dropping Runa hard on the floor.

"Tor?" Hella feigned surprise at the attack. "I didn't do this to Runa. Her soul brought her here. She deserves to be here. Maybe we all do? So says the God in Heaven, and his angels that protect his sheep.

"There are others that could have claimed her if she was

worthy of their attention. What about my beautiful Lucifer? Is there nothing he could have done for her?" The light dimmed in the hall, and the smell of death fouled the air. "Maybe she'd have preferred Freyja or Odin? Believe me, the lost souls of Folkvangr and Valhalla gnash their teeth, just as they do in Hel. If you really believe there's glory in death, then let her go, for my army will be as prepared for Ragnarok as Odin's, I promise."

Tor lunged to grab Runa's arm, but Hel snatched her up again. "How much innocent blood does it take to pay for one's soul? Apparently more than your wife offered." She slung Runa's limp body like a pointer as she pretended to search the hall. Runa's sacrifices may have bought her favors in your world, but 'the gods' must not have noticed." She smiled smugly. "So, she's mine now."

Tor let Ice Breaker sing. With all his might he cut and slashed. His only care was to stay clear of his still dangling wife.

But Hella slipped and slithered, too fast for his assault. Her arms broke out into blue vines, snapped around his wrist, and twisted, until the tip of the sword hit the floor.

Blood from new wounds dripped onto his blade. The lady smiled. "I like you, Tor. You're almost as handsome as Baldr. And you are fearless. Everyone I see is so frightened. Stay with me, and I'll make you a prince here, the leader of my army. The smell of death left the air, the stone hall dissolved again, and the twinkling lights shined like stars on a clear night.

She was a demon and a liar.

Tor touched Runa's face, then stroked her hair. She was ice-cold. He thought back on their failed marriage, on their daughter—and his sons. He wiped his eyes with his sleeve. He had failed her. How had it all gone so wrong so fast? As he felt a lifetime of regret trickle down his cheeks, he looked for the gate.

"You said you can't kill? Then I'll see you when I'm

dead." Tor lifted the body of his wife off the table and started making his way toward the gate. His wife was dead, and he was lost. He didn't have a plan. Just figured he'd try walking away and get Runa out of there — or die trying.

When Runa's body shifted, he nearly dropped her.

"Runa! Are you there?" He started walking faster.

The sky darkened and turned. The light dimmed, and the gate faded to stone.

"Oh, beloved," laughed Hella, "you speak as if your strength gives you power, as if you saying something gives it meaning. Death gave Runa to me, and now Runa's going to give you to me, too."

When Tor got to the wall, he gently laid Runa on the ground. "No, no, no!" He wiped his face and scratched harder between the stones. He'd never felt so helpless.

"Get away from it," said Svikar from his crooked angle against the wall. "That ain't your wife no more."

HELLA'S DEFENSE

"This hurts. My prince is leaving me for another woman." Hella turned her cold attention to Kiara. "But none, my dear, must feel as betrayed as you." She started laughing hysterically as she pulled at her fine gold- and silver-plated necklace. "What did you do for God to send you here?"

Tears blurred Kiara's vision. With a chair and a cup as her only defense, she was surrounded by a string of walking weeds, Hella—who was some kind of angry demon and possibly insane—and a Viking who was scratching at stones with a sword he might use on her next.

"Did he send you here to hurt me?" The white woman slinked around the table toward Kiara. The draugar parted and dropped their empty cups and pitchers in deference as she passed.

Kiara looked hopefully toward Slegge, but the dwarf still looked unsteady, and his hammer was still on the table.

Hella pushed her closer and closer to the ledge and the draugar. When she neared the curtain of vines, she felt the warmth of the rising air.

Kiara tried to push the throne aside to keep her distance from the curtain, but it wouldn't budge. It was a glimmering chair fashioned of souls—even Tor couldn't have moved that.

She held her breath. She was going to have to try to squeeze in between the throne and its deadly backdrop. But on the other side of the seat were the draugar. She was caught. She looked beyond the curtain and down into the abyss.

No chance.

She thought of the heeled dwarf hanging there, like a bloody marionette. She had to try. Kiara led with her left leg. Putting her chest right up against the chair she pulled herself closer, when her foot bumped something. She froze and slowly drew it back, praying she hadn't just kicked a vine.

Why hadn't she noticed it before? A chain passed through a fist-sized hole in the center of the chair, around shoulder high, down past the curtain, and into the abyss.

Just as she considered whether she could make it down the chain without getting snatched up by the vines, Hella turned and circled back the other way.

Kiara stepped away from the chasm.

Thank you, Lord.

Keeping her distance, Kiara mirrored Hella as she made her way back to her throne.

"He must be toying with me now," Hella argued with herself. The more she did, the more the façade of the place slipped in and out of view. She kicked cups and knocked chairs over as her pacing tramped a path in the stone floor.

Away from the throne, the chain was nearly imperceptible, pulsing in and out of view with the illusion of the starry sky. *If she could just get to the dwarf.*

Hella pulled at the rings on her necklace, making her choker seem more like a leash.

She scratched her nails into the wooden tabletop, as if remembering something awful.

"Did you call me a demon?"

She pulled a sword from behind her throne's high back and laid it on the table.

How did I miss that?

"You know I wasn't always like this. My beloved pleaded with God to elevate him above man." With a fingernail, she started tapping into the table like a nervous woodpecker. "He bargained and made offerings." Her eyes raged like stormy seas. "God didn't understand. He didn't know your souls were broken. He didn't know you would betray him. Don't you see? The cost of silence was too great.

"To say *nothing* would've been the *greatest* sin of all!"

The table splintered. Her agitated finger tapped harder. Faster. "And when our God chastised him, my perfect angel, for *what*? For loving him enough to tell him the truth? What was I to do? Just watch? Bow at his feet like the rest of his sheep? While broken creatures like you were anointed above such a perfect creature as my beloved? As if you were his children, and we were just servants? *Unbearable*," she seethed. "I lashed out. I raised a hand to him, and this is my reward."

She jerked her chain of rings and slammed them down on the table with a resounding crash that rippled through the curtain of vine.

The ringing seemed to help Slegge find his wits. His legs steadied, and he made his way to the hidden door.

Kiara could almost feel the pressure of Hella's heartbeat in the dank, disturbed air, polluted with anger and resentment.

"And because I started the war," Hella vented on, "and my beloved raised his sword in my defense, God Almighty gave us exactly what we asked for. He always does." She put on a wry, distant smile. "Just not the way we imagined. We, the most loyal, were cast out, made to earn our inheritance — to have dominion over lost souls, and those given of their own free will. Masters of the proud, and strong, and rich." She wrenched at the necklace of soul rings hanging around her neck. "My beloved has been out to prove to him that the price was too high ever since. Even now, he scours the nine worlds to collect enough rings for me to taste freedom again."

Kiara was confused. "Scours the nine worlds? The

Vikings killed more in my village in one day than there were rings in that dwarf's sack."

Hella slammed her sword on the table. "You know nothing."

She's lying to herself. Kiara thought of how Orlaith defended the Viking who'd gotten her pregnant. How he left her behind without a family or a home.

Hella started walking slowly toward her, dragging the blade along the tabletop as she did. She screamed at the ceiling as she narrowed the gap, still tugging on that chain around her neck.

The room pulsed between light and darkness.

"Sometimes I wish I could take it back." Hella gnashed her teeth. Her sword's tip dropped to the stone floor, leaving a trail of sparks to trace her path. "We stopped nothing. We, the most loyal, cast out like common thieves to live among the dead with your dirty, cracked souls."

The dwarf lowered his eyebrows as he eyed the dead woman lying near the Viking's feet.

"So now I rule the barrows of the nine worlds. Like a common landowner, I wait for my sharecroppers to bring me my share of the harvest. Soon, I will have enough souls to negotiate my freedom—or build an army." Hella grabbed one of her draugar by the throat, then pulled out its gold soul and held it between her fingers. "For those final days, when Ragnarok comes, we will be ready."

DEPARTED, EXPOSED, ALLOWED, DOOMED

R una felt tired but awake. Stronger, but not better. *Felt* meant something new now. Everything became an itch she could no longer scratch. Her fingernails cut into skin that no longer bled. She felt trapped like a moth in a cocoon or a chick ready to peck away at the inside of its egg.

Unsteady, she got to her feet. She felt so clumsy. *Need drink. So thirsty.* Her jaw wasn't working. Nothing was. She couldn't speak. Her awkward body fell into one of the vine figures rummaging around near the troll's head on the floor. The thing was small. In life, it might have been a dwarf.

"Get away from her!" Tor slashed the draugr in two with his sword. Runa did not care for it, or Tor for that matter. Her attention was drawn to the clinking its soul made as it bounced along the floor and into the pit. The other draugar recoiled their half of the vine back in like a fishing line, leaving the soul-less part on the floor, lifeless as a piece of rope. With a shaking hand, Tor cut a piece off and stuffed it in his mouth before Svikar could stab the rest with his tongue and suck it into his ugly head.

Runa turned up the same cup the draugar had been testing. *Empty.* She grabbed another cup. *Empty.*

"They're all empty, sweetheart," said Tor. "Can't you see?"

Runa ran a dirty finger along the inside edge of the cup and clumsily stuck it into her mouth.

"We've got to get out of here." Tor stood over her, sword raised.

"Get away from her, Viking," yelled Svikar. "She's like them now."

"Runa." Tor grabbed her arm and tried pulling her to her feet. "Over here now."

Tor smelled good to her. He was warm. She felt so cold. She grabbed his arm and pulled, and when he jerked away, his arm opened up as if raked by briars.

"Aaagh!" Tor sounded hurt.

She licked the tips of her fingers. Amidst her unfeeling, his blood was warm. The fingers came out dry and were chased, not by her tongue, but by a tendril of vine. She turned a blank face toward her husband. Then the prickly blue tongue started to crawl out like a snake from its den.

"Runa!" Tor backed away.

Runa sensed his blood pressure rising. She could feel his panic. She was drawn to it, like the cup. Only he was no empty vessel. *So thirsty it hurts. Just a little closer. If I could just warm myself against your chest.* She wished she could explain.

The sword cut, and Tor recoiled as the tip of the vine crawling out of Runa's mouth fell to the floor.

Runa swatted at her husband. *What are you doing? You could've killed me.* The pain of the cut was sharp and quick. Then only confusion remained. *Where are you going? Help me!* She was so thirsty, so cold. Tor looked so warm. She felt like she was watching from some other place. She sensed anger and fear. Then she was crushed to the ground, as Slegge the dwarf buried his hammer into her back.

Runa felt her spine snap from the hammer, her ribs crack from the stone floor, but felt very little physical pain. Instead, she burned, the way her feet felt when the snow was wet and there was still a long walk home. She felt it deep inside. It was anger at the dwarf. Disappointment in her husband. And sadness, as all the loss she'd ever felt for her father and her daughter. It all welled up inside her, and it hurt. The unbearable weight of loss and regret filled her hollow soul, and it burned. Worst of all, she couldn't cry.

The burning pointed her to Kiara the way her soul drew her to Hella. She had to drag herself along, but she made her way to the girl.

While Hella drove the girl her way, Runa could sense her fear. She knew what Hella wanted. Hella would take the thirst away in exchange for the girl's soul. She didn't know how, but she knew that's what she was supposed to do. While Kiara was backing away from Hella, Runa tripped her to the ground. *Clumsy girl.* Runa lunged awkwardly on top of her and swiped at her ring. *Nnng!* Kiara's ring added to the burning of Runa's soul.

The girl punched and kneed and kicked and crawled away toward Tor.

Kill the girl, Tor! Why aren't you helping me? Wh-what's wrong with me? Runa looked at her hand. Her unresponsive fingers were twisted. Her wrist hung limply, shattered from the struggle. She stared at it. No pain.

"Runa, stop!" Tor sounded angry at *her.* His blood was pumping harder now.

Runa didn't feel her hand, but she did feel. The more she burned inside, the colder she felt. And the *thirst*—she tried to spit. Nothing. Then she looked at the girl cowering safely under her husband's protection. She thought about all the ways he'd let her down over the years.

He's lost, like he was on the farm. I know how to bring him back. Make him love me, like so many times before. She reached out to him. Just need to get my arms around him. She wanted to wring his neck sometimes when he didn't understand. Put down that sword. The severed shoot stretched out of her loose jaw, reaching toward her husband. She reached for his head, the pulsing vein on his temple audible in the fog. It's going to be alright, Tor. Just stay right there.

Tor was yelling, but she couldn't tell what he was saying. Just stay still for a —

"Tor, look out!" Kiara screamed.

Runa hissed at the girl. *That's my husband! You should be scared.* Runa sensed Kiara's fear as clearly as she could hear a baby cry. She held out her broken hand. *Do you see what you did to me?* The ring hanging above Kiara's chest gave off a different, repulsive light.

Her senses weren't working right anymore, but she did know things. She knew thirst, she knew cold, and she knew the pain of the burning in her chest. She knew the disappointment and fear, and it filled her emptiness.

Put that away, and give me a squeeze. Runa grabbed Tor's wrist, quick as a snake in summer, and squeezed until he dropped the sword. Her prickly tongue caressed his ear. *Don't fight, husband. Just — sleep.*

DRAUGR WIFE

Slegge's hammer crashed upward, breaking teeth and splaying rooted tongue. The old dwarf's follow through decimated Runa's face, leveling the left side of her skull and pinning her to the wall. The snap of jaw and skull and neck echoed off the cavern walls.

Kiara screamed as Runa slunk to the floor, lifeless.

As soon as Tor was free from Runa's grip, he began throwing punches. He wailed down blows of anger with all his power, but the stout dwarf shielded himself with arm and hammer.

"You're too late, Tor! Let 'im be!" called Svikar, lying precariously under the two. "It was too late as soon as we sat at her table."

"That was my wife!" Tor stomped on the dwarf's arm, jerked the hammer out of his hand, and threw it to the side.

Even at her place near the table, Kiara had to jump to keep the hammer from breaking one of her ankles.

"She was already dead!" grunted the dwarf between blows. He grabbed Tor by the leg and rushed him to the ground with an *umph*. "She was going to kill you, stupid fool! I saved your life."

Tor rolled and kicked Slegge off. He sized up the stout dwarf, half shocked by his power. Then he felt a tug on his foot. He slid around to her, forgetting everything else. "Runa?" But she didn't answer. She couldn't have. Her crushed head hung limply off the back of her shoulder.

A vine slithered up to fill the hole where her jaw should

have been. Tor's first impulse was to punch it away. Then he felt sick.

"Get away from that," said Svikar. "She's draugr — only she doesn't know it yet."

As a head resembling Runa's filled the void, the corpse playfully flicked a vine at Tor, as if it were her tongue. Probably from the hammering, the gold coin with Freyja's likeness had been knocked out of its frame, and her gold-plated soul rode the tongue like a serpent slipping through a ring.

Her body writhed like a sack full of vipers. Like an adder sloughing off old skin, the vine pushed up through her jaw as a likeness of Runa started to reform. She looked as confused as Tor as she shook off her old bag of bones like it was an itchy dress.

Slegge must've figured he'd done his part because he crawled off on hand and knee toward Kiara, muttering something about a stupid Viking and needing to find his ring.

Tor reclaimed his sword and watched as the draugr hypnotically tried to figure out how to find its form.

Hella watched, giving her draugar just enough leash to harass the troll and the dwarf, but not enough to suck out either of their brains, or whatever they did once they got inside. Twice Tor kicked Svikar out of their grasp, not wanting to see what would happen if one of the draugr actually got into his head.

"Viking," — Svikar stabbed at Tor's ankle with his tongue — "cut Runa's soul free. That'll end her before she ends you." The troll's head lay sideways, useless except for his sharp tongue. Tor knew he was right, but he just couldn't do it.

She was still too familiar. She ran her hands down her front, the exact way Runa always did to straighten out her apron. What would happen to her if he cut her ring free — would he be killing her again?

The draugr was terrible, but it was Runa — all that was left of her, anyway. She seemed interested in him the way she had when they first married, playfully slipping her tendrils out to try to grab his wrists, the way she did before everything went wrong. When she used to flirt.

Tor struggled as Runa pulled him close, as if to kiss him, tongue extending toward his mouth, its black, doll eyes looking intent on making him hers for all eternity.

THE HAMMER AND THE SWORD

Armed with only a torch, Slegge made his way under the table, pushing the fire along the floor to check every loose ring. The dwarf's hammer still lay at Kiara's feet, but she didn't dare touch it. She didn't want to provoke him, and she wouldn't know what she'd do with it, anyway. She thought about the damage that hammer had done to Runa's head and found herself wiping more tears away from her eyes the closer the dwarf got. He wasn't so different than a short, stout man, but still, there was something wild about him. At first, she'd wanted his help, but now she wasn't sure. She didn't know what she wanted anymore but could only pray Slegge would protect her from the chaos. But her prayers felt empty.

The only ally Kiara could count on was the table. Like a valiant knight, it stood resolute between her and the nightmare unfolding in the hall. To her left, Hella seemed to be drinking in the disunity as if it was a fine wine. They may have arrived together, but somehow the lady had cut their ties with her thorns of pain and distrust.

Across the table, the draugar huddled together like prisoners tied together at the ankles, busy fighting amongst themselves over the same dry, empty cups. They were the only things in the room that seemed more hopeless than Kiara felt. Where a door should have been stood Tor, sword in hand, staring at the draugr that used to be his wife as if, somehow, she would spring back to life. Kiara wanted to run over and try to wake him from his trance, but she feared he might turn his blade on her, or worse, watch as Runa's draugr stole her soul.

Slegge was getting closer. He hadn't found his ring but was working his way to his hammer.

Even in her distress, Kiara recognized its beauty. The iron was fine, unlike any she'd ever seen, and the dwarf had patterned the hammer more like a work of art than a lowly stone-crusher.

Slegge didn't seem worried about the draugar. He crawled with his back to them as if they were little more than nuisances to be kicked away with his boot.

Hella called out to a draugr, "Don't let him get to his hammer." The closest, who looked to have also been a dwarf, grabbed Slegge by the wrist, and with a few twists, had him wrapped up tighter than lingonberries in a pannekaker. Slegge cursed the vine the way Tor chided the goats when they wouldn't get off the roof: "Filthy weed!"

A cold chill climbed the back of Kiara's neck. Slegge might be her only hope. She grabbed the handle of the dwarf's hammer firmly with both hands. For such a heavy-looking tool, she was surprised to find she could wield it with on hand, easier than a hatchet in the wood. She slammed it onto the vine.

"Aaoww!" the dwarf howled.

Kiara might have pinched a bit of Slegge's belly fat when she smacked the vine. It was hard to tell — he was wearing loose clothes. It had him wrapped up so tight. She lined the hammer up on the vine again.

"Stop! Don't do that again," Slegge said through gritted teeth. "Just put my torch back in my hand and go help the Viking. We're going to need him."

Kiara guessed that meant the dwarf was a friend. She gripped the hammer tight and took a practice swing. They needed her.

"Svindl!" Svikar yelled angrily. He bit at the female draugr who was getting too close. "I know you can hear me, brother!" His deep, gravelly voice tapered off as he listened past the echoes of his own voice bouncing out into the abyss. "Svindl!" He shut his eyes, hoping for a response that would not come.

Runa seemed to have gotten stronger since she sloughed off her skin like some prison of flesh. Tor was managing to fight her off without using his sword, but Slegge was right; they needed him now.

Kiara swung the hammer with both hands, planting it firmly into the side of Runa's new head. The sledge disappeared into the nest of weeds pretending to be her hair. The hammering didn't slow the draugr. It continued dragging Tor in for a kiss with its barky tongue.

Hella laughed at the entertainment.

Svikar barked at Kiara. "Put your soul into it!"

Kiara jerked the hammer hard to free it from Runa's tangles and fell on the ground next to Svikar.

"Put your ring onto the handle," said the troll, "the way the dwarfs do!"

Kiara had no idea how the dwarfs did it, but she remembered seeing Slegge take his ring off the hammer to show it to Hella.

Kiara pulled out her filthy little soul. She didn't trust the troll, but the Viking and the dwarf were tied up. She had to try.

She took the chain from around her neck and wrapped it around her wrist, then slipped the ring down the length of handle. It locked into place at the base of the hammer. The handle seemed to bend itself to lock the ring tightly into place. The female draugr who'd been harassing Svikar grabbed at Kiara's left arm. Its thorny grip sent searing pain to her shoulder, and she reacted by swinging the hammer down on the draugr. If it had been an axe, she'd have cut its arm off, but instead, the hammer buried it deep into the stone floor. With the weight of her soul, the hammer had an unnatural power. Kiara looked at her cracked little ring, and for the first time, realized there was power in it.

Svikar's draugr retreated. "If you want to stop a draugr, you've got to get their soul away from the vine." She heard Slegge cursing—something about draugar and candle wicks.

The dwarf growled at the vine as he finally got his torch into it, as if he didn't realize fire burns both ways. Once he got it to light, the vine let go so fast it made a crack like a whip. Its soul ring sang as the dry tendril drew it up and away from the flame. Before the vine got away, Slegge warmed his hands by the fire. But the other draugar in the line panicked, slashing at the burner with their thorny fingertips to prune it before it set them all ablaze like a fire running a fuse.

"Tor"—Kiara refocused her efforts on Runa—"I've got to do this now." She swung the hammer hard. This time a new force propelled the hammer through, ripping Runa out of shape as it passed through her wriggling mass, sinking deep into the wall.

Kiara fell away as a chunk of stone the size of a bull crashed to the floor, burying half of Runa's vine down under it. The impact sent out a small crack the length of the floor, separating Hella from her throne. The demon stopped smiling.

Tor was dragged down onto the boulder amidst his draugr wife—who had become nothing more than a writhing, roiling, and firmly trapped vine. Kiara lost some skin when she yanked her arm and the hammer out of the confused vine's grip. As much as Runa tried, she could not keep her. Tor looked like the wall caving in had woken him from a trance, and with a few quick jerks, he broke away from Runa's tentacles—bloodied but free.

False arms formed and reached out. Claws scratched floor to be freed from the weight of the stone. No luck. Then the thing probed the floor's new crack as if seeking a place to hide. Still no luck.

Tor looked horrified, and the weed seemed to notice. It tried to recoil back into a form more like Runa, but at least half of it was sticking out from the other sides of the stone. The side next to Tor had enough to form a chest, a head, and a piece of an arm. The rest of the weed kept on slithering, making Runa's draugr look like it was crawling out of a den of snakes.

Two obsidian eyes looked as trapped and pathetic as the naked vine—helpless, hopeless, and scared.

Tor looked like he wished he didn't recognize her.

While the thing reached helplessly toward her husband on one side of the rock, the rest of her gathered together and slithered off in the opposite direction, probing around the rubble.

"Tor!" Kiara tried to get his attention.

He turned to her and raised his sword. Reflexively, Kiara raised the hammer, not sure what she would actually do with it but keenly aware that she and it had brought down the stone wall that now trapped his wife. Tor had a defeated look and let the anger fall from his face. Ignoring Kiara and the hammer, he turned back to Runa, sad, as if searching to see if there was something else that could be done.

Kiara decided to let him be. He would have to figure that out for himself. She watched as the part of Runa Tor couldn't see sniffed around the dirty floor until it found its missing gold coin, the final offering Runa held in her soul for this very day—to pay homage to the gods and to buy her way to a better afterlife.

The slithering side of Runa managed to free enough of itself to nudge the little gold coin all the way to lady Hella's feet. Along the way, it followed the part of Hella's necklace she'd left strewn along the floor, slipping in and out of its rings as if to bind itself to its master.

But Runa fell short, unable to elevate the gift to Hella's knees. Hella smiled as it tried but wasn't even willing to stoop to accept it. The vine pulled and pulled but just couldn't make it, so it left the offering on the ground next to Hella's perfect toes, even remembering to flip it over to hide Freyja's likeness.

Runa, who had been trying to kill her husband minutes earlier, had lost all aggression. The vine was beaten, trapped, and at the mercy of those around her.

Gently, it wrapped itself around Hella's ankle, probing and stroking as if to gain favor, like a servant kissing her master's feet. The tip of the weed bore Runa's soul, plated in fine yellow gold, bright and reflecting.

Hella paid Runa's advances no mind. With a shift of her left foot, the demon stepped on the snake, crushing its head and pinning its offering, and its soul, to the ground. Runa didn't struggle or pull away. Instead, she seemed to accept her judgment.

With a crunch of the serpent's head, Hella stepped toward Kiara. Tor raised his sword. The goddess smiled and circled, corralling them around the table toward the wall of vines, a prickly veil separating them from the abyss.

"Wait, don't leave me 'ere." Svikar's eyes were trained on Hella's thirsty-looking draugar. "I don't want to be left again," he pleaded.

As Tor nudged Kiara around the table, he kicked the troll's head toward the dwarf as he passed. The crunch sounded like it loosened some of Svikar's teeth, and he flipped nose over ear under the table like a lopsided gourd.

Svikar painted the floor with long licks from his tongue as a sort of makeshift brake as he skidded toward the abyss.

On the other side of the table, the dwarf seemed to have finally found his ring. Seeing its swirling colors in the torchlight, Kiara couldn't believe it took him so long amongst the gawdy gold and silver rejects the lady'd scattered across the floor.

Without lowering his gaze, the dwarf dropped the sole of his boot on the troll's cheek, stopping it just short of the abyss.

The draugar dutifully followed the lady as she pushed Tor and Kiara around the table toward the dwarf. Farther from the door. Farther from escape.

Hella closed her eyes, and the room began to spin and shift; another part of the illusion gave way. The lady stood in front of a clearly visible arched wooden door — the exit Tor had so desperately searched for but just couldn't seem to find. It was too late for that now. Tor was already steadying his feet, trying to hold on to every foot of solid ground. It was hard to tell what rattled him more, the heights behind the curtain, or Hella and her draugr.

Though the air was cool, sweat soaked the hair along the back of his neck. His eyes looked wild when looked over his shoulder. Then he stopped backing away. Widening his stance, he planted his feet and raised his sword up high.

"Lady, I will go no further." The tip of his sword shook ever so slightly, showing this to be a stand of desperation.

Slegge pocketed his ring.

Kiara raised the hammer.

Hella was the only beautiful thing left in the hall, but even that wouldn't last. Kiara gasped when the lady dropped the last veil and let them see the true nature of their circumstances.

Her pale, white skin glowed blue and slithery wherever it was touched by shadow. In the dark, she was ragged, bleak, and grim, a true queen of the lost souls deceived into her eternal service. A glimmering mother of the common draugar swarming together in her wake.

Kiara gagged, as the very air took on the rank, putrid smell of death. A cold shiver climbed Kiara's back, like the touch of a thousand spiders, and for the first time since they were sacrificed, she could see her own breath.

With her deception withdrawn, Hella's necklace, too, shone clearly. The ornate rings of the fallen not only decorated her long neck, but twisted down along the stone floor then up through the headpiece of the throne before pouring over the ledge and down into the abyss.

Hella was as much a prisoner as they were, only she had power, and she kept coming. Her fingernails dragged across the table as she rounded a corner. There was no barrier except Tor and his sword to keep Hella and her draugar from pushing them into the abyss.

Slegge stopped. He'd gotten to the edge. There was no way he could fit behind Hella's massive throne without disturbing the curtain of death weeds. Kiara was probably the only one who could squeeze through there.

Kiara was about to start climbing up over the table when the stout dwarf gave the throne a shove. She wasn't even sure why he tried. Everyone knew mortals couldn't bear another's soul unless it was given in life or lost in death.

Slegge couldn't move that chair—the same way Vidar couldn't pick up Erik's ring in the village hall.

There was something though, because when the dwarf shoved the throne, Hella stopped, and her twisted stare showed a new emotion—fear.

The goddess forced a smile as the dwarf rubbed his hands together. Her chair was icy cold.

"I'll give it to you if you like. It's worth more than its weight in gold, or gems, or whatever else dwarfs waste their lives digging up." She took a step closer, but Tor stopped her with the point of his sword. "Kill the girl for me, and I'll give it to you."

The chill in the air grew colder.

"How about you, Norseman? Sacrifice her to me, and I'll make sure your soul finds its way to Valhalla."

Kiara looked up at the powerful man, sword clenched tightly in his fist. *Surely, he wouldn't. Not now.*

"In life, Orri begged Odin's favor," breathed Tor, "and he ended up no different than my wife—a woman who'd never raided anything more than a chicken coop." He clenched his teeth as he pointed toward Runa, a trapped, shape-shifting vine.

"Orri was no warrior." Hella put her finger on Ice Breaker's tip. "Not like you." *Was she flirting?* "Besides, it's too late for them—but it's not too late for us."

Tor grabbed Kiara by the arm and pulled her close.

"What is it about this girl, that you would bribe us to kill her?" Tor's grip loosened. "And who would be next, me or the dwarf? Why don't I just kick the troll over the edge while I'm at it—save the last of us the trouble?"

"Would you, a mortal, soul-less man, refuse mercy again?" Hella jerked hard on her necklace, but the chain snagged, and the throne rocked forward. "I only dared condemn the guilty—and for that I was exiled here by God. Do you think you deserve anything less?"

"My wife was a devout follower of the gods and look what that got her."

Hella jerked the ring of the closest draugr, sending a ripple through their ranks. "Do you think these pathetic souls forgot to make their sacrifices?"

"I'm done trying to buy your favors. If I didn't earn Odin's protection after every terrible thing I did in his name, then I will renounce him unto my dying breath." Tor stepped toward the lady. "I will make no sacrifices to you or any god if this is the reward you offer."

Svikar just grumbled from his place under Slegge's boot.

"Take your ring off the hammer, then give it to me, lass." Slegge whispered to Kiara. "The Viking and I will handle this."

Kiara finished her silent prayer, then whispered something to Tor. He shook his head.

Kiara raised the dwarf's hammer, kissed her ring that was banded around its neck like a striated decoration, and stepped up next to Tor.

Hella's eyes narrowed, and her features tensed. Raising her sword higher, the lady took a step backward.

Like a child stepping out on the ice for the first time, Tor lowered his body and slid back toward the precipice — and the throne. His breathing was heavy, sending white clouds of fear rolling over Kiara's shoulder.

"Tor," — Kiara stepped back — "you've got to do it now."

The lady slithered forward toward Kiara.

Tor stood up straight, then stabbed Ice Breaker down through one of the rings of Hella's necklace as it passed out of the back of her throne. He let his body collapse to the floor and immediately started crawling back away from the abyss.

"You're not so bright, are you, Christian?" Hella mocked. The gold and silver rings of her chain kept time — *click, clack, click* — as she reeled in her necklace, until it was piled up at her feet. "Don't think it's long enough to reach you?" With Hella's final tug, Kiara could hear Ice Breaker knock against the back of the throne. "I can still reach any place in this hall." Hella's perfect figure gave way to lumps, like random knots popping out on a skinny tree. Something began shifting from side to side under her gown, like a dog's nervously wagging tail, and her face grew ugly and sinuous. "No mortal soul escapes the pain of death!" hissed the hag.

"But not every soul goes to Hella!" Kiara screamed as she sent the dwarf's hammer crashing into the back leg of Hella's throne.

The leg bent inward, crippling the chair and sending it backward until it flipped through the veil and down into the abyss.

Hella's jaw dropped as the slack in her chain spiraled off toward the brink. She stabbed sharp fingernails from one hand into the tabletop and grabbed the throat of one of her draugr with the other.

The rings of Hella's leash thundered as they passed, cutting a narrow trench into the ledge like a saw. Kiara watched the crippled throne disappear into the darkness, then felt a tug on her ankle. It was Tor, lying flat on his stomach, jerking her away from the abyss, as if he couldn't stand to see her so close to the edge.

Hella let out a shriek of terror just before her lovely necklace finally struck taught. The speed of her departure cracked her body like the tip of a whip. Her face mirrored the terror of the draugar as the shock jerked her and them in succession over the edge and down into the darkness.

The draugar unwound like she'd pulled a piece of yarn out from a series of loosely-knitted soldiers. Every time the tension hit a draugr, whether fashioned as a man, woman, or dwarf, they would be strung out into a rope that would unwind the next and the next and the next until the last in line cracked like a whip as it was jerked over the edge.

One after the other they unraveled, each making a twanging sound like a plucked string before unwinding the next. The rings couldn't keep up with the speed of the serpents' retreat, and were left spinning on the stone floor, likening Hella's exit to that of a spoiled child, scattering her toys in a tantrum after being sent to her room by her father. The final trace of her was her sword, left spinning on its tip like a top.

"Mmmph!" came a muffled, gravelly voice from the void.

"Owww! You stupid troll."

"Mmmph!"

The muffled groans snapped Kiara back to the present. The table was missing, as were many of the chairs.

Tor still had a strong grip on Kiara's ankle. His face was buried in the stone floor, and his free hand clung to the edge of a cobble stone as if the floor had tilted toward the abyss during Hella's descent.

The curtain of vines hung peacefully, pulsing their pale phosphorescent blue light.

Kiara helped Tor to his feet, then fell into his arms.

"Are you alright?" He was still shaking, but he was strong, and suddenly, she felt overwhelmed. The fear and the anxiety and the anger filled her heart till it burst, and her eyes filled with tears. She clung to Tor like the last time she hugged her father. "I want to go home."

DWARF FISHING

"If you break skin, I'm going to put my other boot right across your big, ugly nose!" Slegge's angry voice thundered up from the abyss.

"Mmmph!?"

Tor pulled Kiara back gently by her shoulders, but he took no steps closer to the ledge. "Is that you, dwarf?"

"Down here."

"Mmmmmmmph!"

"Give us a hand, eh, Viking? Before I lose my foot."

"I am not Viking."

Kiara stepped around Tor, whose feet were rooted to the ground like a tree, and eased toward the ledge, leaned over, and nearly fell backward.

"There!" She held the torch out near the curtain and pointed down, but Tor took a step backward every time she leaned out farther over the edge. "I think that's them. Slegge, how'd you get down there?"

"The lady knocked us over with the table — me and this head biting my boot."

"Mmph!"

Slegge translated. "The troll asks that you kindly help us up."

"How is it that the vine hasn't taken you?" She narrowed her eyes. The Vikings' destruction of her village hadn't taught her skepticism — Runa had when she'd given Kiara to Skadi, as if she were nothing more than a broom. It broke her, somehow, and she wondered if she could ever trust again.

"Maybe you can help us up, first. Then we can talk about our luck after. I've got a pretty strong grip, but even I can't hold here much longer."

Tor stayed back away from the edge. "How far down are they?"

Kiara looked him up and down. "About three of you."

"Watch those vines, there! They'll snatch you up, those will," echoed the voice of the dwarf. "Try to find a thin one with fine hairs instead of thorns — somewhere up along the walls. It'll be thinner than a blood vine, smaller around than your finger."

Kiara scanned the room, then saw a vine hanging sideways along the inside wall of the cavern. "I think I've found one. How do I know it won't grab me?"

"You're going to have to trust me. Those aren't the blood vines. The thin ones are Ymir's beard. They're safe."

"Doesn't look very strong."

"Then you've got the right one. Trust me, it won't turn on you. The thin ones are safe."

"I don't know if I can..." Kiara hovered her hand over the little vine. Thoughts of the draugar filled her mind, of what they did to Orri — what Runa had become.

"Mmmmmmmmmph!" grumbled Svikar.

"We don't have much time," the dwarf pleaded. "You can't kill a goddess, not this way, anyway. She's got to be pissed."

Kiara smacked the vine with the dwarf's hammer. A few stones showered her head, but the vine didn't move. She put the hammer down, pulled her ring off its handle, and removed the leather thong from around her neck. Carefully, she looped the leather through the ring, then back into itself before putting it back on. She admired its fractured, mottled surface, seeing it differently now that she knew its power — that creatures like Hella might want it for themselves. Kiara put her ring to her mouth, held it between her lips, closed her eyes, and blew into it. The sound was shaky, and weak, but it brought her peace.

With a finger, she poked the thin vine, like a child playing with fire. Nothing happened. Again, she blew across the ring as she put her fingers, one by one, along the thin vine. Nothing. Kiara began to pull, slowly and steadily. *Pop, pop, pop.* The vine was covered in fine hairs that gave it a strong grip.

"Alright, this one isn't trying to kill me—yet!" Kiara yelled out, as if it was the dwarf who needed to hear it. She pulled, then yanked, even using her foot to push against the wall, but she couldn't break it free.

"Tor, I need some help."

Tor didn't respond. He was standing near the boulder, near what was left of his wife.

"The vine doesn't want to let go," she said as she stared at the sad man. "It's stronger than it looks."

"See if you can find something to pry it off the wall," echoed the dwarf.

Kiara picked up her torch and scanned the dark, dank room. *I can't believe Hella made this feel comfortable.* Without the lady's spell, it was barely more than a cave.

"Ah!" Kiara saw a glimmer of gold and polished iron. *The lady's sword.* "She must have dropped it in the falling."

"What did you say?!" yelled the dwarf.

The sword was light and finely made. She returned to her spot, then thought better of it.

"Hold on." Kiara made a cut. The sword was so sharp it sliced through the vine and scratched the stone. She pried it away from the cave wall, and slid the sword between the wall and the vine, cutting through the strong fine hairs as if they weren't even there. "It's working." Kiara stopped prying the vine from the wall just short of the edge.

The curtain of blood vines blocked the opening. "I can't," she cried down. "There are vines." Then she caught a glimmer from the sword. She turned back to Tor, but he was in another world. "Just pull back and cut. You've swung a sword before," she whispered to herself.

But she had only swung the training kind before. She used to play "Knights" with her brother when they were young. She looked at the shimmer of the pale, blue blade and was reminded she'd really never swung a real one, and never at a column of vines with the power to snatch her up and take her soul.

"What's going on up there, girl?!" yelled the dwarf. "I'm not going to be able to hang here much longer."

"I've got the lady's sword."

"What?!"

"I'll have to cut through these vines, but I'm scared they'll grab me."

"You can do it, girl. They're harmless unless they taste blood or touch your soul. Just use a nice, smooth swing."

Kiara hid her ring inside her shirt. "I'm afraid."

"Why am I not talking to the Viking, right now?"

Kiara turned back to Tor. He was on his knees now.

"I-I think I can manage." Kiara pulled the sword back, said a prayer, and with all her might swung high and across. Using that sword on the curtain of weeds was like choosing to use an axe to cut bread. The sword only slowed when it cut into the stone of the wall over Kiara's shoulder.

"Watch it, clumsy!" shouted the dwarf. "Can't you tell the difference between a sword and a hammer?"

Kiara looked at the blade. *Not a scratch.* She couldn't help but think that if they'd have had weapons like these back in Ireland, how different her life would be now. Kiara laid the sword on the stone floor next to the hammer gently, so as to not bring the walls down on their heads. "Now what?"

"Pass down that strand of Ymir's beard." Slegge sounded tired, or maybe a little sad. "I'll do the rest."

HELL FIRE

The only sound Tor could hear was that of his own shallow breath and the dragging bark of the vines as the curtain swayed from the cold breeze rising out of the abyss. As Hella fell, she took the warmth of the place with her, along with the rest of the façade. Hel, as it turned out, was a frigid place, and Runa's draugr had already picked up a layer of white frost along its bark.

"I won't let Hella hurt you." Tor tried to sound strong.

The draugr reached out a hand, no longer Runa's supple, pale skin, but one of rough bark, with talons of thorns where her nails should have been.

Tor thought about loss. From his parents to his first wife. His daughter. His sons out there somewhere facing the bitterest time of the Norwegian winter on their own. And now Runa. "What a mess this is." He slowly extended a hand.

The draugr ran a coarse branch down the length of his finger, tracing a line across his palm. Tor managed a smile from the tickle. She was still there. He could see something of Runa in the draugr's cold, black eyes. Then, as if to crack bone, it clamped down tight on his hand, and a tendril began to slither up his arm. The eyes did not change. Runa was still inhabiting the draugr's blank, slithering face. Tor grunted as thorns pierced his skin.

The draugr slipped out of her cloak of humanity the way Runa might have dropped her dress to the floor during happier times. As the façade fell, the draugr rose up tall above her husband before wrapping him up to squeeze him like a constrictor. With lungs crushed, he could only manage to grunt for help.

Then the shock of it sank in. Rather than fight his wife, Tor gave in to her. He even managed to slip his fingers out between the crushing weed and hold on to a part of her, even if she no longer could. Tor closed his eyes and began to pray.

He thought back to the life he had lived, to what he had and hadn't done. Valhalla was a lie—he always knew it. But it was a way to avoid the truth. No. He would spend his eternity with this woman—this draugr. This was what he deserved.

Runa moved, her tight grip dragging him along with her.

He opened one of his eyes and realized she was dragging him toward the ledge.

His entire body broke out in a clammy sweat as he thought about the seemingly bottomless pit.

"Runa!" Tor could only cough out his appeal. It felt like his watery eyes might bulge out of his head.

Closer, closer she dragged him. Briar's dug into his back, his chest. With each twist, his weight pushed into more thorns, piercing his flesh like a thousand needles. The pain was the only thing keeping him sane as she drew him closer to his worst nightmare.

"Slegge! Slegge, come quick!" Kiara turned to help the dwarf up, but there was no need.

He ran past her, hammer at the ready, slamming it down on the vine as Tor frantically tried to squirm away from the edge. It didn't work.

Tor hung headfirst out over the ledge. Runa seemed vindictive, stabbing him with his worst fear. No sharper blade could she find.

Four trails of blood painted the stone floor where he dug in his nails to cling to solid ground.

"Help me!" yelled the dwarf. Kiara grabbed the sword

and raised it high overhead.

"Don't." Slegge pushed her to the ground. "They'll both fall if you cut her away from the stone."

Tor howled, half pulling away, half holding on.

Kiara dropped the sword, wrapped her hands in her cloak, and started pulling on the vine.

The only part of Tor still clinging was his legs. Working his toes frantically back and forth, he tried everything to help win the tug of war of his life.

Slowly, the team began to outpull the vine. Tor bit at it, stripping and spitting bark between gasps for shallow breath. When his hips finally touched the edge, he squirmed side to side to help the dwarf and the girl with the pulling.

"Owww!" howled Svikar when Kiara stepped on his ear. Either from the shock of his voice or the squish underfoot, she lost her footing, and the vine lunged forward.

Tor froze. He was staring straight down into the abyss. A blast of icy air blew up into his face, sending a shiver down his spine. Acrid fumes rode the arctic wind, burning his nostrils and freezing the tears in his eyes.

"Bite the vine, troll!" yelled Slegge.

"You left me here, dwarf," replied Svikar.

"Grab it!" yelled Tor and Kiara in unison.

Svik snagged a piece of the vine with his long, forked tongue and pulled it into his mouth. Tor heard the crunch of his chomping. With an angry whip of its tail, the vine sent the head flipping toward the pit.

Kiara dove across the vine to stop the head from going over. When she regained her footing, the rope turned taught, pulling Svikar up off the ground, then down again, as if the squishy head were a bouncing ball.

Slegge rolled around behind the hunk of wall to anchor the vine to the other side.

Tor shifted his legs back and forth like a frog as he slid and scratched his way to solid ground. Next to him, Kiara raised the sword, sweat dripping from her brow.

Crack! She severed the part of the vine that had Tor from its soul.

Tor pulled himself to his feet and fell back against the large stone. Gasping for air, he ripped the prickly vine from his clothes and skin. It made a wet, popping sound as he freed it thorn by thorn. Then he shook off the remains of the lifeless draugr like a pile of prickly rope.

Kiara limped over and put her head on Tor's shoulder. Blood pocked their clothes and skin where the thorns had ruthlessly scratched and stabbed during the struggle.

With a high-pitched clink, Kiara let the sword fall to the floor and hugged him. "I'm so sorry," she cried.

"Kiara, listen." Tor faced the girl. "I didn't—"

Kiara mimed a silent scream—the other side of the undead vine had slithered up and grabbed her by the throat.

Tor caught the tip before it could slip into Kiara's soul. Blood dripped from his hand as he tried to pull it loose.

Slegge hammered down to snare the vine, but it slipped and slithered, leaving the dwarf crushing nothing but stone.

"Runa!" Tor pulled at the vine until he saw he was crushing Kiara's windpipe. He snatched up Hella's sword. "Don't make me."

"Do it!" The thing had caught Slegge by the wrist.

Tor slid the sharp blade between the vine and the girl's throat. He looked for something to reason with, but all he saw was its hollow black eyes and her gold ring riding along the slithering viper like a ship on a rolling wave.

An image reflected off the side of Runa's soul ring. Despite its covering of gold, Tor could distinctly make out the image of a serpent. Like the knot art he'd personally carved into the doors of Pedar's hall. Like the interwoven bodies of dragons carved along the hull of almost every Viking ship. He'd carved the design himself no less than a hundred times, but not in Runa's soul. No knife was sharp enough, or strong enough, to do that. *Why had he not noticed that before. Had Runa?*

Tor thought about how Hella's pale fingers had changed into slithering vipers. His eyes turned to fire. "Go to your goddess, draugr!" he yelled. His hand shook as he strangled the vine. Then, with tears in his eyes, he pulled back on the sword.

Kiara fell to the floor coughing and wheezing for air as she pulled the piece of dead vine from her throat.

But a piece in Tor's hand stayed strong, wrenching and cutting his palm in its struggle to hold on.

Pinning the thing down onto the stone floor, Tor cut and stabbed, cursing and taking out his anger on Runa for what she had become. The anger he felt at himself for watching her change, slowly over the years, into this *thing*. With every cut, he realized she'd become this long ago, a writhing mess of anger and unforgiveness and spite, covered in the facade of a pretty face and a bit of gold.

Like a cornered viper, the last of the vine struggled and bit at Tor, wrapping itself around his arm and clambering for his neck. Tor pinned it to the wall, trying to figure out a way to end it, then froze when he saw the glimmer of Runa's gold-plated soul slipping up and down near its head.

From over Tor's shoulder, Slegge shoved a torch into it. It's dry bark aflame, what was left of Runa loosed her grip in a frenzy of self-preservation. Tor threw the fiery worm over the ledge, where it got tangled inside the curtain. The hanging vines sprang to life at its touch, one of them pushing itself though her ash-infested soul ring. Finding new life, a new fiery draugr began to pull itself together, coiling into Runa's likeness.

The curtain became a sort of twisted stage. Runa had been born again, but this time into a world of flames. She roiled in agony and anguish like a fiery marionette. Her fire spread across to the other vines as she reached out to escape the burning.

The vine burned through, and the shape of his wife fell away when her soul dropped down into pit. The wall of fire she left behind filled Hella's hall with light and heat, as if it was an oven.

Slegge covered his eyes in the brightness of it all, and Svikar used his tongue to drag himself toward the door.

"I couldn't let her hurt you anymore," Kiara cried.

"I should have stopped her long ago." Tor hugged Kiara tight, lifting her up high off the ground. *Maybe I could've saved her if I had.*

"If you two've made up, we really need to get going." Slegge used his hammer to break down the door out of Hella's hall.

The smoke siphoned out the open door, a toxic leader pointing the way.

"Who knows what else lurks in the world's dark basement," said Kiara as she handed Tor a belt she'd quickly woven out of a strand of Ymir's beard.

"I know what lurks in the dark," came the voice of the disembodied head.

"I'm sure you do, troll," Slegge scoffed.

Kiara picked Svikar up, brushed off his dirty head, and looked at Tor like a child who'd found a lost pup. "We can't just leave him."

A face like Svikar's benefited from shadows and bad lighting, and the bright wall of fire highlighted every bit of the ugly.

Slegge shook his head. "Does your own life mean so little that you'd sacrifice it for a troll?"

Kiara fashioned a sling around her chest, like a mother preparing her baby to leave the house. "You still stink, Svikar, but I couldn't live with myself if we were to leave anyone behind."

"What about your son, Slegge? Is there any hope?" Tor thought he saw Slegge's head shaking as he led them out the door.

"Wonderful," said Svikar. "Wandering through Hel with a depressed dwarf, a farmer with a borrowed sword, and a little girl armed with a troll's head in a sling. This ought to end well."

"Ah, troll, you're more than just a head in a sling," Slegge shouted back. "We've got your pretty eyes to help us see, your pointy ears to help us hear, and your lovely, lengthy nose to help us smell. What could go wrong?"

TO TRUST DWARFS OR TROLLS?

An icy fog had settled across the entirety of Hel.
"The air has g-gotten s-so cold I feel like I could freeze." Kiara had her hands as close to a torch as she could manage.

"Hella must've warmed it up for your arrival," said Slegge, "'cause this is the way she keeps it. What's so special about you, anyway?"

Kiara silently shrugged.

"Move faster. It'll warm you up." Slegge waddled on short legs, a pace somewhere between a walk and a trot.

Tor was glad he hadn't forfeited his coat while Hella's spell had it feeling like spring. Since she'd gone, the bubbling creeks had frozen solid, and the columns holding up the ceilings were dressed in coverings of ice, making it feel like they were escaping through a crystal forest.

"How do you know where you're going?" Tor asked the dwarf.

"Because I know many ways to Svartalfheim, both the front doors and the back." Slegge tapped a calloused finger to the side of his nose.

Tor stopped short. "Is this the best way to get us home? I need to get back to my son Toren before he returns to that witch we've betrothed him to."

"And to Erik—" Kiara got very quiet and lowered her gaze coyly, as if she'd almost let out some great secret.

"Ja." Tor looked at the strange girl. "I've got to settle a few things with my neighbors before my sons return."

"To Midgard?" Slegge looked back, then nervously down at the troll. "I'd never take you there." Then he turned to follow the river off the path. He'd picked up his pace.

"You're not taking us home?" Tears froze to Kiara's cheeks. She looked ready to wake up from this nightmare.

Tor understood how she felt, but he found himself looking over his shoulder now, too.

"Never been to your world," huffed Slegge. "Dwarf's don't leave the caves." The stone pillars were getting thinner, and there were more of them, and the space between them was narrowing, too, like the way tall, skinny scrub pines will take over an abandoned pasture after years of neglect.

Without any prodding, the troll blurted, "Don't look at me. I never been to Midgard, either."

"Right," the dwarf mumbled as he skated out onto the icy river.

As Tor tested the ice, he kept an eye on Svikar. The troll's ears kept cocking backward, and so did his eyes. He didn't seem at all nervous about the ice, nor should he have been, for it was thick enough to drive a horse and wagon over it.

When Svikar noticed Tor looking, he started running his mouth again. "But I know some who have—gone to Midgard, I mean."

Everything about Svik just *felt* unreliable. Kiara grabbed the back of Tor's coat for balance. Even with his long strides and a lifetime of experience dealing with ice, Tor was having a difficult time keeping up with the surprisingly fast dwarf. Amidst a forest of pillars that were getting thinner and thinner as they went, one that was massive and out of place emerged from the frozen river, splitting the flow in two.

"Make a left, dwarf," Svikar ordered. "I'll take the lead from here."

Slegge slid to a stop, ending with his hand on the massive column. "Well, I'm going right."

"Good luck to you, then." Svikar's attention was behind them. "Alright, girl, no time to waste," said the troll, "Let's pick up the pace a little. I'll tell you where to go from 'ere."

"You aren't fool enough to let that head lead you into a troll hive, are you?" The dwarf cocked his head back as if he heard something, then slid his way to the right of the tree. "Follow a troll and you might as well cut out the middleman and wait for Hella back in the hall."

"Tor"—Svikar's speech was hurried—"what do you know about dwarfs?"

Taking his cues from both untrustworthy guides, all of Tor's attention was behind them now. "I don't know anything about dwarfs, Svik, but I've never had one lead me to the gates of Hel. Do you want us to leave you here or kick you as far as we can down the left branch?"

Kiara looked at Tor like he was being cruel to their worthless guide.

There was a sound behind them, like a distant storm. Even Tor could hear it.

"No, don't do that." Svik's eyes twitched, and he gulped hard. "I'll stick with you, my new friends."

Tor moved Kiara's hand over to grip the back of the dwarf's cloak and pushed them off to the right. The sound was getting louder. It was like a heavy rain. Tor looked back, almost expecting the stone columns to be swaying like trees. They weren't.

"Like the troll said"—Tor started using his sword to push off the ice and get more speed—"we need to pick up the pace."

"Well, dwarfs are no friends to trolls, I'll say that. They're not friends to anybody, not even other dwarfs half the time." Svikar knew he didn't have a leg to stand on, but still the troll felt the need to sow his seeds of discord.

Tor noticed Kiara passing judgmental glances between all of them. Even him. But it was worse still to see the new fear in her eyes when she craned her neck back toward the rumbling.

"What is that?! Sound's like a storm!" Kiara shouted over the noise.

"You won't have to worry about it!" Slegge dodged the question. "We'll be gone before they get 'ere!"

"Will we be safe if we get to your country, Slegge?!" she asked.

"I can't say!" Slegge may have been blunt, but that was better than lying. "But you'll be a lot better off there than here!"

Tor looked over his shoulder. Blue stars were dropping out of the sky and into the sea of fog. The haze was beginning to light up, like a thin sheet held up in front of a blue flame. He came to a halt. To either side of the river of ice, the spindly columns had become so tightly packed they were like prison bars holding them to the frozen path. Ahead, great masts—as massive as the one they saw splitting the river earlier—rose up high out of the black nothingness.

The world was ending.

"Dwarf!" Tor could feel his heart beating harder with every step. "We've got to stop!"

Kiara let go of Slegge's coat like it was on fire. Without him for balance, she fell and slid till she swirled to a stop.

The dwarf skidded to a stop not twenty paces from the edge. "We're almost there." He skated back to help Tor pull Kiara to her feet, but his eyes were on the storm. "We don't have time for this."

Tor heard the rumbling closing in and could see the reflection of the blue light bouncing off and through the icy trees, but his fear was in front of him. While Kiara found her footing, he found himself easing down to his quaking knees.

The dwarf had led them to the top of a frozen waterfall, its crystalline floor bending down over the edge of Hel. Suddenly, it felt like the ground was tilting. Nobody else seemed to notice but Tor. With a resounding crunch, he stabbed the tip of Hella's sword deep into the thick ice to keep from sliding toward the edge.

"Maybe we should have gone *left*." Tor thought about everything that brought him to this point, and blamed Svikar. *Only a troll could be less trustworthy than a dwarf, hocking souls to the queen of the underworld.*

HEL'S BACK DOOR

"There's a trail up ahead. I promise you'll be safe."
Safe? Closer to the edge? Tor couldn't make the two concepts fit.

"A trail?" asked Kiara. "Where?"

"Swear you'll keep me safe. No executions, no prisons," Svikar demanded.

"Prison?" Kiara looked horrified, of the noise behind them or the statement, Tor couldn't tell.

"Tor, you need to get up!" Kiara screamed.

Tor spun to see streams of vines slithering through the pillars like a flash flood, pulsing blue. *It's too late.*

"Promise me!" yelled Svikar.

"You have my word," Slegge agreed.

The slithering was deafening.

Tor looked at the edge, paralyzed. He couldn't take another step. "Take care of her!" Tor spun on his knees to face the swarm. "I'll buy you some time!" His knees shook like a newborn fawn as he eased his way to his feet.

He turned to Kiara and kissed her cheek. "Stay with Slegge!"

"There's the Viking!" hooted Svikar. "I knew he was still in there. Kiara, follow the dwarf. Your God has saved you again!"

Like a falling star, the first vine dropped down from above, then another came, and another. Tor slashed one, two, then three in half, then bit the head off another. The chaw was dry, but by the time Tor was able to spit, it had taken the edge off everything that was happening, and the prospect of what was yet to come.

Tor knew he was going to die, but he wanted it to mean something. He wanted Kiara to have a chance to get home. "What are you waiting for? Go!" He wanted them to at least try. All he could do was give them that chance. He had to part the waters.

Upstream, the river raged, deep with a flow of phosphorescent vines. The first trickle slid past their feet, biting at ankles to try to keep from sliding over the brink. Tor kicked and slashed. Clearing the early arrivals felt good. Like taking the first chinks out of a log the breadth of a door. Some draugar tried to draw themselves up into their human forms before getting within blade shot but were drowned underneath the next wave of vines swimming through.

Tor scraped frozen sweat from his forehead. Fog from his breath clouded his vision. He figured they had less than a minute before being swept off their feet and drowned in a torrent of vines as they were carried over the icy falls. There were so many that every swing was a reaction, a second more he could stay on his feet.

"You've got to trust me!" Tor heard the dwarf yell.

It was way too late for that.

Fully-formed draugar had made themselves flat so they could walk through the cage of pillars lining either side of the river. Tor aimed for their souls. Gold- and silver-coated rings pinged off the sword when his stroke hit its mark.

Tor considered cutting Slegge down for blowing Kiara's only chance of escape. He turned just in time to see the dwarf bury his hammer deep into the ice.

THE FALL

Kiara kicked and stomped at any vine sinking its talons into her ankles, relieved when she sent any of them sliding over the edge of the frozen falls. She did what she could, but she was unarmed except for the troll's head. Svikar, also unarmed, was not worthless—his biting and snarling knocking many an unsteady draugr off their slippery, slithery feet.

Tor was a true Viking warrior, slashing every draugr that slithered anywhere close by. He parted the river of vines like Moses parting the Red Sea.

Slegge just had time to take them to the path. Kiara could see the spot, a small break in the columns just at the precipice of the waterfall. There was no way Tor would've gone that close to the edge without Slegge hitting him on the head with his hammer first. Kiara could see in the dwarf's angry eyes that, for whatever reason, he wasn't leaving Tor behind. That was good, because Kiara couldn't leave him, either.

The dwarf grabbed Kiara by the arm and opened his mouth wide, took in a deep breath, held it, then let it out slowly. His eyes were desperate.

He wanted her to hold her breath.

"You've got to trust me," he shouted. He grabbed a vine by the throat, bit through its neck, and spit its soul onto the ice. He raised his fingers one at a time, and on three he took another deep breath. When he saw Kiara do the same, he raised his hammer with both hands and slammed it down hard.

The ice shattered underfoot.

Kiara tried to hold on to the side, but the current of water and slush pulled at her legs until it dragged her under the icy floor. The shock of cold wrung the air out of her contracted lungs. Her feet kicked wildly, and her arms flailed for anything she could grab to pull herself out, but there was nothing there—just a slippery ceiling of ice. She watched in horror as the glowing hole the hammer had made drifted out of sight.

Blue bioluminescent light pulsed from draugar that had also fallen in. With each spark of light, she could see Tor, covered in draugr, slamming the tip of Hella's sword into the ice to break his way out. The blade came dangerously close to hitting Svikar, who was still strapped tight to Kiara's belly. The last thing she saw was Tor dragging the sword against the ceiling in a panic.

Then she fell.

WELCOME HOME

K iara crawled to shore, coughing and gagging and wheezing until she finally filled her lungs with air. That first breath was deep and dank and delicious. Then she retched, and a steady stream of fluid poured out onto the stones. The spasms didn't end until the water had been wrung out of her like a dishrag. The coughing and wheezing kept on until her lungs were filled with only air again.

The air was fresher but fouled with fish. Kiara looked up and saw three dwarf children with fishing poles, staring at her as if she was a mermaid. Her mind was so foggy she checked to see if she had fins. *Nope.*

"Tor?" She rolled over, then saw him face down on the worn, stony shore. She crawled to him, her body too weak to stand, and pulled him over to his side. It took everything she had. She was shivering, and her fingers were numb, but she warmed when she felt his shallow breaths against her pale, blue skin.

A tear soaked into his shirt, then another. She was exhausted and crying. They were alive.

The children stared on.

"Help!" Kiara heard Svikar's gravelly voice. "Don't let it—"

Before the blue vine could slither into Svikar's nose, Slegge's hammer pinned its soul hard against the ground.

"How 'bout letting me borrow a knife, boys."

Three knives nearly stuck his boots as they skipped by.

He shook his head as he fished the knives from the water, and cut the draugr off from its soul. The vine stopped wriggling. Slegge tossed the knives and half the vine up onto the shore for the three boys. Then he picked the hammer off what was left, examined the draugr's ring, and put it in his pocket.

"All right then, show's over little dwarfs. How's about helping a helpless head over to dry land before another draugr comes swimming this way again?" Svikar asked.

The children, oddly more comfortable with the head of a troll than with Kiara, used their fishing sticks to roll the head high up on the bank, as if they'd been doing that sort of thing their entire lives.

Maybe it was the warmth of the stone. Maybe it was the sight of three children fishing as if nothing could be wrong in the world. But suddenly, Kiara's eyes burned with tears and fatigue.

"I'm going to get a cart." Slegge was coiling the other half of the vine into a loop. "Now kids, this lot is with Slegge if anyone's asking. Keep 'em safe. And cut the rings offa every draugr you catch swimming outta them falls, ya hear? The rings are mine." He picked up one of their sacks, poured its contents on the ground, and with some muffled cursing, wrangled Svikar's head inside. He looked a little guilty. "If you forget you ever saw that head and you do what I asked, then I'll split the blood weed with you, fifty-fifty." He looked at the vine, bit off a piece, and spit it in the bag. He bit off another piece for himself and begrudgingly threw the rest to the kids.

Slegge walked off with Svikar in the sack, threatening and occasionally cracking him with his hammer's handle until the troll finally shut his mouth.

Kiara's eyes were heavy, and she drifted off, dreaming of rubies twinkling in the sky.

TO WOUNDS THAT NEVER HEAL

T or sat up straight and gasped. To his surprise, his lungs inhaled sultry, smoke-filled air. So hot. He ripped open his shirt. What was he wearing? His stomach was wet with sweat, and the cut across his chest had been dressed in bandages.

His left hand ached, and he held it up. Also bandaged. His right held firm to Hella's sword. His fingers cracked when he loosed his grip. His palm was still wet from his icy bath in the falls.

The last thing he remembered was the glint of Slegge's hammer and being swept under the ice — just one more nightmare to add to the list of things that would haunt him for the rest of his life.

He was lying on a thin mat in the corner of a dark, musty-smelling room. Waves of heat rose from a glowing forge that put out too much warmth and not enough light. The space wasn't small, just cramped, with tables covered with all different sizes of hammers and vises and stones — it was a workshop.

The crowded shelves were filled with fabrications made of iron, copper, and bronze. And there were finer things, collected things — silver and gold, meticulously crafted. There was a scale with arms as long as Tor's, one side piled high with what looked like rubies, opposite a smaller pile of circularly carved stones.

"I didn't mean to wake you, Viking." Slegge walked to a stone door, pushed it open, whispered something to someone on the other side, and let it close, nearly silent, on its stone hinges.

Slegge had a hammer in his hand. He made his way back to the forge and pulled something glowing from the fire. Snarling, he pushed it back in and laid his hammer on the table.

Slegge handed Tor a drinking horn—its bronzed tip stamped with a goat chewing on a vine. Then he filled it with a sour-smelling mead from a matching bronze pitcher. Tor looked at the dwarf suspiciously. *Was this horn from one of his goats?* For all he knew, he was the most prodigious producer of runaway goats in all the nine worlds. *Maybe they left because they didn't like the snow.*

"Where's Kiara?"

"She's in better shape than you, I'd say." Slegge took a slow draught of mead.

Tor did not join him.

"My sister Ruby's taking care of the girl. She requested a hot bath. I believe you could use one yourself."

"What about the troll?"

"Shhhh," Slegge whispered as he put a calloused finger in front of his bearded face. "Ruby's cleaning that filthy bugger up, too. It's against the law to harbor his kind in Svartalfheim. They're trouble. Gotta try to keep him hidden or things are going to get a lot worse for us all."

"You promised we'd be safe." Tor stood up, and immediately pulled his robe tight. He was wearing something like a yellow bedsheet that covered him to just above the knee.

"You're safe, she's safe." He lowered his voice again. "And the head's safe, too." Slegge looked over his shoulder at the closed door, then whispered on. "You and the girl were seen, but I'm not sure about Svik. His kind have always been forbidden. The only time I've ever even seen a troll in the Red Fields was after the war, when Pyrrhus sent his ambassador to establish his government here. That elf had one in his retinue." Slegge furrowed his brow. "There seem to be a lot of them in the government these days."

Slegge cleared his throat and raised his horn. "To getting home." Tor clacked his horn to Slegge's. Getting home was something he could drink to.

The ale poured like fire. "Str-*uhm*-strong," Tor coughed. "What is it?" His face cooled as the fire flowed through his veins down to his fingers, and all the way to his toes.

"Firewater," said Slegge.

"This isn't firewater." Tor's eyes shut and his shoulders fell. Feelings he didn't know he had burned away. All the fear and disappointment and anger that'd been brewing inside him since the Vikings arrived melted away like a spring snow. He hadn't felt that way since his raiding days—worry free, uncaring, and invincible. His eyes opened to the sound of his own knuckles cracking from squeezing the hilt of Hella's sword. He forced himself to ease his grip.

"Dwarfs work hard," said Slegge. "We leave more of the fire in it. Any you've ever tried was likely brewed by a witch and weaker than goblin piss." He smiled. "You know, when Rotinn was a boy..." The joy left his face, and he silently stared into the fire.

"Thanks for not leaving me behind back there." Tor dried the sweat from his cheeks. "Years ago, Runa and I lost our little girl. Before, in the caves, she actually thought she saw her. She was talking to her, same as I'm talking to you now." The fire glowed orange and hot, and the smoke drifted silently out a hole in the corner of the ceiling. "It was terrible what Hella did to your son."

Slegge's lip started to quiver. "Life would be so much simpler if it were only our enemies that could cause us pain."

Tor always found it best to drown the awkwardness of sentimentality with a drink. "To wounds that never heal."

The dwarf answered by wiping his eyes with his sleeves and emptying his horn.

"Time you get cleaned up, Viking. We've got to honor our dead."

DWARF FUNERAL

The spring that fed the pool was hot and smelled of svovel, and it felt good. Tor had never taken such a hot bath. Back home, he was accustomed to washing in Cold Creek, near the farm, or out of a bucket in the house in winter. Never had he been fully submerged in water that wasn't the icy result of glacial melt or an unsunned, underground spring — and it soothed his weary bones.

A horn filled with firewater awaited him as he left the bath. He was also glad to see his clothes again — cleaned and even mended from where the thorns had made their cuts. He'd taken the sword to the pool, not letting it out of arm's reach since they'd escaped Hel, but beside his clothes lay an accessory, a fine new baldric and scabbard. The scabbard looked to be of a reptile's hide — tough, yet more supple than any tanned leather he'd ever felt. The baldric was woven out of Ymir's beard. Dressed with rubies, it fastened over the shoulder with a brooch of solid gold, enough to buy a ship back home. The adornments brought unnecessary attention to the sword, but perhaps that was Slegge's intent. This new setup was surprisingly balanced and light, allowing him to move much more freely compared to any he'd worn before.

Had it not been for the business at hand, and being so far away from home, he might have felt better. He wondered how Slegge planned to have a funeral when they didn't have anything to bury.

As soon as Tor walked through the door, Kiara wrapped her arms around his neck. Her hug warmed him better than the firewater and the hot bath and the clean clothes combined. He couldn't help but think of Gefn.

When Kiara let go, she smiled, curtsied, and spun on her toes. No mended clothes for her. She was wearing a red dress that set off the strawberry of her hair. And her hair — Tor had only seen it wild and untamed — was now clean and shiny, and her big curls had been braided to lie neatly over one shoulder. She was beautiful. He wished Erik could've seen her like that.

Slegge's sister Ruby put down a finely woven sack, dyed green as a winter pine, held to with golden twine.

When she released the knot, the pretty green cover fell away to reveal Svikar, growling like an angry pup. He had lost most of his stink, and his nasty hair was clean and frizzy and standing on end.

Kiara snickered and Tor spewed firewater on his clean shirt. Even the troll was spoiling his somber mood.

"What's this all about, eh?" asked Svikar. "There ain't no bodies, now is there? So, what's the hurry? You're supposed to be finding these two a guide to get them home, and I'd like to go, too, while you're at it."

"Do you take me as a dwarf who would take council from a troll?"

"Maybe we should wait," Kiara agreed.

Slegge cleared his throat. "I've lost my son." He wiped his eyes and stood up straight. "It must be done in Rødfelt. And it must be done now."

Ruby gave Svikar some blood weed to chew on and hid him away in a back room.

After Slegge locked the door, he led them through a labyrinth of tunnels and excavation sites. The roughhewn walls reminded Tor of the corridors that led them to Hel, sending a chill up his spine.

Slegge stopped at a doorway so short even the dwarfs

would have to bow to get through. Tor turned when Slegge's eyes turned back. Some distance behind them, red armor plate reflected an orange glow. They were being followed.

"Go on," said Slegge. "They won't stop us."

A warm breeze blew across Tor's face as he crawled through the door and into a dark tunnel.

"What was that?" Kiara was close behind.

For a brief moment, the floor glowed orange. There was light ahead, and Tor pushed toward it.

"Tor?" Kiara sounded worried.

The floor erupted with color as a school of glowing fish swam by on the other side. Sweat dripped from the tip of Tor's nose as he remembered the shock of breaking through the ice before the falls bore them out of Hel. The floor they were crawling on was like that ice, clear as polished glass, only not as cold. And the only way out was forward into a room full of dwarfs. Tor was beginning to wonder if Slegge had set them up.

"The floor's crystal," said one of the two dwarfs who helped him to his feet.

"Would hold a giant looper if you could figure out a way to get one inside," said the other.

Looper? Tor didn't want to know.

After Tor helped Kiara to her feet, Ruby and Slegge walked out of the tunnel in a bow. Six dwarfs dressed in red armor plate followed close behind.

The room was a massive underwater bubble — ceiling, walls, and floor. Somewhere between the little door and the end of the tunnel, they'd left the world of stone behind. Tor could see it, though, just there, through the wall, a great stone cliff. The bubble was balanced atop an obsidian spire that disappeared into the depths, and water gurgled out onto the floor where they mated.

"Shut that door before you drown us all," the captain shouted to his Red Guard. As soon as the little door echoed shut, the breeze died down, the bubbling stopped, and the standing water drained back into the base of the well.

Tor lead Kiara to the well, where Slegge stood with his arm around Ruby. "Are we safe?" They were surrounded by dwarfs, hats in hand.

"Rotinn grew up in Rødfelt. When one family mourns, we all do," Ruby's voice cracked. Kiara took her hand.

Slegge pulled two tanned sacks from his belt. He opened the larger and held it high.

"Too many have been lost in Svartalfheim." Slegge placed the larger sack, brimming with tiny blue pellets, on the side of the well.

"Too many," the dwarfs nodded and muttered their agreement. Some of the mothers hugged their children. Some wept.

"Too many sons and daughters of the Red Fields have given their souls in the name of order and peace."

Ruby stiffened. The room grew cold as uncomfortable dwarfs shuffled their boots and looked away.

Slegge emptied the smaller sack into his hand. With a gnarled finger, he counted out two gold pellets and gave them to Ruby. "For Job and for Goldie." She hugged him, soaking his shoulder with tears. He gave a white pellet to Tor. "For Runa," he said. Another went to Kiara.

Tor stared at the little white pellet. Can this be all there is? Tor felt so foreign as he looked down on the room full of dwarfs. Why are we here?

Kiara bowed her head and closed her eyes, put her soul to her lips, and breathed a prayer. The quiet, pure note rippled across the water in the well.

The last two pellets looked like glistening ruby shards. "For Rotinn and Kort." Slegge watered them with tears as his whispers echoed in the quiet chamber. "I'm so sorry Kort. It's your turn to watch over him now, my love." As the tears filled his calloused palms, they began to radiate a brilliant red. "I'll make it right. Promise I will."

Tor's eyes widened as he watched the dwarf ease them down into the water. Like two embers of a fire, the shards burned brighter as they sank. They swam in circles around the well until the light burned upward, as if from a torch.

Ruby eased her gold pellets in next, adding a new color to the show. By then, the two reds had slipped out into the crystal water underfoot, circling the bubble at a feverish clip. Within a lap they'd grown to the length of hands and had taken on long, graceful fins.

When Ruby's golds escaped the well, they put on luminescent scales and long, radiant tails and joined with Slegge's reds. Ruby nodded to Kiara and Tor.

The whites turned to living silver as soon as they hit the water. Tor stood over the well as the glowing spawn began to swim around and around, faster and faster, until they burned brilliantly. After they escaped the well, they swam fast as arrows around the crystal bubble. The fish were exquisite, like nothing Tor had ever seen—lending light to dark waters like fireflies on a summer night.

Ruby edged them toward the tunnel so the others could take their turn. Each dwarf added a pellet from the larger bag Slegge left behind. Blue eels swam out of the well, coalescing into a vibrant, glowing school. The original red, gold, and silver fish hunted the eels, putting on a show of bubbles and light. The boiling water attracted other colorful fish, thousands more, until the entire room was filled in a fiery light from the feeding frenzy happening outside.

Kiara was in tears when she leaned into Tor's chest. For the first time since they'd left Slegge's house, he took his hand off the hilt of Hella's sword—and put it around her shoulder. "This is the most at peace I've felt in a long time. I think Runa would've liked this."

"God is good," she whispered to herself.

"God is—" Tor quieted as he caught sight of something on his periphery, like a shadow passing underfoot. He pulled away from Kiara and put his hand back on the sword.

"There," said a voice from the crowd.

"Water looper," said another.

The chatter rippled through the dwarfs.

Tor followed the pointing fingers in time to see a shadow rise to ambush the school. Red, gold, and silver reflected off its white underbelly. Four massive fins left trails of bubbles as they propelled the assassin into the fray. Its long, stone-gray neck swiped, sending red and gold lamentations raining down as it targeted the darting silvers.

Teeth flashed, survivors scattered, and it was over. How could they have missed a monster like that lurking in the shadows? Tor realized the irony of his thoughts. His own village had embraced the lure of Vidar. Hadn't he himself been blind to the threat of Old Erik, and Anja? He thought about his sons, alone in the wilderness. What would they find? What would they come back to? With his hand back on the hilt of his sword, he looked around at the room full of wide-eyed dwarfs, and at the Red Guard. He thought about how he himself had been both predator and prey. Which was he now?

While the creature finished off the dead and dying, Tor pressed Kiara toward the door.

The Red Guard had the exit blocked.

Tor's mood had been spoiled, and he wanted out. He drew the sword.

Confused looks gave way to a trained response, as the guards pulled into formation and raised their hammer-axes across their chests.

"Whoa, whoa, what are you doing, Tor? Put that thing away." Slegge shook his head in Tor's face, staring up at him as if he was insane.

"I've got to get out of here." The bubble felt like it was shrinking. The blade shook in Tor's hand. He hated guards—always too loyal or stupid to know when to step aside.

Slegge snarled, then turned to reason with the captain. "This man's a stranger here. He doesn't understand."

No response. All eyes stayed on Tor—and the sword. Even the creature outside circled the bubble to track a glint reflecting off the blade. Tor noticed. Slegge didn't.

"He's lost his wife...and I my son. Now let us pass, eh?"

"Sir?"

"Not now."

Drops of sweat dripped down the guards' faces as their eyes followed the looper stabbing its head toward the glimmer running along on the glass. Tor pretended not to see it, twisting the blade until he had the creature chasing it's light like a big, twisted kitten with jaws large enough to swallow a goat. Slegge, oblivious, seemed emboldened, as if they were backing down from him.

"Captain?"

"Hold the line, boys."

"Boys? Well look around you, boys. This isn't the time or the place to test this man." Slegge got right up in the captain's face, nose to nose, like two cocks sparring outside a henhouse. "You know where he got that sword, don't you? I know you know."

Tor played with their fear, fixing the glint on the closest guard's red helmet. The color must have resonated, because the monster went wild and started slamming its head into the bubble from above. The dwarf mourners cowered around the exit, yelling at the guards to let them pass. Thump, thump, thump. It was like being inside a drum. Teeth the size of daggers scraped against crystal, leaving deep scars the length of most of the dwarfs. The room shook.

"Let them pass!" The captain fell when he tried to lean against guards that had already scattered.

Ruby was already pushing the screaming Kiara out the tunnel. But Slegge impressed Tor. He took his time, like it was a hot day and he was looking forward to a swim. After

Tor sheathed the blade, the creature hovered, its long neck like a snake looking for something to strike, then turned and swam underfoot, pursuing a red glow fading in the distance. The old dwarf bowed, never breaking eyes with the cowering captain, before leading Tor to the exit.

As they made their way back, Tor felt callous and feral, like he hadn't felt in years. "I'm thirsty. Have you any more of that firewater?

"At home," said Slegge, "but I'm not sure you should be drinking it. Can bring out the worst in you."

"I'm going to need it if I'm ever going to get home again. I've got to end what's started."

When they arrived back at Slegge's, a gravelly voice grunted out of the shadows, "What'd I miss?"

"Just a dwarf funeral." Hands shaking, Tor drained a horn full of firewater and filled it up again. "Beautiful — until the monster showed up."

GET FREE STORIES AND EXCLUSIVE CONTENT

Building a relationship with my readers is the very best thing about writing. Join my VIP Readers Club for information on new books and deals plus a free Saga of Souls novella: How Ubbi Lost His Tongue.

How Ubbi Lost His Tongue

Everything sounded easy enough. Sneak in to a Pict village, steal a holy stone, and claim a Viking's honor. One night—in and out—and Ubbi would never be seen as a stable boy again. What could go wrong?

You can get your copy **for free** by signing up at my website.

Just visit www.dereknelsen.com
Subscribers get free stories and exclusive content.

ENJOY THIS BOOK? YOU CAN MAKE A BIG DIFFERENCE

Reviews are the most important tools in my arsenal when it comes to getting attention for my books. Much as I'd like to, I don't have the financial muscle of a New York publisher. I can't take out full page ads in the newspaper or put posters on the subway.

(Not yet, anyway.)

But I do have something much more powerful and effective than that, and it's something that those publishers would kill to get their hands on.

A committed and loyal bunch of readers.

Honest reviews of my books help bring them to the attention of other readers.

If you enjoyed this book, I would be very grateful if you could just take a minute to leave a review on the book's Amazon page. (It can be as short as you like.)

I've left a link to the Amazon's review page for you on my site: www.dereknelsen.com/review/
Thank you very much.

ABOUT THE AUTHOR

Derek Nelsen is the author of the Saga of Souls series.

For more information:
www.dereknelsen.com
derek@dereknelsen.com

Printed in Great Britain
by Amazon

77925585R00274